BY DARKNESS
FORGED

For more information or to leave a comment about this book,
please visit us on the web at:

www.solarclipper.com

Publishers Note:

To William Cruz Carroll, Sr.

A great fan, a dedicated player of games that I like,
and a good friend

The Golden Age of the Solar Clipper

Quarter Share
Half Share
Full Share
Double Share
Captains Share
Owners Share

In Ashes Born
To Fire Called
By Darkness Forged

Milk Run
Suicide Run
Home Run

South Coast
Cape Grace*

Tanyth Fairport Adventures

Ravenwood
Zypherias Call
The Hermit Of Lammas Wood

* Forthcoming

BY DARKNESS
FORGED

NATHAN LOWELL

Durandus

CHAPTER ONE
PORT NEWMAR: 2376, JANUARY 13

Malloy Gaines lounged in his chair, waiting for my answer.

"A snake doesn't miss his skin," I said.

Gaines merely tilted his head a degree to the left.

"It's a snake," I said. "It lacks the higher cognitive function."

Gaines's lips lifted at the corners, just a smidgen. Not enough to really be a smile but enough to tell me he wasn't buying it.

I looked around his office, taking in the framed degree above the desk tucked into the corner. A rack of cushions took up most of the space in another corner. We sat facing each other in the center of the room, an oblong rug marking the ring we verbally sparred in.

"What are you thinking, Ishmael?"

"I never thought of us as sparring before."

He gave a short, surprised laugh. "Are we sparring?"

I shook my head. "I don't know. I just noticed the layout. The rug as our ring."

He glanced around and nodded. "I can see that. Do you see us as adversaries?" He leaned forward in his chair and rested his elbows on his knees.

"No," I said. "It just struck me as odd and you asked what I was thinking."

"So, maybe you can take off the gloves?" he asked. "Maybe cut out the ducking and weaving a little?"

"A snake sloughs off its skin because it doesn't fit," I said. "They just leave it behind because it's of no use."

"That wasn't so hard, was it?"

I felt myself shrugging. "People aren't snakes."

He sat back. "No. People aren't snakes. Your mother was a literature professor?"

1

"I get the metaphor, if that's what you're asking." I leaned back in my seat and looked at the overhead. "My past is a snake's skin. It's actually healthy for me to leave it behind."

"Some of it," Mal said. "Some of it is part of you. You can't leave it behind any more than you'd leave behind a foot."

"A snake only sheds the part that doesn't fit."

He grinned. "Go on."

"I have to figure out what parts don't fit."

"Snakes have it easier," he said. "When are you shipping out again?"

"Two days."

He nodded. "Not much time."

"I don't get paid unless I deliver."

He raised an eyebrow. "That's your excuse?"

"Not really. I just feel better underway."

"Planets bog you down?"

"It's not that so much. I just feel more focused out there."

He frowned a little. "We have a couple of ticks. Talk about that."

"About what?"

"Focus. Why do you feel more focused there?"

"Fewer distractions. I've a ship to run. Something to do."

"You could take up knitting," Gaines said. "What about being out there is different?"

"It's the only thing that matters. Making a mistake means people die."

"People die everywhere," he said, settling back into his seat again and peering at me across the narrow gap. "You feel differently out there than you do here."

"Yeah, I do. It's hard to explain."

"Try."

"I've got a job. I've got focus. I get satisfaction out of delivering goods, earning value for the company."

"Is that who you are? A delivery guy?"

The words stung a little but I saw where he was going. I paused for more than a few heartbeats to consider the question. "I guess that's true."

"Is that who you want to be?"

I leaned back again to stare at the overhead. "I don't know."

"Have you always felt this way? Like a delivery guy?"

"I don't know that I feel like a delivery guy now." I pulled my gaze down from the acoustic tiles above.

"What do you feel like?" he asked.

I stared back at him. I didn't have an answer.

"That's the problem, isn't it?" he asked.

"Yeah. I think so. I've always had this sense of purpose. In the beginning it was just to survive. To keep from being ground up by the gears of commerce."

"Poetic. You're talking about Neris?"

"Pretty much. After that—on the *Lois*—it was always improving my chances for the next job. Getting the next rating."

"But you were still almost put ashore," Gaines said.

"I was."

"Then you went to the academy and graduated into the meat grinder."

"Yeah. I was pretty green. I've seen it happen to others enough that I can see it in myself now."

"Were you happy?" he asked.

"Happy?" The idea seemed foreign, a concept that had no roots in reality. Was I happy on the *Lois*? The *Tinker*?

"I see the wheels turning in your head but you're not talking," he said. "Let it out."

"I don't know," I said. "I'm actually a little distressed that I don't know."

"Think back to the early days on the *Lois McKendrick*. Give me some words."

"Scared. Fun."

"Anything else?" he asked. "Challenged, maybe?"

"Well, yeah."

"What about now? Are you challenged?"

I sighed. "Not as such. No. We have our moments of terror, but daily? No."

"Why is that?"

"I'm the captain. I have people to run the ship and my job is to stay out of their way."

"That your rule?"

"That's my *role*. Where are you going with this?"

Gaines steepled his fingers in front of his mouth. "You're bored."

"I'm—" I started to argue with him but bit down on the thought. "I'm the captain." It sounded weak, even to me.

"What's that mean?" he asked. "Not the regulation answer. To you. What's that mean? The captain."

"I'm in charge. I make the final decisions."

"How many final decisions are there in your average day?"

"I don't know."

"You have people to do that," he said. It wasn't a question.

"Yes."

"Answer without thinking. What was your favorite ship?"

"*Agamemnon.*"

He grinned. "Now, why?"

"I don't know. I answered without thinking."

"Think now. Why *Agamemnon*?"

"It was my first command."

"What made it fun?"

"The crew," I said. "Definitely the crew."

"Why? Were they really good?"

"They were a lot better than they thought. Getting them to change that was a tremendously gratifying challenge."

"What about the *Tinker*?" he asked.

"What about it?" I shook my head. "The before and after there was night and day. Not even the same ship."

"You worked up to captain there, right?"

"Yeah. Went aboard as a green third mate out of the academy and left after Fredi deGrut retired. Her replacement left the opening on the *Agamemnon* for me to move up to captain."

"Back to the *Tinker*. How do you feel about the early *Tinker*?"

"That was horrible. I was an idiot. I probably should have been cashiered for insubordination."

"Why?"

"I thought I knew all the answers and I was arrogant enough to spout them."

"Did you?"

"Spout them? Yes. Actually know them?" I shook my head and sighed. "No. I knew my answers and assumed they applied to the ship. They didn't. For all that Burnside was an ass—and a dangerous ass, at that—he followed the letter of the regulations for running the ship. He violated the spirit every day and his misogyny blew every idea of crew management I ever believed in right out the air lock."

"But?"

"But?" I asked.

"But what about Burnside? Do you agree with him now?"

"Oh, hell no. I couldn't treat people like that. His duties? Yeah. I was wrong in a lot of ways but every ship has its own culture. You mess with that at your peril. That was true even on the *Lois*."

"But Alys Giggone's culture wasn't Frederica deGrut's, was it?"

I had to think about that for a few heartbeats. "Not exactly. No. Each captain brought their own culture to the ship."

"Perfect," Gaines said, grinning at me. "Generalize that statement."

"What?"

"Make it a generalization about captains."

"All captains bring their own cultures to their ships?" I asked.

His grin widened. "What sense did you take to the *Agamemnon*?"

I shrugged. "I don't really know. The ship had a bad reputation. Bad actors in the crew. Marginal officer corps."

"You didn't believe it," Gaines said.

"Let's just say I was skeptical."

"Why?"

"Reputations are tough. Once you blow it, it's really hard to get it back. You don't even have to really be what the reputation says you are. Once enough people believe it, you're stuck digging your way out of a hole you may not have made to begin with."

"Bitter voice of experience?"

"Not really," I said. "Just observed it enough growing up in the university enclave on Neris."

"Why didn't you believe with *Agamemnon*?"

"At first, I'm not sure I didn't believe. They were supposed to be the worst ship in the fleet. I was ready to go and clean house the way Fredi had with the *Tinker*. It was the chance for my first command. The next step on the ladder."

"How fast did you change your mind?"

"When I saw the ways the crew acted out. Those guys—and it was all guys when I took over—those guys were just acting out. Not acting up. Everything they did, they did to get a rise out of the first mate. They were brilliantly diabolical."

"Why the first mate?"

"I wondered that, too, until I met the captain."

"What about him?"

"He wasn't there. He didn't understand his crew—or even have much to do with them." I stopped.

"Don't stop now. You're on a roll," Gaines said.

I took a deep breath. "He was only the guy who lived in the ship's cabin. He meted out punishments." My stomach felt like I'd just filled it with ice water and acid.

"So the crew acted up," Gaines said, spearing me with his gaze. "Because Delman had people to run the ship for him while he stayed out of the way? He made the big decisions? Is that what you're saying?"

I couldn't seem to find my voice. I just nodded.

"Something to consider, eh?" Gaines said. "You ready for some homework?"

"I'm not sure. It feels like I just took a punch in the gut."

"You did," he said. "First part of your homework is to think about your life on the *Lois McKendrick*. Ask yourself the question 'How did it make you feel?'"

"How did it make me feel?"

He shook his head. "Second person, as if you were asking somebody else."

"How did it make you feel?" I asked.

"Just like that. You said it was fun, challenging. Remember what it felt like. Having fun, rising to the challenges. Being scared." He paused. "Try it now. Close your eyes. Remember the mess deck on the *Lois*. Remember the sounds, the smell. Ask yourself silently."

I did as he instructed.

"Don't answer the question," he said. "Just ask it."

Emotions bubbled just under my heart. A strong sense of belonging. Of gratitude. "How do I not answer the question?" I asked, my eyes still closed.

"Oh, you'll answer it," he said. "Just try not to. Let the feelings wash over you. Different days will give you different feelings. Just feel them. Think of different parts of that experience. Sometimes focus on a face. Sometimes a sound or a smell. Just notice the feelings but don't try to name them, categorize them. Just feel them."

I let the question loose in my head again and tried to remember how it felt.

"Now," he said.

I opened my eyes, surprised at the sudden transition. Like I'd been asleep and woke up suddenly. I blinked several times, trying to find my focus.

"Now," he said, more gently the second time. "Culture. Remember that?"

"Yeah. Every captain brings their own culture."

"What culture did you bring to the *Agamemnon*?"

I shrugged my head. "Acceptance? Inclusion? I don't know how to classify cultures."

"Usually they have a collection of shared values. A shared aesthetic."

"Profit," I said. "We focused on the bottom line. Ran a contest, even."

Gaines raised that one eyebrow again. "But you found your first mate was nearly deaf and got her some help."

I shrugged. "Well, of course. She was hardly effective when she couldn't hear what people were saying."

"So it was profit that made you have her hearing checked?"

"I thought she had some good skills," I said. "I hated to see her miss out."

"And the cargo officer? Wyatt?"

"You've done a lot of homework on a patient you only see once in a blue moon."

"It's a weakness," Gaines said. "Answer the question."

"Wyatt might have been somewhere on one of the cognitive spectrums. Asperger's, autism. I'm not sure. He could look at data and tell you what the answer was. Even without the question. Guy was brilliant as a cargo picker. He just never got the chance until I made it his job."

Both of Gaines's eyebrows shot up nearly to his hairline. "Wasn't that always supposed to be his job?"

"Yeah. On most ships it would have been but he didn't come from a culture that promoted that behavior." I smiled, acknowledging the use of the word "culture".

"You're getting the hang of it," he said. "Now the second part of your homework."

I braced myself in the chair.

"It's not that bad," he said. "Cultures have values, beliefs. They have things they'll accept. Behaviors they'll fight. I want you to think about your various ships. What were the cultures? I suspect they all shared a basic core set of values."

"I can do that."

"That's not your homework," Gaines said. "While you're thinking about the other ships' cultures, I want you to think about one question. 'What will *your* culture stand for?'"

"My culture?"

He nodded, a broad smile pasted on his face. "Remember? All captains bring their own culture?"

"Yeah," I said, suddenly sure where this was headed.

"Well, you're the captain on the *Chernyakova*. It's your culture to mold. What will it be? What will you fight? What will you support? What will you stand against? What will you stand for?"

A quiet chime sounded.

"Just in time. That's all for today. Let me know the next time you're inbound to Port Newmar and we'll set up another appointment." Gaines stood and offered a hand. "Good luck on your next voyage, Captain."

CHAPTER TWO
NEWMAR SYSTEM: 2376, JANUARY 16

I sat in the captain's chair on the bridge and stared out at the Deep Dark beyond the armorglass. I kept running Malloy Gaines's questions through my mind. *How did it make you feel? What will your culture stand for?*

"Captain?" Al asked, looking over at me from the first mate's station.

For a moment I wondered if I'd missed something, too wrapped up in my own head to notice something critical on the bridge. "Yes?"

"Did you say something, Skipper? You made a noise but I couldn't make it out."

I chuckled, more to myself than anything. "No. Just musing over something I heard back at Port Newmar." I shook my head and made a show of looking around. "How far are we from the safety limit?"

She consulted a screen on her console. "I make it just about another stan and a half, Captain." She looked over at me with a sly grin. "You getting spoiled by jumping in and out of the Toe-Holds?"

"Maybe," I said. "You have to admit stations on the outer fringes make for easier jumps."

She nodded. "I'll give you that. Not having to follow the CPJCT limits on when we can put up our sails doesn't hurt either, though, does it."

"That's true enough," I said. I pulled off my seat belt and stood up, stretching my back and rolling my neck around to loosen up the muscles. I walked forward and stood, staring out.

How did it make you feel?

I loved looking out at the stars. The endless night provided endless fascination. Why had I stopped looking out? When had I stopped looking out?

A reflection in the armorglass caught my eye as Chief Stevens stepped up beside me, her hands clasped behind her back. She stared out into the Dark.

"Chief."

"Skipper."

We stood there for several heartbeats without speaking.

"You all right, Ishmael?" she asked, her voice barely louder than the environmental blowers.

I glanced back at the bridge crew—Mr. Reed on his astrogation console, Ms. Fortuner at comms, Ms. Torkelson at the helm, and Al tucked away behind the watchstander's console. None of them seemed to be paying attention to anything but their duties. "Yeah, I think so. Why?"

She shrugged, shoulders rising and falling so quickly I wasn't sure she'd done it. "You've seemed pretty quiet since we got underway." She looked over at me. "Something on your mind?"

That startled a laugh out of me. "When isn't there?"

A patient smile graced her lips and she turned back to the Deep Dark outside. "Captains always have things on their minds," she said. "I just wondered if there was something new."

I debated for a couple of heartbeats before speaking. "Gaines gave me new homework."

"Your therapist?" she asked. She made it a simple question, no judgment.

"We see each other rarely so he gives me things to think about while I'm out here."

"I remember," she said. "The snake and his skin."

"Yeah."

"Did you reach any conclusion on that one?" She glanced up at me out of the corners of her eyes. "You don't have to answer that. Sorry."

"It's all right. I did, actually. It was pretty obvious once I tumbled that it was a trick question."

"Good." She rocked on the balls of her feet a little bit, forward and back. "I'm surprised you had time for a visit. We didn't have much time planetside this trip."

"I scheduled it as soon as we jumped in. Gave him a few weeks to find me a slot while I was down there."

"What's the new homework about?" She glanced up again. "If you don't mind sharing."

"Two questions that don't seem like they should be related but I can't stop thinking about them."

She gave me another side-eyed glance but didn't speak.

"The first is 'How did it make you feel?' in reference to my time on the *Lois McKendrick* as a crewman."

"Classic Zen," she said. "Interesting approach."

"What?"

"The question. It's a classic question from an ancient Buddhist school of meditation. He didn't ask you to answer it, did he." It wasn't a question.

"No, I'm not supposed to answer it. Just feel it."

She grinned. I could see her teeth gleaming in her reflection. "It's phrased to break your focus, to give your mind a split second of a break from overthinking. To put you in touch with yourself in ways that most of us find difficult. Tai chi does the same thing using the movements as focus."

"I haven't done tai chi since the *Iris*, I don't think."

"We should take it up. I'm a little rusty myself."

"The spine?" I asked.

"There's enough room there, I think. I used to do tai chi between the Burleson drives and there's less room there."

We stared out while I thought about it. "You're a woman of surprising insights," I said.

"Nothing surprising," she said. "I'm old. You live long enough, you pick up stuff."

"Even Zen Buddhist practice?" I asked.

She gave me a crooked smile. "What's the other question?"

"What will my culture stand for?"

"Your culture?" She did that birdlike tilting-of-the-head thing. "Not your civilization?"

I replayed the conversation in my head. "No. Culture. We were talking about how every ship has its own culture. How the captain bears the brunt of enforcing cultural norms."

"Ah," she said. "Do you believe that?"

"About captains?"

"Yes. Is it the captains by themselves or the interactions of the captain with the crew?"

I had to think about that. "When I was on the *Tinker*, the change from Rossett to deGrut took a largely dysfunctional ship and turned it into a great place to live and work."

She nodded and gave a small shrug. "Maybe she simply amplified the crew gestalt. Taking what was there and focusing it."

I shrugged. "Either way, it's the captain who makes the difference. Whether it's something they bring to the job or something they do with the crew."

"What did Rossett bring to the *Tinker*?"

"I'm not sure he's a good example. He just came out of the cabin when he had to. The first mate, Burnside, was the bad actor. Rossett just enabled the behavior."

She looked up at me again, both eyebrows raised.

"What?" I asked.

"While you're contemplating your culture, remember what you just said." She patted me on the shoulder and returned to her console, focusing on her screens with an enigmatic smile.

I turned back to my contemplation of the infinite outside the armorglass but her words echoed in my skull. Was I behaving like Rossett? Was I letting Al establish the ship's culture? Was that a bad thing?

"Skipper, we've reached the safety limit," Al said.

"Thank you, Ms. Ross. Chief?" I crossed the bridge and settled back into the captain's chair.

"Securing the kickers and powering up the sail generators," the chief said.

The low rumble from the large rocket motors aft faded out.

She tapped a few more keys. "Sails deployed."

"Status, Helm?" Al asked.

Ms. Torkelson checked her console and nodded. "Helm responding. We have steerageway."

Al looked at me. "Captain, the auxiliary engines have been secured and the sails deployed. Helm reports steerageway."

"Thank you, Ms. Ross. Secure from navigation stations and set the normal watch throughout the ship."

"Secure from navigation stations. Set normal watch. Aye, aye, sar." She lifted her mic and made the shipwide announcement.

"Log it," I said.

"Logged at 1730, 16 January 2376," Al said.

I stood up again and headed for the ladder, stepping aside to let the incoming watch section climb up to the bridge. I caught a glimpse of Chief Stevens as I dropped down the ladder. She looked at me with a crooked smile and one eyebrow raised.

She wasn't exactly subtle unless she wanted to be, a thought that gave me pause as I ducked into the cabin.

CHAPTER THREE
NEWMAR SYSTEM: 2376, JANUARY 20

Five days out of Port Newmar, I had just finished up the daily logs when Al knocked on the cabin's door frame. "Gotta minute, Skipper?"

I'd started leaving the door open, following Fredi deGrut's habit of randomly opening and closing the door. I felt a little funny about never keeping the door open, truth be told. The conversations with Mal Gaines and Chief Stevens chafed like a grain of sand in my shoe. I couldn't quite ignore them, but didn't stop to address the root problems.

Somewhere in the back of my mind, a little voice kept trying to get my attention.

I waved her in. "What's on your mind, Al?"

She plopped into one of the two visitor's chairs and ran a hand over her cropped hair. She stared at me, not quite a challenge but resolute. "I'm going to retire."

That bald statement caught me by surprise. "When?"

She shrugged and looked down at her knees. "Sooner rather than later. Probably not this trip or the next. I won't leave until you've got a replacement lined up." She looked back up at me. "But I need you to start looking for one."

"You have anybody in mind?"

She shook her head. "I'm kinda out of the loop. Have been for a while. After being beached at Breakall, I lost track of what was happening in the sector. It never seemed important. Since we've put the *Chernyakova* back together?" She shrugged. "We haven't put down roots anywhere so it's been hard to get re-established. I'm not sure I want to."

"What will you do?" I asked.

"Art," she said. "I've always been a closet artist. I've got sketchbooks going back decades."

"You carry them with you?"

She laughed. "No. I sketch and scan. Digitized, they don't take up much room. The stuff I picked up at Mel's reminded me that I'd been ignoring it for a long time."

"I understand," I said. "I should probably retire myself." I found myself staring at the backs of my hands instead of looking at Al. I had to force myself to look up.

"Why?" she asked.

"Why retire?" I asked.

She shook her head. "Why do you think you should?"

"I'm ..." My voice petered out as I ran out of words.

"I thought you were doing better," Al said. "Something happen?"

"Gaines set me up with new questions. They're challenging me."

Al settled back in the chair and folded her hands over her chest. "You've never dodged a challenge as long as I've known you."

"I'm bored." The words slipped out before I could think about them.

Al gave a breathy little chuckle and her eyes sparkled in the overheads. "About time."

"What?"

"I said it's about time. You've got your head up your backside about not getting in the way so you hide here in the cabin. It's no wonder you're bored. We've talked about this before."

I sat back in my chair and stared at the overhead. "What would Alys do?"

"Alys? Alys Giggone?" she asked.

"Yeah." I looked back at Al. "Fredi was an amazing captain but Alys Giggone was my first."

"You always remember your first," Al said with a crooked smile. "What's your sharpest memory of her?"

I felt the blush running up my face.

Al blinked. "You're blushing?"

"The *Lois* had a steam room. We called it a sauna but technically just a steam room. The whole crew used it."

Al's eyes grew wide. "You and Alys Giggone in the steam room?"

"It's not like that. Everybody used it. We weren't naked or anything. Towels and trunks generally. The off-watch sections, day workers, officers and crew. It was just what you did."

"So your sharpest memory of Alys Giggone is her wearing nothing but a towel in the steam room?"

"You have a dirty mind."

"It's your memory," she said.

"The memory is that was the first time that I realized that clipper captains are captains even when they're not in uniform. She was wearing a towel but nobody would have mistaken her for one of the crew, even then."

Al settled back in her seat. "Then why were you blushing?"

"I knew how it would sound."

She nodded. "I'll let this one slide. You were chasing what's-her-name at the time as I remember."

"Alicia Alvarez," I said. "She signed my letter of application for the academy but I never saw her again after that night."

"So did you ever think you'd be a captain?"

"Never. In the beginning I never considered attending the academy. That was for spacers and I was an imposter." I took a breath and shrugged. "I guess I still feel like an imposter."

"That probably won't go away," Al said. "But your history says you're a spacer. Your training says you're a spacer. You own this ship and run it. The only time you go planetside is when we dock at Port Newmar." She shook her head. "If that's not being a spacer, I'm not sure any of us are."

I laughed. "All right. You got me." I leaned my forearms on my desk and sighed. "How long before you retire?"

"I want to go now, but I wouldn't do that to you," she said. "The chief isn't going to hang around very long after she finds whatever it is she's looking for out here."

"You don't think she's looking for the mega?"

Al shrugged. "Only indirectly. Whatever she's tracking isn't the ship. We're the wrong vehicle for that kind of search. It might be something connected to the mega, but it's not the mega itself."

"You have any basis?"

"Hunch," Al said, screwing her lips into a grimace. "We were close at Telluride. Why aren't we going back there now?"

"Pip got a can heading for Mel's Place."

Al made a rude noise with her lips. "He could have gotten a can heading for Telluride just as easily. Breaking the blockade there has opened that sector up in ways it hasn't been for two decades."

"I'm sure, but Toe-Hold cargoes aren't exactly up-front in the High Line." I shrugged. "If I were a gambler, I'd wager Mel's is just a stopover on the way out to Telluride and we'll end up there soon."

Al frowned for a moment but nodded. "Probably true."

"Where do you want to get off?"

"When you find a new first mate, I'll get off there. Doesn't really matter. Anywhere in the Toe-Holds is fine."

"Not the High Line?" I asked.

Al considered me for several long moments. "I've got nothing calling me back here. If I'm going to start over, I'd rather do it out there."

"Fair enough," I said. "You think I'll find a first out there?"

"Absolutely," Al said. "Finding somebody who can pass CPJCT muster might be a little harder, but the officer corps out there is generally top notch."

The idea struck me as odd. "Why's that?"

Al shrugged. "The bad ones die early."

Her answer rocked me, but I could see her point. "I guess I didn't think of it like that."

"You're used to the CPJCT ways of doing things as demonstrated by some very good officers. It works great for them. Without the formalized structures, the Toe-Holds rely more on experience and reputation than credentials. It doesn't hurt that a large proportion of Toe-Holders send their kids to the academy for their education. Most of them have degrees from one academy or another, even if they graduate, go home, and never darken a CPJCT dock again." She stood up. "Sorry to spring it on you."

"I'd rather know," I said. "I knew you were thinking about it. I'm glad you made a decision you're happy with."

She opened her mouth as if to speak but closed it again. She gave me a short nod and headed for the door, leaving me sitting there wondering how I could replace her.

Most of me didn't want to, but there was a tiny corner that reminded me that it was her choice to make. It was my job to respect it. I debated about telling her that I'd put her up for captain, but decided to let it play out. There was no sense in getting her hopes up and then not getting the invitation.

I stood up and slipped my tablet into its holster. Thinking about the *Lois*—and Alys Giggone in a towel—made me realize I knew exactly what Alys would do. I wasn't sure if it was what I was supposed to do, but it was much better than moping in the cabin.

I closed the cabin's door as I left and climbed the ladder to the bridge. Mr. Reed had the watch and I wanted to check in with him before I set out on my own little voyage of discovery.

CHAPTER FOUR
NEWMAR SYSTEM: 2376, JANUARY 20

Thomas Reed had always seemed like a perpetual second mate. He loved astrogation, didn't seem inclined to pursue his first mate's ticket. As I climbed the ladder to the bridge, I wondered how much of that was true and how much was just my own projection on the situation.

"Captain on the bridge," Reed said as I topped the ladder.

"As you were," I said. "You know you don't have to do that, right?"

Reed nodded. "Yeah, but it's fun."

I laughed. "Ms. Cheuvront?"

Casey Cheuvront looked up from her helm. "Yes, Captain?"

"What's your next rating?"

"My next rating, Captain?"

"Yes, Ms. Cheuvront. You're what? Able spacer?"

"Yes, sar. Have been for a couple of stanyers."

"Next step would seem to be a spec-three of some flavor," I said.

"Well, Mary is our ship handler already," she said with a shrug. "Not much call for two on a ship like this."

"Ms. Torkelson's ratings aren't your problem," I said. "Having the rating means you could step into her job if she decides to move on."

Ms. Cheuvront looked up at me, craning her head around. "Seriously?"

I shrugged. "If you have the rating, your options open up. Without it, not so much."

"I guess I hadn't looked at it like that," she said, settling back into the helm. "She didn't mention anything about leaving."

"She hasn't said anything to me either. It's just a hypothetical. We may get to Mel's and there's a ship with her name on it and poof." I smiled at her. "Just think about what you might like to move up to. Ship handler? Astrogation? Systems? You could also change divisions if there's something you'd rather do."

"I've always been interested in astrogation, sar." She glanced up at me again, a troubled look on her face. "You're not trying to get rid of me, are you?"

"No, no. Nothing like that. Just planting the seed. I really like to have crew working toward something and not just doing the same job by default."

She didn't look convinced but she gave me a tentative nod before addressing the ship's helm.

I crossed to the watchstander's station but Reed spoke before I could. "Forget it, Skipper. I'm a good second mate. I like being second mate. I'm not going for first."

I held up my hands in surrender. "Fair enough. I won't twist your arm."

"You need something, Captain?" he asked. "Other than my career goals?"

"No. Just wanted to let you know I'm going on a tour of the ship. Bip me if you need me."

He eyed me, then glanced at Cheuvront. He lowered his voice and leaned into me. "You're not going to ask everybody about their career paths, are you?"

I leaned into him. "Maybe. Why? That a problem?"

"Something bothering you, Skipper?"

"Yes. I'm bored. I'm tired of it."

He blinked at me several times as if trying to process what he'd heard, as if it were a foreign language he had a rudimentary grasp of but couldn't quite parse.

I patted him on the shoulder. "It's fine, Tom. I'm just going to do a little walkabout. I used to do that as part of my normal shipboard routine, but I've been a bit lax lately."

"If you say so, Skipper."

I nodded and gave him what I hoped was a jaunty grin. His response made me wonder if I shouldn't just go back to the cabin and practice grinning in front of a mirror.

I dropped down the ladder and headed aft down the spine. There certainly seemed like there'd be enough room for the chief and me to resume our tai chi practice. Our long form had a lot of side-to-side movement, but the spine had enough width that we could face the bulkhead and have sufficient room for the forward and back.

I stopped at the chief's office as I exited the spine. She looked up as I stood in her opened doorway.

"Captain? How can I help you?"

"Just stretching my legs," I said. "Would you like to accompany me on a tour of the aft nacelle?"

Her eyebrows rose slowly as she stared at me. "Finally got bored enough?" she asked.

"Finally," I said. "I used to do this all the time on my other ships. I kinda fell out of the habit in the yards."

She nodded. "A good plan. You don't need me to show you around. Have fun."

"I'll try not to scare the troops."

She laughed.

The main engineering watch station lay just down the passage from the chief's office, down a couple of steps. When I stuck my head into the compartment, all three watchstanders turned to look with various stages of shock and dismay. The lead, a spec-one with a fields rating badge, started to stand but I waved her back. "Murakofsky?" I asked.

"Murawsky, Captain."

"My apologies. I can't read your badge from here and I clearly need to get out more."

She smiled. "I've heard a lot worse, sar."

"As you were. Watchstanders have a higher priority than building up a captain's ego."

They laughed—somewhat nervously, I thought, but they laughed.

"Sound off, please, so I know who you are?" I asked.

"Spec-one Fields Sheryl Murawsky, sar," the woman said, nudging the man next to her.

"Spec-three Grav Derek Bell, sar." The man looked me in the eye and gave me a nod.

The last man turned to me and offered a tentative smile. "Machinist Barrett Dent, sar."

"I know I've met you all before, but thanks for reminding me so I can try to put names with faces."

They looked at each other before settling on Murawsky. "Is there something we can do for you, Captain?" she asked.

I shook my head. "Is there something I can do for you? Any of you?"

"Can we get a coffee mess down here?" Bell asked.

I thought Murawsky might lose her eyes, they bugged out so far. Dent looked surprised for a moment but turned to me.

"A coffee mess?" I asked. "Like what? An urn?"

Murawsky poked Bell but he didn't shy away. "Nothing that elaborate, Captain. Just, I don't know. A carafe with some mugs? It's a long way to the galley during the midwatch."

"Have you asked the chief?" I asked.

Bell's head jerked up and he stiffened in his seat, his eyes round as shaft bearings. "Dr. Stevens?"

"Well, I call her Chief Stevens since she's on my chain of command, but yeah. Her."

Bell shook his head. "No, sar. I couldn't. I mean. She wrote the book ..." He swallowed hard, as if realizing what had rolled off his tongue.

"One tick," I said, holding up a digit. "Lemme check." I trotted back up the steps to the chief's office.

She looked up from her console. "Something wrong, Skipper?"

"What are you feeding these people, Chief?"

"Why?"

"You got a moment?"

She shrugged and stood to follow me back to the watchstanders. "Now, Bell? Is it?" I asked.

His face grew even redder and if Dent slouched any farther into his chair, he'd slide all the way under his console.

I looked at the chief. "Mr. Bell here has a question for you."

"Bell?" she asked, frowning as she looked back and forth between Bell and me.

"Ah," he said, stopping to clear his throat. "The captain asked if there was anything he could do for us and I mentioned a coffee mess. Sar. Chief. Dr. Stevens."

The chief stepped into the crowded compartment and looked at the top of a cabinet against the far bulkhead. "You're supposed to have one," she said. "There. On the top of that cabinet. It's a long damn way to the galley and back on the midwatch." She turned to me. "Have you been forward on your tour?"

"Not yet. Hit the bridge and then came aft."

"Would you mind asking Ms. Sharps about setting up a tray for here? They should have a standard coffee mess tray that fits right on that cabinet. Carafe, some creamers and sweeteners. A few mugs."

"I'd be glad to."

She looked at the three watchstanders. "I'm really sorry. You should have said something sooner. How long have we been sailing together?" She shook her head. "Anything else you've noticed that's out of whack?"

They all shook their heads, somewhat hurriedly.

"Well, if you do, don't wait for the captain to make his way aft to check on us, all right?" She grinned at me.

"Yes, sar." Their unison was perfect.

I stepped out of the hatch frame and let the chief exit. "I'm gonna go peek into environmental. I'll stop by on my way out."

She nodded and sent a quizzical glance back at the watch-standers.

"I'll fill you in," I said.

She nodded again and headed for her office, moving slowly and shaking her head.

I dropped down the ladders, past the main engineering deck, and into the environmental section.

"Captain on deck." A machinist rose from the watchstanding desk just inside the hatch, coming to full attention just as his console bipped. He appeared hung in indecision for a moment.

"As you were," I said before he hurt himself. "Better get that ASIC alarm before it alerts the bridge."

"Yes, sar." He plunked down on the chair and started clearing the automated systems integrity check.

A spec-one stepped out of the small office and grinned. "Captain. What brings you to the swampy side?"

"Penna, right?" I asked, offering a hand. "I remember you from Breakall."

He beamed and shook my hand. "Yes, sar. Jorge Penna."

"How's life in the swamp?" I asked, taking in a lungful of the musky, green-tasting air.

"Oh, you know how it is, sar." He paused and looked at me.

"You're just knee-deep?" I made it sound like a frog's *nee-deep* croak.

He burst out laughing. "Not where I was going, but that about sums it up, sar."

"One of my earliest jobs on ship was environmental."

He frowned at me. "I didn't realize environmental was an officer billet, sar."

"It's not. I was a spec-two. Well, probably wiper when I started, but I made spec-two environmental before I left that division." I looked around the compartment. "Been a while. I started out changing the algae matrices on a multi-freight hauler over in Dunsany Roads."

"Wow," he said. "We haven't used those for—what? A decade?"

I grinned at him and he flushed. "Probably more," I said. "I started young."

"Sorry, Captain."

"Nothing to apologize for," I said. "Seriously, though. How's things down here? Anything you need that you haven't asked the chief for?"

He looked around the compartment as if taking inventory. After a few moments he shook his head. "Nothing I can think of. The chief and I came to an arrangement back on Breakall. I know what needs doing down here. She knows what needs doing up there." He jerked his chin in the direction of the overhead. "Long as she can't smell it, she leaves me to take care of it." He grinned. "She hasn't come down to find out why it stinks, so I figure I'm doing all right."

"Doing environmental long?" I asked.

"I started young," he said with a grin. "Tagged after my parents around the station since I was old enough to ask 'whazzat?' Drove my mother crazy, but Dad just kept answering."

"Which station?" I asked.

"One of Kondur's mining platforms over at Dark Knight."

"Never wanted to try your hand at mining?"

He shook his head and gave a mock shudder. "You never flew in a barge, I take it?"

"No, why?"

"Horrible boats. Not enough room to change your underwear without everybody getting their noses in it. Filled with dust most of the time. Air filtration is a nightmare. Environmentals are all plug and glug." He shook his head. "No, thank you very much."

"Well, I have some understanding of what goes on down here beyond the normal deck officer's 'what stinks?' kinds of questions. Let me know if there's something I can help with."

He nodded and smiled. "Thanks, Skipper. I appreciate that."

I turned to the watchstander, sitting bolt upright and stiff in his seat. "I'm Captain Wang," I said and held out a hand. "Mr. Schulteis, is it?"

The man jumped like I'd slapped him before standing and shaking my hand. "Yes, sar. Well, no, sar. Schul-tyes, not Schul-tees."

"Thank you, Mr. Schulteis," I said, emphasizing the corrected syllable. "I'll remember." I looked at his rating plaque. "Wiper? How'd you get assigned to environmental?"

"Drew the short straw, sar." He shrugged.

I looked at Penna. "Short straw?"

Penna sighed. "Chief Stevens had all the ratings pick their preferred slot based on seniority. Mr. Schulteis is the sole wiper and the most junior member of the crew. He had to pick last and got stuck with me, I'm afraid."

I looked at Schulteis. "How are you doing down here?"

He shrugged. "Quarter share, sar. Shares have been good. It's not too demanding, and honestly, nobody bothers me."

I looked to Penna. "Who else you have in the section?"

"Two half-shares. Carla Moore and Dave Larson. We didn't get any other environmental specialists hired on."

"You want a raise?" I asked, looking back at Schulteis.

Schulteis blinked at me. "A raise? What? To like half share?"

"Yeah. Just like half share. Maybe full share."

Schulteis looked at Penna who shrugged.

"Sure. What do I have to do?"

"Pass the exam," I said.

"That's it?" He asked. "Don't we have to have a billet for it?"

"Usually, yes. Here's the thing." I looked at Penna. "We're rated at minimum High Line crew levels. That means you're rated for at least one spec-three watchstander. You don't have any. You don't even have a full-share machinist, do you?"

Penna shook his head. "No, I don't, sar."

"You know how to get them?" I asked.

Penna shook his head but Schulteis seemed to light up.

"Pass the test," he said.

"Exactly," I said. "You know you don't have to pass each test in order, right?"

Penna's eyes grew wide, but Schulteis just grinned wider.

On my way past the chief's office, I slipped in and closed the door behind me.

She looked up and grinned. "Dish."

"Seems there's a bit of hero worship among your engineering staff. Apparently nobody wanted to bother Chief Dr. Margaret Stevens who wrote the book, etc."

The chief rocked back in her chair like I'd slugged her. "That's insane."

I shrugged. "That's what happened. I don't know how long that's been going on but it seemed like the coffee mess issue had been banged around before."

"Nobody ever said a word, I swear."

"I believe you," I said. "What do you know about Penna?"

"Best environmental tech I've seen outside of the academy. Why?"

"He has no spec-threes."

"The ship has no spec-threes for environmental."

"Weren't there any in the hiring pool?" I asked.

"Nobody I'd be willing to hire," she said, voice flat.

"Good enough for me, then. What about getting some of them moving on their ratings?"

"Out here?"

"Sure. As long as we grab the curriculum off the CPJCT before we jump into Toe-Hold space. They can prep out there as well as here. Grab the schedule and certify our own exams in deep space."

She nodded. "We could have been doing this all along."

"We probably should have been," I said.

"Sorry, Captain. That slipped by me."

"Not a problem. I may have tipped off Schulteis that he can take the spec-three exam as soon as he can pass it."

"Tipped off?"

"He seemed pretty resigned to having drawn the short straw for environmental."

"I let the ratings sort it out among themselves. There was a little arm-wrestling involved. I had to override a couple of them, but by and large they picked the slots I'd have assigned them to. Including Schulteis, if I remember correctly."

"He said he's pretty happy there. It was the 'short straw' comment that made me dig a little more."

She nodded. "I can see where it would."

"I asked if he wanted a raise."

The chief leaned forward. "What did he say?"

"Well, about what you'd expect. I asked him if he knew how to get one. Penna seemed a little out of the loop on the training rules."

"He probably would be, given his background. I'll fix that," she said, typing something in her console.

"I think we've got that handled, but expect Schulteis to make a quiet inquiry about the spec-three environmental curriculum."

"He's going to try to go from wiper to spec-three?" she asked.

"I think so. I hope so."

She ticked her head to the side. "Really?"

"Yeah. I do. I want everybody looking for the next rank, the next rating. Anybody wants a lateral across divisions, let me know."

Chief Stevens sank slowly into her chair as she stared at me across her desk, her eyes narrowing. "Wanna talk about it?"

"What?" I asked.

"Whatever lit a fire under you."

"Al," I said. "She wants to retire."

"We knew that."

"Soon as I can find a replacement," I said. "Here in the Toe-Holds."

The chief's eyes widened. "That's new. Did she say why?"

"Not really. Just that there's nothing to take her back to the High Line so she may as well stay in the Toe-Holds."

The chief pursed her lips. "I'll see if I can sound her out. One old woman to another."

"I don't necessarily want to convince her to stay," I said. "But if there's something wrong, I want to know if we can help."

The chief nodded. "Understood, Skipper."

I stood. "I have to go see Ms. Sharps about a coffee mess. See you at dinner."

When I got to the galley, I found Ms. Sharps looking over the steam kettle.

"Something wrong?"

She looked up and shook her head. "Hi, Captain. No, nothing wrong. Well, nothing serious. This could be cleaner."

I crossed to where she stood and looked. "I hated cleaning these."

She stared at me. "Did they make you do galley duty at the academy?"

"Yes, actually. They had these huge vatlike steam kettles in the galley there. I've seen smaller bathtubs. Not important. What are they missing? The fitting on the foot?" I leaned down to look at the underside where the steam came up from the boilers below.

"That's always a problem," she said. "The kettles stay warm for a long time. Getting down under there while the kettles are hot is a safety hazard. We do a weekly cleanup evolution there along with degreasing the range hoods."

"Then what?"

"The brushes we got are too stiff. I'm afraid they're scoring the inner surface." She leaned into the big stainless tub with a small hand light. "See the scratches?"

I leaned in and saw what she was looking at. "The scratches collect contaminants?"

"That's what I'm afraid of. These things aren't cheap. Getting it clean and keeping it clean is a priority."

"How much do you use it?" I asked, thinking back over the menus.

"Couple of times a week."

"We've only got what? Thirty crew?" I asked.

"I plan for thirty, but I think the actual count is only twenty-eight. Yes."

"What if this wasn't here?"

"What do you mean, Skipper?"

"Cap it. Don't cook anything that needs it. What does that do to your menu planning?"

Sharps looked at me and then stared at the kettle. I could see the gears turning in her head.

"Not that much," she said after a few long moments. "They're really too big to make a full kettle of anything."

"You could use the big stock pots, couldn't you?" I asked, nodding at the heavy cookery lined up under the prep counter.

She laughed. "Normally, I do."

"What would you use this space for if the kettles weren't here?"

"Cabinet and prep counter," she said. "But we just came out of the yards."

"That's my problem, not yours. Don't you have enough counter space?"

She laughed again. "You worked in a galley. Do you ever have enough?"

I looked around and grinned. "No," I said. "And never enough cabinets." I looked around again, really looked. "We can't do anything right now, but secure the kettle for now. Don't use it unless you absolutely have to. See what that does to your meal prep and planning. There's yards where we're going. Let's see what we can do."

"You're serious?" she asked.

"Yes. First principles, Ms. Sharps. Feed the crew. Feed them well. The ship can't sail if the crew can't sail her. If the gear isn't working, or isn't right, I want it fixed."

"Well, thank you, Skipper."

"Is there anything else I should know about?" I asked.

Sharps looked around as if taking inventory. "Not that I can think of. The kettle has been a problem from the beginning, but I never considered it might be a problem to be fixed."

"Fresh eyes sometimes see better," I said.

"Can't argue that," she said. "You wanted something, sar?"

"What?"

"Was there something you needed, sar? I don't see you in here very often."

"Oh, yes. The engineering division would like to have a coffee mess for the watchstanders. You know anything about that?"

"Nobody's asked for one."

"Chief Stevens seemed to think there might be a tray here. Something about this big?" I measured out the size with my hands. "Room for a carafe, some creamer and sweetener, and a few mugs?"

"Oh, sure." She crossed to a cupboard on the far side of the galley and pulled out a handled tray that looked pretty close to the size I remembered. She set it on the counter and pulled out a carafe, snapping it into a dimple in the surface. "Nonskid," she said. "There's a magnet in the base so the carafe won't sail away if there's a gravity failure." She reached under the counter again, pulled out a smallish box, and clicked that down beside the carafe. "I've got creamer and sweetener packets that'll fit in this. Room for half a dozen covered mugs."

"Do the mugs have magnets?" I asked.

"The ones we have don't, but I can get some that do."

"How many of these trays do you have?" I asked.

"Three in this size. I use a smaller one to deliver to the cabin."

As soon as she said that, I recognized the tray.

"How much of a pain is it to set this up?"

"Filling the carafe is the worst. Other than taking it down the length of the ship."

"What if the watch picked it up and returned the dirties when the watch changed?" I asked.

"Midwatch is the only time there's no staff here. There's always somebody here every other time." She grimaced. "If I were on the mid, I'd really want coffee."

"Can you prep the tray so they only have to fill the carafe and go?"

"Oh, sure. That's autopilot and a tail wind."

"Perfect," I said. "Show me how this goes?"

"What? Now?"

"Yes, please, Ms. Sharps."

She shrugged and pulled the carafe off the tray. "Here. If you'd fill this at the urn, Skipper?"

It only took a tick to fill the carafe and snap the safety lid down. By the time I got back into the galley, Ms. Sharps had placed six clean cups on the tray and filled the box with creamer and sweetener. I snapped the carafe into its spot.

"That's it," she said. "It's ready to go."

"Thank you." I picked up the tray and headed out. "If you'd have another ready for the watch change, I'll make sure somebody picks it up and brings this one back."

"No problem, Skipper." She gave me a quizzical look. "You're going to take coffee to the engineering watch?"

"Why not?" I asked.

"You're the captain, sar. Shouldn't you have people to do that for you?"

I paused at that. "No, Ms. Sharps. It needs doing. I'm here. I'm able. Nobody else is available. They'll have to keep up with it going forward, but this time's on me."

Sharps smiled. "You're the captain, Captain."

"Damn straight," I said and took the tray aft to engineering.

Chief Stevens saw me as I passed in front of her door and followed me down to the watch station.

"Here?" I asked, lowering the tray onto the cabinet she'd pointed out before. It fit perfectly and even clicked down onto the surface with a magnetic tug.

"Yes, Captain. Exactly there."

The watchstanders all looked at me like I'd grown a second head. Bell's jaw hung from his face.

"Here's the deal," I said. "Providing this meets with Chief Stevens's approval." I looked at her and she nodded, waving a hand for me to continue. "All right. Here's the deal. This tray, along with the carafe, any litter, all the cups—clean and dirty—goes back to the galley when you're relieved. The incoming watch will find a fresh tray just like this one on the counter just inside the galley door. Midwatch has to fill their own carafe. So long as nobody forgets to return the tray or pick up the fresh one, you'll have coffee available here. Questions?"

"Covered mugs only," the chief said.

I picked up a mug and flipped the handle on the lid a couple of times. "These mugs, not the normal galley mugs." I handed the one I held to the chief. "There's even enough for you."

She grinned at me and took the mug. "If you empty the carafe before the end of your watch, junior watchstander refills it," she said, eyeing Dent.

"Aye, aye, sar," he said.

"Pass the word to the other watch sections," the chief said. "I'll post a memo. Police yourselves because you don't want one of us doing it."

A round of aye-ayes went around the room and I followed Chief Stevens back to her office.

"You didn't fill it," I said, nodding at the cup.

"I'll let them have first draw," she said. She looked at the mug and then at me. "That was unexpected."

"I know, but it shouldn't have been," I said. "I'm going to try to fix that. Nobody should be afraid to ask for what they need on this ship. Even if they need to come to me to ask for it."

The chief nodded slowly. "Yeah. I need to deal with that here. I'm pretty distressed by it."

"You are a pretty big deal in the engineering world," I said. "You wrote the book. Among other things."

Her lips tightened. "Other things that they shouldn't even be aware of."

"Trust me when I assure you, writing the book is more than enough." I shrugged. "You still have Mr. Go, right?"

She grinned. "He's a peach."

"See if you can enlist him in making you human."

"You telling me how to run my division?" The question came with a smile instead of a sting.

"Not me, Chief. He just seemed like a good choice since he's clearly a fan but not star-struck."

She nodded again. "You're right." She glanced at the cup and then looked at me with pursed lips. "You wanna tell me what happened?"

"I'm not sure. Something Mal Gaines said."

"The culture thing?" she asked.

I shook my head. "How did it make you feel?"

Chapter Six
Mel's Place: 2376, February 1

The docking clamps chunked onto the ring just before the lunch mess. The chief said, "Shore ties established. All engines secured and safeties set."

"Thank you, Chief," Al said. "Mr. Reed?"

"Station authorities recognize the vessel and grant unlimited visa."

"It seems we have arrived, Captain," Al said.

"Log it and let's get some lunch," I said.

Al clicked a few keys on her console. "Logged, Captain."

"Any further business?" I asked.

"We're done, Skipper," Al said.

"Secure from navigation stations. Set all normal portside watch throughout the ship. Declare liberty for 1300," I said, unbuckling my seat belt and standing to stretch.

Al pulled the mic up and I heard her voice echoing through the passageways under my feet.

"Thank you, people. Well done." I slid down the ladder to clear the way for the bridge crew to depart and ducked into the cabin to wash up before lunch.

When I came out of the head, I found Pip sitting in front of my desk. "Eating aboard or would you like to go ashore?" he asked.

I checked the chrono and settled into my chair. "Let's go out for dinner. I need to make some inquiries for yardwork."

"The steam kettle?" he asked.

"Yeah. The chief doesn't think it'll be a big thing. We have the personnel to pull it out ourselves. We can patch and paint, but I'd just as soon pay for a local yard to do it so the engineering crew can get liberty."

"And if something goes pear-shaped, you already have outside help aboard," he said, finishing my thought for me.

"Yeah." I paused. "I also need to start figuring out how to recruit crew out here."

His eyebrows rose. "We losing somebody?"

I gave a little shrug. "Not immediately, but soon-ish."

"Al?" he asked.

"Keep it under your hair, but yeah. She wants to retire and would prefer to retire out here. How'd you know?"

"Lucky guess. If it had been engineering, the chief would have brought it up in the wardroom. Al would have done the same with deck division. It's not Tom. He's having way to much fun to leave us. Kim took the second-mate exam. I'm pretty sure she passed, so she's likely to move when she finds something she likes the look of." He shook his head. "We're going to lose the chief as soon as we find whatever it is she's looking for, but we haven't found it yet."

"Can we bump Kim's pay up to second mate?" I asked.

"Probably be smarter to just move her to the top tier of third," he said. "She's making so much in shares that pay is probably the last thing on her mind."

"You been studying up?" I asked.

"What? You think I don't know how to manage a crew?"

"Could have been somebody in Sharps's area," I said.

He shook his head. "That whole division is still recovering from being beached for too long. The yard availability didn't help restore their financial resources. We've got them for another few months. At least."

"Speaking of the chief," I said. "You have any insight on why she's still here?"

He shook his head. "I thought she'd leave after Telluride. That was a pretty big deal."

"She says she's not through with us yet," I said.

"Clearly."

"She said she wouldn't leave without lining up a replacement for us," I said.

He grinned. "I'll admit that I'm looking forward to seeing how she pulls that rabbit out of her afterburner. Chief engineering officers, fully qualified CPJCT-rated chief engineering officers, are hard enough to come by in the High Line. Out here?" He shook his head. "If she can do that, she's a real magician."

The chrono ticked over to noon and I stood. "Come on. Let's not keep the rest of them waiting."

He stood, following me out of the cabin and down the ladder toward the mess deck. "I have a new cargo," he said. "Handlers will pull the current can tomorrow morning. We'll have the new one in the afternoon."

"That's fast."

"They contacted us three days ago. Can of mining spares. Nice delivery bonus."

"What's the catch?"

He shrugged. "None that I can see."

"Where's it going?"

He stepped to the side to make way for a couple of the crew in civvies to pass us. "You'll love this," he said. "Telluride."

"That doesn't seem suspicious at all," I said.

"It makes a certain amount of sense," he said. "A decades-long embargo gets lifted, new trade routes are going to happen. Mel's Place is the closest of the large stations. The most likely to have the kinds of stuff Telluride might be interested in."

"Oh, I grant you that. If I were trying to keep a low profile, that's exactly what I'd do. Arrange a shipment from someplace logical and wave a bonus in front of the crew I wanted with me."

"You're thinking the chief?"

I shrugged. "Either her or the people she works for. It wasn't you, was it?"

He shook his head. "No."

"Would you tell me if it was?" I asked, stopping in the passageway again to look at him.

He nodded. "Yes. I would." He made a crisscross gesture over his heart and held up his hand, palm out. "If I know, I'll tell you."

The skepticism must have shown on my face.

"I know," he said with a grin. "It's a work in progress."

The mess deck only held a few of the crew. Glancing around, I felt pretty sure they were almost all the duty watchstanders. We filled trays and joined Ms. Fortuner at the unofficial officers' table.

"You pulled first watch?" I asked, sliding into a seat beside her.

She shrugged. "Volunteered."

"Volunteered or voluntold?" Pip asked.

"Teered." She took a swig of coffee. "It's the short watch. We'll change again at 1800 and I'll be free for two days."

"I'm surprised Al didn't take it," Pip said.

"I'm not," she said. "She wanted to go pick up some art supplies this afternoon. She'll be back in time to take the watch at 1800. She's looking forward to some quality art time."

"Have you ever seen any of her work?" I asked.

Both of them shook their heads.

"Curious," I said, addressing my lunch tray.

"Why's that?" Pip asked.

"Al isn't usually one to hide her light."

"Art's different," Ms. Fortuner said. "It's often private. Personal."

"Voice of experience?" Pip asked.

She grinned and shook her head. "Not directly. I had a girlfriend who was an artist. Before the academy. She got all squicky if somebody wanted to see a piece before it was done."

"According to Christine Maloney, Al is a known quantity in the Diurnia art scene," I said.

"She's damn good, then," Ms. Fortuner said.

"You know that scene?" Pip asked.

Ms. Fortuner gave a noncommittal shrug of the shoulders. "A little. Enough to recognize that Christine Maloney is one of the best curators of art in the sector—probably the Western Annex. She's got the money to do it right, the aesthetic sense to recognize talent when she sees it, and the knowledge to bring it all together. She runs an annual arts gala that draws the very best from all over and funds an artist-in-residence program for under-recognized talent."

"Al was a semi-regular participant in the gala," I said.

Ms. Fortuner gave me a side-eyed glance. "Al tell you that?"

"No. Christine Maloney implied it when she was here helping paint the cabin."

"Interesting," Ms. Fortuner said. "Wonder if that's why she's thinking of retiring."

I returned the side-eyed glance.

Ms. Fortuner grinned. "Don't look so surprised. You're not the only one she talks to."

"You don't have any insight into her decision?" I asked.

"No." She frowned into her coffee cup. "If I had to guess, it's frustration."

"With the system?" Pip asked.

"Something like that." She wrinkled her nose and shook her head. "She was a second mate for a decade. Did you know that?"

I nodded. "Been a first for another. It's in her jacket."

"She got burned. She had the first-mate rating long before she got a billet."

"Any idea why?" I asked.

Ms. Fortuner shrugged and gave me another glance. "You'd have to ask her."

I translated that as "yes, I know but I'm not telling" and filed it away for future reference.

"She's got enough time in grade for her master's ticket," I said.

"She's not interested," Pip said.

"You sure?" Ms. Fortuner asked. "Is she not interested or just doesn't expect she'll be given consideration?" She scraped the last of her lunch off the tray, drained her coffee cup, and stood. "I want to go check on Bentley at the brow."

"He a problem?" I asked.

She grinned. "Nope. Funny guy. Prankster, but not a problem. Just want to make sure he knows I'm watching out for him." She took her tray to the return rack, refilled her mug, and sauntered off the mess deck.

"She's going to want a second-mate billet soon," Pip said.

"She's going to make a great captain someday," I said.

Pip started at that. "Why do you say that?"

I shrugged. "Hunch."

"Wait, Bentley? I thought she had Cheuvront as a watchstander."

"She and Tom swap back and forth as the whim takes them. Long as everybody's happy and somebody covers the duty, I don't care who's on which watch."

Reed slipped into a seat beside Pip. "Did I hear my name?"

"Just talking about the watch rotation," I said.

"Why do you change it up so much?" Pip asked.

"It's not really that often. Both Cheuvront and Bentley want to go for their astrogation rating. We swap every voyage so each gets a chance to work with me while we're underway."

"How are they coming along?" I asked. "Should I be looking for a few new able spacers?"

Reed cast a glance at Kris Cross on the other side of the mess deck. "Might try prodding some of these SAs to move up. We've got three ables, three apprentices, but no ordinary."

I frowned. "Kim is the education officer?"

Reed nodded. "She's tried to get all three of them to move on their training modules without much luck."

"Is there an issue?"

Reed shrugged. "I haven't gotten into it with her. I know she's frustrated."

"She'll have some action down in engineering. I put bugs in a few ears," I said.

Reed shrugged again. "I'm just focusing on bringing up the next crop of spec-threes."

"Free labor," Pip said, half into his coffee mug.

Reed grinned. "Don't knock it. Anybody want cargo training?"

Pip shook his head. "Not that I know of."

Reed chuckled and addressed his lunch.

CHAPTER SEVEN
MEL'S PLACE: 2376, FEBRUARY 1

I had no sooner settled into my desk when the chief knocked on the open door frame. "We're all secured aft. Replenishment order's placed. Spares order coming tomorrow morning. Tanks will be topped off by end of the working day tomorrow."

I waved her in. "Gotta minute?"

"You're the skipper, Skipper." She grinned as she plunked down in one of the guest chairs.

"How do I recruit out here? There's no central repository that I've found."

"Al?" she asked.

I nodded.

"Don't do anything rash," she said. "I've got my eye on a candidate for her slot."

I blinked, trying to catch up with the conversation. "You've got a candidate?"

The chief grinned. "It may come as no surprise that I keep tabs on up-and-comers in the Toe-Holds."

"And the High Line?" I asked.

She shrugged. "Not so much. CPJCT does a pretty good job of tagging people."

"But you have a candidate?"

"Potentially," she said. "I think you'll like her. Young woman. About halfway to captain at this point, I think. Not sure what she wants long-term. Not sure she knows."

"She have any problems with our operational mode?"

"What, half in, half out?" the chief asked.

I nodded.

"She's doing it herself to a lesser degree. Has a pure profit motive."

"So not playing games with TIC or related entities?"

"Nope. Nothing like that."

"Got a name?" I asked.

"Yes, but I'm not sharing it yet."

"Got a replacement for you yet?" I asked.

"Me? Am I going somewhere?" she asked.

"I'm pretty sure you're leaving as soon as you find whatever it is we're looking for out here. You promised me a replacement."

She chuckled. "Yeah. Well. We haven't found it yet and it may take a while for the dust to settle again."

"You didn't answer the question," I said.

"Yes. I have a replacement in mind." She frowned, bit her bottom lip, and looked at her hands.

"But ...?"

"I'm not sure about her."

"Technical issues?"

"Oh, no. Bloody brilliant engineer. If she were interested in research, I'd be worried for my reputation."

"What, then?"

"She's got a cushy job, owns her own shipping company. I'm not sure I can convince her to work for you."

"And she's an engineering chief?"

"Oh, no. Not yet. First officer."

I raised my eyebrows. "How would that work?"

"She could have written the exam. All she needs is somebody to sign off on her."

"No name," I said.

The chief shook her head. "Sorry, no. Not yet."

"Back to my original question. How do I recruit out here?"

"Station net has a bulletin-board system. There's a classified ad section. Credit a word a day for ads."

"I can find crew? I may need to hire some spacers."

"Somebody leaving?"

"No, but both Cheuvront and Bentley are working on spec-three astrogation. They may move on."

"They won't go," she said.

"You think?"

"I know," she said. "Bentley's got his wagon hitched to your star. Cheuvront's making credits hand over fist on the shares here. It'll take a pretty big offer for her to accept, and she's got no incentive to look."

"Any advice on my spacer apprentices?" I asked.

"You lit a fire under Schulteis on your own. I'd check to see if any of the quarter- or half-shares want to change divisions. Offer some laterals if they can pass." She paused and peered at me. "Why do you care? They don't need ratings out here. They're the rank you say they are."

"They won't always be here. Getting rated is like money in the bank."

"You thinking of sending any of them to Alys?"

"What?"

"Alys Giggone. Remember her? Commandant at Port New-mar?"

I sat back in my chair trying to wrap my head around the idea.

"Never thought of that, huh?" the chief said with a grin.

"No," I said. "It never occurred to me. We've been in and out of the Toe-Holds. I've got no connections to the other captains the way Alys does."

"Do you need them?"

"Well, she pushed my name to the top of the list by getting captains I'd come in contact with to recommend me."

"She got *officers* who knew you. Al wasn't a captain. Most of the people who signed for you weren't captains, were they?"

I tried to remember who had signed, but she was right. The only two captains I could remember off the top of my head were Alys Giggone and Cassandra Harrison.

"You know captains who trust you."

"I do?"

She shrugged. "Recommendations only need three officers. You're an overachiever and an exception to the rule. You've got a fine of-ficer corps here. Even Pip, for all his other flaws, knows which end the fire comes out of. Even at that, do you think Fredi would refuse to back a candidate that you recommended?" She paused for a breath. "Do you think Alys Giggone would turn down one of your recommendations?"

"Why would Fredi take a chance on somebody she doesn't know?"

"She wouldn't be. She'd be taking a chance on somebody she thought enough of to put up for captain at a tender age. Somebody she herself helped grow into the role. Somebody she entrusted her grandfather's stars to."

"How do you know that?"

"Fredi and I go back a ways."

"Is there anybody you don't know?" I asked.

"Quite a few, actually," she said. "You'll gather as many or more before you're my age."

"So, that's two, assuming I can get in touch with Fredi."

"If you can't figure that part out, I'm not sure you're sitting in the right chair on the bridge," she said. "You also know Christine Maloney. Your reputation with DST keeps growing even if you're not there."

"I can't see asking Rossett," I said. "Or even Delman."

"Rossett's gone. He died five stanyers ago. Surprised you didn't hear about it. Hordes of heartbroken romance readers descended on the funeral. Three of them were killed in the crush. They had to give his widow planetary security when they found out Lenora Rossetti was actually a man." She shrugged. "Delman's cashiered. I don't think he's worked since he got tossed out of DST."

"I knew he was booted but never knew why."

"Does the name Vonda Behr ring any bells?"

"Yeah. She moved up to be first mate after I took over the *Agamemnon*."

"Delman made some bonehead moves to try to discredit her after failing to get into her shipsuit."

"Idiot."

"Yeah. That, coupled with the continual erosion of the *Tinker's* performance and a revolving door at crew berthing, convinced Jarvis to step in."

"Ames Jarvis?"

"The same. Rumor has it that Christine might have had some input."

"Yeah, I'd bet on that much."

"Anyway. DST didn't have a deep enough bench. They brought in a new-ish skipper from Dunsany. One of your old pals, actually."

"Not von Ickles," I said. "He's still running for Federated Freight, isn't he?"

"Jillian Avril," the chief said. "She made captain the stanyer before you did. Built a solid reputation at DST. Remembers you fondly, by the way. So does Cassie."

"Cassie?"

"Captain Cassandra Harrison? Well, Cassandra Adams now. She signed your ticket for the academy?" The chief's brows gathered in a little frown. "I never did get the low-down on that one, but she sends her regards. She's still sailing. Senior captain, of course. Silver stars and everything."

"Alicia Alvarez?" I asked.

"Allie's now Alicia Montoya. Married her first mate. They run a family ship over in Dunsany Roads. Their kids are old enough to sign the articles. I expect she'll ask you for a recommendation for her eldest in a couple of stanyers."

I felt a little bit like I'd been hit with a hammer. "How do you know all this?"

She gave a little self-deprecating shrug. "Comes with the turf."

"But you don't know everybody."

"Of course not. Something between ten and twelve billion people call the Western Annex home." She shook her head. "I don't think even High Tortuga knows them all, but we were talking about sending people to the academy. Think about it."

I took a deep breath in through my nose and blew it out. "Sure. Right. Yeah. I'll think about it."

"You'll find the bulletin board on the station net. It'll all be local talent, of course. Is there anything else I can help you with?"

I shook my head.

She stood and smiled at me again. I got the feeling I amused her. She strolled out of the cabin and pulled the door shut as she left.

I needed a moment to process everything she'd laid out.

Then I dug into the station net to find the bulletin board. I wasn't looking to hire anybody, but I wanted to see what options I had.

CHAPTER EIGHT
MEL'S PLACE: 2376, FEBRUARY 1

Pip dragged me out of the cabin at 1730. "Come on. Get civvied for dinner. I'm hungry and want to check in on that steak and brew place."

It only took a few ticks to slide into the suit. I caught a glimpse of myself in the mirror and just shook my head.

"What? You're not going to wear the hat?" Pip asked, resplendent in an iridescent gold tuxedo.

"I might need sunglasses," I said. "The hat? No."

"What? You think this is too much?" he asked, looking down at himself.

"For you? Not at all. I'm surprised you're not wearing a diamond stud in your ear."

His hand went to the side of his head and he swore. "Knew I forgot something. Be right back." He disappeared down the passageway only to return almost immediately, fastening a diamond stud in his ear.

"That's not a real diamond. Is it?"

He shook his head. "Cubic zirconium. Costs almost as much as the real thing."

"Chief says the ship will be ready to go tomorrow evening," I said as we cleared the lock and started down the gallery.

"We'll have cargo by then, too, I suspect," Pip said.

"Should we pull out earlier?" I asked.

Pip shook his head. "It's not going to be a long jump to Telluride from here but we may as well go in rested. Why you asking me?"

"Partner. Thought I'd be polite. I wasn't going to leave early unless you had some overriding reason to do so."

"What'd you talk with the chief about?" he asked.

"Recruiting."

"What else?"

"That's it."

He stopped in the middle of the gallery and put his hands on his hips. "She was way too self-satisfied to have it only be about recruiting."

"She has some candidates for us. She wants me to consider recommending crew to the academy."

"I figured the first. Why does the second surprise you? How did you get in?"

"You know how I got in. Alys Giggone."

"Yes, and now Dear Commandant needs recommendations from captains in the fleet to fill out her rosters with people who have more going for them than rich parents who aren't afraid to exercise their largesse with clipper skippers."

"Really?" I asked.

"Really what? Of course, she does."

"No. 'Clipper skippers?' You actually said that?"

"You like it?" he asked grinning over at me.

"Two goudas."

"I'll raise you a cheddar and two slices of swiss. The imported stuff."

We arrived at the blank door, but Pip remembered to knock and say "Joe sent me."

"Joe who?" the shadowy figure behind the door asked.

"Oh, sorry. This is new," Pip said. "Can I get a hint?"

The man slapped the panel closed.

Pip sighed and knocked again.

"Yeah? Whad'ya want?"

"Quentin sent me."

The man behind the door leaned closer to the opening. "Quentin?" he'd dropped the accent and seemed genuinely confused.

"Quentin Carstairs. I'm his nephew and I'm hungry."

The man's eyes opened so wide I thought the orbs might roll out of the sockets. He slammed the panel closed and swung the door open wide. "Sorry, Mr. Carstairs. Your uncle didn't mention he was expecting you."

"Happens. He's sometimes a little scattered. Surely you've noticed?"

The doorman coughed into his hand but offered no other commentary beyond "Right this way, sirs."

"Your uncle?" I asked.

"He owns the place."

"I didn't know we were meeting him," I said.

Pip shrugged. "I didn't either, but if he's here, he's buying."

The doorman showed us to a private room, knocking before entering. "Mr. Carstairs? This person claims to be your nephew."

Everybody in the room looked up, expressions varying from surprise to anger. Quentin stood up from the table and swept us all out before I got a good look at the attendees beyond Pip's aunt.

With the door firmly shut behind him, Quentin smiled at Pip and nodded at the doorman. "Yes, he's my nephew. I wasn't expecting him, but he's mine."

The doorman looked at the closed door and back at Pip. "Sorry, Mr. C. I didn't realize."

"Not a problem, Clive. Pass the word that Pip and Ishmael are my guests?"

Clive nodded and stopped to speak to a member of the staff on the way back to the door.

"Pip," Quentin said. "Sorry. Negotiations with some of the more skittish Toe-Holders."

"I'm sorry, Uncle Q. The doorman just brought us in thinking we were part of your party."

"How did he know you were my nephew?"

"I didn't know Joe's last name so I gave him mine."

"You knew I owned this place?"

"Sure. Doesn't everybody?" Pip asked.

Quentin frowned and pinched his lower lip between too fingers. "No. Actually they don't. Who told you?"

"Rachel, I think. I'm not sure, actually." He shrugged. "Last time we were here at Mel's we tried it out. We just got in this morning and thought to try it again."

"Odd," he said, but shrugged. "I need to get back in there and soothe some ruffled feathers. You and Captain Wang have a nice evening. Order what you like, just don't mention that you saw us here?" Quentin held a hand out for me to shake. "Nice to see you again, Ishmael. Sorry it's in such awkward circumstances."

I shook his hand and laughed. "I fly with Pip. There are no other kind of circumstances when he's around."

He chuckled and waited until the staff returned to show us to a table before re-entering the private room.

We did the necessary with the staff to get beer and beef moving toward the table before Pip leaned across to me. "Who did you see in there?"

"Nobody I recognized beyond your aunt and uncle."

"Tall guy. Going fashionably gray? Vandyke beard? Seated to the left of Aunt P?"

"Yeah. He seemed really put out."

"You caught that, too?"

I nodded.

"Recognize him?"

"Should I?"

"That's the guy who tried to outbid us for the *Chernyakova*. Vagrant."

I shrugged. "All right. And ...?"

Pip shook his head. "I don't know. He's got a bad odor here in the Toe-Holds for some reason I'm not privy to. It's not much better out in the High Line."

"Well, he's in a conference with your Aunt P and Uncle Q. With any luck we didn't screw up some kind of business deal."

"It would explain why he bought this place," Pip said.

"Cover for meetings?"

Pip nodded.

"He's not exactly a prominent individual, is he?" I asked. "Is anybody even looking at him?"

Pip sat back and took a pull from his pilsner. "Hard telling."

"Not our problem," I said. "We're looking for—what? Exactly?"

"I'm still hoping we're going to get a lead on the mega," Pip said.

"Why?"

"Because I get a reward for finding the lost ship."

I blinked. "That's new."

"I'm breaking about sixteen different NDAs by telling you, but I'm trying to be a little more forthcoming," he said. "Just keep it between us."

"You're not worried about somebody overhearing us in here?" I thought I was teasing him but he didn't seem to get the joke.

"Not really. There's a white-noise generator running in here to keep the conversations from spilling over. We're not talking very loud, I've got a jammer in my pocket, and the nearest live ear is about three meters that way." He nodded behind me.

"Really?" I asked. "A jammer?"

"You want to see it?" he asked, reaching for his pocket, his normal, bantering tone turning acerbic.

"Nope. I wouldn't know what I was looking at anyway."

The server returned with our steaks and we let the rest of the evening pass around us without additional commentary on what Pip's aunt and uncle might be doing with some kind of semi-criminal financier behind a closed door in what amounted to a private club.

As we left, replete with good food and great beer, I asked, "Did you recognize anybody else?"

He shook his head. "Not by name. At least two of them were bodyguard types. The woman across from Vagrant looked vaguely familiar, but she's either eye candy or distraction."

"You got that from a glimpse?"

"Of the half dozen people in there, she was the only one who didn't look pissed off when the door opened."

"Which means what?"

"Well, it could mean she has excellent hearing and heard us outside before the knock so she wasn't surprised and had a chance to compose herself before we crashed the meeting," he said.

"You don't think so."

"No, not really. It's more likely she was just bored and looking for something to entertain her."

We walked along in silence until we got to the docking gallery. Pip walked past our ship without stopping.

"We going somewhere?"

"Small ship dock."

"Checking up on the family?" I asked.

"Something like that. I want to see if they brought the *Bad Penny*."

"What's your thinking?"

"The *Penny* is too well known." He shrugged. "If they're doing something they want to keep quiet, they'll have brought something else."

We reached the small ship docks and began working along the locks, looking at the lock designators. "Most of these are blank," I said.

"Yeah."

"What do you hope to see?"

Pip shrugged. "Maybe nothing."

We reached the end of the small ship docks without finding a single ship with the name showing at the lock panel.

"That was a bust," I said.

"Was a long shot at best, but we walked off some of that food and beer." Pip shrugged again and headed back down the docking gallery toward the *Chernyakova*.

"Maybe not. Isn't that your cousin, Roger?" I asked.

Pip looked up. "Looks like. Let's go say hello."

We strolled along toward Roger. I could tell the exact moment he saw us coming. It was the stutter-step in his gait.

When we got close enough, he said, "Pip. To what do I owe the pleasure?"

"We were just in the neighborhood. Dropping off a can of machine parts. Taking a stroll. Just another day in the life. What brings you to Mel's Place?"

"We ran into Quentin at the restaurant," I added, hoping to forestall any attempt at dissembling. "He bought us dinner."

"He did. That's a great place," Pip said.

"I'm stuck holding down the ship, as always," Roger said. "Just stepped out for some takeaway." He held up the bag.

"Well, don't let us keep you," Pip said. "Nice running into family out here. How long you going to be on station?"

"Probably gone in the morning," he said. "You?"

"We've got a couple more days. Some yard upgrades. Give the crew liberty."

"What are you sailing around these days? I saw the *Son* at Port Lumineux. Your father said you weren't using it anymore."

"You remember Ishmael?" Pip presented me with a wave of his hands like I was some kind of game-show prize. "He and I are in business together. Picked up a used Barbell and we're just getting our feet wet in bulk freight." He paused. "I'm surprised you didn't hear about it."

"How's that working for you?"

"We got a good deal on the ship itself. Auctions can be fun. We've almost paid off the notes. There's a lot more money in bulk freight than I thought. Even with the crew costs and all. It's giving me a chance to test some of my theories on nondiversified cargo distribution."

Roger's eyes started to glaze over. I really understood his point of view.

I pulled Pip's arm. "Come on, Pip. Roger's food's getting cold and we should really head back and make sure nobody's stolen the boat."

Pip nodded. "Great seeing you, Roger. I'm sure we'll run into each other again." With a jaunty wave, he led the way along the docking gallery. He pulled his tablet out and began fiddling with it. He shook it a couple of times, frowned, tapped it on the side of his hand.

His antics had positioned him just slightly behind me so I had to turn to see what he was doing.

"Has he continued on his way yet?" Pip asked.

A quick glance over his shoulder revealed Roger staring after us. "Not yet."

He handed me his tablet. "Here, you fiddle with it a little. See if you can get it to light up."

"Powering it up would probably help," I said, noting the switch on the side.

"Well, yes, it probably would, but then why would we be standing here in the docking gallery?"

Out of the corner of my eye, I saw Roger shrug and continue along. "He's moving."

"How far down?"

"Coming up on the third lock. That's the one. He's keying it open."

"Did it actually open or is he just fiddling with the lock?"

"Fiddling," I said when the lock didn't actually open.

"He's being careful. Gimme the tablet back?"

I handed it to him.

He flipped the switch, lighting up the front panel. "Ah. There!" He held the tablet up so I could see it. In the process he glanced over his shoulder and offered a final wave to his cousin who still watched us.

Pip continued on our way, pulling me along in his wake as if by gravity. He kept waving his tablet around in the air. First in front of his face and then off to the side. It took me a moment to realize the camera was open and showed the view over his shoulder.

We hadn't gone more than a dozen meters down the gallery before Roger finally opened one of the locks and slipped inside. The lock door swung closed behind him but not before Pip flashed a digital of the open lock.

"All right," he said, securing the tablet. "We know which lock is theirs."

"Is that important?" I asked.

"Maybe. I don't know right now, but something smells off."

"How so?"

"First, Roger wasn't happy to see me. Second, he was really surprised when we said we'd met Uncle Quentin. Third, he walked past the real lock and pretended to open a different one. That by itself makes my curiosity bump itch."

"You sure it's not your scalp adjusting to not being abused by bleach every few days?"

Pip sighed. "Reasonably, and I suppose I had that coming."

"What makes you think he didn't just get the wrong blank lock?"

"They're numbered. Would you walk to the wrong numbered lock in a strange port?"

"Maybe," I said. "If I was flustered enough."

Pip chewed the side of his mouth. "All right. I'll give you that much." He paused and looked back down the gallery. "Something is just weird."

CHAPTER NINE
MEL'S PLACE: 2376, FEBRUARY 2

Mid-morning, station time, found me in the chandlery office looking for some installation help.

"You want to do what again?" the chandlery supervisor asked.

"I've got a steam kettle in my galley. I want it pulled out and replaced with a cabinet and some counter space." I shrugged. "Anybody around here who can handle that?"

"You know what kind of cabinet? Got the dimensions?"

"Not on me. I figured I'd see if I could find somebody to do the work before I got too far into the well."

"Well, there's a refit yard on the far side of the station, but I don't expect you'd need that much yard work for a minor refit." He rummaged in the top drawer of his desk. "Ole Man Douglas is probably your best bet. I'm looking for his magnet."

"Magnet?"

"Aha!" he said and pulled out what looked like a chunk of rubber shaped like a pipe wrench. "Here it is. He's left these all over." He tossed it down on his desk where it stuck with a snap. "Got his name and address on it. He takes on odd jobs. Does good work." He peeled the rubber off his desk and tossed it to me. "Here. See what he says."

I caught the thing and looked at the top. "Douglas and Sons, Refit/Refurb/Return" with an address. "And sons?" I asked.

"Well, his sons got fed up and left about ten stanyers ago. Left him here."

"All right, then." I waved the rubber in the supervisor's general direction and headed back to the ship. I wanted to check with Pip before I did anything rash.

I got about halfway down the docking gallery toward the *Chernyakova* before a pair of familiar figures levered themselves off the bulkhead. "Aunt P. Uncle Q," I said. "Fancy running into you here."

"Gotta minute, Skipper?" Aunt P asked.

"Sure. This about Pip and me crashing your party last night? I'm really sorry about that."

She shook her head. "No. Well, not exactly." She stuck her hands into her pockets and glanced at Quentin. "How much do you know?"

"Depends. What are we talking about?"

"You pulled a hot iron out of the fire in Telluride. You didn't just happen onto that with a load of beef."

"You must know what Pip knows. He turned in his report at Lumineux."

"Yeah, so did Maggie Stevens," P said. A small herd of able spacers ambled along the gallery and P pulled me aside to let them pass. "Why'd you come back out?"

"Back out? I'm not exactly following this." I offered an apologetic shrug. "I'm not up on all the spycraft stuff."

"Spycraft?" P asked.

"Whatever you call it. Pip and Chief Stevens are both looking for the mega, as nearly as I can tell. Pip mumbled something about a reward. I don't know what Chief Stevens is getting out of it."

Aunt P shook her head. "Why are you back in the Toe-Holds?"

"I just told you," I said, trying to read something in either Aunt P or Uncle Q's face.

Aunt P frowned at me then looked at Uncle Q.

"You're looking for the mega?" Uncle Q asked.

I nodded. "Well, and we're piling up credits. Another few runs and we'll have paid off the ship."

"Why were you at the restaurant last night?" he asked.

"Dinner. We just got in yesterday. Went out to dinner. We ate there the last time we were here. The door guy asked for a different phrase than the one Pip remembered. Pip knew you owned it so he tried to pull on the Carstairs name." I shrugged. "Thanks for dinner, by the way. It was just as good as I remember."

"Why'd you go snooping around the small ship dock last night?" Aunt P asked.

"All Pip. He wanted to see which ship you flew out in."

"Why?" she asked.

"I have no idea why Pip does anything. I just tag along. Sometimes it's amusing. Sometimes it's just Pip getting into mischief. Once in a while he gets us both in hot water." I shrugged again.

"You bought the *Chernyakova* with him," Uncle Q said.

"Yeah. He talked me into going into business with him over a stanyer ago with some story about a missing mega freighter. I didn't even know about the Toe-Holds except as some vague historical reference. I went along with it because I needed something to do and—well—I thought maybe I could exorcise some ghosts from my past by putting the old girl to rights."

"Did you believe him?" Uncle Q asked, more curiosity and less confrontation in his tone.

"Not at first. I'm not sure I do now. He seems to be trying to be a bit more truthful."

"How'd you get out of Telluride?" Aunt Q asked.

"We almost didn't. You must have read Pip's report."

"Pretend we didn't," Aunt Q said.

"We jumped in, scouted around the periphery of the system, and discovered we were being stalked by another ship. A miner warned us off and our stalker put a missile into it. We jumped out immediately and made our way to Port Lumineux. Chief Stevens and Pip both filed reports. We sold the can of beef to the station there and picked up a can going to Port Newmar."

"That's it?" Aunt P asked.

"I don't know what else there might be."

"Last night. Did you see anybody at the table?" she asked.

"You two, a woman, and a guy with a goatee," I said. "There might have been others in the room but I didn't see them." I grinned at Uncle Q. "You hustled us out pretty quickly."

"Did you recognize anybody besides us?" Aunt P asked.

"I didn't, but Pip recognized the guy as being one of the people bidding against us for the *Chernyakova*. Some High Line outfitter named Vagrant."

The two shared a look and Uncle Q shrugged.

Uncle Q put a paw on my shoulder and stared at me. "We aren't here. You didn't see us. You didn't see Vagrant. You never talked to Roger."

"Who?" I asked.

He frowned and opened his mouth but stopped himself, offering a grin. "Thanks," he said.

"No problem. Will I ever find out what this is about?"

"Ideally, no," he said.

"Can I ask a question?"

He shrugged. "I may not be able to answer."

"Where is David Patterson?"

He frowned. "I don't know."

"But you know the name," I said.

I caught the quick glance that Aunt P shot him before he answered. "Yes."

"If you needed to hire him, how would you go about it?"

"He's not a freelancer," Aunt P said, breaking in before Uncle Q could answer. "The people he does business with all know him and he knows them."

"You don't do business with him," I said.

They both shook their heads.

"You know somebody who does," Uncle Q said. "But he's in prison."

"Simpson," I said.

He nodded. "Can *I* ask a question?"

I grinned at him. "You've been doing pretty well at it so far."

"Why do you want Patterson?"

"I don't really know," I said. "Having you two here without Pip, it seemed like a good opportunity. I'm going to have to deal with him sooner or later, I think."

Aunt P's eyebrows shot up. "Deal with him?"

"He killed my engineer," I said. "TIC is saying it was an accident. Nobody was supposed to die. Pip was trying to convince me that my search for Patterson is my cover for coming to the Toe-Holds. Vengeance and all that. He's also made it clear that there's damn little I can do about it out here, even if I find him. He's been making the case that Patterson works for TIC and that Simpson was just a side job."

"She was a lot more than your engineer," Uncle Q said.

I nodded. "She was."

Aunt Q leaned forward. "Out here, identities are liquid. You can be anybody you need to be. The High Line? That's different. Every hatch you open, every bill you pay. Every time you put your thumb print down. It's you. They track who, when, where. They can't do much about the why but they know the rest." She spoke quickly, words spraying like water from a hose.

"I figured that out long ago," I said. "The question that devils me is how does Patterson have an alias?"

"The answer to that is High Tortuga," Aunt P said.

"The bank?" I asked.

She gave me a wolfish grin. "The data center."

Uncle Q's tablet bipped. "Time to go," he said, offering a hand. "Thanks."

I shook his hand. "I've kept your secrets before. I can keep these. Safe voyage."

CHAPTER TEN
MEL'S PLACE: 2376, FEBRUARY 2

The odd conversation with Pip's aunt and uncle stayed with me all the way back to the ship. By the time I got back to the cabin, I'd almost forgotten Douglas and Sons. I dropped the magnet beside my keyboard and sent a message to the station address. I didn't expect much, so began my search for a refit yard.

When I started digging into it, I found plenty of yards. Nothing like I needed to just pull out the kettles, patch the deck, and install a cabinet, though. Apparently it wasn't a thing people did in the Toe-Holds. Or at least not a thing Toe-Holders hired out. It occurred to me that I hadn't actually asked the chief about it.

With a sigh at my own short-sightedness I pinged her tablet and sat back to think about what I'd learned from Penny and Quentin Carstairs. One phrase echoed in my head. "Out here, identities are liquid. You can be anybody you need to be."

It made sense but it also implied a couple of things. First, my assumptions about identification seemed to be built on sand. Or, maybe, water. Second, it must be possible to change identities. Aunt P's comments about High Tortuga pointed to the source. Not so much the visible financial structures but the actual data management needed to support those structures.

I wondered if my understanding of the hard-coded, inviolable ship transponders was equally liquid.

But I knew those transponders, inside and out. The chips in them weren't rewriteable. Once they were burned, the ship's identity got stored on glass. They couldn't be updated.

The answer smacked me in the back of the skull. I hadn't updated the transponder when I registered the *Iris*. There was no need to. The hull identification stayed the same. The data on the chips never changed.

The registration simply changed the name associated with the records so that once the records updated through the system, everybody saw the ship as the *Iris*.

I looked at my thumb, my gaze working through the loops and whorls. All I needed to do to change my identity was to change the record my thumbprint pointed to. Everybody thought that was impossible, but I was sure I knew somebody who'd done it. Probably more than once.

The console bipped as the chief knocked on the cabin's door frame.

I blinked at her, trying to refocus from looking at the ball of my thumb.

"You all right, Skipper?" she asked.

"Yeah," I said. "I think I am. I just had an epiphany."

"Did it hurt? You look like you've been clocked with a spanner."

"No. It didn't hurt but I'm kicking myself for not tumbling sooner."

"You needed me for something?"

"Oh, yes. Galley. Ms. Sharps. Gotta minute?" I asked.

"Going ashore for lunch in a bit but I've got time."

I led her down to the galley where Ms. Sharps was working dough in the big mixer.

"Ms. Sharps, can you walk through the problem you showed me earlier with the steam kettle?"

"Sure. Hi, Chief." She nodded to the chief before crossing to the kettle in the corner. "It's this kettle. If you look closely, you can see that it's wearing already. I'm pretty sure the cleaning brushes are too stiff."

Chief Stevens leaned into the opening, using a small handflash to illuminate the surface from various angles. "Yeah. I see the problem." Her voice echoed oddly in the kettle. She straightened up and turned off the light, tucking it back into a pocket. "You got one of the brushes?"

Ms. Sharps took us over to the gear closet and pulled out a standard, plastic-bristle scrub brush. "Just one of these. We use them on everything where we need a little extra scrub."

The chief took the brush and ran her hand over the bristles, combing her palm through them. She shook her head. "It's nothing you're doing. The kettle's flawed."

"How can that be?" Ms. Sharps asked.

"The kettles are supposed to be pure stainless. The metal is supposed to be polished smooth, which cuts down on microbe-sized flaws in the surface. Metal isn't a good growing medium for much but surface flaws can catch stuff that is, which is why so many things that need to be sterilized are made of polished stainless."

"If it's not the brush, what's causing the scratching?" Ms. Sharps asked.

"I think there's a coating on the surface. It's not bare metal. It's thin. Probably only a few microns deep." She shook her head. "It shouldn't be there. How much have you used the kettle since we've been out of the yards?"

Ms. Sharps shrugged. "Maybe a dozen times. It's a pretty specialized piece of gear. Great for making big pots of stew or soup, but even at that, it's overkill for a crew our size. The captain suggested I stop using it altogether."

"Not a bad choice. What would you like in that space?" the chief asked.

"We'd discussed a cabinet and prep surface," I said.

The chief nodded, her gaze sweeping the area around the kettle. "I could see that. Sure." She pursed her lips and nodded. "You want that or do you want the kettle fixed?"

Ms. Sharps worried her lower lip between her teeth, looking at the kettle and then looking around at the rest of the galley. "I hate to waste the investment in the kettle."

"Chump change," I said. "What's important is having a galley that does what we need it to do. This is probably some default kitchen arrangement the yard uses all the time. I know I didn't sign off on the layout. Did you, Chief?"

The chief shook her head. "Most of what's here was either here to begin with and upgraded or rebuilt according to the yard standard with modern gear."

"The expense is not your concern, Ms. Sharps," I said. "Your concern is what you need to make this space as functional as it can be. My concern is that we have a galley you love to work in, not one the yard gave us by default."

She nodded and looked around. After a moment, she looked at me. "Really?"

"Really," I said.

"Gut it," she said, looking from me to the chief and back again.

Her response choked a laugh out of me. "Gut it?"

"Yes, sar. Well. Not entirely, but there are work flow problems here that trip us up every day."

I looked at the chief who appeared to be stifling a grin. "What?" I asked.

"Be careful what you ask for, Skipper," the chief said.

My tablet bipped. "I'm apparently needed at the brow. Hold that thought, Ms. Sharps. Can you stand by, Chief?"

They both nodded and I made the short trip down the passageway to find Torkelson with a guy in a mostly clean but ragged coverall with the name Douglas stitched over the left breast.

"Sorry to bother you, Captain. Mr. Douglas here said you wanted to talk to him," Torkelson said.

I nodded. "Thank you, Ms. Torkelson. I do." I held a hand out. "Thank you for coming, Mr. Douglas. I hope it won't be a wasted trip."

He grinned. "One of those, huh?" He nodded a couple of times. "Been there before. What's twisting the bilges?"

I nodded toward the passageway. "Why don't we look it over in person and you can get the skinny direct from the source?"

He nodded. "Always best," he said. "Always."

I led him back to the galley where Chief Stevens and Ms. Sharps were waving arms and measuring spaces. Both seemed to be in good spirits. "Chief Margaret Stevens, Ms. Melanie Sharps, this is Mr. Stan Douglas. He's a local craftsman. They recommended him at the chandlery and I contacted him earlier this morning."

"Chief. Ms. Sharps." Douglas nodded at each. "I wouldn't go so far as to call myself a craftsman. Tin-knocker and bolt-twiddler, maybe." He looked around the galley. "What do you think the problem is?"

I laughed. "Ms. Sharps has a problem with the layout of the galley. Chief Stevens has the say-so on the physical plant. Depending on any decision we reach this morning, we might be doing some remodeling over the next couple of days."

Douglas nodded again. "Ms. Sharps? Wanna tell me what you think should happen?"

"I can tell you what I'm having problems with," she said. "Maybe you can tell me what has to happen."

He grinned at that, lighting up like a proximity alarm in a docking bay. "Do tell," he said. "Do tell."

Ms. Sharps led him on a tour of the galley fixtures while the chief and I stepped back out of the way.

"I suspect this wasn't anything like what you had in mind," the chief said, leaning close and speaking softly.

"Not even in the same sector, but I'm not complaining. At least not yet."

"How familiar are you with Barbell galleys?"

"I've only ever seen the *Tinker*'s and this one. I can lay out the *Agamemnon*'s from memory and could probably still navigate the *Lois*'s in the dark with my eyes closed. It never occurred to me that this layout wasn't a standard one."

"It may be," she said. "The larger question is whether or not a chef has ever been consulted before."

"Good point."

Douglas trailed Sharps around the galley for the better part of a quarter stan, every so often stopping to ask a question or take a note on his tablet. When they got to the steam kettle, he chuckled. "Damn fools put these in everywhere. Never saw the purpose on a ship like this. Too big for cooking, too small for bathing. How many do you feed a day?"

"Thirty-ish," Ms. Sharps said. "Three main messes and snacks in the cooler for the mids."

Douglas nodded, pursing his lips. "Standard Barbell crew. Some skippers try to skimp on crew. Always bites them in the ass."

"Recommendations, Mr. Douglas?" Ms. Sharps asked.

Douglas looked around, nodding his head every so often. "First problem is traffic. These islands are too close together. You'd be better off with a single, slightly larger one that lets you and your staff all work either on the island or at the periphery—like there at the stove-top or over managing the ranges without stepping on each other or getting banged with a hot pan." He walked to the middle of the galley and held his arms up like he was conducting the orchestra. "Was me? I'd put it right about here, shift it forward toward the door to make that alley in front of the sinks and ranges a bit wider. Still has room for the serving line and your prep and staging areas on that side of the galley but gives you a lot more options for how you're going to work on the islands. It's actually going to give you more floor space and less island top, but you're going to be more efficient in that use because you can reach it all. Right now you can't reach the middle of either of these islands from the side. They're too wide."

"If they can't work across from each other, won't that limit the number of people who can work on the island?" Ms. Sharps asked.

"How many people do you have?" Douglas grinned.

Ms. Sharps blinked a few times, her gaze sweeping back and forth. "Oh. Of course."

"Shouldn't be more than three of you here at a time, right?"

Ms. Sharps nodded.

"Floor space counts as much as prep space, and right now you could park a shuttle on the counter space you have but the pilot has no room to get out." He shrugged.

Ms. Sharps took a deep breath and blew it out, her head on a gimbal as she scanned back and forth. "I'm trying to visualize how it would look."

Douglas pulled out his tablet. "Can I take some digitals?" he asked, looking to me.

"Whatever you need," I said.

"I need a coffee," he said. "The digitals will do for now." He moved around the galley, taking snaps on his tablet from all angles. "I assume you want this done with a minimum of downtime and as soon as possible."

"Doesn't everybody?" I asked.

"Well, most people want cheap, too," Douglas said, taking one last picture from the open galley door. "There. That should do it." He flipped through the screens, apparently checking the pictures. "Lemme grab the measurements." He pulled a yellow stick from a pocket and rested it on the nearest work island. He took a picture of it and nodded. "That'll do."

"Now what?" Ms. Sharps asked.

"Now, if it's not too much trouble, I'd like to take a seat out there on the mess deck and run up some plans for you to see."

"Here? Now?" she asked.

He eyed the chrono on the bulkhead. "You're about two stans from lunch mess. I need about half a stan to run up a prototype for you to see. Easier to do it here. Saves me running back and forth from the shop."

Ms. Sharps blinked a couple of times and looked at me.

"Don't look at me, Ms. Sharps. It's your galley."

"Would you like a pastry with your coffee, Mr. Douglas?" she asked. "I have some fresh muffins. Just made them this morning."

"Call me Stan, Ms. Sharps." He grinned. "A muffin sounds terrific."

"You're welcome to stay for lunch, Mr. Douglas," I said, showing him to the lock.

"Obliged, Cap'n, but I need to get this prototype loaded into my metal bender. I'm going to use almost all of what you've got in there now, but I promised Melanie some extra drawer space which you don't have. I'll have them fabbed up by morning."

"This wasn't your first galley, was it?" I asked.

He laughed. "I've lost track of how many galleys I've done. After the first twenty, I realized that damn few yards understand how a galley is supposed to work. Mostly they have the same problems you all have here. Too much island, too little foot space. Planning for a crew that's too big and a galley gang numbered in the dozens instead of single digits."

"Sure you can get this done between breakfast and lunch tomorrow?" I asked.

He shrugged. "It'll be tight. I should be able to do it all in three stans, if Melanie does the prep I've asked for. I could do it overnight tomorrow night. Start after the dinner mess. That would cause less stress, but this way I'll be around to see how things are working for lunch. Leaves the afternoon to make any adjustments."

"I still don't see how you're going to do all that in a couple of stans."

"Said it yourself, Skipper. Not my first galley."

I keyed the lock open for him while Ms. Torkelson logged him off the ship.

He stopped just at the top of the ramp. "You didn't haggle much. You want to renegotiate?"

I laughed. "I'm as tight as anybody, but I know the value of a happy crew. That woman back there is the key. Having her in a galley she *loves* is almost priceless."

He gave me a little laugh. "I shoulda asked for more." With a grin and a wave he headed down the ramp. "See you in the morning, Skip."

I went back to the galley where Ms. Sharps and Mr. Franklin were rolling the lunch mess out. She smiled in my direction but didn't pause in her work. I caught the chief's eye and we adjourned to the cabin.

"You all right with having Douglas work on the ship?" I asked, settling behind the desk and digging into the bit that gave me the most heartburn.

"You afraid you've hurt my feelings, Ishmael?"

I shrugged. "A little."

She laughed. "My forte is engines. Jump drives. Inertial compensators. Getting crews trained and keeping them on their toes. Remodeling ships? Yeah. I can. Douglas? You saw him. He's an artist in the truest sense. He's not creating a galley. It's going to be a work of art that will make every crew member who works in it feel something. Something good." She shook her head. "I can't even pretend that I could do what I'm pretty sure Stan Douglas is going to do to that galley."

"Should we have him do the mess deck?" I asked.

"Ask him what he thinks tomorrow. Why stop there? What about crew berthing?"

I thought about it for longer than I should have, probably.

The chief waved her hands in front of my face. "We've got to move cargo, Skipper."

I laughed. "All right. I'll tuck that away for 'someday' planning."

"Speaking of getting underway, we're going back to Telluride," the chief said.

"Yeah. I'm sure it's just coincidence that we brought a can from Newmar and—voilà—we find a can going to Telluride."

"Not as unusual as you might think," she said. "Mel's Place is a key trans-shipment point. They've got the docks, warehouse, and storage space to support most of the Western Annex by themselves. Mel's, Dark Knight, and The Ranch handle almost eighty percent of all traffic in the Toe-Holds. If anybody had a can going to Telluride, it would be here. Probably a dozen more still waiting."

The percentages surprised me, but I had already recognized that Mel's was a key player in the region. "What do you know about Malachai Vagrant?"

Her eyebrows flashed upward. "Vagrant? Why?"

"Pip says he's in bad odor in most of the Western Annex."

She pursed her lips and frowned. "Yeah. He was a major player in the High Tortuga pantheon at one time. Got caught with his hand in the cookie jar. He keeps mostly to the High Line now. Nobody is aware of any CPJCT regs he's broken so they can't touch him." She stared at me. "Where did you see him?"

I shrugged and wondered how much I could tell her without violating my promise to Quentin Carstairs. "Pip thought he saw him last night on station."

"You don't?"

"I don't know him well enough. He was bidding against us at the *Chernyakova* auction on Breakall. That's the only reason I even know the name."

"So why the question?" she asked.

"A bad actor bidding against us for the ship suddenly shows up at Mel's Place in Toe-Hold space where CPJCT can't touch him at the same time the *Chernyakova* is here?"

She shrugged. "You're still thinking like a High Liner. Mel's Place is bigger, has a larger population, and handles more cargo than any single orbital in the High Line. It handles more than almost any two orbitals you could pick at random. The confederation port at Dunsany Roads is probably the nearest comparable and that's only about sixty percent of Mel's." She shook her head. "If you want to disappear in a crowd? Mel's is the station you want. If he's going to be anywhere in the Toe-Holds, it's most likely to be Mel's.

"His brother, Zachary, has some connection with Dark Knight. Verkol Kondur runs the place but Zachary Vagrant provides some services to him. I don't know exactly what, but Vagrant flies a mixed-freight hauler that may have as many hidden compartments as legitimate holds."

"We've been to Dark Knight. Seemed pleasant enough."

"Trade flourishes when the traders have no concerns about the station or its inhabitants," she said. "Kondur likes it that way and keeps it that way."

"So Mel's Place is the great cross roads?"

"One of only a few, yes."

"If I was looking for David Patterson, I should be looking here?"

"You're full of surprises today," she said. "Are you looking for David Patterson?"

"I'm not sure. Pip seemed to think I should be. It was his argument for getting me to buy into the *Chernyakova* scheme in the first place."

"But ...?" she asked.

"But he's been working to convince me there's not much I could do about it even if I found him."

"Probably more truth than not in that statement," she said. "What would you want him for?"

"Take him back to the High Line for trial."

I saw the veil drop across the chief's face. It was subtle—a shift in the tension around her eyes, a fractional tilt of her head.

"I see," I said. "So I'm not sure. There's damn all I can do about him. Probably the best thing is forgive and forget."

"You could forgive him?" she asked.

I shrugged. "Here's the thing. Exacting retribution means I have to become like him. I have to be acting on impulses that are antithetical to my basic philosophy. If I can't be the white knight or the good cop or whatever metaphor applies to dragging his sorry butt back to the authorities to answer for his actions, and I can't wreak personal vengeance on his hide without becoming like him, the only alternatives are to let him continue to connect to me through my animosity, or forgive him and move on with my life." I shook my head. "I'm done having his pollution cloud my vision. I guess I have to forgive him so I can cut him out of my life again."

"What about Greta?" she asked.

"I'll always have Greta inside, but she's gone from this universe. I miss her. I regret being a dunce where she was concerned and losing time with her that I could have had. Maybe I've learned something. Something valuable." I sighed. "I don't know. Life is short. Love is rare. All those duck-billed platitudes. Captains have to choose their own paths." I paused and listened to that echo in my head. "I don't think it's just captains who have to choose."

"No," she said in a quiet voice. "It's not."

"The cook on the *Lois* told me that, actually. I can hear him in my mind. 'Choose the path before one is chosen for you.' I always knew that was good advice. I just never realized how good." I looked across the desk at her. "He's working at the officer's club at Port Newmar now. I saw him when Pip and I were hatching the scheme that brought us here."

"What do you want to do now, Captain?" she asked.

"We still have some loose ends to wrap up," I said. "I don't know what they are but both you and Pip are working on something. I'm going to trust you'll let me know when there's some part of that you need me for. In the meantime, I'm going to haul freight, take care of my crew, tend my ship, and make money."

She chuckled a little. "That's a plan, but what about you?"

"What about me?"

"What are you going to do about you?"

"I'm going to take it one day at a time. I think I've done some good work today. I'm going to try to do more tomorrow."

She nodded and slapped her palms against the arms of the chair before standing. "I've got an engine room to check on. Holler if you need anything, Captain."

Chapter Twelve
Mel's Place: 2376, February 3

The brow watch paged me at 0700 to sign Stan Douglas and his crew aboard. "Starting early?" I asked.

He grinned. "She's expecting me. You'll see."

I signed him in and led the parade to the mess deck. A few hangers-on lingered but it was only the third day in port. I suspect they were more curious than anything. Nothing travels faster than rumor. Not even light.

I stuck my head into the galley and found the place in a carefully organized disorder. Both islands were bare; the serving line had been secured, and served only to support a variety of pots, pans, bowls, and trays. All the prep areas were covered in similar arrays. The ovens appeared to be loaded with extra bakeware. Ms. Sharps and Ms. Adams had the sink filled with soapy water and were cleaning up after the breakfast mess while the sanitizer ran in the background.

"Oh, good," Ms. Sharps said. "You're here. We're ready for you, Stan."

"So I see," he said. "We'll just get organized a little while you finish up." He pulled a tool bag off the grav pallet of parts and his crew began staging parts on the two closest mess deck tables. The clattering drew a few more observers from the crew, and the chief showed up shortly thereafter.

I took a seat at the de facto officers' table. The chief grabbed a cup of coffee and joined me.

"Come for the floor show?" I asked.

"Wouldn't miss it."

I had to hand it to Stan and his crew. As soon as Sharps and Adams vacated the space, his crew went in with pull bars and started lifting the deck surfaces. I'll confess that I had no idea what was under there, but his assurances made much more sense to me when I realized that the islands and fixtures were not welded to the deck, only latched in with an ingenious hook-and-toggle arrangement. The entire space had notches in the deck to handle a set of standardized building blocks. As long as you knew how big the blocks were supposed to be and had the blocks you needed, replacing the fittings became a question of lining up the pieces the way you wanted and toggling them down. The two islands came apart, only to be reassembled into a single unit, displaced for clearance around the sides and ends. The kettle just unplugged and lifted out of the decking. Douglas even had the plumbing fitting to secure the open pipe in the deck.

"He's good," the chief said.

"Yeah. Talk about exceeding expectations."

One of the pieces Douglas brought was a correctly sized top for the newly configured island. It snapped into place, secured by the same fasteners that the old tops had used. The crew fitted the new cabinet into place where the kettle had been, latched it down and snapped in a metal prep top. The finish matched so well, I couldn't really tell that it hadn't been original. The only clue was a rubber grommet that ran along the metal seam at the top where the two pieces came together.

The chief nudged me and nodded at Sharps. "I think we have a winner."

Ms. Sharps surveyed the process from the side. Her eyes gleamed as the crew pulled the new configuration into being before her eyes.

"I think you're right," I said.

Douglas's gang finished up with half a stan to spare. He'd attracted a small crowd. Ms. Sharps and her attendants all stood by the serving line, peeking between the pots and pans to watch the final touches. While his helpers towed the grav pallet with the excess pieces out of the way, Douglas waved her in.

"What do you think?" he said. "I can put it all back if you want."

Ms. Sharps looked shocked for a moment until Douglas's grin escaped. "It's—" Her voice choked off. "I don't know what to say. It's beautiful."

"You'll curse me in about half a stan when you go looking for stuff that's not where you thought, but I think you'll adapt pretty fast. There should be a logical place for everything now, even if it wasn't where you had to put it before."

"I'm delighted," Ms. Sharps said. "Thank you."

Douglas beamed and nodded. "Lemme get out of your way. I think you've got a lunch to fix." With a final nod to her, he followed his crew across the mess deck, heading for the brow.

I fell into step going down the passage. "Thank you, Mr. Douglas."

"You're welcome, Captain. I've already billed the ship through the chandlery." He glanced at me. "I had to charge an extra ten credits for that rubber grommet. I forgot that on the original estimate. You can dispute the charge, of course."

"Not on your life. Ms. Sharps is over the moon. Under normal circumstances that wouldn't be much of a consideration, but having the cook happy means the rest of the crew is happy."

He chuckled. "You don't need to explain it to me, Cap. I been around the docks long enough to know how this all works. Not just the metal and rubber. You need flesh and blood to make a ship." He winked. "You got any other remodeling next time you're back here, call me. If there's something that don't work right with that galley, I'll make it right. No charge."

"Thanks again, Mr. Douglas."

"My pleasure, Captain. My pleasure."

Cheuvront logged them off the ship and I went back to the galley to check in with Ms. Sharps.

I got there while they were still stowing the cookware. "Anything else you need, Ms. Sharps?"

She straightened up from behind the island, her eyes wide and gleaming. "I don't know what to say, Captain. Thank you."

I glanced at the chrono on the bulkhead. "Will you be able to get the lunch mess off on time?"

"I made a soup last night. It's in the chiller. Portside lunch is soup and sandwich. I've got time to make a nice green salad and bake a cobbler." She glanced at the clock and poked Mr. Franklin. "Alan, grab that cobbler out of cooler two. Put it in the secondary oven at 175, please."

"On it," he said and set words to action.

"I'll get out of your way," I said, backing out of the galley. Chief Stevens stood at the doorway, peeking in past me. "We have a winner."

She nodded and looked at me. "Yeah. I think maybe. What was the bill like?"

"Less than Manchester would have charged for the sheet metal."

She snorted. "I'm not at all surprised. You sure you don't want him to do the berthing areas?"

I glanced back at the happy crew working the galley and shook my head. "No, I'm not sure at all." I shrugged. "Berthing is berthing is berthing and we don't have time to displace the whole crew for that kind of remodel. We're due to pull out of here tomorrow."

"So, I'm hearing a 'not this trip' in there."

I laughed. "Well, maybe. I'm not hearing any complaints about the berthing areas."

"You didn't hear any about the galley until you asked."

She had a point.

CHAPTER THIRTEEN
MEL'S PLACE: 2376, FEBRUARY 3

Pip plunked himself into one of the desk chairs and grinned. "Nice work with the galley."

"Thanks. All I did was pay for it. Ms. Sharps identified the problems. Douglas and his crew did all the work."

"True," he said. "But it's still nice work."

"You have a purpose here? You seem unusually cheerful this afternoon, even for you."

"Thought you might like to take a stroll this afternoon. Last chance before we get underway tomorrow."

"You have any place in mind?"

"Thought we might visit Aunt P and Uncle Q before we leave."

I shook my head. "Not for me thanks. I love them like they were my own but whatever they're doing here, they don't want us involved. I'm going to respect that and stay away."

Pip sighed. "They got to you, didn't they?"

"It seemed pretty clear the other night that neither your uncle nor Cousin Roger wanted anything to do with us."

He looked at me across the desk, his brow slightly furrowed. "What's going on in that head of yours?"

"Nothing much, but I can take a hint." I shrugged. "Your uncle hustled us out of that room so fast, my backside was still going in when my nose had already left. Roger even went to the wrong lock to try to hide where they were. Your digitals probably show which lock so we can walk up to it and ring the bell, but how are they going to feel when they open up—assuming they open up—and find you standing there?"

Pip crossed his arms and slouched into a credible pout. "I just want to know what they're doing here with Malachai Vagrant."

"And they clearly don't want you to know."

"Aren't you in the least bit curious?" he asked.

"Right now, all I'm curious about is what we're going to find in Telluride."

"We're going to find the mega."

"You seem pretty sure of it."

"I am. Brill told us where to find it."

I sat up straight, startled by his assertion. "When?"

He leaned forward—his grin returning, pout apparently forgotten. "She seemed really surprised that the mega was lost. She remembered meeting some of the crew after the ship took off for Margary."

"She wasn't sure of the timing. She also had the wrong port. They were headed for Siren."

Pip's grin broadened. "That's your assumption. What if she's right?"

"What would they want in Margary?" I asked.

"Bona fides," Pip said. "Manchester can't just have a brand new mega-hauler appear out of their backsides. Manchester's biggest CPJCT yard is in Margary. So they announce the new ship in Margary, it swans out from behind a moon and it's now a legit hull."

"Nobody would believe that."

"Nobody has to believe it," Pip said. "That's the beauty. It just needs a legitimate source to claim it, and the company that built it is about as legitimate as it gets. Sure, it wasn't actually built in Margary, but outside of a few people in Margary nobody will know or care."

"TIC might."

He shook his head. "Not much they can do about it without the evidence. They can't get the evidence that's buried in Telluride. They know it was built in the Toe-Holds, but it would have a full registration set from the Margary yards."

"I don't see what difference it makes," I said. "This is all speculation about what mighta, coulda, shoulda happened. The ship never arrived. I don't care how big the ship is. The Deep Dark is bigger. How do we find a ship we don't know is even out there?"

He tsked me. "We've been thinking that the ship got lost in the Dark. What if it didn't jump at all?"

"If it didn't jump, where is it?"

"Mind game. What happens to the *Chernyakova* if we get out to the Burleson limit and the drives fail? They don't explode or anything. They just don't bend space."

The idea boggled me. It was always a possibility. It was why we had two drives. "We just keep going," I said.

"Right. We've been operating on the assumption that the ship was bound for Siren because that's where TIC found the spares. Anybody tracing that vector out from Telluride wouldn't find anything. What if they weren't headed there?" he asked.

I shook my head. "Whoa. Slow down. That system has only been opened up for—what, a matter of a few months? Who's been looking anywhere? Is anybody actually looking for the ship besides you?"

"Well, for one, TIC wants to know."

I nodded. "I'll grant that point."

"Back to the mechanics of it. How long would it take to kill that much momentum?"

"That depends on how much momentum it had gathered. If it started on the outer edges of the system, it wouldn't need much. Just enough to get through the hole and complete the jump."

"Right. They'd have to use the kickers to slow the ship. That's going to take a lot of fuel to pull the ship down to something approaching a stable orbit."

"Wait. Orbit?"

Pip nodded. "If I'm right, I think the mega is still out there. It would have taken stanyers to slow that ship down. It probably didn't have enough fuel to do it in one go. We sure don't carry enough to reverse our outbound momentum on the *Chernyakova*. They'd have had to get refueled at least once. Probably several times. It would need a lot of supplies to keep even a skeleton crew going, but that would explain how Brill met members of the mega's crew after it left. What if it's out around Telluride's Oort cloud—or maybe part of it?"

"So your idea is that it's out there in a deep space orbit around Telluride's primary?"

Pip shrugged. "It's a theory. All the facts we have line up."

"How does this help? It's been—what? A decade or more?"

"That's the beauty. What's the orbital period on an object that far out? Say a hundred AU."

"For that system, I have no idea."

"It's going to be around 1000 years," Pip said. "Twice that for a hundred and fifty AU. I checked and the Burleson limit for us is about fifty. It's not going to be much farther for them regardless of how much bigger their mass."

I sat back in my seat. "So you're proposing that the ship set off on a course for Margary for its grand debut, sailed out to the Burleson limit, fired up the drive and it just choked out."

"Yes," he said.

"Over the next few stanyers, they used their kickers to push the ship into an orbit around Telluride to keep it from wandering off into the Dark," I said.

"Yes," he said. "Properly equipped local ships could have serviced it using a combination of kickers and sails. If they knew where it was, a tanker could have jumped to it from outside to get the proper vector and kept it supplied with fuel."

"So, if they succeeded, the ship is still out there, crawling along at a few meters a stanyer?" I asked.

"Exactly," Pip said.

"What's it doing out there now?"

"That's my question as well." The chief walked into the cabin and took the chair next to Pip. "Brilliant work, Pip."

"You knew it was out there, then?" Pip asked, looking at the chief.

"I had strong suspicions. I couldn't figure out how to find it. Like everybody else, I assumed that it jumped and the drive failed somewhere in the Dark," she said.

"But you had reason to believe it wasn't destroyed," I said.

She nodded. "Nothing solid. No string to pull on, but a lot of circumstantial details. Enough to bring us to Telluride originally. Since then, I've gotten a handful of data points. The crewmen we supposed had been lost with the ship have been turning up in various locations in the Telluride system. We started looking and found payroll records for almost all of them running through last month. There's a suspicious absence of officer records, but the crew roster is complete."

"Where are the officers?" I asked.

She shrugged. "Easy enough to make them disappear. New identities, new ships, cushy jobs. Buying them off is ultimately cheaper than killing them off. Fewer explanations required should it all go pear-shaped."

"What do we do if we find it?" I asked.

Pip and the chief shared a look.

"Depends on what we find, I guess," the chief said.

Pip nodded. "Yeah. Empty ship? Yay. Salvage. I don't know how we deal with it but it should be worth something, if only for the scrap metal."

"The technology should be worth a lot," the chief said. "I suspect the consortium that built it would pay to keep it quiet, if nothing else."

"You mean Manchester?" I asked.

"Manchester, Pravda, Mellon-Merc." The chief ticked them off on her fingers. "They'll all have some piece of that."

I considered her point for almost a tick. "Why do you want to find it?"

"I'm just closing a loop," she said.

"Uh huh," I said. "I think we need to bring Al and Mr. Reed into this conversation. If the *Chernyakova* actually did service the mega, there should be a record of it. If anybody can find it, they can."

"Wouldn't we have found it already?" Pip asked.

"Nope," I said. "We've been looking for the wrong thing."

Chapter Fourteen
Telluride System: 2376, February 10

I couldn't help having a little trepidation about jumping into Telluride. After the last visit, I kept thinking there might be some residual animosity. "How's it look, Mr. Reed?"

"We're right on the mark, Captain."

"Ms. Ross?" I asked.

"Calibration shows us in Telluride. Give it a few ticks and we'll have some decent scans. There's nobody near us at the moment."

I settled into the captain's chair, dividing my attention between the brilliant pinpoint ahead of us that was the system primary and the repeater screen showing the short-range scan expanding outward.

"Telemetry link with the comms buoy," Mr. Reed said. "We have a data packet for transfer."

"Thank you, Mr. Reed," Al said.

"Any trade data in the stream?" I asked.

Mr. Reed pulled a couple of windows up and nodded. "Routine-looking trades. I'm seeing cans, large and small. Some twelve-meter containers. Even a couple of tanker loads."

"Route to cargo, please?"

"Already done, Skipper."

"Thank you, Mr. Reed."

"Skipper?" Al said, pointing to the short range.

"What you got?"

"That ship is holding station just inside the outer belt." She looked at the screen again, then back at me. "It's got no designator and it's about our size."

"That's the guardian," the chief said. "Ignore it. Pretend it's not there. Just don't run into it."

"The guardian? Is that its name?" I asked.

She shook her head. "The ship assigned to make sure the powers that be here don't do anything rash."

"All right, then," I said. "Mr. Reed, make sure we give this ship that's not there plenty of room."

"Plenty of room, aye, Captain."

We docked at Telluride just before the dinner mess on the twentieth. We were a lot farther into the gravity well than I liked, given our history. We'd be another two weeks digging ourselves out. In truth, I recognized that the paranoia causing my anxiety had no basis. Neither traffic control nor the station personnel gave me any cause to suspect some nefarious counteraction against us.

I met the station security at the lock.

"Welcome to Telluride, Captain." The official could have come from any of the stations we'd visited in the Toe-Holds—carrying a tablet and wearing a tired, liveried jumpsuit and a bored expression. "Purpose of visit?"

"Trading cans," I said.

She ticked off a form. "Length of stay?"

"Probably four standard days."

She ticked off another form.

"Number of crew?"

"Twenty-eight."

She entered the number and turned the tablet toward me. "Thank you, Captain. Limited visa for four standard days. You can extend it at any time by notifying our office. Please instruct your crew to observe the red lines. Don't cross them unless escorted by a resident. Thumb here."

I did as instructed.

She looked at the screen, nodded. "I'll send a copy to the ship. Welcome to Telluride."

"Thank you, officer. Have a good day."

She snorted, turning away to stroll on down the docking gallery.

"Not exactly the welcoming sort, eh, Captain?" I turned to find the chief standing on the lock ramp.

I shrugged. "Felt a little odd. There can't have been that many ships docking here over the last decade or so. She seemed like it's a job she's been bored with for far longer than a decade. I'd have thought she'd have exhibited a little more excitement to have new faces show up."

"Maybe she's just jaded. She knows you're just here to take advantage of the trade situation and won't be staying around."

I shrugged. "Possible. Whatever the reason, we're here." I walked back into the ship and found Al waiting by the brow. "You heard the red line restriction?"

"Yeah. A bit more restrictive than I would have thought," she said. "Their station. Their rules."

"Go ahead and declare liberty for the top of the hour. Make sure they know the visa restriction," I said.

She nodded and proceeded to make the announcement while I climbed up to the cabin. Pip waited for me there.

"Don't you have a stateroom of your own?" I asked.

He shrugged. "Yeah, but I know I can find you here pretty much any time I want to talk to you."

I settled across from him. "What's up?"

"Wanna hit a pub tonight?"

I shrugged. "Something interesting?"

"Local brews. Jazz trio. Thought maybe we could collar Al and the chief, maybe Kim?"

"I like that. Give me a chance to sound her out about her second-mate ticket."

He nodded. "You're thinking of moving her up?"

"Well, I can't unless Reed moves. I don't think he's going to, and the chief claims to have a candidate so I'm not supposed to really hire anyone."

"Did you look?" he asked.

"I got a little distracted by the galley overhaul."

"So why talk to Fortuner about her ticket?"

"Because she can't stay third mate forever," I said.

Pip grimaced and looked off to the side. "That's a problem, you know."

"What? That she has to move up?"

He looked back at me, shaking his head. "That you think you know what's right for everybody. Of course they have to be working on their next rating, their next position. It's what everybody does, right? That's what you did, so everybody has to? Whether they want to or not, move up or move on?"

His words drove me back in my chair. I just sat there, stunned, unable to speak. I finally said, "That's how you see it?"

He shrugged and looked away again. "That's what it looks like from where I'm sitting."

I couldn't help but wonder if he was right. My fundamental perspective said that I should encourage my crews to skill up, to move along the career ladder. The idea of "whether they wanted to or not" never occurred to me. The notion that he had me dead to rights did not sit well. "Thanks," I said.

"Thanks?" he asked, staring at me. "Are you being sarcastic or something?"

I shook my head. "No. It's a perspective I never even considered. I should have."

"Well, you know my opinion on it now," he said. "So? Dinner?"

"Tom has the duty?"

Pip nodded. "I think so, yeah."

"Al, the chief, Kim, you, me?"

"If they all want to come with, sure."

"You don't have any ulterior motive or anything?" I asked.

"Well, I didn't have any ulterior motive back at Mel's. It just blindsided us when the doorman crashed Uncle Q's party." He shrugged.

"Granted. Fine. Let's do it." I keyed an invite to the other officers and tapped the send key. "How are we looking for cargo?"

"Locals say they'll collect the can within the next twenty-four stans. Probably first thing in the morning, station time. I found a lot of outgoing cargo but cans heading toward Margary are a bit sparse."

"I suspect anything going anywhere in Dunsany Roads would be close enough," I said.

He nodded. "It would. Everything I've seen come by since we jumped in has been going to Dark Knight or Mel's. Not exactly in the right direction."

"Let's get together with Tom before we head out. See what he came up with for a likely location for the mega."

Chapter Fifteen
Telluride Station: 2376, February 20

I changed into my civvies around 1800 and wondered, not for the first time, if I'd done the right thing with the outfit. It seemed like the right thing to do at the time, but looking down at the burgundy fabric—well—the patterned fabric seemed more like upholstery than clothing. I felt a little like a sofa. Was I furniture taking up space in the cabin? Inherently useful but only when people needed someplace to sit?

I found the thought disconcerting.

Coupled with Pip's observations earlier in the day, I wasn't in the best of spirits when I found Mr. Reed at the officers' table on the mess deck.

"Going ashore or coming back?" he asked.

"Going. Al, the chief, Pip, and Kim are all going. Pip found a jazz club that serves dinner."

"Sounds like fun. Lemme know if it's any good."

"Will do. What's your favorite cuisine?" I asked.

"I'm partial to food," he said. "I don't really care what kind as long as it's tasty and plentiful." He grinned at me around his coffee cup.

"Have you found any place that looks likely in terms of the mega?"

He shook his head. "I've got a couple of possible candidates but I want to spend a little quality time with the database to see if there are any better ones tucked away in obscurity. My hunch is that a hidden landing zone isn't going to be labeled 'X marks the spot,' if you know what I mean."

I laughed. "Yeah. Probably not. Anything I can do to help?"

He shook his head. "Space and time. Two things you'd think we'd have plenty of but we always seem to run out." He glanced at the galley. "That was inspired, by the way."

"What? The galley?"

He nodded. "I didn't even know she had a problem with it."

"I didn't either until she showed me the steam kettle."

"Serendipity still counts, Skipper."

"It does that." I stood. "Holler if you need us, but I don't expect we'll be out late."

"Will do, Captain. Have fun."

"I'll do my best."

"You're not wearing the cap?" he asked, eyeing me up and down.

I shook my head. "Honestly, I'm not sure about the outfit but we'll see."

"It's a change of pace, no question," he said.

I gave him a wave and headed toward the lock. Along the way, his "change of pace" comment kept echoing in my head.

The place—a literal hole in the wall named Bass Clef—fell just on our side of the red line. One more door down and it would have been off limits. I wondered if that was on purpose.

The host showed us to a table not too close to the stage and distributed menus. "Mike will take care of you. He'll be along momentarily."

We thanked him and he disappeared back toward the front.

"What's with the décor?" Ms. Fortuner asked. "Black paint everywhere? It's like a cave in here."

"Been in many caves?" the chief asked.

"You know what I mean," she said. "Actually, I have been in a few real caves. They're dark but there are some really spectacular places to see when you get them lit up."

The chief nodded and looked around. "I do know what you mean," she said. "I suspect it's some cultural reference. I'm not sure."

A guy in black jeans and T-shirt stepped up to the table on Kim's blind side. "Howdy, folks."

Ms. Fortuner almost jumped out of her chair. "Don't do that!"

To his credit, the guy seemed mortified. "I'm so sorry. I didn't mean to startle you."

"Black clothes. Black walls. Are you trying to be sneaky or something?" Her face sported a red flush.

"I'm really sorry, ma'am. Can I get you a drink? On me for scaring you?"

Ms. Fortuner shook her head. "Thanks, not necessary. It just flipped me out for a sec."

The chief leaned over and said in a loud whisper, "Take the free drink, dear. He's cute."

The server took a deep breath and bit his lips together for a moment. "Well, shall we try this again, from the top? I'm Mike. I'll be taking care of you all this evening. Can I get you started with drinks while you look over the menus?" He smiled brightly, a slightly goofy grin that made us all laugh.

"You got a local beer?" Pip asked.

"Several. What's your preference? Heavy, light, dark, hoppy?"

"What's your light?"

"We have a nice pilsner and there's a great brown ale. A little heavier on the malt but still well shy of porter or stout."

"I'll try that," he said. "Can we get a pitcher?"

"Of course, sir." He looked around. "How many glasses?"

"Coffee for me," I said. "Black."

He nodded and looked around, counting raised hands.

Ms. Fortuner said, "Is the coffee any good here?"

He grinned at her. "I like it. Depends on what you're used to, I guess."

She nodded. "I'll have that."

The chief asked, "Do you have any specialties?"

"I have several," he said, winking at her. "But the house has a couple of specials tonight. We just got some really fine pork ribs with a smokey barbecue sauce that are on offer this evening. The prime rib is great, it's served just on the pale pink side with a dollop of our house horseradish and choice of sides. Vegans? The chef makes a killer vegetarian chili. Asian fusion. Heavy on the beans and tofu with a fermented soybean paste sauce. Hot, medium, or mild. The hot will make your eyes water but it's a local favorite."

A short pause as everybody looked at everybody else but nobody spoke.

"Drinks for now," I said. "Give us a few ticks to check out the menus?"

He grinned and nodded before fading into the background again.

It took us almost no time to sort through the various menu options. By the time we were done, Mike had returned with our drinks. He left with the food orders and Pip did the honors with the beer. I took a sip of the coffee. It wasn't half bad. I was so used to bad coffee in restaurants, it was a pretty low bar to begin with. I just didn't feel up to beer.

Pip held up his glass. "The *Chernyakova*."

"Don't start," the chief said, but raised her glass and we clinked glass and china around the table. When it looked like he was going to try again, she put a hand on his forearm, holding the glass on the table. "Really. We've a long night ahead on a strange station."

Pip relented, giving her a small nod and sitting back in his chair. The action was so unlike him, I sent a sharp look in his direction.

He gave a shake of his head. "What shall we talk about?" he asked.

"Next steps," Ms. Fortuner said.

I leaned forward and placed my elbows on the table. "I like this. What kind of next steps?" The chief and Pip both gave me odd looks but I focused on Ms. Fortuner.

Ms. Fortuner shrugged. "We're here. The ship's doing well. We could be close to finding what the chief and Pip have been angsting over. What do we do if we find it?"

Chief Stevens gave me a wide-eyed stare.

I gave her a shrug and a shake of the head.

Ms. Fortuner looked around the table. "It's not like I'm not paying attention, you know."

Al leaned forward. "It might not be where we're looking."

"I know that," Ms. Fortuner said. "It's a long shot but at some point we'll find it. Then what?"

Pip frowned but the chief hid behind her beer glass, leaving Al staring at me with a "your turn, boss" look on her face.

I stared into my coffee cup for a couple of heartbeats. "It's probably a bad precedent, but to tell you the truth? I hadn't thought that far ahead."

She hooked an arm over the back of her chair. "Did you think we wouldn't ever find it? That we'd be some kind of *Pequod* forever chasing the mythic white whale?" She gave me a saucy grin. "Are you sure you're not Ahab instead of Ishmael?"

"Who's Queequeg?" the chief asked.

"Don't look in my direction, girly," Al growled in mock fierceness.

Ms. Fortuner laughed. "It's a terrible metaphor. We're on a quest. I hope it doesn't take a tragic turn the way *Moby Dick* did."

"Why do you ask?" I asked, leaning forward to hear her over the sound of the jazz trio beginning to set up at the back of the room.

She fiddled with her coffee mug for a few moments, staring at it as if in a trance. "I don't know. It's something I've been thinking about for a while. I'm pretty sure we're on the right track." She paused and looked at Pip. "We're off the ship, can I call you Pip?"

"Only if I can call you Kim."

"Of course," she said. "I think Pip's analysis is spot on this time. I mean he comes up with some harebrained schemes, but based on what we know, I think it's way better than his usual stuff."

The chief leaned over and looked into Ms. Fortuner's mug. "You sure that's just coffee in there?" She grinned at the young woman. "I happen to agree with you. On all counts."

"Harebrained?" Pip asked.

The chief gave him the stink-eye and he retreated to his beer.

"So, I suspect the chief will move on." She looked at the chief. "Not that I wouldn't sail with you forever, but you've got other places to be. Even I know that."

The chief frowned a little and sat back in her chair, a calculating look in her eye—like she was re-calibrating her opinion of our third mate. "Go on. Please, I think this is the most I've ever heard you say in all the time we've sailed together."

Ms. Fortuner shrugged. "Well, third mate. I don't get much face time with senior staff. Wardroom meals and navigation stations." She looked up at me. "I'm not complaining, Skipper. Sailing with all of you has been wonderful and I'll do it as long as you let me."

"Keep going, Ms. Fortuner," I said. "You're not the only one who's learning from our relationship."

The chief shot me a sly grin and Al kicked my leg under the table.

"So, I know Al wants to retire to be an artist." She looked at Al. "You do, don't you?"

"How do you figure?" Al asked.

"You're always sketching. Sometimes I smell the paints you use. I've seen you staring out at the stars when I come up to relieve you sometimes. You seem far away then."

"What about the retiring?" I asked.

Ms. Fortuner looked at Al. "I'd bet you've been sailing longer than I've been alive."

Al snorted at that. "Don't pull any punches, do you?"

Ms. Fortuner paled and her eyes widened. "Sorry, I didn't mean it that way."

Al grinned at her. "I didn't take it that way. I suspect you're right. I've probably been sailing longer than the captain has been alive."

Ms. Fortuner nodded. "But you never made captain. I don't think it's because you wouldn't make a good one. I'd sail with you in a heartbeat." She looked at me. "No offense, Skipper."

"None taken," I said.

"Why do you think?" Al asked, her voice soft and low.

"I think it's because you kept getting passed over."

"Have you ever gotten invited to the board?" I asked.

Al shook her head.

"Would you want to be?" I asked.

She stared at her beer glass for a long time while we all sat, silent, waiting. She lifted the glass in salute to Ms. Fortuner, then drained it, snapping it down on the table beside Pip for a refill. "For a long time, I thought I did," she said, talking to the middle of the table. "Now? I'm tired. I could probably get a berth in the Toe-Holds." She looked at me. "You're a captain. Even with your head up your ass, you're a captain." She looked away and took the refilled glass. "Where I used to find joy in plotting the tight course, in keeping the ship and her crew on good terms with each other? Now I find myself treasuring that quiet time in my stateroom with my charcoals or my sketch pads." She looked at Ms. Fortuner again, a soft smile on her lips. "You're right. I want to retire and be an artist."

Mike showed up with food and broke the mood, but I found the chief looking at me across the table with a raised eyebrow. I didn't know how to answer her. The chief was the only other person who knew I'd put Al up for the captains' board back at Dree while we were still in the yards.

"Is there anything else I can get you?" Mike asked, having distributed the food.

Pip held up the empty pitcher. "This seems to have a hole in the top where the beer falls out into our glasses."

"I'm afraid all of them do," Mike said. "Can I refill this one?"

"I thought you'd never ask." Pip grinned at him.

"I'll be right back," he said.

I'd only barely begun exploring my plate before Mike returned with a full pitcher. "There you go. I'll be back in a little while to see if you need anything."

The food service completed, I looked at Ms. Fortuner. "What about you, Kim? What's your next step?"

"Second mate, I suppose," she said. "I don't expect Tom will move up, though, so ... I'm not sure."

"You want second mate?" the chief asked.

Ms. Fortuner finished chewing and swallowed before answering. "It's the logical choice. After going through the academy and all. I passed the exam already."

"Do you like it, though? Being a deck officer?" I asked.

"Yeah. Being comms and systems isn't the most fun, but it's necessary. I feel like I help keep the ship moving. Watches are watches. Does anybody like them?" She looked around the table.

"Sometimes it seems like that's all there is," Al said with a grin. "Watches and drills. I actually like bridge watches. Torkelson's a good helm. You want to swap Cheuvront?"

"No, she's good. I swap between Cheuvront and Bentley every other trip as it is."

"How's that working?" I asked.

Ms. Fortuner shrugged. "I kinda like it. Bentley hums sometimes, but it's usually quiet. Cheuvront doesn't say much. We get along fine on the mids. That's kinda the test. Doing the midwatch cleaning."

Al looked at Pip. "What about you?"

"Me?" Pip looked up from his plate. "What about me?"

"What's your next step?"

"We need to clear this white whale out of the way before I can think that far ahead." He grinned at Ms. Fortuner. "Hopefully without sinking the ship."

Al nudged his arm. "Come on, give. You don't do anything without having the next ten steps staked out."

Pip looked across the table at me and then at the chief. "I'm going to focus on Phoenix Freight. We've got a good start on a profitable business. I'm not exactly sure how, but we've made a metric buttload of credits while we're just thrashing around out here chasing our tails." He looked around the table with as sheepish a look as I've ever seen on his face. "Kinda makes me wanna see what we can do if we actually focus on it."

The chief gave him a long look.

He saw her looking and gave a little shrug. "That's all I got at the moment."

"Captain?" Ms. Fortuner asked.

I shook my head. "I'm going to try to keep flying as long as I can. It's all I've known since I left Neris. There's still a lot I have to learn."

"Captains are supposed to be infallible, Skipper," Al said.

I chuckled. "On the ship, I'm infallible. Ashore?" I thought back to all the mistakes I'd made. "Well, let's just say I've got a ways to go." I took a sip of coffee and looked around the table. "What *should* we be doing?"

The chief looked at me with a little frown. "The galley remodeling seems to have struck a chord."

"I lucked into finding Stan Douglas," I said. "Ms. Sharps really did the hard work. If she hadn't noticed the scoring in the steam kettle, nothing would have happened. It's made me wonder who else has spotted a problem but not said anything."

The chief carved a bite off her prime rib and grinned at me. "Surprising what a captain can hear when he listens, huh?" She tucked the beef into her mouth and chewed.

She had a point, and it sank deep into me.

I looked at Al. "You do murals?"

She almost choked on her food and grabbed her beer to wash it down. "Murals?"

"Yeah. Big paintings on the—"

"I know what they are, Skipper," she said. She put her beer down and stared at her plate. "I've never tried a mural."

"Why not?" Ms. Fortuner asked.

She shook her head, as if to herself before looking up. "I never owned a wall, I guess."

"Are there any regs about how we paint the inside of the ship, Chief?" I asked.

"None that I know of. We have to be a little careful painting on equipment. Heat, conductivity, those kinds of things can get messed up—sometimes just by painting the casings. Bulkheads? Fair game as far as I know."

Pip squinted at me, like he was trying to see inside my head. "You have a wall in mind?"

"Mess deck," I said. "It's mostly blank bulkheads."

"Spine?" the chief asked.

Al's eyes grew round. "Wait. The spine is huge. Painting around all the structural members there?"

"*Moby Dick*," Ms. Fortuner said. "I don't go down there very often but the supports always make me think of walking down a literal spine, each section a vertebra."

Pip tilted his head and stared at her. "That's a little creepy, but I like it."

"Mess deck, huh?" Al asked.

"It's one of the common crew areas. It's got blank bulkheads without a lot of fixtures to work around. Seems like a good canvas," I said. "A mural in there would liven everybody's day."

"Like the cabin?" the chief asked.

"I need to do something about that," I said, speaking without really thinking.

She blinked a few times and tilted her head. "You mean change the paint scheme?"

I shrugged. "Yeah. At least."

"What would you change?" the chief asked.

"For one, I'd start using the couches."

Everybody laughed.

"Seriously. I had them installed instead of a boardroom style table. I never sit there. I'm always at my desk unless I'm in my rack."

"What about the shearwater?" Al asked. "That's pretty classy."

"It's pretty dark," Ms. Fortuner said.

I nodded. "It is, isn't it?"

"It doesn't match your suit," Al said.

"What?" I looked down at my outfit. "This suit?"

"Yeah," she said. "There's a disconnect. That suit says you're one thing but that mural says something else." She stared at her beer glass, spinning it around with her fingers. "Nothing wrong with having different facets. Do either of those represent you? The real you?" She shrugged and looked around the table. "Don't mind me."

"What do we stand for?" I asked.

"What? Like when the captain enters the room?" Ms. Fortuner asked.

I shook my head. "No. Like what's one of our core values?"

"Oh, like truth, justice, fairness? Like that?"

"That's three," I said. "Do any of those things matter to us as a crew?"

"*Liberté, égalité, fraternité,*" the chief said, almost under her breath.

"Profit," Pip said, raising his glass in salute.

Al grinned at him. "You say that, Mr. Moneybags, but at what cost?"

Ms. Fortuner looked at me. "At the academy, they told us captains aren't just the people who makes the decisions for the ship. They shape the shipboard culture."

I gave a short laugh. "Crew Management 200?"

"I think so," she said. "Dr. Frobisher. I can still see her standing at the podium. Was she ever a captain?"

"Adele's one of the key thinkers about how to keep people sane and productive in space," the chief said. "She was a deck hand for about ten stanyers in her youth. Banged around most of the Western Annex before she decided to pursue higher education. Got an undergrad degree in psychology. University of Ciroda, if I remember correctly. Did her graduate work at the Teaching Hospital at Tellicherry. Earned her doctorate in psych research by studying the interactions of officers and crew. She wanted to know why some ships had rich and flourishing culture and others were—well—barely functional."

Ms. Fortuner's jaw hung open. She closed it with a click. "I forget you taught at the academy."

"Still do on occasion," the chief said. "I've been kinda busy of late." She shot me a smile. "I should probably do a rotation there again soon. I need to finish the revisions to the next edition of the textbook first."

"Anything exciting in it?" I asked.

"I did some work a few stanyers ago with recovery of damaged hulls. We got a prototype running and I've been trying to get a production model out. I've reached some new conclusions on hull integrity and the positioning of the Burleson emitter pylons as a result." She glanced around at the glazed eyeballs. "Sorry. It's pretty exciting to me."

"So why are you out here with us instead of working on that?" Ms. Fortuner asked.

"Who says I'm not?" the chief asked. "I've got an Unwin yard in New Caledonia working on it. They're giving me yard space for development in return for a cut of the design royalties."

"You can do that?" Ms. Fortuner asked, her eyes narrowing.

"Oh, yes. It's pretty common actually."

"But you have to invent something first?" Ms. Fortuner asked.

The chief laughed. "Yeah. That's kind of a prerequisite. I find being out here working in actual engineering spaces to be inspiring. It's why I spend so much of my time in space." She leaned closer to the young woman. "Also good for writing new texts. Not much else to do between watches."

"I had a captain who wrote romance novels under a pen name," I said, thinking of Rossett. "He retired."

The chief snorted. "Yeah. Retired."

Ms. Fortuner looked back and forth between the chief and me. "Do I ask?"

Al shook her head. "No."

"It was my first berth out of the academy. To say it didn't go well would be an understatement," I said. "I suspect, one of these people will gladly fill you in once I'm not at the table."

"What do you do, Captain?" Ms. Fortuner asked. "Besides reports and such, I mean."

"Ms. Fortuner?" Al said. "Maybe rethink that question?"

Ms. Fortuner colored. "No, I didn't mean it that way. Al does art. The chief designs stuff and writes textbooks. Pip is constantly fiddling with math and data."

Pip stiffened and stared at Ms. Fortuner.

She glanced at him. "What? You do."

"How do you know?" he asked.

She gave him a wide-eyed exasperated look. "You leave your compartment door open half the time. I can't tell you the number of times I've walked by and seen the formulas on the screen. I don't know what they are, but I know they're some kind of vector analysis. Your tablet is always covered with scribbles. You even bring that drawing thingie to the mess deck sometimes and fiddle with it there."

Pip stared for a few heartbeats before sitting back in his seat. "Carry on, Ms. Fortuner."

Al looked at me. "We've got to find something for this woman to do."

"I don't know," I said with a shrug. "Seems like she's doing pretty well on her own."

The trio in the back finished setting up and began riffing a down-tempo blues number. I couldn't place it, but it seemed familiar. It put the kibosh on further conversation, and not a moment too soon. Ms. Fortuner's question—not to mention her spot-on assessment of her fellow officers—echoed in my head.

CHAPTER SIXTEEN
TELLURIDE STATION: 2376, FEBRUARY 24

We got the cans swapped and the crew back aboard without any issues. So far, Telluride felt like just another station in the Toe-Holds.
Watching people in the passageways, I saw a lot more company-
liveried workers. People with the Manchester M on their backs or
the Pravda wheel on their chests. It made me think of Brill's comment about being locked in. About it being a pretty cushy prison
that paid really well. About it not being that much different from
the High Line.

I looked down the table at the assembled officers. "Chief? We
ready to go?"

"Tanks are topped. We're short a few spares but we're within
parameters, Skipper."

"Al?"

"Crew's all present. We're not leaving anybody behind, Cap.
Stores are stocked. Ms. Sharps reports we're at CPJCT standard
levels."

"Mr. Reed? Astrogation?"

He looked startled. "I've got a course locked to the location Pip
gave me. It's a short jump so I'll need to tweak it just before we
push the button. We'll also need to make a short adjustment to
line up for Dark Knight."

"Ms. Fortuner?"

"System backed up. Logs burned to glass. We can't do much
with off-site backups here. It's something we should think about if
we're not going to be hitting a home port very often, Captain."

"Good point. Thank you, Ms. Fortuner. Let's do a little research once we're underway. It must be a common problem that
somebody else has already solved."

She nodded. "Aye, aye, sar."

"Mr. Carstairs? I thought we were looking for a can to Margary."

"Close as I could find leaving on our schedule, Skipper." He shrugged. "You'll like the profit margin on it."

"Fair enough. Anybody have any reason we shouldn't get this boat underway at 1300?" I looked around the table. Nobody raised so much as an eyebrow. "Good. Then let's get on with getting out of here." I stood and left the wardroom, freeing up the rest of them. Before heading up to the cabin, I took a swing through the mess deck.

Liberty expired at 0600 so almost the whole crew lingered over their coffee. Ms. Sharps had laid out a spread of pastries to keep everybody happy while they caught up with each other's escapades. The noise levels weren't painful but I caught an earful long before I stuck my head in the door to the mess deck.

"Captain on deck!"

"As you were," I said before anybody had a chance to move. "You'll be working soon enough. Finish your coffee."

I got some laughing "aye-ayes" as I passed through into the galley.

"Good morning, Skipper," Ms. Sharps said.

"How's the remodeling holding up?"

She smiled and nodded. "Stan was right. We cursed him for about half a day because nothing was where it used to be. Half the places we used to have stuff weren't even there anymore. Now?" She looked around, surveying her domain. "Fewer corners to clean. Easier access to everything from coolers to cleaning gear. I don't know how we did anything with the old layout."

"Al says we're good on stores?"

She shrugged. "We're within parameters but not full-full, if you know what I mean."

"I do. Any problems getting supplies?"

"The prices are fair, but they didn't have a lot of selection. We've enough for about three months. We're topped off on staples like root veg, flour, frozen goods."

"Coffee?" I asked with a grin.

She laughed. "Standard varieties, Skipper. I think I've got enough to keep us all revved without pulling out the back up stock."

"We're going to navigation stations at 1300. That's going to crowd your luncheon."

She shrugged. "Our stations are here so it might slow cleanup by a few ticks but won't matter much. We'll strap in for the pushback, but we can work around it once we get pointed outward."

"Thank you, Ms. Sharps."

"Thank *you*, Captain."

I stepped back out into the mess deck.

"Captain on deck."

"Sit," I said.

They did, silence descending immediately.

"Anybody hurt?" I asked.

My answer was a lot of shaking heads.

"Hung over?"

A few people grinned at their bleary-eyed companions.

"Any problems you know of with the ship? Any reason we shouldn't dust off and go make some credits?"

More shaking heads.

"All right then. We're getting out of here at 1300. Don't linger over lunch. Pay attention to your department heads. Anybody has a problem they can't handle, bring it to me. Anybody causes a problem they can't handle, bring them to me. Anybody doesn't like it ... you can walk home."

The room erupted into laughter.

"One last thing. You've all seen the smiling galley crew. I didn't really expect to do an overhaul of the galley while we were at Mel's, but it happened. I'm more than pleased with the result. If anybody has any ideas about what you might like to see? Take it up with your department leads. Poke them up the chain of command. We're making credits. We can afford to make our home more homelike. If you have an idea, share it." I paused to let it sink in. "Let's get on with it, then."

The crew returned to their post-liberty festivities and sufferings and I headed for the brow.

"Did you get breakfast, Mr. Bentley?"

He looked up from his screen and stood. "Yes, sar. Thank you."

"How's it working out with trading watch sections?"

He frowned a little. "It's going really well, sar. Is it a problem?"

"Not in the least. I think it's a great idea. Is it hard to make the adjustment between voyages?"

He shook his head. "Going from portside to underway schedules is such a jolt, I hardly notice I'm in a different watch section, Captain."

"How are you coming on the coursework?"

"I'm about halfway through the spec-three book, sar. It still seems a little bit like magic and we rely so much on the computer to give us the data. It's ... not what I expected."

"That'll change as you move up. Spec-two goes from math-less to math-lite. Spec-one gets nasty. The second-mate exam? That's a bugger."

He grinned.

"Carry on, Mr. Bentley."

"Thanks, Captain."

I left him settling back onto his seat and bringing the spec-three book back up on his screen.

The stroll back down the passageway, past the somewhat less crowded mess deck, and into deck berthing took only a couple of ticks. The passageways along the way looked clean, even in the corners and along the edges. With Al riding herd on the operation, I wouldn't have expected anything less, but it still gave me a warm feeling to see it.

I stepped into the deck berthing area, inhaling the aromas of fresh laundry, floor wax, and deodorant. Low voices came out of the head. I looked around, trying to see the area through new eyes. Was it space efficient? Was it effective? I wondered what Stan Douglas would have done with the space.

I backed out of the area and crossed the passageway to engineering berthing. The two spaces mirrored each other with identical bunk, locker, head setups. Engineering always had a tang of machine oil to me. I never knew if it was actual or just a mental overlay. Even when I worked in the environmental section of the *Lois*, I always thought the berthing area smelled like machinery.

"Captain on deck!"

"As you were. I'm just visiting."

A spec-three fields with Verde on his name tag stepped out of one of the quads. "Is there something I can help with, Captain?"

"Thank you, no, Mr. Verde. I'm just taking a tour of the ship before we get back out there." I smiled at him. "It's a habit I haven't done that much on this ship." A few more heads peeked out around lockers and over partitions. "Carry on. I'll show myself out."

I left the berthing area to a chorus of quiet chuckles and made a mental note to tour the berthing areas when the crew was on liberty. They didn't need me sticking my head in while they were getting ready to get underway.

The tour took me back to officer country and I followed Al up the ladder.

"You lost, Skipper?"

"No, why?"

"I thought I saw you down by the berthing areas."

"Just getting reacquainted with the ship before we get under-way."

She headed into her stateroom, one door down from the cabin, the ladder from the bridge between them.

"Do you have any pieces you might show me?" I asked.

She stopped. "Skipper?"

"Artwork? Anything you'd be willing to share?"

"Why?" The question carried no heat, just curiosity.

"If I'm going to lose you to your muse, I'd like to see some of your work." I shrugged, feeling suddenly foolish for prying into what might have been private.

She nodded and held the door open for me.

I followed her in and stopped just inside. I don't know what I expected. Sketches everywhere, maybe. She could have painted the walls in exotic patterns. Instead I found a gallery.

The first mate and engineering officer got a bit more room than the other officers, even the cargo master. The compartments could never be considered spacious. Al's was painted a pale gray, the decks a charcoal nonskid. An easel leaned against the bulkhead nearest her bunk, but the rest of the bulkheads held art. A few were paintings. Most were sketches. Spacescapes. Some portraits. I recognized Chief Stevens in one, bent over a water pump, sleeves up and a streak of grease across one cheekbone.

"Has she seen this?" I asked.

Al shook her head. "Nobody's seen any of it. It's all since our first trip out to Mel's when you bought me art supplies."

"You've done all this since then?"

She shook her head. "This is only a fraction of it." She reached down beside her desk and pulled out one of the sketch pads I remembered from Mel's. She lifted the cover and started flipping through it. It was mostly full.

My expression must have registered.

She shrugged. "It's a long time between watches."

I looked around the stateroom, my gaze slipping from one piece to the next. "I'm sorry," I said.

"For what?" she asked.

"I put you in for the captains' board while we were still in the yards at Dree."

"You what?" she asked.

I looked her straight in the eye. "I thought I was doing you a favor. I put you in for the board."

"That was months ago," she said.

I shrugged. "Apparently it takes a while. Fredi said she put me in long before they responded. Months."

She lowered herself to the bunk, staring at me. "Why are you sorry?"

"Well, the other night at dinner ..." I didn't finish.

"You didn't say anything then."

I shook my head. "I didn't want that to be public knowledge. Even now, I'm not sure I should have told you."

"Why not?"

"What if you're not called?"

Her head shook slowly from side to side. "I don't know."

"Now this." I waved a hand around the paintings and the sketches. "All this. I understand why you want to retire to be an artist."

She stood again. "Skipper, I'm an artist now. It's as much me as this chunk of stainless in my ear. I just happen to earn a living as a first mate."

"But you're planning to retire."

"I've saved enough. I've got some investments. I don't exactly live the system-hopping, high-flyer lifestyle. Never have. Never wanted it. Out here, I could live comfortably on investments, selling a painting or two. I talked to some folks while we were at Mel's. I had some digitals of my older work that one of the gallery owners wanted to exhibit."

"What are you saying?"

"You put me in for captain."

"Yeah, I actually just told you that."

"Why?" she asked, suddenly frowning. "Why would you do that?"

"You mean other than your skills, knowledge, experience, and heart?" I laughed. "Fredi put me in and I've only got half of your skills and experience. We're aboard ship, so pretend I'm not saying this but every day I find some other way I've screwed up."

She took a deep breath and blew it out, still staring at me. "Do you know how many of my skippers have put me up for the board since I became qualified?"

"Five? Ten?"

"One," she said. "Just one."

"That's ... disturbing. Who was it?"

"You."

"Why in the world? What's wrong with that picture?"

"Nothing. I had some great skippers. Some just wanted to make sure I stayed in their crews. Some gave me really nice raises. Some were dicks. I thumped one of them. Busted back to second mate. I don't regret it."

"You were lucky he didn't just toss you out the air lock," I said.

"We were portside in a bar at the Junk Yard. CPJCT would have probably yanked my ticket but the station security sided with me and wrote him up. Fined him a few thousand credits. Kicked him off the station."

"So he got his revenge by busting you back to second mate," I said.

"Yeah. I left them at the next port. Got a decent ride for a few stanyers. It worked out."

"You've been at this job for decades."

She nodded. "I'm old."

"You're not old. I'm just trying to get my head around the scope of this."

She laughed. "Good luck with that part."

"Why did you stay so long?"

She bit her lips between her teeth and looked around the stateroom. "This," she said at last, jerking her chin toward the artwork displayed around her stateroom.

"This is the Alberta Ross that Christine Maloney knows," I said, comprehension dawning.

"Yes. I've been entering the show for at least a decade. I don't know how long. Never got anywhere until she took over managing it. I've sold a few pieces there. She's offered me space in her gallery in the past."

"You missed last year."

She nodded. "Breakall wasn't a good place to be beached."

"What do you want to do about the captains' board?"

"Well." She laughed. "They have to invite me first."

"Fair enough," I said. The moment turned awkward so I backed out of her stateroom, admiring the work from different angles as I left. "The mess deck needs a mural," I said.

She grinned. "I'm thinking about it. You all right with it being dark?"

"You mean the Deep Dark?"

"Yeah."

"I got no problem. Do you have enough black paint?"

"I'll figure something out."

"We've got it in the ship's budget, next time we're docked."

"I'll figure something out, Captain."

I left her staring at her own artwork as I latched the stateroom door behind me.

Started to head aft, but saw the chief lounging at the foot of the bridge ladder. "Something up?" I asked.

"Maybe. The cabin?"

I led her in and we settled in the normal places. "Something new?"

"Something old. Al. What are you going to do?"

"You mean about putting her up for captain?" I asked.

She nodded.

"Funny you should ask.

"I heard you talking. Did you come up with any ideas?"

"You know she's never been put up? Ever."

"Wasn't that what she said at dinner the other night?"

"No, what she said the other night was that she'd never sat for the board."

"Isn't that the same thing?"

"No. You know as well as I do how this works. She might have not gotten the invitation to sit. It's a black box as far as I can see."

"Alys would know more about it," the chief said.

"No doubt." I felt the anger building in my chest. "Not one of the captains she flew for put her up before this."

"That surprises you," the chief said.

"Of course it surprises me. That woman has forgotten more about running a clipper than I've ever learned."

The chief held up a fist and ticked off her points as she went. "First, she's a woman. Second, she's not a pretty woman. Third, she's hard, sometimes crass. Fourth, she has more ink than a yeoman's office and more stainless steel than our galley." She paused. "Do I need to go on?"

"You say that like these are bad things."

"Ships are business. Running them is politics," the chief said. "She's been on the wrong side of the politics for every captain she's sailed under. She doesn't fit the mold. Won't do for a recruiting poster."

I took a deep breath and let it out slowly. "I guess I knew all that."

"You don't think about it because you don't need to think about it. You're young, good looking, talented, smooth as polished glass. The academy knocked most of the rough edges off and Fredi groomed you for the better part of two decades."

"You seem pretty sure of that."

The chief chuckled. "You remember me at *Sifu* Newmar's studio?"

"Of course."

"Margaret Newmar had you tagged then. I saw Fredi the week after she took over from that piss-ant Rossett. She was only staying with the ship to make sure you grew into a captain."

"And you've been showing up at opportune moments, too, haven't you?" I asked.

She gave me a one-shoulder shrug. "Timing matters."

CHAPTER SEVENTEEN
TELLURIDE SYSTEM: 2376, FEBRUARY 24

Telluride's tug, one of the ubiquitous Moran "bumblebees" so called for their yellow and black livery, released us almost as soon as we got lined up on our outbound vector.

"Ms. Ross?" I asked. "How soon can we put up a sail?"

"About another stan at this velocity," she said. She consulted a couple of screens and shook her head. "Mr. Reed, do you have any data on how far we need to go before we can jump?"

"A normal exit, we'd need a couple of weeks. This short? All three accelerometers indicate we could make our jump now if we wanted to."

"That's what I thought," she said. "Captain, local regs ask that we move a few thousand kilometers off the station before jumping."

"If we stay on a ballistic course?" I asked.

"About a stan. It'll give our sails a bit more clearance but by then jumping would be the logical action."

"Well, let's coast on ballistic for a bit. I'm still not comfortable jumping this close to an inhabited station."

"Stay on ballistic, aye, aye, Captain," Al said. "Ms. Torkelson, mind our course."

"Aye, aye, sar. Minding course."

I spun the captain's chair around to look back the way we'd come. Telluride Station looked more like a CPJCT orbital—minus the planet under it—than any of the other Toe-Hold stations I'd visited. It felt awfully close to the stern of the ship even though I knew we'd traveled as much as a hundred kilometers from the dock. In space, a hundred kilometers was nothing.

"Who do you suppose built that station, Ms. Ross?"

"Judging from the architecture—and the fact that they were already here—I'd go with Manchester, Captain."

"You can tell it's a new station, though, can't you," I said.

"Well, it seems obvious to me," she said. "I've seen a lot of old stations. What features lead you to draw that conclusion?"

"For one thing, it doesn't look like it was cobbled together from cargo containers, baling wire, and good intentions."

"Don't say that too loudly at Mel's Place," she said.

I laughed. "I think it's high praise that an edifice build of common and mundane materials can be as majestic as Mel's." I swung the chair back around, facing forward. "Telluride feels a little sterile. Like a house that's not lived in. Or a hotel room. Nicely appointed, but not really a home."

She looked back at the receding station. "I get your point, Captain. Functional but lacking character."

"That's it," I said.

She smiled at me. "It's more like an orbital than a station." She glanced back at it. "It's not a bad design. Just not a good one."

I sipped my coffee. I tried not to obsess too much on what we might find at that first jump but the farther we went, the more anxious I got. Finally, I couldn't take it anymore.

"Mr. Reed? How long will it take us to come to the next course?"

"Minimum of a stan, Captain. Maybe as much as three depending on where we find ourselves in that pocket."

"Can you extend our current vector along our course line? Find a clean hole we could jump to almost immediately?"

He glanced over his shoulder at me but nodded. "One tick, Skipper."

It took him less than that. "I've got a hole just over one BU beyond our target, Captain. Deep Dark location on a line to Blanchard in the northern part of Venitz."

"Do me a favor and get that course loaded as soon as you can after we jump if you please, Mr. Reed?"

He looked at me. "That will delay our course adjustment, Captain. I can't plot the burn for Dark Knight."

"Understood, Mr. Reed."

He nodded and turned to his console.

Al stepped over to me, standing by my chair. "Something on your mind, Skipper?" Her voice barely carried over the sound of the blowers.

"Paranoia, I hope. I don't know what we're going to find in that hole. If we find something nasty, I want us out of there as soon as possible. Trying to come about in tight quarters with somebody who's not happy to see us isn't on my list of things I want to do today."

She nodded and moved back to her station. "Ten ticks to jump, Captain."

"Thank you, Ms. Ross."

Pip topped the ladder and took a seat at the auxiliary terminal. "Couldn't stand the suspense," he said.

The chief snorted.

"Well, the gang's all here," Al said. "Let's hope we don't lose hull integrity on the bridge." She grinned in the darkness.

"Morbid thought," the chief said.

"It's a gift," Al said, still grinning. "One tick to jump, Captain."

"Carry on, Ms. Ross."

"Mr. Reed, are we ready to jump?"

"Course locked and ready, Ms. Ross."

"Ms. Fortuner?"

"Systems ready."

"Chief?"

"Sails secure. Burlesons charged and ready."

"Ship reports ready to jump, Captain."

"Ready about, Mr. Reed. Hard a-lee."

Reed punched the button but nothing happened for a few heartbeats. I was just about to speak when the stars shifted around us.

"Sorry, Skipper. Should have warned you. We were about three seconds early. Timer needed to run down." He tapped keys on his console. "Verifying position."

"Anything on short range, Ms. Ross?"

"Nothing yet, Captain. We'll need a few seconds to get a ping out and back."

"Capacitors, Chief?"

"Barely put a dent in them, Captain. We can jump again immediately."

"Where are we, Mr. Reed?"

"Right on the button, Skipper. Short jump. Small error."

"Al?"

"Bingo. One large damn blip about a half-million kilometers." She stood and looked to port. "That way somewhere."

"Anybody else here?" the chief asked.

Al bent over the short range again. "I'm getting sporadic returns near the ship. I can't tell if it's just noise or some small craft."

The chief caught my eye and nudged her head to the side.

"Mr. Reed. Reload our jump to Dark Knight. How long until we can get lined up?"

"Checking, Skipper." He tapped keys for a few heartbeats. "Less than a stan."

I glanced at the chief who gave me the slightest of nods.

"Execute, Mr. Reed."

"Aye, aye, sar. Executing course correction." He hit a couple of keys. The stars outside the armorglass appeared to shift in position as we rolled and yawed to point the bow in the direction we needed to go, while the heavier thrusters along the keel worked to change our vector. I could feel them rumbling under my feet.

"Anything changed, Ms. Ross?"

"Negative, Captain. Still have the intermittent returns but the big ping hasn't budged."

"Record a track for it, best you can. We're not going to be here long enough to get a good read, but I think we've proven the hypothesis about what happened to the mega." I looked at Pip. "Happy now?"

He grinned at me. "Almost, Skipper. Almost."

"Captain, those are small craft working around the larger ship," Ms. Fortuner said.

"Explain, Ms. Fortuner."

"I've run some post-processing on the data. I believe their movement causes the flicker effect as they maneuver." She paused, peering at the screen. "There's also a possibility that there's at least one object between us and them."

"Wouldn't we see it on short range?" I asked.

Ms. Fortuner looked at Al.

Al shrugged. "It's a long way off. If it's close enough to the mega, we may be seeing the effect of its shadow but not actually resolving it as a separate entity."

"Thank you, Ms. Fortuner," I said. "Any way to get a better resolution on the short range, Ms. Ross?"

Al shook her head. "Only by getting closer. I think we're maxed at this range."

"Ms. Fortuner? Any number magic on the data?" I asked.

"Nothing else I can see, Captain."

I settled back in the captain's chair and pondered the short-range repeater screen on the overhead. "Anything on long range?"

Al flipped some windows around on her console. "We're clear out to five light minutes," she said. "I'm getting a grainy return beyond that. How big is this hole we're in, Mr. Reed?"

"Nothing in the data, Ms. Ross. Big enough to jump into."

I raised an eyebrow in Al's direction.

"Yeah, we're going to want to leave here before we find out how small it is, Skipper."

"How long until we can bend space, Mr. Reed?" I asked.

"Five ticks and a bit, Skipper."

"Lemme know when it's down to just a bit, Mr. Reed. We've got all we're going to get here and there are people waiting for this can at Dark Knight."

"Aye, aye, Captain."

Chapter Eighteen
Deep Dark: 2376, February 25

The second long jump all but drained the capacitors. "How many jumps to Dark Knight, Mr. Reed?" I asked.

"Two and a short one, Captain."

"Capacitor time, Chief?"

"We can jump again in about three stans, Captain. We'll have full cap in six."

"How short is short, Mr. Reed?" I asked.

"Just under one BU, skipper." He looked over his shoulder at the chief. "Those first two are at our jump limit at six BUs, Chief."

"Recommendations, Chief?"

"We won't have enough to make the last jump without at least a stan of recharge time, Captain."

I checked the chrono. We'd been at navigation stations most of the afternoon. "Here's my plan, people. Secure from navigation stations now. Give Ms. Sharps time to get the evening mess put together and taken down. Come back at 2000 for one of the jumps and secure for the night. At 0800 we come back and finish our run into Dark Knight. Any problems there?"

Nobody spoke.

"Chief?" I asked. "Will that give us more than enough time for a full charge?"

"It will, Captain."

"Mr. Reed? Any problems in astrogation?"

"No, Captain."

"Ms. Ross, secure from navigation stations. Set normal watch throughout the ship."

"Secure from navigation stations. Set normal watch. Aye, aye, Captain."

I stood and stretched my back out a little while Al made the announcement. "Chief, if you'd join me in the cabin when you've secured here?"

"I'll be right along, Skipper."

"Thank you, Chief." I dropped down the ladder to clear the way for Cheuvront to go up.

She smiled on the way by as I ducked into the cabin, leaving the door open. I had time to hit the head and get settled before the chief showed up at the door.

"Come on in. We've got things to discuss, I believe," I said.

She closed the door behind her and settled into a guest chair.

"What do we need to do now?" I asked.

"Continue as planned," she said. "I've got a report to make when we jump into Dark Knight. There's not much I can do until then."

"What happens now that we've found the mega?"

"Now we focus on hauling cargo and making stockholders like me happy."

"What about Pip?" I asked.

"What about Pip?"

"He's been driving this since before we had the ship. It was all about finding the mega."

She shook her head. "He'll file a report. He might collect a reward."

"We're not going to have to do anything rash like board it, take it over? Put in a salvage claim?"

"I'm going out on a limb here." She settled back in her seat and folded her hands across her chest. "No. The last thing you want to do is take this ship back into that area of space."

"Can you say why?"

"That would be the last thing you would do."

It took me a couple of heartbeats to parse her words. "I see."

She raised both eyebrows.

"No, I don't actually see the connection between those two ideas," I said. "I trust that what you're telling me is literally true and accurate. Since I have other things I might like to do in the future, I'll pass on making another run through that particular place."

"Even if Pip insists on it?" she asked.

I opened my mouth to agree with her but closed it with a snap.

"Good. You thought that through," she said. "You need to know so I'm telling you. Emphasis on 'need to know' and 'you.' Not Pip. Not Al. You."

I nodded. "Message received."

"The people on that ship had at least one nuclear device they used to extort funds from stations around the Toe-Holds. We know that because they made a mistake with one and wiped out a station along with one of their ships. We recovered the ship—or what was left of it—and the crews they left behind. We know they acquired at least one more because they've been up to their old tricks. We don't know how many they have, how many crews they have working, or much about the scope of their operation. All we know is that it's operating—and I quote—'out of the biggest damned ship I ever saw.'"

"The mega," I said.

She shrugged. "Given the source? Almost certainly."

"So you've been looking for the ship to shut down this gang?"

"Your words, but I won't contradict them."

"How long have they been operating?" I asked.

She shrugged again. "Hard to say. We know some stations disappeared. Well-established, well-run stations. We've nosed around and found some places that admitted they'd been the victims. Our data analysis suggests there are at least four others that are still paying them but won't admit it."

"So they have some way to keep the pressure up," I said.

"Hence my insistence that this ship never go back there. They have no reason to make trouble for us. We didn't linger. We didn't get close enough to see much. We scrammed almost immediately."

"You don't believe in 'twice is coincidence?'" I asked.

"I don't believe in sticking my head in the oven when I know the gas is on," she said. "If I'm right, these people have blown at least eight Toe-Holds out of existence and extorted Maude knows how many credits from even more. They're not going to think twice about causing an unarmed freighter to not make it to its next port."

I nodded. "So, you're leaving soon?"

She shook her head. "Not immediately. I still need to verify that that was the mega, that its home base to a pack of rabid weasels, and that we've shut them down permanently. I'll be here until that's all settled."

"You're going to do all that from your stateroom?"

"Me? I'm just a chief engineer who happens to be an expert on starship propulsion. Where would I be if not working on a clipper?" Her grin would have looked right at home on any white-haired, storybook grandmother.

"Oh," she said. "I'm trying to push that engineman into the academy. I've got his application filled out, but I need one more officer to sign it."

"Which engineman?" I asked.

"Chong Go?"

"The guy who'd read everything you'd ever written?"

"That's the one. He's wasted as crew. His application is in your inbox," she said.

I pulled up the inbox and found the app. A couple of quick keystrokes added my digital signature to it and sent it back to the chief. "Done."

"Don't you want to know why I recommended him?"

"I know why."

"Really?" she asked.

"Yes. You've observed him in his duties. You found him to be unusually competent, curious, and willing to learn. He works well with others and exhibits higher-than-normal levels of initiative and leadership, even when he's not in positions of actual authority."

She blinked at me. "You didn't read that on the application."

"No," I said. "I didn't read that on the application."

"Then how did you know?"

"Am I right?"

"Yes, actually. Damn near spot on."

"I just thought of all the reasons you would have made such a recommendation. They're the same ones I'd use. If he hadn't had most—if not all—of those characteristics, you wouldn't be asking me to endorse him."

She grinned. "You realize you just explained why Alys Giggone recommended you to the academy?"

"Of course. It's also the list of characteristics I need to be looking for in the current crew for my own recommendations." I sighed. "And the reason I haven't found them yet is because I haven't actually looked."

"How's it feel?" she asked.

"Terrible," I said.

"If it didn't, you wouldn't be healing," she said.

"Intellectual understanding doesn't obviate emotional pain," I said.

"Big words." The chief grinned.

"Mother was an ancient lit professor. She liked to challenge me."

"She did a good job," the chief said.

"She didn't have much time with me," I said. "I haven't thought of her in stanyers."

"She'd be proud," the chief said.

I sighed. "Maybe. I still have a long way to go, I think."

"We all do, until that last day," the chief said. "And then we don't have any farther. I think you're doing better than you think. Just keep going."

A knock sounded on the cabin door.

"Enter."

An SA opened the door and peeked around the edge. "Is this a bad time, sar?"

The chief stood and nodded to me. "I've got an engine room to run. Thanks for the signature, Skipper."

"Come in," I said.

The SA stepped smartly to the side as the chief edged her out of the way. "Step forward. Stand at attention. Announce your name and rank," the chief said in a stage whisper as she left.

The young woman looked startled for a moment and then came to her senses. She took three steps forward, coming to a halt two steps from my desk. "Spacer Apprentice Kris Cross, sar."

"Relax, Ms. Cross. Have a seat."

She stared at me for a moment and then slipped onto the edge of one of the guest chairs. "Yes, sar. Thank you, sar."

"How can I help you, Ms. Cross?"

"Well, Captain, it's about the other day. In the mess deck?" She paused so I nodded for her to continue. "You said if we had any ideas about the ship?"

"I remember, Ms. Cross. Do you have one?"

"Yes, Captain. I do."

"I'd like to hear it."

"It's the spine, sar."

"What about the spine?"

"It's boring."

"Boring?"

She nodded. "It's long. It's bland. You get partway down and you can't tell which way is which. From the middle, both ends look the same. Captain."

"Really? I never noticed." I stood, perhaps too suddenly because she flinched. "Show me, please, Ms. Cross."

She stood and I waved her ahead. She marched out of the cabin and I swung the door closed behind me. She marched down the spine. Literally, marched. I changed my footing and she matched it. I did it again and she matched it but glanced up at me.

"Sorry, Ms. Cross. That wasn't very nice of me."

She bit down on a smile and shrugged. "You're the captain, Captain."

"People keep saying that."

She laughed and stopped about halfway down the spine. "Look at both ends from here, sar. Don't they look the same?"

I peered forward toward the bow and aft toward the stern. "I have to admit you're right. They look very similar."

"Now what if this were an emergency, sar? Seconds matter."

"I may not be the best person for this, Ms. Cross."

"Why, sar?" she asked.

"Because I know which end is which."

"Try it this way, Captain. Close your eyes. Please. Sar?"

I closed my eyes and felt her tugging on my sleeve, spinning me around in place a few times.

"Now, open your eyes and point to the bow, sar."

I opened my eyes, looked both ways, and pointed forward.

She frowned. "How did you know, sar?"

"I used to work in environmental," I said.

"Environmental, sar?" She frowned. "I don't follow."

"One of the duties an environmental watchstander has to do is tour the ship every so often."

"Yes, sar. Visual site inspection, I know about that. I see them all the time."

"The spine is one of the places they have to check. It's tedious but it's part of the tour."

"I'm with you, Captain. How does that help you?"

"There are nodes around the ship. Part of their job is to check the nodes, and collect the data from them."

"I didn't know that part, sar."

"You also probably don't realize that they're all along the spine. Every few frames there's a node." I pointed to the nearest one. "There's one there."

She stared at it, then looked up and down the spine. "Are they all on the port side, sar?" she asked.

"Good eyes and a valid conclusion. Yes, Ms. Cross, they're all on the port side."

She looked at her boots and shook her head. "I feel so dumb. I'm sorry for taking up your time, Captain."

"Tell me your idea, if you would, Ms. Cross?"

"Sar?"

"You had an idea about the spine. It's boring and easy to get lost in. Seconds count." I shrugged. "So, what's your idea?"

"Paint, sar."

"That's something of a coincidence, Ms. Cross. I was thinking about paint just the other day. What's your pitch?"

"Port and starboard, Captain. It's kind of redundant now that I know where to look."

"Go on," I said.

"The grab rails make handy markers dividing the bulkhead on both sides. The deck is skid-grip anyway and the lighter overhead makes everything brighter." She really threw herself into the explanation, waving her arms and checking my face frequently to make sure I understood. "These bottom parts, my idea was to paint them red and green for port and starboard, corresponding to the navigation lights."

"I like it, Ms. Cross. What about the upper panels?"

She paused. "I'm not sure, Captain. I thought maybe we could paint them some complementary color, like a pale blue or something."

"How about a mural?" I asked.

"A mural? Like paint pictures on them, sar?"

"Exactly like paint pictures on them, Ms. Cross. Or patterns or whatever."

"Who?"

"Who what? Who would paint the pictures?"

"Yes, sar."

"You any good with a paintbrush, Ms. Cross?"

"Me?" her voice squeaked in surprise.

"Well, you, some of your colleagues in the deck division. I suspect a few of the engineering crew might be convinced to spruce up the space."

She looked at me and then up and down the spine. "That's a lot of pictures."

"It would be yes, but maybe a design. Something that isn't really fussy. Maybe something that represents the ship?"

"So like gears for engineering, stars for deck?"

"There's stewards and cargo, too. I'm not sure how much representation Mr. Carstairs needs ..."

"Sar, he's the guy who makes it all happen. Without him we wouldn't have any reason to be out here."

"Really, Ms. Cross?" I asked.

"Well, no offense, Captain, but we *are* a freighter."

"You're dead right, Ms. Cross."

She stood there looking anywhere but at me. "So, that was going to be my pitch, Captain."

"It's a good one," I said.

"What?" she said.

"It's a good pitch. We should do it."

She gave her head a little shake. "But why. You just showed me how easy it is to find the direction."

"I did, Ms. Cross, but how many crew are in environmental?"

"Four?" She shrugged. "Sorry, that was a guess."

"Good guess. It's four." I paused to let that sink in.

She looked at me, her brow furrowing for a few long moments. Suddenly her eyes shot wide. "Oh. Oh!"

"You see where I'm going with this?" I asked.

"I didn't know to look for the nodes because I'm not in environmental. I'm guessing that's pretty specialized knowledge, huh?"

I shrugged. "I only knew it because I used to be an environmental watchstander. I suspect the chief knows because she's the chief. It's her job to know."

"But nobody else on the ship knows," she said, finishing the thought.

"Nobody may be a bit of an overstatement, Ms. Cross, but I'm relatively certain the number of people who don't know far exceeds the number who do."

"So? What are you saying, Captain?"

"I'm saying, Ms. Cross, well done. You've identified a possible safety hazard. If we were to lose power with a member or three of the crew in the spine, the disorientation caused by a loss of gravity, possibly lighting, even briefly, could be catastrophic."

She blinked a few times. "Is that likely, Captain?"

"It's happened to me once. It's scary as hell to be finding yourself walking along the deck one second and swimming through the dark the next."

Her eyes practically bugged out of her head.

"I wasn't in the spine, so I didn't have that problem to deal with but even knowing where the nodes were wouldn't have been half as useful as the color-coded bulkhead."

"You've had some experiences, Captain."

I laughed. "Yes, well, that comes with the job. You kinda have to have had experiences before they let you be captain."

She colored and bit her lips. "Yeah. I should have probably figured that. Sorry, Skipper."

"No harm, no foul, Ms. Cross. The question for you is the one I asked before."

She paused a couple of heartbeats. "Am I any good with a paintbrush?"

"That's the one."

She looked up and down the spine again. "Captain, I'm a spacer apprentice. I live paintbrushes, swabs, sponges, and brooms. It'll take me forever to do this, but yeah. I'm pretty darn good with a paintbrush."

"Good," I said. "So you won't have any trouble showing others what needs doing?"

"Showing others?"

"Of course, Ms. Cross. I'm putting you in charge of this project. There's not much you can do until we dock and can order the red and green paint. That'll give you a chance to recruit some shipmates to help. Not all of them will be spacer apprentices, so they may need some instruction on painting. They can help with the big swaths of color and work with you to design the upper panels."

The horror on her face nearly made me laugh but I held it in. It only lasted a moment before I actually saw her backbone stiffen. She surveyed the spine once more, this time like she owned it. She looked back at me. "Thank you, Captain. I won't let you down."

"Let me know if you run into any snags," I said, and walked back to the cabin leaving Ms. Cross to survey her new domain.

CHAPTER NINETEEN
DARK KNIGHT STATION: 2376, MARCH 11

The run into Dark Knight went like clockwork. Once we got there, our luck took a bit of a turn when Pip couldn't get an outbound cargo.

"No cargo?" I asked. "We've been here two days. You had a week and a half before that?"

Pip shrugged. "I've never seen the beat of it. Apparently there's been a parade of Barbells through here in the last two weeks. When we jumped in, two had just jumped out and three more had already left the station. The dockmaster is shaking his head."

"What are the odds?" I asked.

"A station this size?" He shrugged. "There's usually a choice of cans. Some aren't really worth taking but even a bad cargo is better than none at this point."

"How would we find any new cargo coming up through the system?"

He shrugged. "I suppose we could ask the mining company. Or the refining people."

"There have got to be empty cans here somewhere," I said.

"You thinking of jumping empty?"

"It's that or wait for a cargo, but without some way of predicting what that might be, I'm stumped," I said.

Pip screwed up his face as if to say something and then didn't. He just looked down at his hands where they lay in his lap.

"Spit it out," I said. "Whatever you were about to say."

"Ask the chief?" He shrugged. "Long shot but she's got connections I don't. I don't know what they might be but everybody in the Toe-Holds seems to know her."

"I thought the same thing about you," I said.

He smiled. "Thanks. I know a lot of people. I'm known on all the major stations and some of the minor ones. At least on the docks and with the brokers. She knows the people who run the stations."

I tapped a message into my console and sat back. "Can't hurt to ask."

The chief popped into the cabin almost before I spoke. "What's up?"

"That was fast," I said.

"I was in my stateroom working on the edits."

"Have a seat," I said. "We have a problem."

Pip outlined the situation to her, her face growing darker by the tick.

"So, the station master says there are no cargoes?" she asked when he got done.

"Yeah. That the station has been picked clean."

"You believe him?" she asked.

"It seems odd," Pip said. "But I haven't seen a new can come into play since we jumped in. No, that's not accurate. There was a can, but the last ship picked it off before I could put in a bid. They'll be jumping out of the system in the next day or so. The problem is I can't imagine what we may have done to incur any kind of retribution."

The chief settled back in her chair, stretched her legs out in front of her, and frowned at the toes of her boots for maybe a whole tick. "So the cans dried up after we showed up."

"Circumstantial, but that's an accurate statement," Pip said.

"We're wanted," she said.

"Wanted?" I asked. "By whom?"

"By somebody who wants us to run a cargo someplace. It's either a cargo we wouldn't otherwise take or a destination we wouldn't sign up for," she said.

"That's what, not who," I said.

"There are a couple of people with that kind of clout here. We should probably find out which one it is."

"How do we do that?" Pip asked.

"We ask," the chief said. She looked at me. "You and I need to make a call on the station owner. If it's not his cargo, he'll know who's pushing the buttons. Grab your civvies. Forget that suit. Go drab. Jeans and jersey." She lifted herself out of the chair and headed for the door. "Pip, find the dockmaster. Tell him the captain's going to see Kondur."

"Then what?"

She stopped at the door. "Then see what he says. We'll be back as soon as we can, but hang around the dockmaster's office. You know, just in case he finds a lost can somewhere."

It took next to no time for me to skin into jeans and a jersey. I snagged my tablet and met the chief coming out of her stateroom. "We're going to just drop in on the station owner?"

"He's expecting us."

"You lead, I'll follow," I said.

She grinned at me and led our short parade off the ship and onto the docking gallery. We headed for the station's designated Main Street, walking past Marc's on Main where I'd gotten the fancy suit that felt more wrong every time I saw it in my wardrobe.

She led me to a dive tucked between a couple of shops. Two guys lounged beside the door—one on either side. They weren't exactly casual observers. The one on the left wore a pair of rough trousers and a T-shirt with no sleeves. His arms had sleeves of ink and each bicep looked bigger than my thigh. He eyed the chief, giving her a little smile.

His buddy didn't strike me as the bouncer type. A slender, wiry build almost got lost under a couple layers of shirts, coats, and trousers. They weren't bulky enough to hide the holstered weapon in his armpit. They probably weren't meant to. His eyes practically revolved in their sockets as he seemed to be looking everywhere at once and no place in particular.

"Chief," he said.

"Afternoon, Sydney. Is he in?"

"He is to you. Who's the stiff?"

"That's the captain."

Sydney's eyebrows raised just a notch and he focused his wandering gaze on me, shipboots to scalp and back down. "Zat so? Where's the other one?"

"Waiting at the dock master's office. We can get him."

Sydney shook his head. He jerked his head toward the door. "You know where to find him."

She looked at the beef. "Norman. How's your mother?"

"Chief. She's going good. Still on the circuit. Up for the championship next month if all goes well."

"Nice," the chief said. "Give her my regards when you see her and remind her to keep up her right guard."

The man rumbled a laugh. "I'll do that, Chief."

She pushed forward through the door and into the dimness beyond. We stood there for a moment. I couldn't see anything until my eyes adjusted a little. The place smelled of good beer and fresh coffee, not the scents I'd expected. I got enough vision back to see the chief strike off between the tables, heading for a booth in the corner. I ambled along after her, hoping I didn't trip on somebody's foot or elbow a drink into somebody's face.

The chief stopped beside the booth and nodded at the bodyguard standing against the wall.

He nodded back but otherwise gave no indication that we stood there.

"Maggie, how are things with the spooks?" The voice came from the guy sitting in the booth. He blended into the upholstery so well that I might not have seen him but for the shining teeth and a silver earring gleaming in the dark.

"Good afternoon, Verkol. Same as ever. Never see us unless we say boo."

He gave little heh-heh laugh. "Have a seat. Introduce me to your friend?"

Maggie slipped into the booth opposite him, sliding in far enough for me to sit beside her.

"Verkol Kondur, station owner. He's the original Dark Knight," she said, leaning toward me. "This is Captain Ishmael Wang of the *Chernyakova*."

"You've been here before, Captain," Verkol said.

"Yes, we've docked here before. Rather enjoyed the visit."

He smiled. "Good. I've heard good things about you and your ship. You're welcome here any time."

"Thank you. We try not to be one of the troublemakers. Everybody has too many of those and I don't ever want to get on that list."

"A good practice," he said. He looked at the chief and back at me. "How can I help you today?"

The chief sat back and looked at me. "Skipper?"

"It seems that Dark Knight Station has absolutely no outgoing cargo."

His eyebrows shot up. "That seems unlikely," he said. "How do you come to this conclusion?"

"My cargo chief has been working with your dockmaster. We delivered a load, the can has been taken off, but it seems there are no cans to put in its place. The *Chernyakova* is a Barbell."

"Ah," he said. "I see your problem. The weakness of the Barbell."

"Indeed."

"You can't leave without a can. The longer you wait, the more docking fees you incur," Kondur said.

"In a nutshell," I said. "The chief suggested that we come see you to try to resolve this problem."

His eyebrows rose even farther. "Me? I own the station. I leave cargo to the cargo people. Life as a station owner has enough challenges."

"Pity," the chief said. "I thought perhaps there might be a can tucked away safe. Maybe something that needed special handling."

Kondur's brows lowered into a frown. "Now that you mention it," he said. "I seem to recall just such a shipment. It's been languishing so long, I'd nearly forgotten." He looked at me. "Perhaps you could do a favor for me? Since you need a cargo and I happen to have one."

"Where does this can need to go?" I asked.

"That's the difficulty," he said. "It needs to go to a place that's not really a place."

As soon as he said it, I knew where it was going. "I'm going to guess the place that's not really a place is not exactly Telluride?"

The chief stiffened beside me and Kondur's face went blank.

"I can't deliver a can and return without one," I said.

Kondur stared at me for so long with that flat expression I wondered if I'd overplayed the hand. "That's not a problem. There's a can waiting for you."

"I see," I said.

"Do you?" he asked. "Really?"

"You want this can—which I'll hypothetically call a can of supplies—delivered to a ship between stations. It's not lost so much as stranded in a location which you happen to know and will tell me when I agree to take this can. I am to deliver this can of so-called supplies to this ship and return here with a can of something—which I will call merchandise."

"Hypothetically," Kondur said.

"Hypothetically," I said with a nod. "Are there any other stipulations? Problems I might encounter? Requirements for this delivery?"

Kondur shook his head. "Other than your discretion. The parties involved are ..."

"Reclusive?" I asked. "Shy?"

"Exactly," he said. "Shy. Yes."

"And in return for this favor?" I asked. "Should I agree to do it?"

"Well, you will have a can and my thanks."

"I can't pay my crew with good will," I said. "Surely you have the same problem?"

"What would such a deal cost, hypothetically?" he asked.

"Three hundred," I said.

"Three hundred thousand credits? That seems very fair."

"Three hundred million," I said.

"Are you mad?" he asked.

I shook my head. "I made that much on a single can of black malt delivered to Mel's recently. Surely this small favor is worth as much as a can full of beer-making supplies." I paused. "To say nothing of our discretion."

He stared at me and a smile grew on his lips. "Both ways," he said.

"Both ways. Three hundred million credits. Half on departure, half on return," I said.

He held a hand out across the table. "Deal."

I shook the hand. "Deal."

As we slipped out of the booth, Kondur spoke again, his voice low, barely audible. "You know the cost of failure?"

I looked at him. "The wages of sin."

An odd expression crossed his face but he nodded. "Safe voyage, Captain. I look forward to your return."

"I'm glad we could reach some understanding," I said.

The chief led the way out of the dive and halfway down the block before she spoke. "Are you mad?"

"I wouldn't go that far. Maybe a tad peeved."

She snorted out a short laugh. "You know where he wants you to go?"

"Yeah. Shoots down my plan for never going back there."

"And we're bringing back a can full of stolen goods. Do you have any idea how much trouble that's going to put us in?"

"Yeah," I said. "I think I do. Particularly since we're not supposed to actually return."

"No? It seemed pretty obvious that's what he's asking."

"Yeah, that's what he said. He doesn't expect we'll be back. He gave in too quickly on the negotiations. He's going to pay us half up front but we're never going to collect the other half."

"Why not?"

"Because I suspect we'll be dead."

Chapter Twenty
Dark Knight Station: 2376, March 11

We didn't say anything else until we got back to the ship. The chief followed me into the cabin and closed the door. "Do you know what you're suggesting?"

I sat behind the desk before answering. "Call me paranoid but he just held us up to deliver a can to the one place most likely to want us gone."

She plunked herself down across from me and stared. "Explain."

"All right. Start with the idea that you're right and that an extortion ring has co-opted the mega. How that happened? No idea. I don't know if Manchester is in on it or even if they know. It's irrelevant to the current problem. We jumped through their space, close enough for us to see them on short range, presumably close enough for them to have seen us."

"How would they have known where we were headed?"

"They had almost a stan's worth of trajectory data. I could have extended that line to Dark Knight myself, so I'm sure they could. We should have just jumped straight out." I shook my head. "Hindsight."

The chief frowned and sat back in her chair. "So, why?"

"Why what?"

"Why would Kondur go along with this scheme? He's got a rough reputation but he's never been a criminal."

"I don't have your resources, but just connecting the dots? We're up against a gang that extorts stations by smuggling nuclear weapons aboard. Somebody who knows they're sitting on a nuke might not behave normally. Kondur is behaving oddly." I shrugged. "They have a reason to want us removed. The last thing they want is somebody who knows where they are."

The chief went very still.

"I've overlooked something," I said.

She nodded. "We're not the only ones who know."

The implication washed over me like a bucket of ice water in the face. "Kondur."

She nodded again.

"Would they blow the station to silence him?" I asked.

"I don't know," she said. "They'd almost have to because they can't tell who else might know. Dockmaster might. Some of Kondur's people must know they're being extorted."

"How do we find the device?" I asked.

She frowned and steepled her fingers in front of her nose. "Depends on how leaky it is."

"You've never found one intact?"

She shook her head. "Closest we've come is recovering most of one of their delivery ships. A Barbell, as it happens."

"Assume the gang is only marginally competent. That they've got their hands on some fissionables and a do-it-yourself kit."

"Lead is the easiest shield. Our fusactor cores are lead-lined," she said.

"What about the triggers? Don't they need some shaped charges to trigger the reaction?"

"That'll be inside the shielding."

"How big are we talking?" I asked.

She shrugged. "Hard telling. Bigger than a breadbasket. Smaller than a boxcar. I'm not an expert on this stuff."

"You have anybody on your team who is?"

She shook her head. "Not close enough to do any good. We're not under any obligation to get underway immediately. How long can we stretch it?"

"Couple of days should be easy enough. What's that buy us?" I asked.

"I need to know if Kondur is a voluntary participant," she said.

"How do we do that?"

"Ask him," she said. "But we need a lever."

"What kind of lever?"

"I'm thinking the same one that's being used on him. If we can remove that, we've got a chance."

"Doesn't that mean we need to find a bomb that may not exist?"

She nodded, frowning. "That's the catch. Finding it proves the point. Not finding it proves nothing."

"How do we find it? Didn't you just say we won't be able to detect it?"

"No," she said. "I said we hadn't found one yet. This is actually the first chance I've been privy to the potential before the event." Her eyes narrowed as she stared into the distance. "I wonder if I have some data." She threw herself out of the chair and headed for the door.

"What's up?"

She stopped at the door. "We recovered a ship about five stanyers ago. We think it was the delivery vessel."

"You mentioned that before."

"I've got the forensics data with me. We might be able to reverse engineer the bomb's profile."

"How?"

"Residual radiation patterns. One of the anomalies we found. I need to look again to refresh my memory, but the level of residual radiation should tell us how leaky the device was and where they stashed it."

"If it leaked enough to leave traces, wouldn't that be enough to kill the crew?"

She shook her head. "Not right away. They may not realize the problem. A lot would depend on how they picked their crews, how often they delivered bombs, and whether or not they ever picked them up."

"I'll get Pip moving," I said.

She stopped halfway out the door. "Pip?"

"Yeah. If the bombs get delivered in cans, specifically Barbell cans? You don't just roll a can into a station like this. It needs to be unloaded, the cargo stored or distributed. Pip has the connections to figure out that process."

"You're thinking it might narrow down the locations we need to look?" she asked.

"Can't hurt. Might turn up nothing, but it's a chance."

She bit her lip and nodded. "We should also invite Kondur over for dinner."

"Get him out of the station? You think he's worried about being overheard?" I asked. "Is that even likely? He must sweep that bar three times a day."

"Paranoia digs in deep," she said. "We might be surprised."

"I'll get Pip going on the cargo handling. You figure out how to get Kondur aboard."

She nodded and ducked out the door.

I reached for my keyboard but Pip came in before I had a chance to do more than put my fingers on the keys.

"I thought she'd never leave. What's going on?" he asked.

"What did you find from the dockmaster?" I asked.

"You were right. We've got a can coming in from the marshaling yard. Should be here by tomorrow's morning watch." He sat in the chair and stared at me. "What's going on?"

"Kondur froze us out until I agreed to take a can for him."

"That's odd. He could have just hired us."

"Oh, he did but he wanted to make sure we understood that this was a special cargo and that we're trading this specific can for another specific can at the destination."

Pip frowned. "That shouldn't have been complicated. He could have just sent a note."

"The destination is the mega."

He blinked, one slow blink, eyelids pressed hard and then opened. "The mega."

"Yeah."

"What's he paying?"

"Three hundred mil. Half on departure, half on return."

Pip sat back, his eyes staring into space. "So, we jump through the mega's location. Come straight here only to find that the station owner wants us to take a somewhat clandestine cargo back to the place we just came from?"

"And return with a can of cargo from them."

"What are we allegedly taking out?"

"Supplies."

"That doesn't sound suspicious at all," he said.

"We need to find out how the station handles Barbell cans."

"What do you mean?"

"What's their work flow? A can comes in, then what?"

"Typically, it goes to the marshaling yard," he said.

"Yes, but after that? The cans are built for bulk cargo, but how many times have we had a can of 'machine parts' or 'electronics?' The shipper didn't throw parts into the can."

"No, they're usually in shipping containers and the containers get stacked in the cans. That undercuts mixed-cargo ships, but it requires that the whole cargo goes to one place. It's a tradeoff that's been around since the Barbells first rolled off the line at Unwin."

"Right," I said. "So that also means that they must have someplace to unload them and procedures to control where the shipments wait until they're claimed."

"You want to know where that is."

"I do. Preferably someplace centrally located on the station."

"That shouldn't be hard to find out," he said.

"Good. Find out."

"Where is this going?" he asked.

"I want to know if there's a package that came in on a Barbell in the last five stanyers that hasn't been claimed."

"Why would anybody ship something here and then not claim it?"

"I can think of a couple of reasons. The addressee might have died. Might not have gotten the notification that it was in. Heck, it could have been shipped to the wrong station by accident and the original owner asked for a reshipment."

Pip shook his head. "You don't believe any of that."

"No, but those are all good suggestions for things you can tell the people who ask you why you want to know."

"They won't believe me either."

"I don't care if they believe you as long as they tell you where that hypothetical crate might be."

"How about this? I'm an insurance adjustor looking for a lost shipment. I've traced it to Dark Knight and need to look over their cargo holding depot."

"You can be the emperor of the Western Annex for all I care."

He sighed. "Something has you spooked and I suspect Kondur is the cause. When I get back, I'm going to want to know what the hell is going on."

"I'll tell you as soon as I can. You're part owner, after all."

"I wasn't going to play the owner card."

"You'd have gotten around to it. Work with me. How many times have I followed you into the dark?"

He paused and tilted his head to the side. "That's fair." He stood and headed for the door. "I should be back for dinner."

Chapter Twenty-one
Dark Knight Station: 2376, March 11

The chief popped through the cabin door with a grin. "Found it. The ship had residual radiation on the aft side of the forward nacelle, just about where the inspection hatch would fall on the container. Nothing on the spine so it wasn't strong enough to reach there."

"So, they filled a can, tossed the nuke in as an afterthought?"

"That's my working theory. It probably had a remote detonator and depended on the can being close enough to the station to be useful."

"So it had to be used during loading or unloading," I said.

She frowned. "That's true."

"Do you know what was in the can?"

"I only have the manifest records. It could have been full of wet sand. There wasn't anything left of it by the time my forensics team got there."

"I've got Pip running down the work flow for incoming cans. He's on his way to the dockmaster's office now. With any luck he'll parlay that into the freight-handling process. He's looking for an abandoned cargo container."

"Why abandoned?"

I shrugged. "Less risk. Ship it in. Put it in a box that would be routed to long-term storage, but relatively near some critical infrastructure. It doesn't need to be too close. It's a nuke, after all."

She grimaced. "Granted."

"Ship it to somebody you know isn't going to be on station. Mark it 'hold for pickup' and never pick it up. It's here until it's needed."

"That's only going to hold so long."

"Yeah. I'm guessing it only needs to hold long enough to make the initial demands. Once you're over that psychological hurdle, it's easier to keep paying. How long would such a device be viable?"

"Depending on the device, maybe a couple of stanyers. They're not exactly meant to last very long."

"How long ago have you got records of this gang?"

"Earliest reports in '66. We recovered this ship in '68."

"So a decade. Plus or minus. That corresponds roughly with the time the mega went missing."

She nodded. "Raises the question of whether the mega failed or got hijacked."

"I'll leave that to you," I said. "I'm just trying to get a handle on how long Dark Knight might have been working under threat."

"Because if we knew that, we'd know how long ago that container had been shunted to the back of a warehouse somewhere."

"Yeah."

"We need to invite Verkol to dinner," she said.

"You seem to know him well enough."

She frowned and chewed on the idea. "Do we have an SA you can send with a note?"

"Seriously?"

"I've got some letterhead card stock. It's hard to trace paper electronically. Harder still to intercept it."

"You're assuming a pretty deep incursion into his infrastructure," I said.

"I am. If I'm wrong, no problem. If I'm right, we dodge the bullet."

"Will he respond?"

"Yes," she said.

"I have an SA, if she's not already ashore." I pulled up my console and paged Kris Cross.

Cross reported to the cabin within a few ticks. "SA Kris Cross reporting as ordered, Captain."

"Have a seat, Ms. Cross. What's your schedule this afternoon?"

She settled on the front edge of the empty chair beside Chief Stevens. "Having lunch aboard and then heading over to Main Street for some shopping, sar. Probably have dinner ashore and then go bar hopping. I'm off until 0600."

"Would you run an errand for me while you're there?" the chief asked. "I need to drop a message off for a friend but I'm going to be tied up here all afternoon."

"Of course, sar. What do I have to do?"

The chief picked up a small paper envelope from her lap and handed it to Ms. Cross. "There's a dive bar on Main Street."

"The one with no sign? A couple of doors past the brothel?" she asked.

The chief nodded.

"I'm not supposed to go in there," she said.

The chief blinked a couple of times. "Who said?"

"The bouncer. Big, beefy guy with tattoos up his arms."

"He turned you away?" the chief asked.

She nodded. "Yes, sar. He was nice about it. Pointed me to the spacer bar just down the lane. The Playground."

"His name is Norman," the chief said.

Ms. Cross's jaw hinged open as she stared at the chief. "You know him?"

"Yes. He's a nice man whose job it is to look mean. His friend is named Sydney. You might have seen him."

"Skinny guy? Wears a lot of layers?"

"That's him. What I want you to do is take that envelope and give it to either of them."

"What if they're not there?"

"If you go this afternoon, they should be. In any case there will be a bouncer there. Hand the envelope to whoever it is and say 'I was supposed to give this to Sydney but you'll do.'"

"That's it, sar?"

"Yes, please."

"What if Sydney is there?"

"Just smile, hand him the envelope, and say 'It's from Maggie.' Then walk away."

Ms. Cross flipped the envelope over in her hands. The initials – V. K. — the only inscription. "This is real paper?"

The chief nodded. "A dinner invitation. In writing. An old custom."

"Why don't you deliver it in person?"

"I'm tied up here with my book and need to finish working on the revisions. The invitation is for this evening, so I need to get it to him sooner rather than later. Since you're going in that direction ...?"

"Of course, sar." She looked at me. "Is there anything else, Captain?"

I shook my head. "Just let me know when you've dropped it off."

"Of course, Captain." She stood and nodded to the chief before leaving.

"Now we wait," I said.

"Are we being too clever to send it with her?" the chief asked.

"Maybe." I pondered it for a moment. "The risks are low. She's not going to attract the same attention you or I might. It's just a simple invitation to dinner, isn't it?"

The chief nodded. "Nothing anybody would look twice at."

"Except it's on real paper," I said. "Carrying a message that could have been sent more easily electronically."

"It may come as a surprise to you, Captain, but some officers of a certain age engage in private correspondence using mashed and dried cellulose fibers."

"Kondur is an officer?"

"He was," she said. "A long time ago. Seems like a lifetime now."

"Before he took over the station?" I asked.

"No. He owned the station before going to the academy. Graduated near the middle of his class. Engineering, actually, with a minor in closed-ecosystem environmental science. Came back to the Toe-Holds and focused on making the station one of the top places to live in the Western Annex."

I settled back in my seat and pondered that.

"Changes your perspective on him, doesn't it," the chief said.

I nodded. "It's completely at odds with the image he projects."

"Protective coloration," she said. "It's not just for insects." She stood and headed for the door. "I don't want to make myself a liar. I better go see if I can finish another chapter or two of edits."

"I'll ping you when Pip gets back," I said.

She just nodded on her way out the door.

I went back to contemplating Verkol Kondur, wondering if he was actually being extorted—or if he was behind the gang currently inhabiting the very large hull on the outskirts of Telluride.

Chapter Twenty-two
Dark Knight Station: 2376, March 11

Pip showed up just before 1600. His pants had a smear of dust across each thigh, and he carried a streak of dirt across his left cheekbone.

"That took a while," I said as he parked himself in a guest chair.

He leaned back and rested his head on the chair back. "I've had a tour of the cargo-handling facility," he said. "Cans move directly to the marshaling yard. The contents get pulled out. Mixed-cargo shipments get broken down. They get transferred to the cargo depot—which is near the chandlery, by the way. They stay there for up to a month. After a month, they go to a long-term storage facility and the routing slips get moved to a storage terminal. Basic data like what, who, when, and any provenance along with the resting place in case anybody comes along to claim it."

"I'm exhausted just thinking about it," I said. "Where's the long-term storage?"

"Oddly enough, under the docks. It's one of the oldest parts of the station. When they outgrew it, they just moved the current operation to the new facility and left the old one to handle the overflow and long term."

"How often do they clear it out?"

"Funny you should ask. They auction off unclaimed cargo after five stanyers. There's nothing there older than that." He shrugged. "Apparently, they wheel out the old shipping crates and bidders get a couple of stans to look them over, see if there's anything they want to bid on. Highest bid wins. The catch is you can't open the crate before the auction. You can look at the outside, but not inside."

"Sounds like fun. You might get a shipment of gold or a shipment of cow dung."

"Basically," he said. "According to the dockmaster, it's pretty well attended."

"When's the next auction?" I asked.

"Couple of months."

"Maybe we should be here for it," I said.

Pip laughed. "You never struck me as a gambler."

"I'm learning a lot about myself this trip," I said.

"So, that's what I learned. Does it help?"

"Might be just what we needed to know."

"Where are we going for dinner tonight?" he asked.

"I'm going to be in the wardroom with the chief and Verkol Kondur, I hope."

"Am I invited?"

"It's just a quiet little get-together to find out how long Kondur's been being extorted."

"Sounds dull," he said.

"Seriously?"

He shrugged. "Kondur's not going to admit anything. You two will have a lovely evening trying to figure out whether or not he's lying. In the end you'll be no further along than you are now."

"You sound pretty sure."

"He owns the whole station, Ishmael. Why would he tell you two anything about his business?"

"Well, mostly because he's setting us up to take a one-way trip to Telluride."

Pip straightened up at that news. "The can?"

I nodded. "It's supposed to be filled with supplies. We're to trade it for a can that's waiting for us and bring that one back."

"But we're not coming back?"

"My guess is no, but that's what I'm trying to get a better handle on. Which is why the dinner with Kondur."

"Why would he set us up?"

"Well, if somebody had planted a bomb on his station that he can't find, he might be willing to take a few shortcuts with an itinerant freighter."

"There's more to the story than that," Pip said. "You mentioned a bomb?"

"Seems there's a band of extortionists working the area. Pay or boom."

"How do you know this?" he asked.

"The chief."

He frowned. "She'd know. You're not supposed to tell me any more, are you?"

"Probably not even that much but you're a business partner."

"And the chief thinks this merry band of bomb-makers operates out of the mega," he said.

"That's the working theory. She's been looking for them since '68."

He nodded, but he was looking over my right shoulder at nothing. "So, your hypothesis is that the bomb-makers saw us do the flyby, and tracked us to Dark Knight where they already had a bomb, so they could extort Kondur to send us back out with a can of supplies and pick up a bomb of our own which would theoretically take us out of the picture permanently? Seems a bit complex, doesn't it?" he asked.

"A bit."

"It supposes that they tracked our course out of the pocket, that we didn't change course after that, and that Kondur would be able to finagle a can just for us."

"That last part was pretty neatly done, you have to admit that," I said.

"What if Kondur's behind it?" he asked. "What if the call he got about us was 'Boss, we have a problem?'"

"That's why I wanted to know where the long-term storage was. If we can find the bomb here, we'll be better set up to talk to Kondur. We'll know he's not the boss but a victim."

"How do you propose to do that?"

"The chief is pulling a radiation detector out of stores."

"A nuke?" he asked, straightening up in his seat. "It's a nuke?"

"Yeah. Working hypothesis only at this point. If we don't find it, we still can't rule out that it's there and we didn't find it. If we find it, we'll be in a better position."

"I can get you into the facility," he said. "But you're going to have to take the caretaker in with you. No unaccompanied visitors."

"The auction?"

"Yes. Some skullduggery in past events. Poisoned the well, as it were."

A quick knock preceded the chief's entry. "I have a detector." She held up a standard wand.

"Pip can get us into the storage facility but we'll need to take a caretaker with us," I said.

She grimaced for a moment. "I can deal with that. Strap it to my leg and run an earplug to hear the readouts." She eyed Pip. "How much do you know?"

"Nukes. One-way ticket. Kondur maybe setting us up." He looked at me. "You know, this could all be a simple trade deal. He needs to get supplies to the ship and get the goods back. They contacted him to broker the transaction because he's the owner of Dark Knight."

"Why us?" the chief asked. "Why now? We just flew by the mega and now Kondur wants us to fly back?"

"I've seen less likely things happen," Pip said.

"Like what?" she asked.

"Ishmael owning the ship he found as salvage and was only able to get it because some shipping bigwig took the final jump, the dead guy's company fired him then sold him a ship cheap, which he turned into multimillions worth of success before selling out to the daughter of the same dead magnate so he had the money to invest in that salvaged ship—which, by the way, he never wanted to step foot in again?" He shrugged. "Worse than that?"

"What time did you invite Kondur for?" I asked.

"Normal evening mess. 1800. We should probably alert Ms. Sharps that we'll be three for dinner in the wardroom."

I checked the chrono on my console and typed a fast message to Ms. Sharps. "Done, I said. Good catch."

"Let's move then," the chief said. "I'd really like to find this before we meet with Kondur."

Pip sighed and shook his head. "I want to see this in action."

"I'll just tape this down." She held up the wand. "Be right back."

We left the ship and Pip led us down the gallery, around the back of the chandlery, and into a dusty office. A middle-aged woman in station livery looked up from a comfy-looking chair in the corner. "Yeah?"

"Ms. Nance, I'm Philip Carstairs. I was here a little while ago asking about the unclaimed cargo?"

She nodded, squinting her eyes at the chief and me. "You brought your captain and engineer?"

"Yes. The reason I was here before was to see what kind of long-term storage you had. We thought maybe a cargo we lost a few stanyers ago might still be here."

"Nothing older than five stanyers," she said. "Told you that before."

Pip nodded. "We're looking for a crate that went missing from one of our shipments. We just discovered the problem during an audit and since we're here, we wondered if it would be possible for us to take a quick look."

She stared at him for a few heartbeats. "Quick look?"

He nodded.

She burst out in a braying laugh. "You folks have no idea what kind of mess you stepped in, but sure. You can go have a quick look." She levered herself up from the chair, grabbed an oversized tablet off the counter, and led the way deeper into the compartment. "Come on. I want to see the expressions on your faces."

She slid a door open and stepped through, turned to the right and started flipping switches. A lot of switches. Overhead lights began coming on high above us. The storage facility stretched almost as far as I could see. "There," she said. "Hope you wore your walking shoes."

Pip whistled. "We could park the *Chernyakova* in here."

The chief looked at me. "Plan B?"

Verkol Kondur showed up on the dot of 1800. Mr. Bentley had the brow and logged him aboard for me.

"Thank you for coming, Mr. Kondur. It's not every day we get to host a station owner," I said.

The chief reached out to shake his hand. "I appreciate your coming on such short notice. I hoped we could have a quiet chat away from extra ears."

His smile looked genuine enough. "Talking with you, Maggie? Always an interesting conversation."

"Right this way," I said.

I led them down the passageway and into the wardroom. I felt a bit like the maître d' in a boutique restaurant, the ship merely creating the ambiance for a special dining experience.

Kondur seemed perfectly at ease. "Nice ship, Captain. Recent refit, as I remember."

"We're still shaking some of the bugs out, filing down some of the sharper edges. I'm getting pretty attached to her."

"Can't say as I blame you," he said.

I crossed to the sideboard. "Can I offer you a drink? I'm afraid our cellar isn't very deep."

He shook his head. "I'm a coffee drinker. Have been for decades."

"Chief?"

She shook her head. "Perhaps later. Why don't you ask Ms. Adams to serve and we can settle in?"

I pressed the call button on the sideboard and Ms. Adams popped her head in through the galley door. "You can serve now, Ms. Adams."

She smiled at me, nodded to Kondur, and ducked back into the galley.

We settled around the table, the chief and I took our customary seats and I waved Kondur into Al's chair. By the time we'd settled, Ms. Adams had the coffee poured, a carafe on the table, and dishes arrayed in front of each of us.

The first course, a salad of fresh greens, started us off. When the door latched behind Ms. Adams, the chief said, "I'm so pleased you could join us tonight, Verkol."

He crunched through a bite of salad and swallowed. "Real paper? How could I refuse?" He speared another forkful. "How are you finding Toe-Hold space, Captain?"

"It hasn't lived down to my preconceived notions." I shrugged. "I didn't grow up as a spacer, so life in the Deep Dark has always been a process of unveiling."

Kondur grinned and lifted his coffee mug, cradling it in both hands. "You've done very well for somebody without the family connections." He took a sip and his eyes widened. "Good coffee."

"Thanks. It might be the only vestige of my youth that followed me into space."

"A penchant for good coffee?" he asked.

"Yes. It was my first job in space, mess deck attendant. The coffee on that ship was atrocious."

He laughed and addressed his salad. He took a bite, chewing while he seemed to consider us. He swallowed and raised an eyebrow toward the chief. "You have things to talk about that you feared might be overheard, Margaret. You're being uncustomarily quiet."

"I'm a little paranoid these days. Honestly, I'm not sure where to begin."

"Why not start at the beginning and continue from there," he said.

"You know about UMS17." She made it a flat statement instead of a question.

Kondur nodded. "Anybody with an ear knows that story. Usoko Mining station got blown to shreds. Rumor is somebody smuggled a nuke—if not on board, then at least close enough to obliterate the station."

She nodded. "My people have been tracking the organization that did it. We may have found them, but I'm concerned there may be other nukes out there. Stations giving in to the extortion."

He finished the salad and wiped his mouth with his napkin. "A rational assumption. I've heard some echoes in the Dark. Stations going missing. Financially secure stations suddenly unable to support themselves. We've noticed a slow trickle of new residents here that are one step above refugee."

"Are we ready for the next course?" I asked.

They both nodded and I signaled Ms. Adams.

She appeared almost immediately, swapping the salad plates for dinner plates of roast beefalo, mashed tubers, and carrots. She hustled the dirty dishes out, closing the door behind her with a click.

"She's very efficient," Kondur said, leaning forward over his plate and inhaling. "This smells divine."

"I'm blessed to have good crew," I said.

He looked at me out of the corners of his eyes. "You may not have grown up as a spacer, Captain, but you're being modest. Good crews aren't a matter of luck. They're almost always a function of picking good stock and developing them into a team."

"You make it sound like breeding cattle," the chief said.

He laughed. "It's not that much different, other than most ships aren't trying to raise the next generation of crews through careful application of genetics. Even family ships crossbreed with others."

"Hybrid vigor," the chief said.

I found the image at once humorous and disturbing, which forced a laugh out of me. It made me think about Pip's family in a new light.

After a few moments of savoring the main course, Kondur looked at each of us for a couple of beats. "Let's stop dancing around the table, shall we?"

The chief placed her fork down. "Are you being extorted, Verkol?"

He smiled around his fork and held up a hand while he chewed. "I suspected that was where you were going." He took an appreciative sip of coffee. "Not directly, but I have friends who are. A threat to a loved one is a dagger to your heart. One of the stations that went dark belonged to a rather stiff-necked colleague. It's been over three stanyers but I still miss our periodic arguments."

"But you're supplying them," the chief said.

He nodded. "I am." He shrugged. "I'm not the only one supplying them, but I've been biding my time. Staying on their good side. Learned a bit about their operation." He shrugged. "Not enough, but some."

The chief frowned. "Like what?"

"Like they have a standing order for potassium iodade tablets."

The chief frowned. "That's not good."

"That's actually rather dumb, isn't it?" I asked.

Kondur smiled at me. "You see the implications?"

"They know they're being irradiated but not what radiation is doing to them," I said.

He nodded. "The iodine pills keep their thyroids from absorbing any radioactive iodine in the atmosphere but does nothing to stop the breakdown of cellular structures through direct exposure to radiation."

"Placebo?" the chief asked.

Kondur shrugged. "Possibly. More likely a solid PR campaign to keep the underlings in line and working. Auto-docs can help mitigate the damage. If the exposures are relatively minor, it could take decades for problems to emerge."

"It also means that whoever is building the devices isn't doing a very good job of shielding," the chief said.

Kondur nodded. "I have no idea where they're getting the bomb cores."

"Pravda?" I asked.

Kondur gave a noncommittal shrug. "Possible, I suppose. They could be siphoning off some of Pravda's cores and converting them to weapons grade." He looked at the chief. "How hard would it be to do that?"

The chief took in a deep breath and blew it out slowly.

I could practically see the gears turning inside her head.

"It's not that simple. The cores don't have the right grade of materials. It would take a lot of cores to get enough base material out of them to make even a small bomb, and then it has to be enriched to weapons grade." She shook her head. "Not impossible, but time consuming."

"They've been at it for a long time," Kondur pointed out.

"There's probably a compounding effect," I said. "Each new device gives them more resources to produce the next one."

Kondur nodded. "They must have had access to a lot of material in the beginning, or they've got a relatively stable supplier. This isn't something you can just dock up and buy from a chandlery."

"True," the chief said. "But start with some decent uranium ore and a breeder reactor. It's not a simple process but it's a relatively well-known one. We've been doing it for centuries. Uranium's not that rare either. Almost every belt in the galaxy has at least some."

"Is it as rare as tellurium?" I asked.

The chief shook her head. "I don't know if you can make that kind of assessment. Some systems have a lot of gold and very little iron. Some systems are basically rust with very little—say—tin."

"Some systems have a lot of tellurium," I said. "What if the answer's right next door?"

"You think they're getting the uranium from Telluride?" the chief asked.

"What if one of the cans was filled with it?"

"That's a lot of uranium," she said.

I shrugged. "I don't know the timing on it, but if the ship was loaded with uranium ore? That would make a hell of a lot of bombs, wouldn't it?"

She blew out a breath and thought for a moment. "It would depend on the quality of the ore and whether or not they shipped raw ore or the refined metal."

"Either way, a rich prize for somebody who claimed it," Kondur said.

"Are we sure that this is connected? Could it be just a bunch of squatters?" I asked.

"They trade goods for supplies," Kondur said. "Where are they getting the goods if not stealing them?"

"You're sure they're not making them? Salvaging them from one of the cans?" I asked.

He shook his head. "No. There's really only one way to be sure and I've never had the wherewithal to push the point. I have a contract with them for supply. They pay me in goods. It's not an unusual arrangement for a small station."

The chief smiled and pressed back in her chair. "That's why you picked us," she said.

Kondur lifted a "who me?" expression to the chief. "I have no idea what you're suggesting, Maggie. You just happened to be inbound."

"Of course," she said. "My mistake. Tell me, how many of these runs have you made?"

"About one every six months. I usually use one of my own Barbells, but those damned girls turned me into a freight hauler."

"Damned girls?" the chief asked.

"You haven't run into them yet? Usoko and Regyri?"

"Oh," the chief said. "Yeah. I've run into them. I thought they were busy running freight themselves these days."

"They are, but when they first came out from the academy, they did a run for me over to Siren. Flushed out some problems in my operation. Once those got cleared up, I discovered I could actually make money hauling myself."

"I never understood why you didn't keep them on the payroll," the chief said.

"Too stiff-necked."

"Who? You or them?"

"Regyri was bound and determined to run that antique as a packet. Never did make it work but I'll give her points for trying."

"UMS17 changed a lot of lives," the chief said.

"It did that," Kondur agreed. He slid his plate back from the edge of the table and reached for his coffee cup. "So, yeah. I never intended to get into actually hauling freight. I kept a couple of Barbells around to haul a bit of ore and pick up some odds and ends." He took a swig of coffee and shook his head. "Those two screwed everything up."

"How's the hauling business going?" the chief asked.

"I've got five ships now. Added a tanker and a couple of Unwin Eight clones. They're killing it in terms of profitable runs."

"What'd you do differently?" I asked. "You must have made some changes if they weren't working before."

"First, I hired somebody who understands freight as a consultant. Second, I brought on a guy whose only job is to oversee that operation. Actually it was one of the Barbell captains. I just pulled him off the bridge and gave him an office, an assistant, and a percentage of the profits." He shook his head. "Damnedest thing. He's hired on some extra people. Filled out the crew rosters and keeps those ships rolling in and out of here as fast as they can unload and load. Crews don't bitch and the ships stay maintained." He paused to take a sip of coffee. "Third, I listened to the first guy. Fourth, I got out of the way of the second." He grinned at me. "You probably know all about getting out of the way."

I caught a sharp glance from the chief out of the corner of my eye but I nodded. "It's a lesson I keep having to refine."

"I'm ready for dessert," the chief said. "Verkol?"

He nodded. "And I think this carafe is nearly dead." He demonstrated by emptying it into his cup.

I signaled Ms. Adams. She cleared, took the empty carafe, and whisked it all away. "Be right back, sars."

"So, yes. This is not the first trip I've made with supplies," Kondur said. "My ships are all out and here comes the *Chernyakova*. I trust our arrangement will be sufficiently rewarding for you, Captain."

"You could have just asked," I said.

Kondur shrugged. "We have no history. I couldn't count on having a simple request being met with the affirmative." I caught the glance he gave the chief.

"Fair enough," I said. "Next time, ask? I may not be able to carry your freight but I'm more likely to say yes when I'm not being arm-wrestled over a barrel of knives."

He laughed as Ms. Adams returned with a carafe of fresh coffee and a tray of assorted desserts. "Here you go, sars." She disappeared again and closed the door.

Kondur helped himself from a plate of brownies while the chief snagged one of Ms. Sharps's crèmes brûlées from the tray.

"Captain?" the chief asked, starting to lift the tray of desserts.

"None for me, thanks, but I wouldn't turn down a return of the carafe."

She grinned and passed it my way.

Kondur finished his first brownie and washed it down with a swig of coffee. "Coffee and chocolate," he said. "Are there any more heavenly pairings?"

I laughed. "Glad we could indulge you."

He took another sip from his mug and looked back and forth between the chief and me. "Now, have I convinced you that I'm not trying to kill you? That I'm not sending you on a one-way trip?"

"Not really," I said.

The chief looked at me like I'd poked her but Kondur laughed.

"Good," he said. "Cautious captains live longer." He looked me in the eye. "I understand your perspective, Captain. In your shoes, I might share your fears. I make no bones about it. These people can be dangerous. I suspect they are dangerous. I've been doing business with them for rather a long time, but it's not because they have hidden a bomb in my station."

"What's changed?" I asked.

"Changed?"

"Yes. Why are you changing a long-standing business arrangement to send us instead of waiting for one of your own Barbells to return from wherever it is now?"

He settled back in his chair and fiddled with his coffee cup. "A couple of stanyers ago. A station went dark. Rawlston. Small place, barely getting started. Some good belts. Lots of potential." He shook his head and took a sip. "My grandson worked on that station. He really liked the idea that he was helping to build something." He shrugged. "Small stations. Small crews. Questionable funding. They disappear almost as frequently as they pop up.

"I kept thinking I'd hear from him. That the station had failed financially or something and he was on Mel's or at The Ranch. Even working for High Tortuga." He shrugged. "I started digging around and every new lead pointed to this group. The same group I'd been working with. At first I thought it was a mistake. The more I looked, the more the evidence piled up." He looked at the chief. "I could have killed them. Put my own bomb in the supply can. Delivered it. Flown away."

"Why didn't you?" she asked.

"I wanted to at first." He took a deep breath and a sip of coffee. "Then I realized that if I did that, I wouldn't be able to look at myself in the mirror. I don't want revenge." He gave a short laugh. "Well, yes, I suppose I do. But that's no real answer."

"What is it you want?" the chief asked.

"I want them to spend the rest of their—hopefully long—lives understanding that what they're doing is a crime against all of us, not just me. Not just the people at Rawlston. Not just the people who died at UMS17 and all the people who loved them. All of us who need to get along to survive out here. All of us who have so much more in common than we have different. I want those bastards stopped and I want them to live in cages like the animals they are for the next century."

He lifted his mug and put it down again. He stared at it, his hand trembling just the slightest bit on the white china handle.

"I can't promise anything," the chief said.

"I haven't asked you for anything," he said, some of his composure returning. "I'm just telling you a story about my grandson."

He took a deep breath and stood. "I'm due back at the office. Sorry to eat and run, but a station owner's life is no more his own than a captain's is."

We all stood and I led him down the passage, stopping to wave at Ms. Sharps. "We're done, Ms. Sharps. Thank you and my compliments to Ms. Adams for a job well done."

She waved back. "Thank you, Skipper."

I turned to find Kondur observing me with a small smile on his lips.

"If you find yourself in need of employment, Captain. I can use a man like you."

I laughed as we continued down the passageway toward the brow. "Thank you, Mr. Kondur—"

"Verkol, please."

"Thank you, Verkol," I said. "But as part owner in this ship, I've got my hands full."

He nodded as Mr. Bentley logged him off the ship. "I understand, Captain—"

"Please, Verkol. Call me Ishmael."

He laughed. "Does anybody ever get that reference?"

"Sometimes." I offered my hand as the lock levered open. "We'll be underway by this time tomorrow, I think."

He shook the hand and nodded. "Next time you're docked at Dark Knight Station, dinner's on me."

Chief Stevens stepped up and gave him a hug and a peck on the cheek. "Take care of yourself, Verkol. I take comfort knowing you're here."

He smiled and patted her cheek. "While I'm glad you're out there." He paused and looked into her eyes. "Thank you, Maggie."

With that he strode down the ramp, picking up his bodyguard outside, and turned toward Main Street and his office, tablet in one hand, his head down.

"Interesting guy," I said.

The chief nodded. "At least we didn't waste time trying to sort through all that abandoned cargo."

I laughed and keyed the lock closed.

Chapter Twenty-four
Dark Knight Station: 2376, March 11

The chief and I went back to the cabin. "Where are we?" I asked, settling into my chair and leaning back as far as it would go. "The question is veracity. Do we believe Kondur, or was that an award-winning snow job?"

The chief grunted. "I need to do some research. I should know some answers by morning. Certainly before we jump out."

"Can you confirm any of his story?"

"I think so," she said. "We've got pretty good data on stations going silent thanks to our friends at High Tortuga. I can see if Rawlston appears on the list and, if it does, what date."

"Where are we on the mega's dates? Do we know if this whole thing started before the mega took its last voyage?"

"I know when the mega left Telluride Station and headed for the Burleson limit. I can guess the date it reached it—months later—and there's probably a few more weeks in there while it tried to slow down and change vectors for an orbital insertion."

"Months, more like," I said. "If we were outbound and the Burleson didn't fire, we'd be a damn long time changing our vector."

"The mega was never going to be a speed demon," she said.

"I'm not familiar with it but just from what I've seen, this was a ship in search of a market," I said.

"You don't think there's a market for a hauler that can jump a million metric kilotons?" she asked.

"There probably is, but not if a single Barbell can make the round trip five times over the same period. Months to get out of Telluride? That's just not viable. I'm trying to imagine a ship like that trying to operate on the High Line." I sighed and straightened up to look at her across the desk. "The *Chernyakova* could carry a million tons between here and Mel's in the time it would take that monster to reach the Burleson limit so it could jump at all." I shook my head. "Either it could actually jump a lot farther, or they never planned for it to get into a gravity well in the first place. The economics of that balancing act makes me think it was a prototype that failed to prove out its concept. Brill said that they didn't lose steam when the ship failed its first space trials. They just took what they'd learned and moved on."

The chief sat up. "Brill said what?"

"It failed its first space trials."

The chief pulled out her tablet and started paging through it. She must have found what she was looking for because she stopped paging and worked down the line on some display I couldn't see. "Those lying bastards."

"Something not lining up?" I asked.

"According to the documentation we got from Manchester, the ship passed its first and second space trials. It failed on what was supposed to be the first leg of the big PR voyage." She shook her head. "If Brill is correct—and I have no reason to believe she's not—that first space trial was in '64."

"Meaning it was loose in space a lot longer than Manchester wants you to believe?"

"Exactly," she said. "Our earliest cases of blown stations started up half-past '65."

"Time enough to get the ship under control, insert it into orbit. Is it enough time to make a bomb and blow up a station?"

"It is if they already had a bomb and the breeder reactor to make more," she said.

"So, we're back to where did they get the uranium? I can't imagine they'd load a few billion credits worth of radioactives into a ship that had never been in space," I said.

"Good point. They have a problem with using Barbells, too," she said. "They can't fly a can out and return without a can to bring back."

"Well, they started with at least four cans, if I understand the construction model."

"Where'd you get that number?"

"Something Brill said. They used four standard two-hundred-metric-kiloton cans for the cargo so they wouldn't have to come up with a new trans-shipment container."

"So it didn't actually carry a million?"

"Not according to Brill."

"So, fly a can out, take a can from the ship and move on," the chief said.

"Tedious process without a way to unload the cans. Or load them, for that matter."

"So, we're taking them a can, getting a can. Where are they getting the uranium and how are they processing it?" she asked.

"Add the question of how are they loading and unloading cans. You don't just open a hatch and shovel stuff out of those suckers." I sighed and rubbed my eyes. "They must have a station."

"Why?" the chief asked.

"Well, the mega is a great place to hide stuff you want hidden. It's a terrible place to do anything that requires cargo handling. It's a hull in space. Granted, it's a big hull, but they'd have to strip out the engineering space, figure out a way to expand the living quarters. Deal with the issue of loading and unloading cans. If they're making their own plutonium, they need a breeder. Even if they're making dirty bombs because they're easier, they still need a fairly sophisticated set up."

A thought grenade went off in my head and I had to close my mouth for a moment to catch my breath and examine the damage.

"I know where their reactor is," I said.

The chief stared at me. "You do?"

"In one of the cans."

"In a can?" she asked.

"Yup. I'll bet you a bottle of rum that's where it is. I kept trying to figure out how they'd deal with all the heavy equipment they'd need and how little space there is in the ship. Even accounting for the larger nacelles. Four cans, probably empty. They can be made airtight easily enough. Would the equipment needed to run full industrial operations to create the enriched uranium fit in a can?"

"With room enough for half the student body at Port Newmar, but that would require access to the cans from the ship," she said.

"It would, yes, but if they used the same mounting scheme on the mega as they do on a Barbell like us? And why wouldn't they?" I paused. "Build out the can at a base. Load it up with everything you need. It becomes a portable base of operations. Attach it to a Barbell and take it where you need it. Pull the can off the Barbell and at least one of the cans from the mega. Plug the factory in and mate the Barbell to the free can."

"Carve an air lock from the bow or stern to let people in or out of the can?"

"Exactly," I said. "The cans latch at the corners and along the spine. The ends are basically metal bulkheads with an airtight door in the center."

She nodded, her eyes focused somewhere else. "It could work."

"You know what else would work?"

She shook her head.

"Building that can and mounting it to a stock Barbell."

"What would that buy you?" she asked.

"A base of operations you could fly anywhere in the Western Annex and nobody would look twice at it." I shrugged. "Living quarters, training spaces, anything you'd need to set up housekeeping."

"Until you docked somewhere," she said.

"Docking is nothing unless you're going to trade cans. There's nothing that says we couldn't fly the *Chernyakova* around the Western Annex until doomsday. Nobody would notice that we never changed the can."

"What would you do with it?" she asked.

"Well, if you wanted to go into bomb-making, it would be pretty good cover."

She snorted but she studied her boots for several long moments. "It could work."

"It still doesn't answer the problem of loading and unloading cans," I said. "It's a start. Maybe we'll learn more when we get out there."

She nodded. "We're going to have to go, aren't we?"

"I don't see how we can avoid it. The more immediate question is whether Kondur is on the level. How long have you known him?"

"Almost a century, I think."

I *felt* my eyeballs bugging out of my head.

"Don't look so surprised. He's a lot older than he looks."

"I have a hard time believing *you're* old enough to have known anybody for a century," I said.

"Nice save," she said. "When you've been banging around the Western Annex as long as I have, you'll be really, really old." She grinned. "Kondur has always been a straight-shooter. It's why he left the High Line. He couldn't stand the idea of CPJCT. He came out here and staked out this system as Dark Knight Station."

"Did he found it?"

She shrugged. "To this day I don't know if he founded it, bought out the founder, or just rolled in and took over. He cultivates a bad-guy image. Works at it diligently. Even the little mustache and goatee. Working out of that dive—which has the best coffee in the Western Annex, by the way. It's all part of his persona."

"What's he stand for?" I asked.

"Besides a pretty woman?"

She got a chuckle out of me. "No, I mean what's his basic value set include? Clearly he was all right with these pirates until they hit his family."

"I'm not sure that's true. Until he had direct evidence, I'm not sure he even knew who or what he was dealing with. He's probably got these deals with cash-poor, resource-rich stations all over the Western Annex. If I had to say, that's probably the best concrete example of what he stands for. Helping the little guy get started. Making sure that the Toe-Holds keep thriving." She shrugged. "You heard him. He believes in the Toe-Holds and the fact that the Toe-Holds have to hang together against pretty much everything. Including these scum."

"Don't beat around the bush, Chief. Tell me how you feel about them."

She snorted and rose from the chair. "If we're leaving tomorrow, I need to get some messages out."

"You need me to stall for a couple of days?" I asked.

She seemed to think about that for a few heartbeats but ultimately shook her head. "I think we can get underway and take our time out and back. There are no delivery bonuses. What kind of training can we do to keep people distracted?"

"What? Our people?"

She nodded.

"Paint the spine?" I asked.

She stopped in her tracks and turned all the way around to look at me. "Paint the spine?"

"One of the SAs came to me the other day. Identified a safety hazard."

"In the spine?"

"Yeah. Unless you know to look for the VSI nodes, if you're too close to the middle, you can't tell which end is which. In an emergency, that could be disorienting."

She frowned. "You're kidding."

I shook my head. "Next time you go to engineering, stop somewhere in the middle, close your eyes, and spin around a bit. Open your eyes and pick the direction of the bow."

"I know which end of the ship is the bow."

"So do I, but without looking at the VSI nodes can you point to it?"

She frowned. "I don't know. Never tried."

"I hadn't either until the other day."

She shook her head. "What's wrong with using the VSI nodes as a landmark?"

"Because, unless you've been trained to look for them by—say, being one of the environmental watchstanders—you probably don't know that they're always on the port side."

Her eyes widened. "That would be almost everybody on the ship."

I nodded. "It wouldn't have occurred to anybody who's in on the secret, and it's one of those dangerous things you don't know you don't know."

"Her solution was paint?"

"Yeah. A stripe of green to port and red to starboard. I suggested some decorative touches."

"Like Al and the mess deck murals?"

I nodded. "Think she'll sit for the board?"

The chief shrugged. "I don't know if she can even get an invitation at this point, but knowing you put her in? Yeah. She'll remember that."

"Think she'll make a good captain?"

"No question in my mind. You better not have any doubts in yours."

I laughed. "I don't. I'd sail under her any time."

The chief gave me one of her looks. "If you think she'd ever let you sail under her, you've missed the point." She headed for the door with a wave in my general direction. "I have some things to do."

CHAPTER TWENTY-FIVE
DARK KNIGHT STATION: 2376, MARCH 12

The day started out pleasantly enough. It started going south when the brow watch paged me to the lock.

"What have we got, Ms. Torkelson?"

"Station security, Captain. I asked them to wait in the gallery until you could meet with them."

"Did you page Ms. Ross?"

"I did, sar. She's out there with them now."

I nodded. "Anybody overdue from liberty?"

"Nobody overdue, no, sar. The watch section is all present and accounted for."

"Thank you, Ms. Torkelson." I walked down the ramp and stood beside Al. "Officers? I'm Captain Wang. Can I help you?"

"Sorry to bother you so early, Captain." His name tag read "Riordan."

"Do I have a problem, Officer Riordan?"

"I'm not certain," he said. "When was the last time you saw Verkol Kondur?"

"Last night about 1930. He and his bodyguard left here headed toward Main Street. He said he had some things to take care of."

"Anybody else see him?"

"We logged him on and off the ship. The watchstander watched him go. My chief engineering officer watched him walk away with the bodyguard."

"His bodyguard?"

"Yes. One moment. Lemme page the chief."

Riordan nodded and I pulled out my tablet and hit the chief with an "at your earliest convenience" request.

She popped out of the lock in less than a tick.

"Officer Riordan, this is my engineering officer. If you'd like to ask her, I think she will corroborate what I've told you."

"When did you see Verkol Kondur last, Chief?"

"Last night around 1930 or so. He logged off the ship, joined his bodyguard here on the gallery, and headed off that way." She pointed toward the main station entrance.

"Did you recognize the bodyguard? Either of you?" the other officer asked.

"I thought it was the same guy we saw him with the other day at his office," I said.

The chief nodded. "Yeah. It was the same guy. Hervé Villarosa. Been with Kondur at least five stanyers."

The two officers looked at each other. "I see," Riordan said.

"Can I ask what this is about?" I asked.

"You can ask, but I can't tell you. At least not yet. You weren't planning on leaving Dark Knight Station, I hope?"

"Soon as we get the can tied on," I said. "Although the can's not here yet so that's going to be a problem."

He gave me a grim smile. "The Barbell's only weakness." He sighed and looked at his partner, a woman with "Marshall" on her name badge.

She shrugged.

"Kondur never made it back from here last night. Far as we know, he came here for dinner and never came back."

"You searched his tablet traffic?"

"We've got somebody tracking through that now," Marshall said. "He gets a lot of traffic and half of it is encrypted."

"I'm not surprised in the least," the chief said. She gave me a little nudge with her elbow.

"Under the circumstances we'll be happy to stay until station security says we can go," I said. "Let us know if there's anything we can do to help."

Riordan tipped his cap in our direction. "Thanks for your understanding, Skipper. Chief. I shouldn't have to say it, but—confidential?"

"Of course," I said. "No need to get the station in an uproar. Right?"

He gave me a wry grin. "Something like that. Yes. Thanks again."

They turned away and headed back toward the main station entrance. Riordan had a radio out, speaking into it as they walked.

"This is not good," the chief said.

"Cabin," I said.

"Yup."

I walked back up the ramp and stopped at the watch station. "Did you log our visitors, Ms. Torkelson?"

"I did, Captain. I logged their arrival and that they asked for you. I paged Ms. Ross as OOD and then you."

"Thank you. They've left. You can log them away, if you would." I looked at Al. "Got a tick or two?"

"It's been a pretty boring watch so far," she said. "I could use the distraction."

"You say that now," the chief said and headed up the passageway toward the cabin.

Al looked at me, shrugged, and followed the chief, leaving me to bring up the rear. I was pretty sure the morning—and probably the afternoon and evening—would be less boring.

I stopped at the mess deck for a coffee on the way. Al followed me and filled two cups.

"Good thinking," I said. "This might take a while."

She looked at me and shrugged. "I've got the duty."

We caught up with the chief in the cabin. She slouched in one of the guest chairs and looked up to take the coffee from Al. "Bless you," she said. "I didn't think to get one on the way by."

"I probably wouldn't have if the captain hadn't stopped."

I closed the door behind me and took my place behind the desk. "How much are you up on, Al?"

"I'm going with 'I have no idea' for now."

The chief and I took turns filling her in.

"So, Kondur arm-twisted us into handling this cargo for him? A cargo that he has always handled personally. A cargo that we're going to deliver to a bunch of killers who've taken refuge in a multi-billion credit boondoggle in slow orbit around Telluride."

"Basically," the chief said. "Kondur being missing is a new wrinkle. I don't know how to read that."

"Warning," Al said without missing a beat. She took a sip of coffee.

The chief frowned. "That would make sense but it only makes sense if there's somebody here, watching."

"That's a no-brainer if you're getting your food from here. You'd want to know if anything threatened your supply line," Al said. "Do we know if any ships left the station?"

"No way for us to know. Traffic control might," I said. "You think they grabbed him?"

"It would be pretty easy," Al said.

"Even with that mountain of a bodyguard?" I asked.

"Makes it easier," Al said. "The mark isn't suspecting anything because of the mountain. Two guys with tasers from behind.

Drop them both. Trank them. Sort out the bodies at leisure." She shrugged. "Easy."

"Station security?" I asked, looking at the chief.

"Cameras on the docks. Selected public areas like the chandlery and Main Street." She shook her head. "Neither Riordan nor Marshall struck me as incompetent. Kondur's been playing the game a long time. He doesn't hire fools." She shook her head again. "No, if they had any better leads, they wouldn't have been knocking at our lock this morning."

"Al?" I asked.

"If it was a warning, he'll turn up before long—probably banged up. Maybe suffering from a drug hangover."

"Bodyguard?" I asked.

"They won't be together," she said. "He's going to be hard to carry so they probably had one of the maintenance carts with a wagon. Toss him in the wagon, throw a tarp over him, and he's just another bag of trash heading for compost or recycle." She took a slurp off her mug and nodded. "That's where I'd leave him. Just park the cart and walk away. Day workers come in and find him when they get around to seeing what's what."

"What about Kondur?" the chief asked.

"He's going to be tougher. If it's only a warning, he'll show up. Beat to hell, probably. A good beating would make him hard to identify. I'd check the auto-docs around the area. They didn't take him far, they only needed him conscious enough for a tersely worded, melodramatic warning before they beat the crap out of him and dropped him outside an aid station."

"You make it sound so easy," the chief said.

Al gave her a sideways grin. "You've been around the docks longer than I have. How would you do it?"

"Just the way you described," the chief said. "Verkol helped by not having a tail on himself. He's safe in his own station, right?"

Al sighed. "If I had a credit for every time I heard that one."

"I don't know whether to be glad you two are on my side or worried at the depths you both seem personally familiar with," I said.

"Those are not mutually exclusive, Skipper," Al said. "Pay attention here. You might learn something you can use later."

"Is there anything we can do?" I asked.

"Doubt it. Where's Pip?" Al asked.

"I haven't seen him today," I said. "That's not exactly newsworthy."

Al frowned and looked at the chief before stepping out of the cabin. I heard her knock on a door. "Pip? You awake?"

I checked the chrono. 0940.

A door opened and closed before Al returned. "Not in there."

I pulled up my tablet and sent him a message. "He's probably holed up somewhere," I said.

Al shook her head. "He doesn't cat around, as a rule. He may come home late, but he almost always comes home."

"He *is* on liberty," the chief said, but she didn't look convinced to me.

I checked with the brow and got a message back. "He went ashore yesterday afternoon just before evening mess." A wash of ice water slid down my back. "Coincidence?"

Al and the chief shared a look.

"Kondur and Pip both missing at the same time? Yeah. That's got to be a coincidence. They're not connected in any way," Al said.

"Well," I said. "They're connected by a cargo container bound for the mega."

"We identified ourselves to that clerk at long-term storage," the chief said.

"You have any new thoughts on how big one of these nukes must be?" I asked.

"Taking out a station? Probably bigger than a breadbox."

"Grav trunk?" I asked.

She frowned. "Not enough data. Stupid designs abound. Poorly executed and you wind up with a popgun instead of a howitzer." She screwed up her mouth in a grimace. "Dirty as hell, but no real ka-boom."

"So anybody with a grav trunk?" I asked.

She gave me a noncommittal shrug. "I don't know. Maybe. Possibly. Mass would give it away but that argues more for something in a shipping crate than a grav trunk. What are you thinking?"

"Just because Kondur hadn't been extorted yet doesn't mean there's not a device on the station he doesn't know about."

"Insurance?" Al asked.

I nodded. "I'm also thinking that the link has to be connected to the dockmaster's office. The woman at the abandoned cargo warehouse saw Pip twice. Suborning a minor functionary like that would be useful. Keeps track of the station. Rides herd on the bomb. Notifies her handlers if anybody comes sniffing around."

"I'd have a cell here," Al said. "What? Three? Five?" She looked at the chief.

"Three is probably ideal. One for brains. Two for hands, eyes, and legs."

"So somebody saw us get the special can and alerted home? Kondur came for dinner and gets grabbed for reasons unknown, maybe a warning. Why Pip?" I asked.

Al and the chief shared a look again. I had no idea how they were communicating. I never even saw eyebrows wiggle.

"Hostage," Al said.

"Make sure we deliver the can without double crossing them," the chief said.

"Can we find him?" I asked.

"He's off station," Al said. "If they want to kill him, it's easier out there. Controlling him in the Dark is going to be easier there than here where he might break loose and raise hell."

The chief nodded. "We really need to know if any ship left the station in the last—what? Fifteen stans?"

I pulled up my tablet. The message to Pip hadn't been delivered. "He's not on the net," I said.

"He could have his tablet turned off," the chief said. "It wouldn't show until he turned it on again."

I started punching keys until I connected with station security.

"Dark Knight security. Please state the nature of your emergency."

"I'd like to speak to Officer Riordan or his boss."

"Riordan is on assignment."

"Can you connect me with his supervisor?" I asked.

The pause lasted for a few heartbeats. "What is the nature of your business?"

"It's about Verkol Kondur," I said. "I'm Captain Ishmael Wang of the *Chernyakova*. Officers Riordan and Marshall visited me this morning. We may have additional information that could help the investigation."

"One moment, Captain."

The line clicked and a woman's voice came over the line. "Oscella, speak."

"I'm Captain Wang of the *Chernyakova*," I said. "One of our officers is missing. He left the ship about the same time Kondur arrived."

"Why do you think those things are connected, Captain?"

"Our meeting with Kondur involved a shipping job. The missing person is our cargo officer."

"You're sure he's missing and not just cuddled up beside somebody?"

"I can only be sure if we find him," I said. "That behavior would not be in keeping with his habit, but I can't rule it out."

She sighed. "If he's not back in twenty-four hours, file a report at the dock security station. It's just off the chandlery."

"Wait," I said. "Have any ships left the station since about 1900 last night?"

She laughed a low, sad laugh. "Probably only a hundred or so, Captain." She paused. "We've already looked. It's a large number that doesn't even give us a comprehensive list."

"I see. Well, our best guess is that Villarosa will turn up in a compost or recycling center near the docking gallery exit. Kondur's probably tucked in an auto-doc as a John Doe not too far away."

The pause went on so long, I looked to see if I'd been disconnected.

"You want to explain that, Captain?"

"We had a business meeting with Kondur last night. He left here after the evening mess. Around 1930. We watched him and his bodyguard, Villarosa, walk away from the ship. This morning we learn he's missing. He wasn't grabbed on the docks or you'd have found it on the security tapes. He didn't get as far as Main Street or you'd have seen that. He must have been taken between those two. The easiest way would be two people with tasers taking them both down at the same time. Villarosa is a big man so they'd have needed a cart like the maintenance people use. It would have been big enough for both Villarosa and Kondur. They take Kondur someplace, beat the hell out of him, and drop him at an aid station where the medics throw him into an auto-doc without looking too closely for an ID. They take the cart with Villarosa to the nearest maintenance depot, park it in line, and walk away."

"I'll give you points for thoroughness, Captain. Do you have a motive?"

"We're contracted with Kondur to take a sensitive cargo out of here. The people we're delivering to have reason to distrust us because Kondur's been using his own ships to deliver for the last few stanyers."

"Why would they distrust you?" she asked.

"Because we're not Kondur."

"That makes no sense."

"That's as much as I know," I said. "Anything else is speculation."

"Speculate for me, Captain."

"It's probably because Kondur's been trading with a group of pirates who aren't happy that somebody new has the location of their operations base. It's complete speculation. I have no direct knowledge."

She sighed. "You realize that who Kondur does business with is no business of ours."

"I realize you're employed by the station, which means Kondur. He makes the rules and you enforce them. I'm not making any judgments here. You asked me to speculate. That's my speculation. It also covers why they would have kidnapped my cargo chief."

"Why's that?" she asked.

"Hostage. We get him back when the cargo is delivered."

"Have they contacted you?" Oscella sounded a bit desperate.

"I'd have started with that if they had."

She sighed. "Look. You're on your ship? The *Chernyakova?*"

"Yes," I said.

"Stay. We'll be there momentarily."

"We're at your service, Officer Oscella."

The connection clicked off.

Al and the chief stared at me from across the desk.

"That was unexpected," the chief said.

"What?" I asked. "She said there are at least a hundred ships that left since 1930 last night. Pip can't be considered missing until he's been gone twenty-four hours. She wanted to know how I came to the conclusion that both Kondur and his bodyguard—"

"Not that," she said. "That she hadn't already put those pieces together."

"Give her the benefit of the doubt. How many times has Kondur been taken?" Al asked. "I suspect the worst they have to deal with here on a regular basis are bar fights and drunks."

"To be fair, there are the occasional murders reported," the chief said. "Some domestic disputes."

"How do they handle those?" I asked.

They both looked at me like I'd asked what color an orange was.

"Courts?" Al suggested. "I haven't looked but all the major stations had local courts. High Tortuga gets right of final arbitration if the station can't settle it."

The chief nodded. "Verkol's got a good setup here. Neighborhood-, station-, and system-wide. Everything goes to local adjudication and it gets bumped up until everybody's happy—or they deal with High Tortuga." She shook her head. "Nobody wants to deal with High Tortuga."

I stood. "Let's adjourn to the ward room. I suspect we'll have visitors in the next few ticks."

Chapter Twenty-six
Dark Knight Station: 2376, March 12

I had just about enough time to stop by the galley and ask Ms. Sharps to set up a coffee mess in the wardroom before the constabulary descended. I greeted them at the lock and had Ms. Cheuvront log them all aboard. Riordan and Marshall came with a diminutive woman with hard eyes who turned out to be Oscella and a security chief named Lawrence.

"Welcome aboard. If you'll follow me, we can talk in the wardroom. I've asked my senior staff to join us."

Lawrence looked like he might want to argue about talking on the ship. He had the "how about we all go down to the station" air about him. Oscella gave him a look while Riordan and Marshall were dealing with getting logged aboard.

I led the parade into the wardroom, grateful that Mr. Franklin was already setting out mugs and carafes. Ms. Sharps followed up with a plate of cookies. "Anything else, Captain?" she asked.

"Thank you, Ms. Sharps. I'll signal if we need anything."

"Of course, Captain." She smiled at our guests and backed out, pulling the door closed behind her.

I grabbed a mug, filled it with coffee, and sat at the head of the table. "Please. Help yourself. Any tea drinkers?"

It didn't take long for everybody to settle. Al and the chief took their customary seats beside me, leaving the rest of the table to security. I would have bet that Lawrence would have taken the foot of the table, just to sit opposite me. Oscella took it instead and I had to shuffle my assumptions about who was in charge.

"Let me make introductions," I said. "Chief Margaret Stevens, my chief engineering officer. First Mate Alberta Ross. We're most concerned about our missing cargo chief—Philip Carstairs. How can we help you?"

Oscella spoke first, just barely cutting off Lawrence. "You ran down a pretty specific set of hypotheses about what happened last night. Care to comment on how you came up with that?"

I shrugged. "Logical extrapolations of observed occurrences."

She looked like she might be waiting for me to say more.

I took a sip of my coffee.

Lawrence grabbed the chance. "You seem to know an awful lot about something you claim no knowledge of."

It took me a moment to parse that statement. I thought the chief snorted, but when I glanced over she had her nose in her cup. "I'm not following, Mr. Lawrence. I don't claim anything. I know some facts. My watchstander logged Carstairs off the ship at about 1730, he hasn't come back yet. He has not responded to electronic communications. The network reports that those messages have not been delivered. I saw Verkol Kondur leave our ship, meet his bodyguard at the foot of the ramp, and walk down the gallery toward the gallery exit nearest Main Street. I met with Officers Riordan and Marshall before I was aware that Carstairs was missing. We tried to figure out where Carstairs might be and along the way wondered where Kondur and Villarosa might have ended up.

"We speculated that his being missing wasn't a function of random behavior since we had security on our doorstep barely twelve stans after he left." I glanced to either side. "Did I miss anything?"

Al and the chief both shook their heads.

"How did you know Villarosa would be at a recycle station?" Lawrence asked, his voice a baritone growl. It was such a cliché I had to take a sip of coffee to stifle the laugh.

"I didn't," I said. "We speculated that it would be the most logical place for his attackers to leave him. Is that where you found him?"

Oscella nodded. "Two maintenance workers found him this morning when they reported for duty. We've got officers querying the aid stations looking for John Does. No luck yet."

"Have them look for Hervé Villarosa," Al said.

Lawrence scowled down the table at her. "What good would that do? We know where he is."

"Do you know where his ID is?" Al asked.

Lawrence threw up his hands, disgust written in the sneer on his lips. "Look, why don't you people leave the law enforcement to the professionals, all right?"

Riordan had his tablet out. In a moment, he lifted his head and looked at Oscella. "It's missing."

"What's missing?" Lawrence asked.

"Villarosa's ID tag."

Lawrence stood and braced his hands on the table, glowering at us like it meant something. "I don't know what kind of game you're playing here, but it's going to stop and right now. Do I make myself clear?" By the end his shouts rang off the bulkheads.

The chief laughed. It wasn't the kind of "hah" you might have expected as a retort. It was a full-on belly laugh.

The red flushed up through Lawrence's face, turning him into a veritable cartoon of an angry male. "You think this is funny?" he said, leaning over toward the chief. "You don't realize what you're dealing with here."

The chief just laughed again—a quiet chuckle. "No," she said. "You don't realize what *you're* dealing with here. If you'd like to keep your job, I suggest you sit down, shut up, pay attention, and stop behaving like a toddler who's had his shiny toy taken away. I've been at this for almost a century and I've dealt with a lot tougher bully-boys than a jumped up jerkwad with a badge who thinks that the person who yells loudest is always right."

"You can't talk to me like that."

"On the contrary. James Kelton Lawrence. Started in law enforcement as a TIC customs agent in 2361. Cashiered for taking bribes in 2364. Moved to The Ranch where you were in charge of shoveling out the barns until you killed your co-worker, David Burnside, by dumping a container of wet manure on him while you were drunk in 2365." She paused there and gave me a shrug before continuing. "You've been here at Dark Night Station ever since, working your way up through the ranks to your current position of 'security chief' which I happen to know puts you junior to the woman to your left, who actually happens to know a bit about law enforcement. Now. Sit down and shut up or I'll tell her exactly how you got that post."

His face paled but he didn't back down. "You're bluffing."

The chief looked at Oscella. "Cecilly Varney. Age twenty."

Lawrence shook his head. "That's a lie."

Oscella looked at Lawrence. "The lady gave you some good advice. I suggest you follow it."

"But she's lying," Lawrence said. "You're going to take her word over a colleague?"

Oscella looked at Riordan. "Call for backup."

"You can't do that," Lawrence said.

Oscella sighed. "I can and I did, Jim. You're relieved of duty pending administrative hearing. Turn in your badge, comm, and weapon."

Lawrence deflated into his chair. His gaze darted from Oscella to the chief and around the table. Even his fellow officers wore stony looks.

Oscella looked at the chief. "I don't know who you are. I suspect I don't want to know but I know enough to listen." She grinned. "I can always arrest you later."

The chief grinned back. "Fair enough."

"Marshall, would you escort Lawrence to the lock to meet the backup team?" Oscella asked.

"Of course." She stood and motioned to Lawrence.

Lawrence gave her a surly growl.

"Come on, Jim. Don't make this any harder than it already is, huh?"

He stood and shambled out of the wardroom, Marshall at his back.

"Wait with him, tell the backup team he's suspended. Have them take him back to the station to clear out his stuff. Then make sure he's turned in his badge, weapon, and comm."

"Got it," Marshall said, closing the door behind her on the way out.

I nodded at Al and the door.

"I'll just make sure they find the lock," she said and followed them out.

"Riordan, would you ask the survey team to look for Villarosa?" Oscella asked.

"Already done. Mallory thinks he remembers that name. He's going back to check."

"Why didn't they kill him?" Oscella asked. "This was a lot of trouble."

"They wanted to send him a message about who was in charge," the chief said. "They aren't any more correct than Mr. Lawrence was."

"We still haven't found Pip," I said.

"He's near," the chief said.

"Basis?" Oscella asked.

"If we're right that he's a hostage, they'll wait until we get back with the delivery to release him. They'll avoid the station where he might get away or have somebody find him, but they won't want to get so far away they can't be sure we didn't follow through."

Oscella nodded. "Makes sense."

"That's how I'd do it," the chief said.

Oscella gave her a look.

The chief just smiled and shrugged. "How would you do it?"

Oscella frowned just a fraction. "I never really thought about it."

"Can you tell me if your security department has anything to do with Kondur's personal security?" the chief asked. "I understand if that's too sensitive to share."

"We don't," Oscella said. "Until today, I don't think anybody ever considered he might be tagged."

"I'll talk to him when we find him," she said. "He knows better. He's just gotten sloppy in his dotage."

"You sound pretty confident," Oscella said.

"Killing him doesn't get them anything. They think roughing him up will."

"Won't it?" Oscella asked.

The chief raised an eyebrow. "Just how well do you know Verkol Kondur?"

Oscella frowned. "Good point."

"Correct me on this," I said, looking to the chief. "Our plan going forward is to take the can to its destination. Swap it for the other can. Get it back here."

"Yes," she said. "We've got some timing issues to resolve. I should have what we need in another day."

"We're going to have to swap cans there," I said.

She nodded. "Covered."

Oscella watched our exchange. "You're leaving the station?"

"Assuming you don't need us here," I said. "We've got cargo to run and we're not getting our man back until we return with the cargo."

"You're just going to leave him?"

"I don't know that we have much choice. We can assume that he's on one of those ships that left—"

The chief gasped. "Maybe not."

"Something?" I asked.

Al came back into the wardroom. "They're on the dock."

"Maybe. Al, what's your second choice for hiding spot?" the chief asked.

"Where you'd least expect it," she said.

"Right. So here?"

"The last place I'd expect is on the station," Al said, nodding.

"Me, too. Now where?" The chief looked at me with a little smile.

"Abandoned cargo," I said. "Nobody goes in without going past that nice little old lady. Nobody stays alone."

"Close, easy in, easy out. No cameras," the chief said.

"You noticed?" I asked.

The chief sighed. "I'm an engineer, dear boy. I notice stuff like that."

"You're more than that," Oscella said. "Care to translate for the cheap seats?"

"We had cause to look through the long-term storage unit where the station keeps abandoned cargo."

"I'm familiar with it. They auction the oldest stuff off every stanyer," Oscella said. "I'm going to overlook my instinct to ask what you were looking for. At least for now."

"There's a caretaker. A woman, older than springtime, younger than winter," the chief said. "Comes across as a little dim, bumbling."

"Doesn't help me," Oscella said. "That describes about a third of our population."

"Point is that if I wanted to hide somebody—just temporarily—for safe keeping, that would be ideal if she was in on it. Care and feeding would be pretty easy. There's probably a head nearby. Nobody has any cause to be in there until the auction comes around except for cargo handlers who might want to turn in a new piece of abandoned cargo," the chief said. "They could keep him there almost indefinitely."

Al nodded. "Good choke point. I assume the freight doors don't open from the outside?"

Oscella shrugged. "No idea. Not my bailiwick."

"How do we get him out?" I asked.

The chief looked at Oscella. "You don't need probable cause here, do you?"

Oscella shook her head but frowned. "Not technically. We operate almost exclusively in the public spaces. We'll break down a door if we need to, but if we show up, they'll know something's up."

"All right. Back to chicanery," the chief said. "Where are the cargo loading doors?"

"They're actually in the chandlery," Riordan said.

Oscella looked at him with a raised eyebrow.

"It's where they run the auction," he said. "They open one of the doors, wheel out a crate. Everybody bids. Winner has to drag the crate off—or pay to get it hauled. Since the chandlery is right off the docks, it's easy to move cargo out of there." He glanced at Oscella. "I drew crowd control a couple of times."

"Uh huh," she said. "But that answers the question. Why do you want to know?"

"Because I want to know where my escape route goes," the chief said. "If we can trick our way in through the front, I want to be able to get out the back, preferably where there are lots of witnesses."

Oscella nodded. "We can help with that much, I think."

Riordan looked up. "They found him. Kondur."

"Auto-doc?" Oscella asked.

"Yeah. Right around the corner from the maintenance station where we found Villarosa."

Oscella took a long, considering look at the chief, then me, then Al. "I don't want to know who or what you are. I'm pretty sure you're not all what you're claiming to be. But you've been on the beam from the beginning. Right now, I need to go make sure Kondur's taken care of. If there's anything you need, call me." She stood and motioned to Riordan. "If you'd walk us out, Captain?"

I stood and led the way out of the wardroom and down the passage. I got everybody logged out. "Thank you, Ms. Oscella. I'm sorry, I don't actually know your rank," I said.

"I should be thanking you," she said. "It's captain. I should have reined in Lawrence long ago, but didn't have the legs to do it. Between your chief engineer and his outburst, he's going to be washing dishes at Kondur's office from now until doomsday."

I chuckled at the image. "Why washing dishes?"

"We don't go in much for incarceration here," she said. "Unless the infraction is a capital offense, almost everybody gets either public service or banishment."

"Kondur's office is public service?"

"He's the boss. I'm not going to tell him otherwise," Oscella said. She shook her head. "He's a funny guy, Kondur. You look at him and you see a thug, almost a warlord. Then you find out he's funding a school for orphans to give them a basic education and also funds their advanced training when they have to go off-station to school."

"What's the catch?"

"They have to come back and work here one stanyer for every year they're away."

"What? Indentured?" I asked.

She shook her head. "No. That's the hell of it. Just come back, get a job. Work here for a stanyer for every year you were gone. I've never asked him about it. We don't exactly rub elbows."

"He does this for the orphans," I said.

"Yeah. Not exactly a thug's behavior," she said.

"Well, he's getting a trained, loyal workforce out of it," I said.

"Some of them, yeah. Some do their time and move on." She shrugged. "Some use it well. Some squander it. Some blow it. Mostly they're just humans."

"I'm not belittling his philanthropy. I think it's great. I also think it's smart."

"Why smart?" she asked.

"What's better for a station? A bunch of untrained, unskilled labor or a bunch of trained, skilled labor?"

"I'll give you that." She paused at the foot of the ramp. "What are you going to do about your missing crewman?"

"I'm going to go check in with the brain trust in the wardroom and see what they advise. Why?"

"Keep me in the loop, would you?" She looked up and down the gallery, anywhere but at me. "We owe you and your brain trust. We'd probably still be looking."

"Will do. When you see Kondur, tell him 'Maggie says hi' for us."

"What are you going to do about the pirates?" she asked.

"What pirates?"

"The ones you're going to trade with."

"I plan to sail out, swap cans, and sail back with as little trouble as possible," I said. "I'd really like to take my whole crew with me, but that's a bias I have about not leaving people behind."

She chuckled and held out a hand. "Nice to meet you, Captain Wang."

"Likewise, Captain Oscella."

"It's Louisa," she said.

"Likewise, Captain Louisa." I smiled at her. "Call me Ishmael."

"Thank you, Ishmael. You didn't answer the question. What are you going to do about the pirates?"

"They're not really in my remit, are they?" I asked. "I mean, sure, they blow up stations, extort goods, and are—by all accounts— snappy dressers, but my job description is basic captaining and providing value for my shareholders."

She stared at me for several very long moments. "You don't mean that."

"Well, I do, actually. Most of it anyway. The snappy dressers part was hyperbole." I shrugged.

"You're going to let them get away with it?" she asked. "Blowing up stations and the rest?"

"I didn't say anything about that. You asked what I was going to do about it. What I'm going to do is my job and leave the pirates to the people whose job it is to make their lives hell. Or maybe end."

I could see in her eyes when the reality of what I wasn't saying struck home.

"It's not *your* job," she said.

"We understand each other, I think. My job is to fly the ship. To deal with cargoes and taxes, payrolls and discipline. I take care of the crew and the ship and the goods entrusted to my care."

"And you fly with some rather astonishing crew," she said.

"Did you know about The Ranch job?" I asked.

She shook her head and her eyes turned to stone. "No, but I knew Cecilly Varney."

"Chief Stevens is an amazing woman. I'm going to lose her soon, I fear. She's heading back to the academy to teach starship engineering."

"What will you do after that?"

I shrugged. "Nothing different. I'll just keep doing my job."

She stared into my face, her gaze going back and forth between my eyes like she was trying to read something written there. A bemused smile blossomed even as her frown deepened. "Safe voyage, Ishmael."

"Good luck with Kondur, Louisa."

She laughed and stepped away. "I'm going to need it."

She started down the gallery. "You're going for Carstairs?"

"Recon first, then decisions."

"I've got your back," she said.

"Much obliged."

I turned to walk back up the ramp only to find Al standing in the lock with a goofy grin pasted on her face.

"What?" I asked.

"Flirting with the head of station security?" she asked.

"Me? Hardly." I looked down the gallery where Oscella had Riordan and Marshall trotting along at a goodly pace.

Al snorted. "Well, she was thinking real hard about flirting with you."

I laughed and pushed into the ship. "Ship and station don't mix. I tried that once. Once was enough. Where's the chief?"

"Gone to her stateroom to draft some messages. What are we going to do about Pip?"

"I think we're going to go back to the abandoned cargo warehouse and look for lost cargo."

I stuck my head into the galley on my way up to the cabin. "Thank you, Ms. Sharps. Sorry for the inconvenience."

"Have we heard from Mr. Carstairs, sar?"

"Not yet."

"I'd hoped station security might have had some answers."

"We've filed the necessary reports, Ms. Sharps. I believe he'll turn up sooner rather than later and we'll be able to sail with a full complement."

"Good," she said. "I'll have Ms. Adams clear up the wardroom in a few."

"Thank you, Ms. Sharps, and my compliments on the cookies."

She beamed and I beat feet. I wanted to grab a couple of those cookies before they went back to the galley. I took enough to share with Al and the chief. It didn't really surprise me that they'd both grabbed a few for themselves.

"Where are we?" I asked, plopping into my chair and wishing I'd brought some coffee with me.

"We still haven't gotten the can tied on," Al said.

"I've sent a few messages." The chief shrugged. "I need at least a couple of days in system for confirmations to get back."

"What are we going into?" I asked.

She looked at me and tilted her head to the side for a moment. "I know people who can deal with the mega's infestation. Unless we can get Pip back—and we're still operating on an assumption that hasn't been confirmed—we need to come back with the can from Telluride."

"We still don't know that there isn't a bomb, either," I said. "Only that it hasn't been used to extort Kondur."

She nodded. "Agreed, which raises another point. Even if we get in, find Pip, get him out, we don't know who else might be involved or where they are. We're going to have to try to find a bomb that we're not sure exists."

Al let her head fall against the chair back. "Unless we find one, we won't know if there is one."

"That's the problem," the chief said.

"How do we logic ourselves out of this?" I asked.

The chief shook her head. "We can cut it off at the root but we don't know where the branches are."

"We need to find the bomb and hope there's only one," Al said.

The chief's tablet bipped. She frowned and pulled it out. The frown deepened as she read the message. "Kondur's conscious and wants to talk to us right now."

"I guess we'll find out what the message was," I said. "In his office?"

"Still in the aid station auto-doc." She held up her tablet. "I have the location."

My tablet bipped and I wasn't sure I'd like what I was about to see. I flipped open the interface. "Oscella," I said. "Wants to know if we can help find a bomb."

Al sighed. "I guess that answers one question."

"Which one? Why Kondur wants to meet or whether or not there's a bomb?" I asked.

"Both, actually," she said and pushed up from her chair. "Shall we go?"

We got to the aid station and found a cordon of station security personnel around the outside perimeter. Inside we found a battered-looking Hervé Villarosa standing beside an auto-doc with an even worse-looking Verkol Kondur propped up in it. Oscella joined us a few moments later.

"Thank you," Kondur said. "The captain here tells me you knew where to find me."

The chief stepped up beside the auto-doc. She reached toward him but rested her hand on the side of the pod. "You really need to fix your security." She glanced at Villarosa. "No offense."

Villarosa shrugged. "None taken. We were sloppy."

"Maggie, listen. They're going to knock me out again in a few ticks. I still need a few more repairs. You were right, this was a warning and they told me there's a bomb. Here. That they'll blow the station if you don't do exactly what they say."

"We figured that much," the chief said.

"But you have to do what you need to do. Do what you can. We need to stop them." His eyes rolled back in his head and he relaxed back into the pod. "I was a fool."

I thought he was out but he opened his eyes and looked at me. "They sent a message for you, Captain. They have a pip. I don't know what that means but they said you will."

"Message received," I said. "Rest. Heal."

He went under in a heartbeat. The med-tech came in and began shooing us out. "That's it. No more. I wouldn't have gone along this far for anybody other than the station owner and I shouldn't have done it for him." He pressed a few keys and the auto-doc closed around Kondur. "Out. Nothing to see here." He glanced at Villarosa, who still leaned against the bulkhead, his massive forearms crossed over his chest. The bandages on his face and scalp, the dark bruising on his face and arms did nothing to make him look any less menacing. "I'll get you a chair. It's going to be a while."

Villarosa nodded.

The tech turned to us. "You're still here. Do I need to call security to throw you all out?"

Oscella raised her hand. "I'll handle it."

He swallowed once and nodded.

Oscella made shooing motions with her outstretched arms. "Move along, citizens. Nothing to see here. Move along."

I thought the grin she wore might split her face but we all shuffled out of the aid station and back into the passageway.

Oscella moved us down the block, away from the security perimeter, and into a huddle. "I could really use your advice."

"There's probably a bomb. It's probably a nuke. It's probably somewhere safe for now, but undoubtedly uses a remote trigger," the chief said. "I think there are three things that need to happen and I'm not sure we can do them all."

"I'm listening," Oscella said.

"If we can find the bomb, we can neutralize that threat. That assumes only one bomb on a remote trigger," the chief said.

"How do we find it?"

"Radioactive leakage. We should be able to detect it unless they've done a professional job of shielding. I have reason to believe they have not."

"I won't ask," Oscella said. "What do we need to do?"

"We believe the bomb is probably hidden in the abandoned cargo warehouse, along with Pip."

"Why there?" Oscella asked. "Couldn't it just be stashed someplace in a grav trunk? In somebody's room?"

"It could be," the chief said. "It would leave a trail back to whoever paid the storage fee. Even if faked, it's going to be there. Shipping a crate to the station with a hold for pickup instruction means the station stores it, the only back trace is on the bill of lading. Those aren't worth much out here if you want to fake it."

"Can't argue that," Oscella said with a rueful grimace.

The chief started to say something but stopped. "You have patrols?"

Oscella shrugged. "Of course."

"You have radiation detectors?"

"Sure."

"Can you issue one to each of your patrols?" the chief asked.

Oscella pondered that for a few heartbeats. "I think we have enough, but this is a big station."

"Your patrols cover a lot of it, though, right?"

"Yeah, but it's not like we cover the whole thing every day. We don't go into a lot of spaces at all. Shops, hotels, private facilities. Not everything here belongs to Kondur."

"I'm just trying to rule out places. Every place your people can cover is one less place for us to worry about."

"We need to keep this quiet," Oscella said.

"Panic?" the chief asked.

"That's my concern."

The chief nodded. "I understand."

An idea kept trying to bubble up in my brain. I kept trying to focus on the conversation but that tickle kept coming back. "Smoke alarms?" I asked.

The chief's eyes widened. "You have a network of alarm sensors?"

"Sure. Smoke, fire, heat, carbon monoxide, oxygen, carbon dioxide, the usual stuff. It's spelled out in the building codes."

"Do you specify a model in your codes?"

She shrugged. "Not really, but the chandlery only stocks one model."

The chief frowned. "Can you show me the relevant code requirement?"

Oscella laughed. "If I can't, there's a big problem." She pulled out her tablet and started flipping through the screens. It took almost a whole tick but she finally held her tablet out to the chief. "There it is."

I glanced over but only saw a wall of text filling the screen.

The chief paged down and down and down. "There," she said, stabbing the screen with a forefinger. "Perfect." She held the device so Oscella could see it. "Shipboard, all the usual stuff includes radiation levels—particles and wave forms. This looks like somebody copied the code from a ship-standard environmental sensor."

"So the station is already wired for it?" Oscella asked.

"Well, probably wireless but yeah. Same idea. Who monitors that network?"

"Every zone has an environmental monitoring station. Twelve zones. Twelve stations," Oscella said.

"Where's the nearest?" the chief asked.

"Near the docks."

"Let's go."

Oscella led the way with the chief striding along beside her.

Al caught my arm. "Skipper, I'm going back to the ship to ride herd. Fortuner's got the watch but with everything in the air ..." She shrugged.

"You know how to reach me if you need me," I said.

Al peeled off and legged it for the dock, and I fell in step behind the chief.

Oscella led us down a few blocks and turned at a cross passage. She stopped at a nondescript door that looked like every other airtight door on the station. She pressed a button beside the handle and stepped back. After a few moments the door handle moved and the door swung open.

"Yes?"

Oscella flipped her badge wallet open, holding it so the woman behind the door could see it. "We need to use your network."

The door swung all the way open, revealing a closet-sized room with a chair, a console, and not much else. "I'm not sure how many of you can fit but ..." She waved a hand. "Help yourself, Captain."

The chief stepped forward. "Actually it would probably be best if you ran the equipment. You know it better than any of us do."

The young woman flipped a stray lock of hair out of her face and grinned. "Inside and out," she said.

"Good," the chief said. "Correct me if I'm wrong but the environmental network here monitors a wide range of factors?"

"Yes'm. Air quality, particulates, gas mixtures—"

"Radiation?" the chief asked.

"Yeah, that, too, but that doesn't change much." She paused. "Well, really, none of them vary much from baseline."

The chief grinned. "I know what you meant. Do you have a map overlay?"

"That shows the various levels at points around the station?" the woman asked.

"Exactly."

"Of course, it's our best tool."

"Could we see it?" the chief asked.

The woman hesitated and looked at Oscella. "Am I allowed to show people?"

"My authority," Oscella said. "It's important."

"All right, then." She dropped into her chair and flipped through a few screens. "Here we go. You want the whole section?"

"Yes, please. Can you isolate radiation?"

"Of course."

The screen changed to show a schematic of the station.

"What are we looking at?" the chief asked.

"We're here." The woman pointed to a spot in the middle of the screen. "This is the area I cover. We're looking at the differential levels of radiation accumulated over the last three stans."

"I'm not seeing anything," the chief said.

"It's because it hasn't changed in—I don't know how long." She pressed a few keys. "Here. This is the carbon dioxide layer."

A layer of pale yellow overlaid the screen, more opaque over the passageways, making the passages all glow a faint yellow.

"Yellow is moderate change. Ten percent per stan upward. Green, if there was any, would be a ten percent per stan change downward." She pointed to the places where there was no color. "These are the passageways and it's still relatively early in the day. They're moving from their overnight levels to the daytime levels. The carbon dioxide gathers in the passageways. You can tell how many people are breathing by the density of the color. This passageway here?" She pointed to a corridor that showed only the faintest tinge of yellow. "There are only a few people using that, but it's a throughway for the cargo carts. The carts put out a lot of carbon dioxide but there aren't many of them. So the levels are rising at the moderate level, but the overall levels are still low. These blocks here? Those are almost all rooftops. There's nobody there. So no change."

"So when we looked at the radiation overlay, there was no change and a negligible level?" the chief asked, leaning forward over the woman's shoulder.

"Yeah. Exactly."

"Do you have any control over the overlay data?"

The woman shook her head. "It's what comes in. I just record it. Watch for hotspots. Once in a while somebody will overheat a cargo hauler. That's always exciting. Fires are the worst but the suppression systems take care of them real quick."

"Can you display an overlay that shows the raw level, not the change?"

"Well that's shown in the density of the color, the transparency of the color."

The chief nodded. "On the standard overlay, but say I'm looking for very low levels of radiation that aren't changing at all. Say, a box of radioactive chemicals that fell off a hauler two months ago? It's not going to be a very high level and it's not going to have changed for, like, two months."

"Is that what I'm looking for?" she asked.

"No, but it'll help me calibrate what we're seeing here."

She gave the chief an odd look but started fiddling. After a moment she sat back. "There's nothing to see because the levels are so low and they're not changing."

"Can you boost the sensitivity? I want to find a few alpha particles."

"I don't know about that, but ..." She tapped some keys and a faint purple haze began covering the screen. "That's as high as it goes. I have no idea what it's reading but the actual levels are really, really small."

The chief nodded and smiled at her. "That, I believe, is the background radiation from the system primary."

"How can that be? We can barely see it from way out here."

"Nothing to stop it from here to there," the chief said. "Even far away that star is cranking out a hell of a lot of radiation. Only a small portion of it is in forms we can see."

"You a physicist or something?"

"Chief engineering officer on a solar clipper," the chief said. "That would classify as 'or something,' I guess." She straightened up and looked around. "The station has the capability. Can we get this display from every sector?"

"Oh, sure," the woman said. "We port all the raw data to environmental main in real time. They're going to be the ones who can use it by adjusting conditions in various places around the station."

"I thought your environmental system was distributed," I said.

"Oh, it is. The things that suck crap in and blow air out? They're all over the place. The control for all of them is environmental main."

"Our next stop is environmental main, I guess," the chief said. She held out a hand to the young woman. "Thank you so much for your time. It's really helped a lot."

The woman beamed. "Glad to help. Not much goes on here. It was a nice change of pace." She cast a considering glance at her console. "I never thought of doing stuff like that before. I may need to play with this." She grinned at the chief and turned to her console.

I took a step back from the door and made room for the chief and Oscella to come out. Oscella swung the door closed and set the dogging handle.

"Airtight doors?" I asked.

"If we lose pressure, we want to make sure these stations are safe and can continue to collect, screen, and collate the data."

"That seems like a really boring job. Staring at screens that only update once a stan?"

Oscella nodded. "It's not a job everybody can do, but it's a foot in the door of the environmental section. Most of the people who start here move on to improve their skills, get new technical ratings, and—sometimes—leave the station to work for other environmental operations around the Western Annex." She beckoned us along. "Let's get some transport and go visit environmental."

CHAPTER TWENTY-EIGHT
DARK KNIGHT STATION: 2376, MARCH 12

Oscella got a wheeled vehicle with station logos on it to pick us up and take us to environmental main. It had to have been a couple of kilometers from the docks, and I was glad I didn't have to try to walk it.

Her badge got us through the door and into a circular control room that had to be ten meters in diameter. Huge screens around the perimeter flashed through various colors and patterns every few seconds. A slender man met us just inside the door.

"Not prone to epilepsy, I hope." He grinned at us. "Captain? How can I assist station security today?"

"Maurice, this is Captain Wang from the *Chernyakova* and his chief engineering officer, Chief Stevens. Captain, Chief, this is the head of environmental main, Maurice Dumaurier."

"We don't get many spacers in here, Skipper. How can I help?"

I nodded at the chief. "She's the one who knows. I'm just the comic relief."

"We have reason to believe that there's at least one, possibly two, radioactive devices on the station. We need you to run a radiation level scan stationwide to see if we can spot at least one of them that way."

His eyeballs practically bugged out of his head as he looked at Oscella. "Captain?"

"You heard her. It's legit. She's trying to help us," Oscella said.

"You've got the raw data, I believe," the chief said.

He nodded. "Sure. Of course. It's fed to us in real time."

"If you can, run a radiation level filter and crank the sensitivity up to where it begins to show the background radiation."

He blinked at her. "I can try. I didn't know it went up that high." He looked at Oscella.

"It does," Oscella said. "We checked."

He shrugged. "All right, then. Let's give it a go." He turned and led the way into the control room, barking orders to the duty staff.

It took a few ticks for all the screens around the room to shift to that same purplish haze we'd seen at the local station. Dumaurier strolled around the perimeter, staring at each screen in turn. "Do I want to know what you're looking for exactly, Chief?"

"If I say yes, I'd be lying," the chief said, following Dumaurier and staring at the screens herself. "If I say no, you'll know what we're looking for."

Dumaurier stopped in his tracks, turning to stare at her. "I want to say 'you're kidding,' but you're not, are you."

"No, Dr. Dumaurier, I'm not."

He nodded and turned back to the screens, walking a little faster. "How did you know I was Dr. Dumaurier?" he asked, an aside to the chief as they continued the circumnavigation of the room.

"Dr. Maurice C. Dumaurier. PhD, Closed-Ecology Engineering with specializations in Water Recovery Technology and Atmospheric Quality Metrics from University of Ciroda in 2362. Your dissertation was a brilliant examination of water fingerprinting entitled *Factors Differentiating Water Source Processing: Suspensions and Solutions*."

Dumaurier stopped again and stared at her, slack-jawed.

"Nice pun, by the way. Your undergrad was—not coincidentally—from the CPJCT Merchant Officers Academy at Port Newmar. Class of '59. Captain Wang was a year ahead of you in the deck officer's program."

"Pay her no mind," I said. "She's just showing off. She doesn't know everybody."

The chief laughed and continued on her way around the room.

"She didn't answer the question," Dumaurier said, as if to himself.

"She doesn't as a rule." I shrugged. "Well, no. Sometimes she does and I've learned not to ask too many questions for fear she'll actually answer them."

"What's this?" the chief said, pointing at a screen.

"Power plant. Primary water treatment facility," Dumaurier said, his attention refocused.

"That fusactor needs tuning. It shouldn't be spilling like that. Put some dosimeters on your people in there to make sure they're safe until you can get the fusactor serviced."

"Oh, holy crap. You're Margaret Stevens," Dumaurier said. "I thought you looked familiar."

She chuckled and nodded. "Busted." She moved on to the next screen.

We made the full circuit without spotting anything else untoward.

"What are we missing?" the chief asked, worrying her bottom lip between her teeth and staring around the room at the screens that steadfastly refused to show anything out of line.

Dumaurier's stance mimicked hers as he stared around the room. "Well, we don't have the whole station covered," he said. "Only about ninety percent of it."

Oscella perked up at that bit of news. "I thought we had the whole place wired. Where are the open areas?"

Dumaurier walked to a terminal and typed a few commands. "Here's the map."

Oscella and the chief crowded around while I tried to make sense of what the big ring of screens told me. "Why aren't the other power plants showing up?" I asked. "Why just that one?"

The chief straightened up and looked at me. "Yes."

"Well they're pretty well shielded," Dumaurier said.

"But we have the sensitivity cranked up so high you're showing levels of radiation that wouldn't trigger a dosimeter. Even the best shielding bleeds a particle or five above background levels. They're not completely covered. How many different fusactors do you have on station? Five? Ten?"

He shook his head. "I really don't know. Environmental has three. The station grid uses seven. I don't know how many backups and other systems might have their own power supplies."

"Are those all represented on these screens?" the chief asked.

Dumaurier nodded. "The main power grid is over there." He pointed at one of the first screens on the tour. "The atmospheric plant is here." He leaned in to one of the screens nearby. "The fusactor is in that building." He tapped the screen.

"Why is it not showing?" the chief asked, more to herself than Dumaurier.

"We have two problems," I said. "Chief, correct me if I've missed something. Part of the station isn't even shown here. Right?"

Dumaurier nodded.

The chief said, "Yes."

"We need to do a closer search on those parts," Oscella said. She pointed to the map. "I can have teams covering those areas with radiation detectors by morning."

"The other problem centers on this display," I said.

"Obviously, it's flawed," Dumaurier said.

I shook my head. "No, it's not flawed."

The chief's eyes brightened. "Of course. It's showing us what we asked for. The problem is that it's not showing us what we think it should."

Dumaurier frowned. "We think it's showing us all the sources of radiation but it's only showing one."

"Yes," I said. "We can prove that the display is not showing us everything we think it should with a simple test."

"Put a Geiger counter beside a fusactor that's not showing on this map?" the chief asked.

"Yeah. If there's enough radiation for a Geiger counter to pick up, it should be on the screen," I said. "If there's that much radiation and it's not showing, there's a problem in the way we asked for the display to render."

"Where's the nearest fusactor?" the chief asked.

"The Main Street power station," Oscella said.

Dumaurier looked at her. "That's halfway across the station from here."

Oscella pulled out her tablet. "It's across the street from the security barracks. I can have somebody there with a sensor in two ticks."

She was as good as her word. "Reading shows traces. Needle flicking but just barely registering."

"Have the deputy take it out in the street," the chief said. "It's not much distance but the extra shielding from the building should amplify the fall-off."

Oscella typed a few lines and waited. "Yeah. It's fallen off."

The chief looked at the screens around her again and then at Dumaurier. "What are we missing?"

I crossed to Oscella. "Can you send a deputy to that fusactor in the water treatment plant?"

"You want to know the levels there?"

I nodded. "If there's a radically higher level there, it would be what we'd expect based on what we think we're looking at here."

Oscella nodded. "If it's not, then that's another indication that we're not seeing what we think."

"Yeah. There's something about this that isn't adding up," I said.

Oscella started tapping on her tablet. "I'll send the same deputy and meter over there. It'll take a few ticks."

I walked over to Dumaurier and the chief where they huddled over a console.

"You're sure it's showing you the current radiation level," the chief said.

He nodded. "I've taken off the filters that measure change over time. It should be just the level. We've got the sensitivity maxed."

I left them to walk through the forest of options and started walking around the screens again. I was halfway around when Captain Oscella spoke up. "My deputy says that fusactor at the water treatment plant isn't very much different from the one on Main Street."

The chief straightened up and frowned at the offending screen. "How is that possible?"

"Why did you think it was leaking?" I asked.

"Look at those levels. There's nothing else like it on the board."

"That's the problem. There should be." I looked at Dumaurier. "What's different about that particular fusactor?"

He shrugged. "Nothing that I know of. If the deputy is right, it's not emitting any more radiation. I can't tell you anything that's different."

"It's newer," Oscella said. "It went in over there, when? A couple of stanyers ago?"

"Yes, but the only thing that changed is the location." He looked at the chief. "We rebuilt that treatment plant a few stanyers ago. It's in almost the same spot but we expanded a couple of the sedimentation pools and made some plant changes to bring up the efficiency. We moved the fusactor across the campus."

I walked over to the screen and started going over the area again. A shadow caught my eye when I looked away but I didn't see it when I looked straight at it. I stepped to the side and looked at an angle. It didn't look any different but when I got straight in front of it I found the shadow again. "Was it right here before?" I asked.

Dumaurier came over and looked at where my finger rested on the screen. "Yeah. How'd you know?"

"There's a shadow there. Just a tiny bit but it's enough to fade out the overlay by just the tiniest amount." I stepped aside. "Look at it. See if you spot it."

He moved into my place and moved his head around a little. "I see it. What the devil ...?"

"Check your filters," the chief suggested. "Radiation isn't like oxygen or smoke. It may have a set that blocks out constant sources. If that fusactor had been there for a while, the system may have learned that filter but hasn't had time to unlearn it and learn the new location."

He frowned. "I thought I'd cleared those."

"That's the first symptom," I said.

"What?"

"When a system doesn't do what you want, the first symptom that you've got excess user head space is the notion of 'huh. I thought I cleared those,'" I said. "Trust me, this is the bitter voice of experience talking."

Dumaurier pulled up a chair and sat at the console. "All right. I'm checking the aspect filter. Radiation is on. Everything else is off. The display is raw level. The sensitivity is max. Filters are off." He shrugged and looked up.

I walked up behind his chair and looked over his shoulder to see a full screen of options. "These are all the filters?" I asked.

He nodded. "You can see, they're all off."

"Scroll down?"

"What?"

"There are more on the next page," I said.

He leaned into the screen as if it would look clearer if his nose was five centimeters closer and scrolled the screen down. Three new filters appeared, one of which was checked. He unchecked it and new radiation sources appeared on screens all around the room. He shook his head. "I'm flabbergasted."

"Doctor, if I had a credit for every time I've been bitten by something like that, I'd have paid off my ship by now." I looked around the room. "So what are all these?"

We started around again. Either Dumaurier or Oscella identified a fusactor or some other fixed device for every source. One was actually a research reactor. We got all the way around the room but didn't find anything that one or the other of them couldn't identify.

"Damn," the chief said. "What else are we missing?"

"Other than it might be in the areas that aren't covered?" I asked.

"Besides that," she said.

"Dead sensor head?" I asked.

Dumaurier shook his head. "They fail once in a while. We get a maintenance alert from the network that it's missing a node and we fix it."

"Look at something else," the chief said.

"What?"

"Bring up a display of something else. Something common. Nitrogen levels. That should be about the same everywhere."

He frowned but clicked keys. In a few moments every screen in the room turned cyan. He clicked a few more keys and pulled the sensitivity down so the solid colors became more like smoke than solid colors. He stood and spun in place to look at the screens. "I don't see what—" His voice chopped off as he looked at a screen that showed a fuzzy oval hole in the cyan.

"That's not right," he said. He crossed to the screen and peered into it. "That's not right at all."

He strode back to the console and clicked a few keys to bring the flawed display onto his local system. A few more clicks and the screen became dotted with four-digit numbers. "These are node IDs," he said. "That node is not detecting any nitrogen." He ran through some keystrokes, making the color change but not the hole. "It's not detecting anything that I've tried."

He opened a command window and ticked off some options. A dialog opened and scrolled a series of what looked like gibberish to me, but the familiar VSI codes would probably appear that way to him. The dialog stopped scrolling. The last message appeared. "Test Complete."

"That node just responded to a full diagnostic reset and query. It claims it's fully functional," he said.

He popped up another screen and columns of numbers started filling it up. All the numbers in every column were zero.

He took a deep breath and sat back in his chair. After a moment he looked up at Oscella. "Captain, this should not happen. That node is not broken. It is not off the network. It appears to be functioning perfectly. Every sensor detects a level of zero for every characteristic it's supposed to measure."

"Why is that not a malfunction?" she asked.

"Because the diagnostic routine checks to see if the sensor is working. It's detecting what it's supposed to, but sending a value of zero for that reading."

"So what? Somebody sabotaged the detector head?" she asked.

"That's what it looks like from here."

"Somebody has something to hide? From a smoke alarm?" she asked. "Who would ever think like that?"

"Somebody who knew it could detect radiation," the chief said. "But didn't know enough about it to only poke out that one eye."

"So they poked out all of them?" Oscella asked.

"Brute strength," I said. "Sometimes it's the best choice."

"Wouldn't somebody have noticed that?" the chief asked. "The nice young woman we met earlier seemed to have a good sense of what she was looking at."

Dumaurier clicked a few keys, erasing the overlay and magnifying the location. "Maybe not," he said. "It's located above a building near the docks. Normal gases like oxygen and carbon dioxide wouldn't show much variation from hour to hour and day to day."

"How long has that sensor been sending zeros?" the chief asked.

He pursed his lips, pulled up a screen of numbers, and started working backward. "A while," he said, still scrolling back. "It's zeros all the way down. I'm into last stanyer." The scrolling stopped. "That's the end of this file. It's all zeros on this head. At least eighteen months."

"You said it was above a building. What building?" I asked.

He brought the magnified image up again and traced an oblong shape off to the side. "That's the chandlery. This building must be one of their warehouses. You have a better read on it, Captain?" He looked at Oscella.

She stepped a little closer and leaned over his shoulder. She frowned and then scowled.

"What is it?" Dumaurier asked.

"Yeah, that's the chandlery," she said. "But unless I miss my guess and Riordan was off on his assessment this morning, that building is the long-term storage warehouse."

"The one they put abandoned cargo in?" I asked.

She nodded, her lips pushed into a grim line.

"Maurice?" the chief said. "What's the process for getting a head replaced?"

"I send a work order to station maintenance with the head ID number and a locator number. They send somebody out to pull the old one and plug in a new one."

"That's it?" she asked.

"That's it. When the new head connects it looks for the nearest mesh node, assigns itself the right number, and starts collecting data."

"How long does that process take?" she asked.

"A stan or two. Depends on the availability of a maintenance worker."

"Where's the local sector operator for that sector?" I asked.

He pulled a new overlay onto his console. "There," he said, pointing to a spot just off the thoroughfare that led to the chandlery.

"Will that operator see the node getting replaced?" the chief asked.

"Not inside the station, no. They don't have any kind of windows."

"How about when the node goes off-line and then comes back up?" she asked.

"Oh, certainly. When this node comes down, the system will flag a disabled node until the new node goes up. If they're looking they'll see the new one go up when it establishes contact with the net." He paused and looked back and forth between the chief and me. "Why?"

"Whoever hacked that node didn't do it by climbing up to it," I said.

"You think they'll just compromise the replacement?" Dumaurier asked.

"Maybe not immediately but eventually, yes," I said. "Who has network access to those nodes?"

He shrugged. "Every operator, including the ones here."

The chief blinked. "All the operators can access any node?"

"Yes. We designed it to provide a redundancy in the event of a catastrophe."

I felt like we took two steps back for every step forward.

"Chief?" Oscella asked. "If this were your operation, what would you do? Forget what we think we know."

The chief shrugged. "It's going to depend on the goal."

"If the goal is to safeguard your logistics supply line? What then?"

The chief shook her head. "First, I'd never rely on only one source."

"How many?" Oscella asked.

"At least two, possibly three. I'd do what I could to control as much of it as I could with my own resources."

"So, right there, we've an anomalous data point," Oscella said.

"Maybe," the chief said. "Barbells aren't cheap. If I had only one and I lost it, I'd have to use less-reliable sources."

"Follow that line," I said.

"First I'd try to mask my actions as much as possible. Operate through ports large enough to blend in," she said. "I don't know that I'd resort to any kind of extortion."

"Even as insurance?" Oscella asked.

The chief shook her head. "I wouldn't but I'm a special case."

"I can't argue that," Dumaurier said, almost under his breath. Oscella grinned at him.

"From the wide-angle view, this is an impossible task," the chief said.

"Break it down," I said. "Captain Oscella, can you get your people out into the areas not covered by the network?" I asked. "That's going to take time."

"They're already out," she said with a grin.

"Thanks," I said. "Dr. Dumaurier, can we look at the display that showed us this node again?"

"Sure, but why?" he asked.

"We focused on this one so quickly, I didn't notice if there were others."

He nodded and pulled up the cyan overlay.

I started with the screen nearest me and gave each one a solid perusal as I walked around the room.

"Here's one," the chief said, standing in front of a screen across the room from me. From that distance I didn't see what she was looking at. "It's a tiny hole."

"Nodes overlap," Dumaurier said. "The most populated sectors have more nodes per square meter so they overlap their fields."

The idea that had been bumping against my brain surfaced. "Zeros. Dr. Dumaurier, can you query that database for nodes sending all zeros?"

"You're thinking there may be more compromised nodes?" he asked, sitting down at his console again.

"Yes, I'm not sure how that helps us, but if there are other nodes out there, they're going to point to places we might want to look at more closely."

The chief's brows furrowed as she frowned at her boots. "Camouflage."

"Chief?" I asked.

She shook her head. "If I were doing this, I wouldn't compromise just one. It would be a big flashing red arrow if discovered."

"You couldn't do many or the probability of detection goes up," I said. "They're easy to spot."

She shook her head again. "Only if you know to look for them. How long did we mess around before we found one? And we weren't operating in the standard mode." She looked to Dumaurier. "How hard would those be to spot using the standard time-weighted filtering?"

He shook his head. "I'd have said 'not hard at all' except for one thing." He pointed to the screen we'd first discovered. "That one has been returning false data for over a stanyer and we didn't notice. It wasn't masked by node overlap. It wasn't particularly hard to find once we stopped using the standard protocols."

"Doctor, would you do the query looking for zeros? Let's see how many there are," I said.

"Yes, of course." He addressed his console.

I leaned over to the chief. "What are we missing?"

"Pip," she said. "We're operating on too many assumptions. I think we need to start testing our hypothesis in a more concrete manner."

"You still like the abandoned freight barn as a hiding place?"

"I do," she said. "We need to find out a couple of things. One, how many people work that overseer job. Two, how often the guard changes."

"What if it's only one?" I asked.

She grinned. "We have an opportunity to do some recon and the local constabulary to give us cover." She nodded toward Oscella. "I don't know how much probable cause she needs to act, but it's likely to be far less than TIC would require."

"Particularly since her boss got rolled?" I asked

The chief grinned and nodded.

Dumaurier waved a hand at me. "I put a priority on the maintenance order. It should be up within a stan."

"Thanks," I said and crossed to Oscella with the chief trailing behind. "Where are we?"

Oscella shrugged. "I've got people out combing the areas not covered by the network. I've also filed an inquiry to the station management board about why there are parts of the station not being covered."

"I wondered about that myself," the chief said. "If you're going to do a firewatch in a closed ecology, leaving spaces uncovered only guarantees that's where the emergency will start."

Dumaurier joined our little scrum. "I've submitted it on the budget every stanyer. It's always denied."

"Any rationale?" the chief asked.

"Not enough money in the budget." He made a sour face.

The chief frowned. "Does Kondur know this?"

He shrugged. "Mr. Kondur and I don't exactly run in the same circles. He appoints the SMB to run the operation but doesn't sit on it."

"How does somebody get on that board?" I asked.

"Kondur appoints them. I just said that," Dumaurier said.

"Yeah, but how does he find candidates? How long do they serve? How many people are on the board?" I asked.

Dumaurier looked at Oscella. "I know there are nine on the facilities planning committee. You know the total?"

"Thirteen on internal security. Nine on space threat analysis and planning."

"How many of these committees are there?" the chief asked.

"One for every specialization area," Oscella said. "There's one for freight management, an operations management committee that governs business regulation and building codes." She shrugged. "I know there are others that I can't think of right now."

"Medical," Dumaurier said. "I think there are five on that one."

"That's quite an infrastructure," I said.

Oscella shrugged. "It's a big station. Verkol Kondur is many things, but even a superman couldn't manage a station this size without delegating most of the management to others."

The chief and I shared a glance.

"Do we wait for the new node to sync up or head back to the ship?" I asked.

The chief looked at the console and around the room before answering. "Let's wait. It shouldn't be long. A few ticks won't matter getting back to the ship, if it shows up nothing."

"You think that's what it's going to be? Nothing?" Dumaurier asked.

She nodded. "I think it's sleight-of-hand. They—the nebulous they—want us looking at these nodes. Why even block out the nodes that leave signposts pointing to your operation when you can use places that have no coverage at all?"

"Misdirection," Oscella said.

"Yeah. That's what I'm thinking." The chief looked at the console again. "I hope I'm wrong but I'm afraid we just tipped our hand to anybody watching that node."

"They know we've tumbled to them?" Dumaurier asked.

"Well, that we've tumbled to one of them. Perhaps ignoring the others with readings all zero will be enough."

"You think there are more?" Dumaurier asked.

"We already found another one. Your query should discover how many more there are," the chief said. "If the replaced node reveals something, then we'll see."

He sat down at the console again and started shuffling data.

"Where is Pip?" I asked, more to myself than to the chief.

She shook her head. "Kondur's message said they had him. We're assuming it's the pirates out on the mega."

"You think we have two groups after us?" I asked.

"Not us, necessarily, but Pip? Wouldn't surprise me to learn there are people looking for him all across the Western Annex." She shot me a look and a shrug. "But it's probably a long shot. They wouldn't have told Kondur if it wasn't related to this shipment."

"We still don't have the can," I said. "Unless they snuck up on the ship and tied it on while we've been here." My brain felt like a rat on a wheel, running and running but getting nowhere.

CHAPTER TWENTY-NINE
DARK KNIGHT STATION: 2376, MARCH 12

The new node came on line, closing the gap on the cyan filter but offering no other information.

"What if there's no bomb?" I asked, leaning close to the chief and keeping my voice down. "What if this is nothing more than a simple assault and warning?"

The chief nodded. "I've thought that from the beginning, but it's a threat we have to take seriously. They have a long history of using explosive arguments."

"Where else could they have stashed Pip?"

"There's always the possibility that we're overthinking it. That they have him out there in a ship tucked behind a rock," she said.

"If we find him, will it change anything?" I asked.

She looked at me. "What do you mean?"

"I mean, they're holding him to make sure we deliver. So? Will whatever you've got behind the curtain make any difference to that process of going out, swapping cans, and coming back?"

"You're willing to leave him here that long?"

"Not my first, or even second, choice. If we get that can on today, we can be underway tomorrow. We'll be back in—what? A week?"

The chief nodded. "Something like that."

Oscella crossed the room to stand by us. "Ideas? I see you two over here plotting."

The chief laughed. "We're both about tapped out. We don't know there's a bomb. That's the problem. We can't prove there isn't one. All we know is that there's a team of at least two people who wanted to send a message to Kondur that they're watching him. We're assuming they tagged Pip to have leverage over us."

"So, we're back to square one?" Oscella asked.

"We need the can before we can get underway," I said. "I thought it was on its way yesterday."

Oscella shook her head. "No idea. I think we've done all we can do here. Is there anything else you can think of?"

The chief glanced at me before shaking her head. "Unless we're overlooking something, there's no unaccounted-for radioactive device here. Your crew may find something."

"That's funny." Dumaurier had a finger running down the strings of data.

"A good funny or an uh-oh funny?" Oscella asked.

"I'm not sure." He stood and crossed to one of the glowing fusactor icons on a nearby screen. He peered at it, then moved to the next one. "The display isn't showing the difference. It's too small to register."

"Difference?" the chief asked, crossing to look over his shoulder.

"This one, it's got the levels I'd expect from a standard fusactor running under an average load. The numbers confirm it." He nodded at the list of numbers on his console and went back to the first one he'd examined. "This one's detecting about ten to fifteen percent more radiation. It doesn't show on the screen because it's too small a raw number. Our eyes can't pick up the difference between this one and that one."

"Is it generating more power?" Oscella asked. "And would that make a difference?" She looked at the chief.

The chief's head already swung back and forth. "No," she said, drawing the syllable out. "Unless the fusactor's case is damaged. The power draw might make the generator portion run a little hotter, but radiation? That's not how they work."

"Where is that fusactor, Maurice?" Oscella asked.

"That's the one we checked manually. It's across the street from the security barracks just off Main Street."

"That's going to be a problem," the chief said.

Oscella paled. "What do we do about it?"

"First, we take a deep breath," I said. "Dr. Dumaurier, can you tell when that sensor started registering the higher value?"

He shook his head. "More than eighteen months ago. It's probably in the last backup, but my window into the past cuts off at around eighteen months."

"Is that significant?" Oscella asked.

I shrugged. "Might be if you have surveillance video of that building during the period when the value changed, but at the moment, we don't know if the change is significant."

The chief nodded. "It's a relatively small change and it's been constant. A different manufacturer, a different production run, or even the age of the unit could account for a change like that." She looked to Dumaurier. "It's still below health and safety levels, right?"

"Oh, certainly."

"So, there's no immediate threat," I said. "If it's been there that long, I don't know what might change the status quo. Especially since we need to go out, leave this can, get the other can, and bring it back."

I spotted the flaw in that ointment as soon as I said it. The look on the chief's face told me she'd spotted it, too.

"What?" Oscella said. "Something happened. Both of you know something."

"We only have to deliver the can," the chief said. "We don't need to bring one back."

Oscella's mouth made a silent "Oh."

"It would probably work in their favor if we just disappeared out there," I said.

"It would be easy to do," the chief said. "Might set them back a few months without the income but an easy solution to implement."

Oscella's expression went from shocked to incredulous. "You're talking about getting killed and how much that would set back your killers?"

"Sure," I said. "We're getting to the stage that our risk analysis needs to step up."

"All right," the chief said. "Priorities. We need to get a look at that fusactor without anybody looking sideways at us. Got some maintenance jumpsuits?"

Oscella dropped us at the dock. "I'll get the coveralls couriered over. It may take a bit."

"Hurrying isn't something we need to be doing right now," the chief said.

Oscella nodded and wheeled her cart around, zooming back up the docking gallery.

"She seems like a nice girl," the chief said with a sly smile in my direction.

I chuckled and keyed the lock open. Al waited at the brow with Torkelson. "You could have, you know, let us know what's going on once in a while."

"Log us in, if you would, Ms. Torkelson," I said and beckoned Al to follow us up to the cabin, stopping at the galley for mugs of coffee on the way.

"Here's what we found," I said, settling into my seat. "That somebody hacked a lot of environmental sensors, that the environmental sensor net does not actually cover the whole station, and that there might be a nuke leaking radiation near one of the municipal fusactors in the middle of—well, I guess we'd call it 'town.' We think that the hacked sensors are there as an early warning system to let whoever's behind this know when somebody starts looking for them. We're not sure. It might just be some juvenile hijinks on the part of hackers-in-training." I paused and took a sip. It had been a long day and the coffee tasted wonderful. "Did I miss anything?"

The chief shook her head. "I think that's about it. We still don't know where Pip is, nor do we know for certain if a bomb even exists.

"We pretty much washed out this afternoon," I said.

"We had some successes," the chief said. She shook her head. "I could wish we had a little more success finding Pip."

"Are we going to look in the abandoned cargo warehouse?" Al asked.

"Eventually," the chief said. "We need some more information about how that's managed. Normally, because it's cargo, I'd say Pip was our go-to for that but ..." She shrugged. "That's a problem."

Al sipped her coffee and frowned into the middle distance. "The can's not here yet. Which I find odd, since it was supposed to be here in time for us to leave and we would—normally—expect to leave sometime tomorrow, right?"

I nodded. "The longer it takes to get here, the more time we have to find Pip."

"If they wanted us to deliver the goods, it would be really helpful if we had them," Al said.

"True." I pondered for a tick or two. "In a little over a stan, the chief and I are going to go see a man about a bomb. We're expecting a package from the chandlery before that."

"A bomb," Al said. "You mentioned that before."

"Something doesn't look right. We don't know it's not a bomb. It could be just a damaged fusactor radiation casing. It's very low level. Hardly noticeable." The chief took a good pull from her coffee and sighed.

"We'll go in as maintenance workers and look it over," I said.

"I'll get you a tool box to carry," the chief said.

"Do I need one?" I asked.

"No. In fact, you probably won't even open it, but nobody looks at maintenance with a tool box."

"Don't you need one?" I asked.

"Don't be silly. Supervisors don't carry toolboxes."

Al sighed and took another swig of coffee. "What can I do?"

"Keep the ship from leaving without us?" I asked.

"I like that idea," the chief said. "Can you find out what the watch schedule is for the abandoned cargo warehouse? Or if there is one?"

"I can try," Al said. She pulled up her tablet. "Should have an hours-of-operation note somewhere. It's a start. Do you really think Pip is in there?"

The chief didn't look up from her coffee. "No, but I want to rule it out."

"Do we need to revisit the 'tucked into a ship' scenario?" Al asked.

"We may need to," I said. "First things first. Make a general announcement that we're going to be laying over another two days. Extend liberty."

Al nodded. "I can do that."

"If anybody asks, it's because we're waiting on a cargo to be brought over."

She nodded again. "No story's easier to keep straight than the truth." She peered at me over the top of her mug. "Is that the truth?"

"Well, we're going to need that can before we can leave anyway, but I'm hoping we'll be able to round up our missing cargo master in that time. CPJCT will be pissed if we go back to the High Line without him."

"When's the waiting period up?" the chief asked.

"Tonight around 1800," Al said.

"We should make a formal report," the chief said. "Anybody's watching, we need to at least behave like we want him back."

"Don't we?" Al asked.

The chief laughed. "That you even thought to ask that makes me happy." She nodded. "Yes, Al. We do. He's quite often a pain in the butt, but he's our pain in the butt."

"He's also an officer in the company, so that's a complication," I said.

"Isn't he CEO?" Al asked.

"Chairman of the board, I think," I said.

"I thought that was Alys," the chief said. "She's the one that approved the additional stock issuance."

"Oh, maybe." I shook my head. "I've lost track."

"You should probably figure that out. I think we're due for an annual stockholders meeting soon," the chief said.

I hunkered down over my coffee. "He must be. We had a conversation about the CEO and the captain not being the same person," I said. "Alys would never forgive me if I lost Pip."

"The orphaned freight storage facility is open during working hours seven days a week," Al said. "I'll wait until about an hour after and ask the chandlery about getting access to a cargo we lost last week."

"Won't they just tell you to wait?" the chief asked.

"I can be persuasive if I need to be," she said. "We're leaving tomorrow and we mixed up the captain's grav trunk with a crate of machine parts. We really need to get that grav trunk back before he skins me alive." She took another sip. "Besides, what I'm hoping they'll say is 'There's not even anybody in there now. You'll just have to wait.'"

The chief nodded. "Might work."

"Also lays the ground work for when I go over there and pound on the door."

"You sure you want to retire?" the chief asked.

Al's glance flickered to me and back to her cup. "I'm still evaluating it."

The chief's eyebrows gave a little dance before settling down to a frown. "I see," she said.

I was pretty sure she did. I grabbed a swig of coffee and savored it. It kept me from putting my foot in my mouth.

Chapter Thirty
Dark Knight Station: 2376, March 12

The maintenance jumpsuits came with ball caps. I pulled mine down low on my forehead while the chief cheerfully parked hers on the back of her head and flipped the bill up like a flag.

I looked at the cap and frowned. "Really?" I asked.

She chuckled and led the way out of the security barracks. "You're looking at the hat, not my face."

Shifting the toolbox to the other hand, I took a few long strides to catch up with her as we crossed the street. "I'm going to feel pretty silly if we've gone through this charade and there's nothing there."

The chief glanced at me. "I'm going to feel pretty relieved."

"We still won't know if there's a device somewhere on the station."

"That's true, but at least we'll know it's not here."

I had to grant her that point, but I couldn't help but wonder what we'd do if it was here.

She stepped back so I could shoulder the door open for my "boss." The inner door needed the badge key that Oscella had given me. I swiped it and the door buzzed.

We pushed through into the vacant building. Our footsteps echoed against the plas-crete bulkheads. The heavy equipment emitted a low hum that vibrated my diaphragm. I spotted the fusactor crouched in the corner, a control pylon rising from the deck beside it. "Holy Hannah," I said. "That thing's huge."

The chief laughed. "You're too used to shipboard systems. This isn't even one of the big ones. Kondur saved himself some credits and increased his power grid's resilience all at the same time."

"More fusactors scattered around instead of one big point of failure?" I asked.

She nodded and crossed to the pylon. She folded her hands behind her back and examined the gauges on the surface. She shook her head and frowned. "There's a Geiger counter in that box. Break it out, would you?"

I put the box on the deck and flipped the latches. I found the meter and pulled it out, flipping it on. I crossed to the chief and handed it to her.

"Thanks, Skipper." She walked the Geiger counter around the side of the fusactor, disappearing behind the green behemoth only to appear on the other end. By the time she rejoined me, her head was shaking back and forth so fast I wondered if her eyeballs rattled. "This isn't right," she said. "These readings are exactly what I'd have expected to see for a normal fusactor of this size."

"Isn't that good?"

Sighing, she gave me a shrug and handed the Geiger counter back to me. "Yes and no. Yes because it's operating within normal parameters as far as emissions go."

"No?" I asked.

She stepped back and put her hands on her hips, her gaze raking the fusactor from one end to the other. "No because the readings we got from Dumaurier's environmental sensor are about twenty percent higher here."

"There's nothing else here," I said, my words echoing from the far wall. "It's a big empty building."

"Nothing else *here*," she said looking up at the overhead. "But the sensor can't tell us where exactly here is."

"What are you thinking?" I asked, tilting my head back to look at the girders above.

She pursed her lips and gave me that sideways tilt to her head. "I'm thinking we need to look on the roof."

My tablet bipped and I pulled it out of my pocket to read the message. "Oscella," I said. "She must be watching."

"What's she say?" the chief asked.

"Ladder in the corner nearest the fusactor. Goes to the roof." A new message bipped in under the last. "I can hear you."

The chief grinned up at the nearest security cam and then struck out for the ladder. "Bring the box, would you?" she asked.

I slotted the Geiger counter back in the tool box, secured the lid, and followed the chief.

The ladder was, in fact, a ladder. One of the vertical kind. A real ladder as opposed to the handrail-equipped sets of stairs we called a ladder on the ship. The chief was already a third of the way up when I got to the foot and wondered how I was going to climb and hold a toolbox.

She looked down at me. "Coming?"

I stepped onto the ladder and grabbed an upright with my free hand. Climbing one-handed felt really awkward but it worked. When I got to the top the chief reached down and took the box from me so I could use both hands to crest the ladder and step onto the roof.

"You all right?" she asked. "You're a little red in the face."

"I should spend a little more attention on physical conditioning," I said, looking back down the ladder. "That was a long climb."

She laughed and I didn't like the sound.

The roof of the building was less roof and more deck-without-a-railing. In the station itself there wasn't a lot of need for weather protection, so the usual stuff I'd expect to find on a space designated as *roof* didn't apply. Several boxy outcroppings dotted the area. One of them fired up with a roar and I realized they were environmental units, probably helping to control the atmosphere in the barn under us.

The chief had the toolbox open and the Geiger counter out. She paced her way toward the first unit and squinted at the counter. She walked all the way around it before moving to the next. Every one of the half dozen units on the deck looked identical but she repeated the walkaround for each. She scanned the last one and frowned.

"What is it?" I asked. "Not here."

"Something's here," she said, walking back to one of the middle units. She showed me the read-out. "This is the baseline level. It's whatever's around up here plus the fusactor under us. We're right over it so it's almost the same as it is down there."

"I'm with you so far."

"When I walk over here, look." She crossed to stand next to one of the units and held the read-out. "If there were a bomb up here, I'd expect it to be higher. It's not. Just here, it's lower."

"Not by much," I said.

"Yeah but that's the thing. It shouldn't be lower at all."

I looked at the decking under us. "This isn't right," I said.

"That's what I'm saying," the chief said.

"Not that. This." I pointed to the deck under us. "This is new."

She frowned. "It's a different color."

"There's a seam here that isn't on any other section of the deck up here." I walked around the unit. "It goes all the way around."

The chief moved the meter over the edge and back a couple of times. "It's shielding the radiation from directly below us."

I looked at the unit and then up at the overhead above us. I could see the network node above us—its power light glowed scarlet in the shadows. "Crap."

"What?" she looked up at me.

I pointed at the HVAC unit. "That's it."

She looked from me to the unit and back at me. "That makes no sense."

"Yeah. It does. What would the sensor see if it looked down here?"

"Obviously just a slightly elevated radiation level. That's what it saw."

"Right. And you're measuring a slightly lower one when you're close enough to the bomb. The shielding under it cancels out just enough radiation to mask it. To make it look like it's just a fusactor here."

"Then why does the sensor measure more?"

"It's only a little more but the node is pulling the average radiation over the whole area it's looking at. The shielding isn't quite balanced to take out exactly the same amount as the bomb is adding in when the surface area of the whole deck is taken into account," I said.

Her eyes went round and she stared at the unit. "Crap."

CHAPTER THIRTY-ONE
DARK KNIGHT STATION: 2376, MARCH 12

My first instinct was to run. I only tamped it down because I knew running wouldn't help. I couldn't run fast enough to get away. "Any ideas about how to deal with this?" I asked.

The chief glanced over at me. "Gimme a tick."

The initial shock began to wear off and I tried to work through the problem myself.

"Faraday cage, I think." the chief said. "Keep the remote from detonating it."

"How do we disarm it?" I asked.

Her eyes squinted down to slits, as if by narrowing them she could see through the outer shell. "We can't exactly evacuate the station." She looked up. "I wonder what's up there."

"What are you thinking?"

"Cutting into it, even to see what's under the casing is going to be risky," she said. "There are no exposed pieces for us to get a handle on."

The blower behind us fired up with a roar, startling me so much I jumped right up against the bomb. Horrified, I peeled myself away and stared at the chief.

"Well, we know a little jostling won't hurt it," she said. "As I was saying, if we can keep it from receiving a signal, then build a cofferdam up through the top of the station here, mount some grav plates under it ..." She shook her head. "Faraday cage, then bring in a couple of people I know."

"How long will that take?"

"Longer than we have, I suspect," she said. "Let's go see Captain Oscella and let her know what we've found."

Getting down the ladder went a lot smoother and it wasn't until we were back in the security barracks that I realized why. I'd left the toolbox on the roof.

Oscella took one look at our faces when we pushed through the doors and hustled us into a conference room. "It's there," she said. It wasn't a question.

"Yeah." The chief sat in a chair and folded her arms on the table. "It's there. It's hidden in one of the atmosphere management units on the top of the building."

Oscella settled into the chair opposite the chief. I took a seat and let the professionals deal with the situation.

"We're thinking a Faraday cage to isolate it until we can lift it up through the top of the station," the chief said.

Oscella pursed her lips. "How did they get it up there?"

"Grav crane, probably. When was the last upgrade on that structure?"

Oscella shrugged. "At least three stanyers. I'd have to check with maintenance to be sure."

"How many people would have had to be involved with an operation like that?" I asked.

They both looked at me. "Say more," the chief said.

"How many people would they have needed to install an HVAC unit like that on the top of the building? Theoretically? Somebody needed to approve it, I assume?"

Oscella nodded. "Somebody would have had to propose it. Since it's station property, the power people would have had to debate it to death with the infrastructure finance group. They'd have had to acquire the unit. Purchasing would need to buy it, bring it in, verify the shipment against the order." Oscella shrugged. "That's even before we get it up on the roof over there."

"I thought CPJCT was bad," I said.

"Maintenance records," the chief said.

"What about them?" Oscella asked.

"Is there somewhere handy we can pull them up?"

Oscella rose. "My office is just upstairs."

We left the conference room and followed Oscella up a ladder and down a passageway. Her office wasn't exactly spartan but it held no personal memorabilia, no pictures on her desk, and no certificates on the bulkhead. She dropped into the chair behind her desk and started to tappity-tap on the keyboard. "Here," she said, sliding away so we could see. "All the maintenance records for that building."

The chief reached in and started scrolling down the list, past all the records for routine fusactor service, lighting fixtures, resurfacing the deck inside. Eventually we found a record for the roof units.

"Is there any detail on this heat exchanger coil?" the chief asked.

Oscella pulled the supplemental record up for the chief to read.

"Reinforced the decking, removed defective coil, installed new unit." She ticked off the various bullets in the work order. "Tested sat." She frowned. "Who tested that unit?"

Oscella shrugged and scrolled to the top of the work order. "A. Norris." She frowned. "Norris? I know that name. How do I know that name?"

"This work was done about two stanyers ago," the chief said.

"I remember that. They had to block off part of Main Street for a day."

"Where's Norris now?" the chief asked.

Oscella sat back in her chair, shaking her head. "I need to double-check but I think he's dead. That's how I know the name. Electrocuted on the job one day."

"That's not suspicious," I said.

She sighed. "If I remember correctly, it wasn't very long after this installation."

"Well, we know they're willing to kill to cover their tracks," the chief said. "That doesn't make me feel any safer."

"They're not going to blow the station on a whim," I said. "It's too valuable."

"Explain," the chief said.

"It's been a reliable pipeline for stanyers. People, materials. They have some access to Telluride that's going to be growing unless we step in, but Dark Knight is one of—what—four or five major destinations in the Toe-Holds?"

"More like twenty depending on how you count them, but I take your point. Probably ten to fifteen percent of all traffic in the Toe-Holds comes through here," Oscella said. "Minimum of exposure because their traffic blends in. Thousands of people in and out of here in a week. I don't even know how much cargo."

I shared a glance with the chief. "What next?" I asked.

The question hung there for a moment before Oscella's tablet bipped a staccato, repeating pattern. She grabbed it off the desk and looked at the screen. "Your man Carstairs just walked off the small boat dock. A security team has him and they're taking him to the aid station next to the chandlery."

For some reason the news didn't even surprise me. "He's hurt?"

"Officer reports that he's ranting about cargo. They're taking him for evaluation."

"That's odd," the chief said.

"What? That he's ranting?" Oscella asked.

"No, that's normal. He's always got a rant up his sleeve. Cargo isn't one of his favorite topics," the chief said.

"We should probably go find out what we can," Oscella said. "Want a ride?"

Oscella grabbed a security cart and we zipped down Main Street to where it ran into the main docking bay. She parked beside a loading dock with a red cross painted on the roll-up doors. A personnel door let us into the back of the aid station where Oscella snagged one of the workers. "Carstairs? Just came in a few ticks ago?"

"Family only," the med-tech said.

The chief stepped forward. "I'm his mother."

The tech gave her a long once-over and a sour smile. "Sure." He looked at me. "And you're his father?" he asked.

"Son," I said. "You gonna let us see Dad or does Captain Oscella here have to arrest you for obstruction of a criminal investigation?"

"Room four. Just down the hall, hang a left. If you wind up in the bathroom, you went too far." He shook his head and strode off in the other direction.

"Think he bought it?" the chief asked.

Oscella laughed. "Come on. He'll have the net back here to scoop us all up in a few ticks."

The aid station looked like every aid station I'd ever visited, although it was the first one I'd ever entered from the loading dock. We found a medic poring over the readouts on an auto-doc. "Can I help you?" she asked without looking up.

"Carstairs?" I asked.

"In the can," the medic said. "We're still running an evaluation. He's got some drug residue, which we're flushing. A bit dehydrated."

"He's been missing for a couple of days now," I said.

"The more I talk, the longer it'll be before you can ask him where he's been," the medic said.

I took the hint and dropped back to the doorway.

"I'm going to go find the officers who brought him in," Oscella said. "They're in the lobby."

The chief nodded and Oscella slipped out.

The medic straightened up and stretched her back before turning to us. "All right. His badge record says Philip Carstairs and not much else. Who are you and why do you care?"

"He's my cargo master. He disappeared about two days ago and hasn't been seen since."

"You are?"

"Captain Ishmael Wang of the *Chernyakova*."

She nodded and looked at the chief. "You?"

"Engineering Chief Officer Margaret Stevens. Also of the *Chernyakova*."

"Well, your man here seems to have been to quite a party. His blood alcohol level is somewhere between 'I can't feel my nose' and 'Is that my foot.' He's been drugged. Not with something most people would take voluntarily, which makes me think somebody slipped it into him when he wasn't looking. No evidence of sexual assault but he's got some fresh bruises on his face. They'd be consistent with somebody smacking him with a stick or—more probable—he fell down and caught a handrail with his head." She shrugged. "Other than that he's in pretty decent shape for a man his age."

"How old is he?" I asked.

She frowned. "How old do you think he is?"

"Forty-ish," I said.

"Yeah. That's how I read it, too." She paused. "You know, I see people like this a lot. Drunk, dragged in barely able to stand. This guy's innards don't match the profile."

"How so?" I asked.

"By the time guys with a booze habit reach this age, I'm already seeing the result of carb poisoning, a little incipient cirrhosis. Lipids all over the place." She shrugged. "The auto-doc can help mitigate it a bit, but he's not showing anything like that. He drink much?"

"Only when he's awake and there's beer within reach," the chief said.

The medic frowned at the chief. "That's what I would have expected to hear."

"I hear a *but* coming," I said.

She shook her head. "But the auto-doc found nothing that would indicate that behavior. Not a teatotaler by any means but if this guy actually drinks more than a six pack a week, I'd be shocked."

I grinned.

"You find that funny?" the medic asked.

"In a way. Runty little bugger lies about everything. Apparently even his love of Clipper Ship Lager."

The chief folded her arms and frowned at the deck for a moment. "How long before he can come back to the ship?"

The medic consulted the panel again. "He should be coming out of it any tick now. I'd like to keep him for at least a couple of stans, just to make sure there's nothing else going on in there."

I nodded and stepped out into the passageway. I pulled out my tablet to notify Al.

The chief stepped out a moment later. "Anything new on the ship?"

"No messages," I said. "I'm taking that as a good sign."

She chuckled. "He's not a heavy drinker."

I leaned against the bulkhead and tilted my head back. "He's never been what he seemed. Or claimed."

"I've known him since he was a toddler," the chief said.

"He acted like he didn't know you back on Breakall."

"He didn't know me. I know him. I know his whole family. You ever meet his sister, Rachel?"

"No." I tried to think back over the decades that I'd known him. "I know his father, Thomas. I met his mother. Tammy? . I know his Aunt P and Uncle Q. Cousin ... Roger?"

"Yeah. Penny has a sharp nose for the business. Roger? Good-hearted lad, but if my back was against a bulkhead, I'd want Pip." She grinned at me. "Rachel. Pure stainless steel. Mind as sharp as a razor and as curious as a bag of cats."

I glanced at her. "You match-making?"

She laughed. "No. You and Rachel would make a terrible pair. You both have the same flaws."

I bit down on a wise-ass retort and thought about that. Before I could pursue it, I heard Pip's voice from the other room.

"There's nothing wrong with me. What do you think you're doing?"

I stepped into the med-bay with the chief on my heels. "Glad to see you haven't lost your sense of humor," I said.

"Ishmael, do we have the can tied on yet?"

"Not that I know of," I said.

"We need to get moving," he said.

The medic stepped up to him and stood in front of his face. "You need to stop thrashing or I'm going to knock you out and button you into this pod again. Copy?"

He drew a big breath and blew it out, giving her the stink-eye. "Capisco." He settled back.

"Good. Now how do you feel?" she asked.

"Like getting out of here."

"You'll need to wait for us to grow you a new leg first," she said.

Pip's eyes went totally round. "My leg?" He tried to look into the bottom half of the auto-doc. "My leg, there's nothing wrong with my leg. It feels fine." The monitors all went haywire with beeps and boops and warning tones.

"I'm talking about the leg your argument would need to stand on before you can convince me to let you go," the medic said.

He stared at her for a very long time as the monitors started evening out and the last of the warnings stopped buzzing. "That was a terrible thing to do."

"Yes." She nodded. "But it worked."

"Sorry," Pip said, looking around as if seeing the med-bay for the first time. "Where am I?"

"Humor me for a few more ticks," the medic said. "Where do you think you are?"

He looked around again. "Auto-doc, of course. Med-bay, probably Dark Knight Station."

"What day is it?" she asked.

"I have no idea. When security brought me in here it was Thursday, I think."

"What time should I pick you up for dinner?" she asked.

He looked at her for a moment. "To be honest, I'm pretty hungry. What time do you get off work?"

"You're fine," she said and turned to me. "I'll be finishing up the paperwork in the office. Please don't press any buttons or let him out of there."

"I have no plans for letting him out, believe me," I said.

She swept out of the med-bay and I heard her shoes *skwiching* down the passageway.

"Damn," Pip said.

"Buck up," the chief said, stepping up to the auto-doc across from me. "She'll be back to let you out. Maybe she's just being coy."

He grinned. "One can hope." He looked back and forth between the chief and me. "So, somebody tazed me when I left the ship. I'd just stepped off the docks and they got me from behind. I have no idea who it was or even how many. By the time I got my muscles under control, they'd already jabbed me with a needle." He angled his head, displaying a red mark just under the jawline. "When I came to, they had me handcuffed to the bunk in one of the staterooms on an Unwin Eight." He held up his right arm. The red abrasion showed clearly. "They tried to convince me the ship was underway. I played along. Either they didn't know I'd lived on an Eight most of my life, or they thought anything that would fool them would fool me."

"Which Unwin Eight?" the chief asked.

"Small ship dock twenty-one," he said. "No idea what name it was but I made it a point to get that. I remember telling security before I got tossed into the thing."

"You were drunk and drugged, according to the med-tech," I said.

"Something in the beer," he said. "They counted on it knocking me out."

"It didn't?" the chief asked.

"Made me loopy. That tipped me off. I pretended to be out of it for a bit and then woke up gagging and retching like I was going to puke." He chuckled. "They had the handcuffs off and me face down in the head in less than a tick."

"How'd you get from there to the docks?" the chief asked.

"I retched and pretended to hurl. It wasn't hard. Whatever they gave me kicked me hard in the gut and made me dizzy as hell. After a while, they started arguing about who was going to stay with me. Eventually one of them slapped his buddy and pulled rank. I heard him stomp off to the bridge so I flopped over on my side, like I'd passed out. The guy watching me swore up a storm but made the mistake of leaning over to drag me out of the head." He shrugged. "Kneed his groin, banged his head on the bowl, rolled him into a corner, and walked off the ship. When I came out of the small ship dock, two security types grabbed me, dragged me to an aid station—which I presume is this one—and they slapped me into an auto-doc."

"They said you were ranting about cargo," the chief said.

"I just said I only had one beer but we had to get the cargo loaded." He sighed. "It might have been loud and slightly slurred. I was heading back to the ship. Were you worried?"

I laughed but the chief nodded. "A bit. We didn't want to leave without you."

"Did they say why they grabbed you? Ransom? Leverage?" I asked.

"I assumed it had something to do with the cargo going to the mega. I asked, but they didn't offer any kind of answer," he said. "So? What did I miss?"

I heard shoes *skwiching* up the hall. "A little of this. A little of that. We'll fill you in when you get back to the ship."

The med-tech breezed into the room. "Out. Time's up. Visiting hours are over. Vamoose."

I held my hands up and backed toward the door. "Contact the *Chernyakova* before you let him out and we'll send an escort to make sure he gets home safely."

She grinned at me. "Will do, Captain. Don't worry. We'll take good care of him."

The chief followed me out to the lobby where Oscella stood with two uniformed security officers. She looked up as we entered. "What's his story?"

"Tazed, drugged, held on a docked ship," I said.

"Yeah, he told us it was dock twenty-one in the small ship area," one of the officers said, holding a tablet. "He repeated it several times along with demanding a beer."

"Demanding a beer isn't unusual for Mr. Carstairs," the chief said. "What's the problem with dock twenty-one?"

"There are only fifteen docking rings in the small ship gallery," he said.

"Any Unwin Eights?" I asked.

"What?" he asked, completely blank-faced.

"Unwin Eight is a model of small fast packet in common use in the area," the chief said.

The officer shrugged. "They could be empty cans of beans for all I know."

Oscella pulled up her tablet and flipped a few screens. "Three empty rings," she said. "Of the rest, one is a Damien Six and the rest are Unwin Eights."

"What about the ships that left?" the chief asked.

"None have left since yesterday afternoon. If he was on one of those Eights, it's still docked."

"Cheeky," the chief said.

"Stupid," Oscella said. She tapped on her keyboard and sent a message. "Those ships are impounded until we get to the bottom of it."

"Can you do that?" I asked.

"Yes," the chief said. "She can."

Oscella looked at the senior officer. "Robarts, you and Stevenson here get some backup. Knock on the locks of everybody there. Speak to all of them. If anybody's not home, then station an officer there."

"What are we looking for?" Robarts asked.

"When they answer, tell them you need to inspect their state-rooms for lice. If they give you any guff, tell them the lice carry a disease and one guy is already in an auto-doc from it. It's just a public health inspection," Oscella said.

"Lie to them?" Robarts asked. He didn't seem to object to the idea. More like he just wanted to clarify his understanding.

"Not at all. The people who've done this are lice. They put Mr. Carstairs in an auto-doc. They're carrying a tendency for violence I don't want loose on this station. Clear enough?" Oscella asked.

Robarts nodded. "Anything in particular we need to note?"

"Handcuffs," the chief said. "Eights have a grab rail on the bulkhead and a safety bar on the exposed edge. Mr. Carstairs has contusions on his right arm consistent with being handcuffed to one of those two rails."

"Would they leave the cuffs there with Mr. Carstairs loose?" Stevenson asked.

"Maybe," the chief said. "The bars are painted chrome. They'll chip if you sneeze on them. I suspect most of them will have minor dings and scratches, but handcuffs leave a ring. The fresh chips of paint will be pretty obvious."

Oscella looked at the chief. "Voice of experience?"

"Over the course of my career I've seen the results of way too many people handcuffed to the bed."

Oscella took a long look at the chief's face and nodded. "You heard the woman."

Robarts and Stevenson sketched a salute in Oscella's direction and headed for the door.

"He say anything else?" Oscella asked.

"He's seen something of his captors but not the people who grabbed him," the chief said. "I'm not sure how much his testimony would hold up at trial, given that he seems to have been repeatedly drugged and fed beer."

"Fed beer?" she asked.

"He never mentioned food. Just beer." The chief shrugged. "They could have fed him but he'd remember the beer."

"He didn't say what kind of beer," I said.

The chief turned toward me but her gaze focused somewhere else. "He didn't."

Oscella frowned. "Is that significant?"

"Might be. If he knows the brand and it's not common, it might help find the right ship," I said. "Lemme go ask him." I trotted back to the med-bay, knocking before entering. I found Pip still clamped into the bottom half of the auto-doc and the tech lounging across the room with an enigmatic smile.

"Captain? I thought I said no more visiting."

"Sorry, I need to ask one question."

She nodded.

"What kind of beer was it?" I asked.

He looked blank for a moment. "Rock-Knocker Red Ale."

"Was it any good?"

He shrugged. "Better than most. Cute label. Has a—" He bit off his words and glanced at the med-tech, who looked me in the eye.

"It's got a mostly naked woman on the label, Captain. She's in a somewhat compromising position," she said. "It's a bit pricey but the people who like it seem to like it for more than the label."

"Thanks for that clarification."

"My pleasure, Captain, now ...?" She raised her eyebrows and made a little finger twiddle motion that clearly said "run along now" without a word being uttered.

I walked back to the lobby. "Have them look for Rock-Knocker Red Ale bottles."

Oscella gave me a double-take. "Rock-Knocker Red Ale?"

"That's what he said."

Oscella shrugged. "I'm not an aficionado but is that like going to a hardware store and looking for a particular screw?"

"If the description of the label is any indication, that might be closer to the truth than you think."

Chapter Thirty-two
Dark Knight Station: 2376, March 12

We left Captain Oscella in the lobby of the aid station and walked back to the ship. "This has been a day," the chief said.

"What are we going to do about the bomb?"

"Well, it's been there for at least eighteen months."

"It makes me nervous just being that close. Knowing that somebody could decide to pull the trigger any moment," I said.

"Nothing we can do about it right now," she said. "I haven't heard from Kondur today. Did he get out of the med-bay?"

"No idea." I keyed the lock and walked up the ramp.

The chief followed me and the lock started closing before I could reach the key. Surprised, I turned to the brow watch and froze. A pale Bentley stood behind the watch station. The woman beside him looked calm and collected. The barrel of her needler fit neatly into Bentley's right ear.

"Welcome back, Captain," she said. "We've been waiting for you."

"Log us aboard, if you would, Mr. Bentley," I said.

"Logging aboard, aye, aye, Captain."

"How cute is that," the woman remarked to nobody in particular.

"So, you're here to make sure we deliver your cargo, I take it?" I asked.

"I heard you were smart," she said.

"Is the can latched on?" I asked.

"We wouldn't be here if it weren't," she said. "The crew's all here except for that irritating man, Carstairs, but you won't need him this trip. He'll have plenty of time to recover from his ordeal."

"Well, then, I suppose there's not much keeping us here." I looked over my shoulder at the chief. "Would you get us ready for pull out? I'll track down Mr. Reed to file our departure." I started to walk into the ship.

"Hold up, Captain. We can't have you wandering around the ship by yourself," the woman said.

"Make up your mind. You want us to get underway or not? I'm happy to do it, with or without that weapon giving Bentley there an earache. I want to get this albatross of a can delivered and return with the other one so I can get back to trading. I've already been tied up here too long because you people can't seem to get your act together. Now, we both want the same thing. You can fight me to make me do it or you can get out of my way so I can be rid of you and get on with turning a profit. Your call." I paused and stared at her. "One thing. I can't fly this ship with half a crew. We barely have enough hands to keep it going as it is. You start getting stupid and none of us will see a gravity well again."

"Big talk, Captain."

I laughed and walked into the ship. "Send your escort. Doesn't matter to me. We're getting underway and once we undock, it's a long walk home."

The adrenaline hit me when I walked past the mess deck and saw the crew seated at the tables, their hands flat in front of them. It took me a lot of heartbeats to tamp it down. Five people in light body armor prowled the room. Each of them carried a needler. Everybody looked at me. I stopped and the chief almost bumped into me.

"Who thinks they're in charge here?" I asked.

The guy in the corner nearest the coffee urns, straightened up from a slouch and gave me what he must have thought was an evil grin. A skinny man with half his hair shaved off leaving a bald scalp trailing patches of fuzz down the sides, he brandished a long gun—a needler model I'd seen before and spent some amount of time with at the academy. The length made it a liability in the close quarters of a ship's passages but quite effective on orbitals where the longer barrel gave it better accuracy. "Nice to see you accepting realities, Captain."

"All I'm accepting is that you people are getting in the way. If you want to get underway, these people need to be working, not sitting here while you prance around like some B-grade holovid villain." I looked at the chief. "Get us ready for a pushback, Chief."

She nodded and stepped around me to look into the mess deck. "Wallace, Murawsky, Wicklund. With me."

The three engineering crew looked at the gunmen. The gunmen looked to the thug in the corner.

The chief sighed. "Seems like they don't really want to leave, Skipper."

I stepped into the mess deck and walked to the cup rack. "You people haven't really thought this through, have you?"

"Shut up," the skinny guy said.

I sighed and pulled a mug from the rack. I crossed to the urns and the leader snapped his weapon around so it pointed at me. I stared at him while I drew a mug of coffee. I took a sip and tossed the rest into the drain. "Ms. Sharps?" I kept looking at the guy who thought he was in charge.

"Yes, Captain?" She sat on the bench nearest the galley.

"The coffee is cold."

"I know, Captain. Sorry about that. The ... guests ... have been hampering our operation."

"I see that, Ms. Sharps. Who's got the duty today?"

"That would be Mr. Franklin, Skipper."

"Mr. Franklin?" I said.

"Yes, Captain?"

"Mr. Franklin, would you get at least one of these urns operational for me, please?"

"Ah, that's going to be difficult, sar."

I stepped up to the skinny guy, walking right up until the barrel of his weapon pressed against my chest. I leaned into it so he had to take a step back. "Son, I don't know who you think you are or how you think you people are going to manage keeping the ship flying and the crew sitting at these tables for the next week but I've got a bit of a newsie for you. You can't. We can't fly the ship from the mess deck. We can't fly the ship if we're hungry, thirsty, or exhausted. You need to make up your mind how you want this to go down. Either get out of our way or start killing us now, because those are your choices." I leaned into the gun a little harder, forcing him to take another half-step back. "Start with me because if you start killing my crew, you're going to have to deal with me in real short order."

"Jack, go with the biddie and her chicks. Make sure they don't do anything funny. Benny, walk behind Jack," the guy said, staring into my eyes.

"Good choice. That biddie and her chicks are going to make sure we get where we're going without suffocating on the way. Now, Ms. Sharps and her mess deck crew need to get into the galley and begin preparing the meals. Unless you're planning on feeding twenty-odd people and yourselves in the process, I suggest you put down the weapons, and get out of our way. I've been threatened by pros and you're not even in the farm league. You've got a lot to learn."

"Oh yeah?" His sneer curled his upper lip almost to his nose. "Like what?"

I grabbed the gun, twisted it away from his trigger finger, broke his hold on it, and wrenched it out of his hands. It took me two tries to get the magazine out and clear the chamber, but I still thrust it back into his chest before he got his jaw closed. "Like don't screw with stuff you don't understand. Take your toy and get out of my way."

I stepped away from him but he recovered enough to try to use the gun as a club. I just sidestepped the windmill, letting him swing it all the way to the deck so I could push him after it. I dropped the magazine in my pocket. I looked at the one he called Jack. "What's this idiot's name?"

"Snake," Jack said.

"Snake. How intimidating and original." I sighed and looked at the chief. "Get us ready to move, Chief. Murawsky, Wallace, Wickland. You're up. Give her a hand. I want us to be ready to go at the top of the stan."

The chief nodded. "Top of the stan, aye, Captain." She waved an arm. "Come on, Jack. You and your buddy need to move a little sharper if you're going to stay with the crew." She turned and headed for the spine with her engineering gang on her heels.

I looked at Jack and Benny standing there, apparently stunned.

"Don't just stand there, idiots. Go," Snake said, clambering to his feet and glaring at me.

I cast a meaningful look at Ms. Sharps, still sitting at the table with her palms flat on the surface. "Well, Snake? Your call. You getting hungry, yet? Need a cup of coffee? I sure do. It's been a long day, it's going to get longer before it's over, and I get really, really grumpy when I haven't had my coffee."

Snake offered me another glare but jerked his head in the direction of the galley. "Don't get ideas, Sharps."

She rolled her eyes and nodded to Adams and Franklin. "Come on. We've got work to do." The three of them stood and went into the galley, leaving Snake and two of his henchmen.

To be fair, the henchmen looked at Snake like he'd lost his mind.

"All right. We seem to be working things out. One last question and then I'll get busy doing what you keep interrupting by telling me I have to do it or—presumably—else. Where are my officers?"

"Next door," he said.

It took me a few moments to parse that as "in the wardroom."
"How many of the crew made it back aboard?" I asked.

"All of them," Snake said.

"First, I know that might be what you believe but I happen to
know for a fact that at least one of them isn't. I only ask because
I need to figure out what to do if too many of them have learned
the ship's being—and I use the term advisedly, because it's really
questionable when somebody holds you at gun point to force you
to do the thing you would have done anyway—hijacked."

Snake's eyes glazed over for a heartbeat.

"I don't *always* talk like that. No. Rather often, I do, yes. I
have a bit of a reputation for it."

Some wag at the back of the room said, "Hear, hear."

I looked at the other two, since Snake seemed to be tied up
parsing. "Who are you?"

The sole female in the group—an undernourished waif sporting
impressive biceps and dark circles under her eyes—lifted her chin.
"Cindy."

I nodded. "Cindy." I looked to the last unknown. "You?"

"None ya damn business." He waved his gun in my direction.

"Well, nice to meet you, Mr. Nunya. I'd appreciate it if you'd
try to stop waving that weapon around. It's pretty clear you don't
know how to use it and I'm concerned you might accidentally hurt
one of my crew." I looked around while he spluttered in the corner.
"Tell you what, Cindy. Why don't you take over watching the
galley to make sure Ms. Sharps doesn't poison us all with too
much oregano in the stew? Stay out from under foot and she might
give you a snack. When was the last time you had a decent meal?"

"I ate this morning, thank you very much," she said.

"Well, be that as it may, Ms. Sharps and her two henchmen
are—at this very moment–plotting to prepare the evening meal.
Unsupervised, if you catch my meaning."

Cindy looked around as if to see if anybody was looking at her.
Answer, only all the people on the mess deck. She sidled along the
bulkhead and scooted into the galley. Ms. Sharps caught my eye
through the galley door and grinned.

"Now, since I'm pretty sure Mr. Snake here wants to keep his
eye on me, Mr. Nunya, that leaves you to guard the mess deck
while my crew prepares the ship for departure." I looked around.
"Who's supposed to be standing watch now besides Mr. Bentley?"

"Ms. Fortuner has the OOD, sar," Bentley said.

Ms. Cross raised her hand as did one of Penna's enginemen and
a spec-three with a gravity insignia on his tunic.

"Ms. Cross, would you go to the wardroom and ask Ms. Ross to join me here?"

"Sar, there are other ... people ... with them."

I nodded. "Thank you, Ms. Cross. Hang tight here, then." I looked at the engineman, "Ms. Moore, isn't it?"

She nodded. "Yes, sar. Carla Moore."

"You're supposed to be in environmental?"

"Yes, sar."

"Mr. Penna aboard?"

She shook her head after a glance at Snake.

I sighed. "Please resume your watch station, Ms. Moore."

She was gone almost before I finished speaking.

"Mr. Bell, right?" I asked.

The spec-three nodded. "Yes, sar."

"Your duty station is unattended at the moment. Remedy that, please."

"Aye, aye, sar." He stood and made a slightly more dignified exit.

"Mr. Bentley, I believe you have the brow?"

"Yes, Captain."

"Would you take your new playmate with you and resume your station, please?"

The woman growled. "I have a name, asshole."

I nodded. "I assumed you did. If you'd share it with me, I'd be happy to call you by it."

"It's Samantha," she said with a glare around the compartment.

"Samantha what?" I asked.

"Grant."

"Thank you, Ms. Grant." I looked at Bentley again. "As I was saying, Mr. Bentley, would you take Ms. Grant with you and resume your station?"

"Aye, aye, Captain." Bentley, ever the gentleman, offered his arm to Ms. Grant, who scowled at him. He shrugged and waved her ahead. She went with Bentley following, a bemused expression on his face.

"All right. The rest of you, hang loose. Ms. Sharps will have fresh coffee up in a couple of ticks. We'll be going to navigation stations as soon as I've checked with the department heads." I looked around and saw a lot of heads nodding. "Mr. Nunya, I trust we won't have any problems while I'm gone?"

"You're going to leave me with all of them?" he asked, his voice perhaps a note or two higher than it had been before.

"Why, yes. Yes, I am. What did you think was going to happen? Do you have a problem, Mr. Nunya?"

He swallowed and looked around. "There's like twenty of them."

"More like fifteen but I take your point, Mr. Nunya." I looked around the mess deck. "Let me make one thing very clear. This ship is under my command. Mr. Nunya is our guest until such time as he and his colleagues decide that their being here is stupid, counter-productive, and uncomfortable. Please make him feel welcome. Anyone caught fighting will be brought before the mast for nonjudicial punishment." I paused to let that sink in. "Are we clear?"

"Yes, sar" echoed in the room.

"Well, there. Feeling better, Mr. Nunya?" I asked. "They won't hurt you. I expect you to offer them the same courtesy."

He gave a shaky nod.

"Good. Mr. Snake, I think we're done here. Come along." I headed off the mess deck, leaving Snake in my wake and scrambling to catch up.

"Hey! You can't just wander off," he said.

I stopped in the passageway outside the mess deck. "You people keep saying that. I'm not wandering off. Pay attention, Mr. Snake. I'm getting ready to put this ship into space. I was under the impression that was what you wanted. Have we failed at a basic level of communication?"

"Yes," he said. "You seem to think you're in charge here."

I felt the stars on my collar. "Yes. Actually that's true, Mr. Snake. These stars mean I'm in charge."

"I'm the one with the gun," he said, poking the weapon into my shoulder.

"I can't argue that," I said. "Tell you what. You're in charge." I crossed my arms and leaned back against the bulkhead.

"What?"

"I'm agreeing with you. You're in charge. Now what?"

"Get this ship underway."

"I was in the process of doing just that, but you insisted you're in charge so ... abracadabra. You're in charge. Carry on, Mr. Snake."

"Don't be a smart-ass. Get this ship underway. Now." He had a sheen of sweat across his forehead and back over the exposed strip over the top of his head.

I sighed. "Look, I don't know who pushed you into this but they chose badly. If you're in charge, that means you're the captain. The captain gives the orders. You want to be in charge, then give the orders. Ordering me to get the ship underway isn't going to do you any good because the process of getting the ship underway means the person in charge gives all the various orders in the correct sequence to cause the ship to leave the dock and sail off into the Deep Dark." I shrugged. "If you're going to insist on the charade that you're in charge, then I'm going to insist that you actually be in charge. Give the orders. Figure out who you're supposed to give them to. Make sure they're in the right order. All of that. You're in charge? Then be in charge."

He opened his mouth but I kept right on going.

"Otherwise I'm going to be in charge, and you can continue to be the pesky puppy humping everybody's leg and snapping at shadows, insisting you're in charge like some toddler with a biscuit making stupid, self-centered demands of the adults in the room, who are ignoring you. Now, Mr. Snake, do you want to be in charge, or do you want this ship to get underway and deliver this can?"

"Get this ship underway," he said, his voice nearly a snarl.

"If you would get out of my way, I'm trying to do just that." I stared at him. "Would it be all right, oh mighty god of all you survey, if I actually got on with it?"

He took a step back and I headed down the passageway, walking into the ward room to find the three mates seated around the table with another of the would-be hijackers glaring at them, his back in a corner and a long gun pointed generally at Al. "Who are you?" I asked.

"Who are you?" he asked back.

Snake came through the door behind me and latched the door closed.

"I'm the captain. You can call me 'Captain' because, well, otherwise I ignore you." I looked at Al. "Report, Ms. Ross?"

"They pushed their way aboard when Bentley answered the lock call. Rounded everybody up from around the ship. We got stuffed in here with Chumly while the rest of the crew is, I believe, on the mess deck waiting for you, the chief, and Mr. Carstairs to come aboard."

"Anybody hurt?" I asked.

"None of the crew that I know of. I think Mr. Bentley might be feeling a bit defeated. He hasn't been able to get into his guard's pants yet."

"Give him time," I said. "Do we have all the crew aboard? We're going to have to leave Pip, but I think he'll find comfort while we're gone."

"We're missing Penna, Verde, Dent, and Keehn, Captain. They went on liberty this morning and aren't due back until tomorrow."

"Cancel liberty and put out a recall, please."

She nodded and pulled out her tablet.

"Mr. Reed, I have it from an unreliable source that we have a can attached. Would you head up to the bridge and make sure it's actually there? You should be able to see the latches set correctly on the cargo master's terminal. While you're there, plot us a course out of here and file a departure notice to Dark Knight Local for the top of the next hour."

"On it, Skipper." Reed started to rise but the bright bulb in the corner stiffened and swung his weapon around to point at him.

"Mr. Snake, would you ask your associate to get with the program?"

"Relax, Frankie," Snake said.

"Is this your first hijacking? If you're going to point that thing at somebody, point it at the one who's the most danger to you," I said.

"Who's that?" the guy asked, looking around as if he'd missed somebody enter.

"The individual holding the gun," I said. "Mr. Reed?" I nodded to the door. "We're going to need that clearance."

He finished getting up and left. I heard his footsteps pounding up the ladder.

"Ms. Fortuner—"

"Hey, Snake's the only one holding a gun in here," Frankie said.

I looked at Snake. "Is he your boss's kid or something?"

"Why?" Snake asked.

"Why would you bring him if he wasn't?"

"Skipper, there's no need to be cruel. They're trying their best," Al said.

I sighed. "You're right. My apologies, Frankie. I appreciate the effort but now I need to ask you both a question."

Snake took a step back. "Does it have to do with getting underway?"

"Yes, although not directly. We need to get the engines up and running. Mr. Reed needs to get the course plotted and laid in. We'll need to clear with local traffic and maybe see if we can get a tug to pull us back. It's all part of the process. We talked about that earlier."

Snake nodded but I was completely sure he had no idea what I'd just said.

"So my question is, did you know you were sent out here to die?"

"Die?" Snake asked.

"That may be a bit over the top. How about to be caught and locked up?" I asked. "That sound better?"

"What are you getting at?" he asked, his gaze flickering around the room like he had a balloon deflating in his head, making his skull flap back and forth inside his skin.

"How many of you are here?" I asked.

"Eight," he said.

"Fine, one I haven't had the pleasure of meeting yet."

"I've met him, Skipper," Al said. She wrinkled her nose and shook her head.

"We've got you outnumbered by four to one. We know the ship. We know each other. We know how this ship works and the dangers of being aboard. What were you thinking that you thought you could push aboard, wave a few toys around, and survive a three-week trip through the Deep Dark with only eight people?"

"We have the guns," he said. "If you get any smart ideas, some of your crew winds up with glass in their ass. I may not be able to threaten you, but some of your cute little girls and boys here?" He grinned. "That's your weakness. Captain."

"Hold that thought," I said. "Perhaps you'll find comfort in it later. Al? We got liberty canceled?"

"Dent and Verde are on their way back. No response from Keehn or Penna."

"Drop them a note. We're pulling out at the top of the hour. Have them get with Pip and wait until we're back."

"Aye, aye, Skipper."

I caught a shift in the ship's vibration. "I think the chief has the fusactors up to snuff. I think we just went off shore power. Ms. Fortuner, can I ask you to check in with Ms. Sharps? I forgot to ask her about stores. We should have enough to last a few weeks, even with a few extra mouths to feed, but would you confirm that for me?"

"Be happy to, Captain." She braced her hands on the table and eyed Frankie. She stood up slowly, never taking her gaze off him.

"Where's she going?" Snake asked.

"She's going to make sure we have enough food to last for the voyage. I'm relatively sure we do, but I like to double-check things like how much air, water, and food we have before heading out into the Deep Dark."

He nodded. "You just keep all that in your head?"

"Lots of practice," I said. "I had to earn these stars by doing the work over the stanyers. Al? I want to get up to the bridge and check the can for myself. Would you join me in half a stan?"

"Sure thing, Skipper."

I turned and motioned for Snake. "Come on. We're going up top where we can see what's happening."

"You need me to do anything before I come up, Cap?" Al said.

"Book a couple of rooms at the Asteroid Arms. Charge them to the company."

Al nodded. "Good thinking."

I held the door open for Snake and followed him out into the passage. "This way." I pushed past him and up the ladder toward officer country and the bridge beyond.

"Hey, wait a tick. You can't just walk around the ship like that."

"You keep saying that, Mr. Snake, but I keep demonstrating that you're mistaken in that belief." I crested the ladder to the bridge and looked aft. "Looks like a can to me, Mr. Reed."

"It is, indeed, a can, Captain. Latches are set green. I've got a preliminary plot out of the system, we can refine it when we actually get moving."

"Local traffic control?" I asked.

"We're cleared for pushback at the top. No tugs are available so we're on our own."

I nodded. "Shouldn't be a problem." I crossed to the watchstander's console and began lighting up the interface. Everything looked normal. I swapped over to the chief's station and brought that online as well. The fusactors were warming and the shore ties were already disconnected. "Looking good here, Mr. Reed."

"I'm double-checking for updates now. We need to get Ms. Fortuner up here to do the system backups."

"I'm here," she said, topping the ladder with four cups of coffee. "Compliments of Ms. Sharps, Skipper. She said you left the galley without one."

"That woman is a saint," I said. "Thank you, Ms. Fortuner."

"Tom?" she said, handing him one of the mugs.

He took the offering with a smile and a nod.

She turned to Snake. "Want one?" she asked, holding a mug in each hand.

He started to take the offered mug but paused and took the other one with a knowing grin.

She handed him his choice of mug with a little smile of her own and took a swig from the cup in her hand. "Backups, Captain?"

"Yes, please, Ms. Fortuner. Clear the comms caches. We'll have time to pick up new traffic on the way out of the system."

"Aye, aye, Captain." She sat at her console and started the backup process.

I planted my butt in the captain's chair and sipped the coffee. "Ms. Fortuner, did Ms. Sharps happen to mention where this coffee came from? It's not our standard brew."

"Oh, yes, she did, Captain. Apparently, Mr. Kondur sent over a couple of tubs of his private roast. She wanted to try it out."

"I'll have to send him a thank you," I said.

Al came up the ladder and took her place at the watchstander's console. "Dent and Verde are aboard, Captain. Keehn is still out of contact with the ship. Penna can't make it back in time. I've booked a suite for all of them. Sent the confirmation to everybody."

"Thank you, Ms. Ross. Anything else I should know?"

"Nothing significant," she said.

"Where's Frankie?" Snake asked.

"Guarding the empty wardroom, last I saw," Al said. "Why?"

The chrono ticked over to 1645. "Ms. Ross, set navigation stations throughout the ship."

"Aye, aye, Captain. Set navigation stations." She pulled out her mic and made the announcement.

Ms. Torkelson climbed up the ladder and took her seat at the helm.

"Captain, Ms. Sharps reports that she'll have boxes ready at 1800 in lieu of an evening mess," Al said.

"Thank her for me, Ms. Ross, and remind her to add enough for our guests."

"Aye, aye, Cap."

"Mr. Snake, you might want to start considering how you'd like to distribute your people around the ship. Once we secure from navigation stations, we'll be setting normal watch. Some people will be sleeping. Some will be on watch. Some will be awake and tending to personal chores."

"What do you mean?" he asked.

"Well, all these people have jobs. The jobs need to be done all day, every day. We don't pull over for a snooze at night. So the people who'll come on at midnight will be catching some sleep until they go on duty. The people who go off at midnight will be trying to relax and unwind before they get some sleep. The galley crew will be going to bed around 2200 and getting up at 0430. What would you like your people to do? Now would be a good time for you to figure that out. Samantha will be the first one at loose ends after we're outbound. Mr. Bentley will secure the brow watch and report to the engine room. Do you want Samantha to go with him, take on a different duty?" I shrugged. "It's up to you."

He didn't say anything.

I let him stew.

"We have green light local, Captain," Ms. Fortuner said.

"Thank you, Ms. Fortuner. Verify shore ties with the chief, Ms. Ross."

"Shore ties secured, Captain. Chief Stevens reports she'll be in engineering main today."

"Thank you, Ms. Ross. Release docking clamps."

I felt the chunk in my feet, the vibration echoing the length of the ship.

"Docking clamps released, Captain. Ship is free in space."

"Thank you, Ms. Ross. Secure the brow."

"Brow secured. Mr. Bentley is on his way aft, Captain."

"Thank you, Ms. Ross. Announce the pushback in ten. Mark."

Al picked up the mic and counted down to the ship.

"Helm, ready to push back," I said.

"Helm ready, aye, Captain."

The countdown reached zero. Al said, "Execute pushback."

"Execute, aye."

Torkelson teased the bow thrusters—once, twice, and again. I could see the delta-vee on Al's console as the ship edged out of the dock and away from the station. It wasn't fast enough to observe by looking out of the armorglass, but we were moving.

"Five meters," Al said.

"A little more thrust, Ms. Torkelson. Bring us up to a meter a second," I said.

"A meter per second, aye, Captain." She pressed the thruster control a couple of times.

I watched the delta-vee on Al's console tick over to a meter per second and settled back with my coffee. "Log us out, Ms. Ross. Report a hundred meters."

"Log departure. Report a hundred meters, aye, aye, Captain."

The station looked more distant and the ships on either side of us at the dock appeared to move away as we slipped out from between them. I turned my chair to look aft as we backed into the traffic lane. "We are clear on the lane, Ms. Ross."

"One hundred meters, Captain."

"Take us out, Ms. Ross."

"Aye, aye, Captain. Helm, yaw one-twenty."

"Yaw one-twenty, aye."

"Mr. Reed, do we have an outgoing track?" Al asked.

"Outgoing track sent to helm," Mr. Reed said.

"Helm, confirm track."

"Track confirmed, Ms. Ross. We are on the beam."

"Ahead five percent."

"Ahead five percent, aye."

The station fell behind us as we angled away toward the Deep Dark. The magic of the math told us which way to turn, how fast to go in order to move away from the station.

"Doesn't this ship go any faster?" Snake asked.

"Most certainly, Mr. Snake. It takes us a while to reach that speed and we probably won't be going all that fast for a while. Ms. Ross, how long to the safety margin?"

"About a stan, Captain. Dark Knight Local advises ballistic to Burleson limit."

"Thank you, Ms. Ross. Mr. Reed?"

"We've a short exit jump in approximately two stans on the current plot, Captain."

"Thank you, Mr. Reed." I swiveled to look at Snake. "There you have it. We'll be another two stans outbound before our first jump. Luckily we're in a system where the station is on the outer edge. We won't be traveling very fast when we jump compared to our top speed, but it's fast enough to get us where we're going."

"How long to get to the destination?" he asked.

"Mr. Reed? Mr. Snake would like to know our ETA."

"Could be as little as a day, Captain, but probably closer to two, maybe three, depending on what kind of jump errors we get."

"Thank you, Mr. Reed." I looked at Snake.

He shrugged and looked around the bridge then over his shoulder at the receding station.

I turned the chair to face front and smiled into my mug.

CHAPTER THIRTY-THREE
DEEP DARK: 2376, MARCH 12

The stars barely seemed to shift at all when we jumped. "Jump complete, Captain. Verifying position."

"Thank you, Ms. Ross."

"Next jump in approximately two stans, Captain. The vector's off a bit."

"Thank you, Mr. Reed. Let me know when the burn is programmed."

"Aye, aye, Cap."

"Position verified, Captain."

"Thank you, Ms. Ross."

"The burn is programmed, Captain."

"Initiate program, Mr. Reed."

"Initiate program, aye, Captain."

The ship twisted in space and the space frame rumbled when the heavy thrusters along the keel fired.

"Time to burn, Mr. Reed?"

"A hundred and ten ticks, Skipper."

"Ms. Ross, please notify the chief of the burn time."

"Notify the chief, aye, Captain."

I settled back in my chair. My coffee was cold. A glance at the chrono showed it to be nearly time for evening mess. I could wait that long. I turned to look at Snake. "So, Mr. Snake. Your first time in deep space?"

He scowled. "I've been in space before."

"Well, technically, you're always in space," I said. "Even planetside. It's just the perception isn't as clear when you're on a planet. I find it easy to forget even when I'm on a station." I looked around. "Up here, with the armorglass all around? It's hard to overlook."

Snake swallowed hard as he looked out, his weapon hanging loosely from his hand. "What happens if we break down?" he asked.

"Depends on the nature of the breakdown," I said. "Almost all the systems aboard have redundancy built in. If one part dies, the redundant part takes up the slack. We can fix most things—at least well enough to get back to a station."

He nodded but he didn't look comforted by the information. "How soon before we're there?"

"Hasn't changed, Mr. Snake," I said. "This course adjustment is small and gives us a chance to recharge the capacitors. The next jump will be much longer and the jump error could be larger or smaller. The jump after that will be another long one with the same chance of error. By then we'll be out of juice and we'll need to wait until we can recharge. When we get in-system on that end, we'll need some time to match orbit. Depending on how close we get, how fast we're going, and our entry vector relative to the destination, it could take a while. Maybe as much as a week."

He stared at me. "A week?"

"Most jumps in the High Line take weeks on each end," I said. "Dark Knight is easy to get out of, but it'll take us at least a few days to dock up there when we go back." I let that sink in for a moment. "If I'm not violating any confidences, Mr. Snake, should I plan on you and your party returning with us?"

"Yeah," he said, not looking at me.

Something about his demeanor, his posture set off alarm bells in my head. I expected him to lie, but something about his lie didn't sit well with me. I turned to face front again, sipping at the cold coffee. My old mantra surfaced. The first symptom of not understanding your situation is you're sure that it's under control.

I pondered my assumptions and looked around for the proverbial other shoe.

We made the last big jump before our destination late in the morning. The chief joined us on the bridge, leaving her crew under the watchful eyes of our guests.

"How are we, Mr. Reed?" I asked.

"A little long and well off vector. I'm calculating the course correction now, Skipper."

"Thank you, Mr. Reed. Chief? How much time do you need before we can make the last jump?"

She looked over at me, casting a glance at Snake lurking over my shoulder. "I'll need at least twelve stans, Skipper."

"That long enough to adjust course, Mr. Reed?"

"Should be. I'm running optimizations to get the best cost-time ratio, Captain."

"Thank you, Mr. Reed."

"Why so long?" Snake asked. "It didn't take that long the last time."

"Because, Mr. Snake. The last time we did what we call back-to-back. We jumped twice in a row without recharging the system. Our course correction only took a few ticks because we hit our mark so we were able to take the next step quickly. Now we're off course and there's no juice to engage the Burleson drives that allow us to move through space. Now we stand down, wait for the course burn to put us on track and the fusactors to refill the bucket."

He fidgeted a bit at that and frowned.

"Anxious to see friends and family, Mr. Snake?" I asked.

He nodded and flattened out his expression. "Yeah. It's been a long time."

His body language screamed what his words denied. I knew in my gut he lied. I knew without any question that we were sailing into a trap. For the life of me, I couldn't figure out what direction the danger was coming from, but I knew beyond a shadow of a doubt that it was coming.

I faced forward. Al and the chief both looked at me. I gave a small shrug.

"How are the sleeping arrangements, Mr. Snake?" I asked. I knew the arrangement was taking a toll on them. None of them looked like they'd had a decent night's sleep since we left Dark Knight. I knew the chief was stretching out our transit, so quietly passed the word to make sure none of the guests got more than two stans of uninterrupted sleep. It was risky but it kept them from thinking too clearly about what was going on around them. I still hadn't met the last member of his gang.

"How do you people do this all the time?" he asked.

I shrugged. "It's our life. You get used to it after a few months. You'll be home in your own bunks by this time tomorrow."

"Not a moment too soon," he said and sighed.

I raised an eyebrow in Al's direction.

She nodded.

That's when I knew they didn't plan on letting us return, but I still had no idea how they planned to stop us.

"Burn calculated, Captain. Eleven stans brings us on course by the time the capacitors top off."

"Thank you, Mr. Reed. Execute burn."

"Execute burn, aye, aye, Captain."

After the familiar twist and rumble, I said, "Secure from navigation stations, Ms. Ross. Set normal watch throughout the ship."

"Secure from navigation stations and set normal watch, aye, aye, Captain." She picked up the mic and made the announcements.

I stood up, stretched, and eyed the chrono. "Chief, Ms. Sharps should be serving the lunch mess at the top. Would you join me in the cabin, when you're secured?"

She nodded. "Of course, Captain."

"Mr. Snake? We need to leave the bridge now." I led him down to the cabin where he took up residence on the sofa, cradling his weapon on his lap. The bottom of the weapon showed that he still hadn't reloaded. The slot where the magazine would be gaped, an oblong mouth hungry for ammunition. I couldn't decide if he was really stupid, just oblivious, or so over-confident that he didn't believe anything could go wrong.

I had time to disabuse him of that belief.

The chief knocked on the door frame and entered when I looked up.

"Close it, if you please, Chief?"

She latched the door and took her customary seat.

"How's the ship doing?" I asked, firing up the console and opening a comms channel to the chief's tablet. I typed: *"They don't plan to let us go."*

"Well enough," she said. "We've got enough in the tanks to make it to Telluride in a pinch. Should be plenty to go back to Dark Knight for Penna, Keehn, and Carstairs." She pulled up her tablet and started keying.

"I'm concerned about scrubber cartridges," I said. "It's getting a bit whiffy. We got underway without Penna, too."

My tablet bipped. Her message read: *"I caught that, too. The question is how."*

"I'll check the console when I get back. I haven't noticed it, but you've got a better nose than I do," she said.

I typed: *"I still haven't met the eighth person."*

"Did we get enough printer stock to run up some cartridges on our own?" I asked.

"We can print the filters but not the frames," she said. "I have an order in for the machine that can print frames but it hasn't caught up with us yet." She typed on her screen.

"I don't think we can expect replenishment this stop," I said.

The message on my screen read: *"He's relieved to sleep but they bring him food. He never gets too far from environmental."*

I wrote: *"If they don't want the can to go back, what are they after?"*

"No, I'm not planning on it. Depending on how long it takes us to match velocities and trade cans we may be a little short, but—like I said—we could always drop into Telluride." She typed again.

The message read: *"Something other than silence?"*

I shrugged.

She nodded.

"Well, keep me informed, Chief. See you at lunch."

She nodded, pocketed her tablet, and left the cabin.

"You people lead such boring lives," Snake said. "How do you stand it?"

I looked at him. "Well, every so often the boredom is punctuated with short periods of sheer terror when we wonder whether we'll live through the next tick. Compared to that? Boredom seems pretty good."

His eyes narrowed and a flat smile grew on his lips.

The expression made me worry that he really didn't understand the fresh hell he believed he was going to rain down on us. Or that we were all—literally—in the same boat.

Chapter Thirty-four
Deep Dark: 2376, March 14

The timer ticked down to the jump. "Ready about, Mr. Reed. Hard a-lee."

The stars moved a bit but I probably only noticed because I was watching.

"Jump complete, Captain," Al said "Verifying position."

"We're in the right neighborhood," Mr. Reed said.

"I have the ship on long range," Al said.

Snake stiffened and shifted his grip on the weapon. "How did you know it was a ship?"

Al looked at him. "What?"

"How did you know we were meeting a ship?"

"Mr. Snake," I said. "We're just inside the Oort cloud for the Telluride system. We're barely anywhere at all. What did you think we were going to meet out here? A marching band?"

He shook his head and leaned back against the bulkhead behind me. He did not look like a man who had just jumped home—his gaze twitched around the bridge, his hands kept shifting on his weapon, and he shifted his weight back and forth like he had to take a leak but couldn't find the head.

"How long before we match orbits, Mr. Reed?" I asked.

"Probably four days, Captain. We're a long ways out and are still building our ephemeris data on it."

"Four *days*?" Snake asked.

"That's actually pretty good, Mr. Snake," I said. "I wouldn't have been surprised with four weeks."

"It's Snake. All right. Just Snake. Not mister anything. Snake." The color blossomed across his face as he ranted. "Think you can remember that, Mister-high-and-mighty Captain?"

"Thank you for clearing that up, Snake. You should have said something earlier," I said.

Benny came up the ladder to the bridge and crossed over to Snake. He asked Snake a question, but his voice was too low for me to hear.

Snake kept his voice down but not far enough. "Four more days."

Benny frowned at the answer and shook his head. He glanced in my direction. "What are you lookin' at?"

"I'm looking at you. What are you doing on my bridge?" I asked.

"I'm conferring with my colleague here. Mind your own business." He edged around so his body blocked the view, his back toward me. He had a pouch slung over his shoulder. It looked familiar but I couldn't place it.

I faced front and glanced at Al. I hadn't noticed any of them carrying anything like it before.

"Any update on the ephemeris, Mr. Reed?"

He glanced at me and I made a stretching gesture with my fingers in front of my chest.

"Updates are still coming in. Looks like maybe seven days. I'll know more when we get the last of the light speed data in."

"Thank you, Mr. Reed."

"Ms. Fortuner, any comms from the ship yet?"

"Nothing yet, Skipper. We're still a long way out and it'll take them time to notice us."

"Ms. Ross, do we have any need to stay at navigation stations?"

"No, Captain. We're here and have confirmed our position."

"Very well, Ms. Ross. Mr. Reed do you have a preliminary course for helm?"

"I do, Captain. Passing preliminary course to helm."

"Ms. Torkelson?"

"Preliminary course received, Captain. We are on the beam."

"Thank you, Ms. Torkelson. Ms. Ross, if you'd secure from navigation stations and set normal watch, we'll all get out of Mr. Reed's hair while he works his magic for a final course."

"Secure navigation stations and set normal watch. Aye, aye, Captain. Tom has the watch anyway."

Reed snorted and didn't look up.

Al picked up the mic and made the announcement. "Secured navigation stations, Captain. Logged."

"Thank you, Ms. Ross." I stood and stretched. The two hijackers stood huddled together at the back of the bridge. Snake appeared to be trying to see everything at once. Benny stared at me. It took me a moment to identify the sneer as contempt. I crossed to Reed's position and leaned down. "More time is better, Tom." I all but whispered it into his ear. "Thank you, Mr. Reed. Carry on."

I dropped down the ladder off the bridge, Snake on my tail and Benny behind him. With the tension ratcheting up with our guests, I wondered if my decision to give them the run of the ship was the wisest. None of them seemed to realize they had the run of the ship only because I hadn't taken any of the opportunities to corral them. I headed for the cabin, but dragged my feet a little to hear what Benny might say.

Snake followed me but Benny stopped at the foot of the ladder. I thought he said something about "Davie" but I couldn't tell what the actual sentence was. I pressed into the cabin and took my usual seat behind the desk while Snake sprawled on the couch. I made a note to have it fumigated.

A quick survey of the reports left me no more informed than when I sat on the bridge. I stood and Snake shot to his feet. "Where are you going?"

"Right at the moment, the head. Why? You wanna watch?"

He gave me a disgusted look and plopped back down on the couch. "Unbelievable."

I slipped into the head and pulled out my tablet, sending a quick note to the chief. *"Are your guests carrying pouches on their backs?"*

I left the head and beckoned Snake. "I'm going walkabout. Come on if you're coming."

He rolled his eyes and clambered to his feet.

I dropped down to the mess deck and took a quick survey. The woman, Ms. Grant, stood in a corner, her weapon holstered and her face slack. She looked like she might nod off given half a chance. I stuck my head into the galley. "Ms. Sharps? How are we doing?"

She glanced at the guard in the corner, and I recognized the face but couldn't remember the name. "We're all just peachy, Captain. Rumor is we're only about a week out."

"That's what Mr. Reed said before I left the bridge. How are we fixed for stores?"

She shrugged. "We're good."

I looked at the guard. "What was your name again?"

"Jack."

"Ah, thank you. I'm terrible with names and faces."

I pulled out of the doorway and almost bumped into Snake. "What happened to Mr. Nunya?" I asked, walking off the mess deck and into the passageway.

"Nunya?" he asked. "Oh, Tim? He's sleeping."

"What about Frankie?" I asked.

Snake frowned. "I think he went aft. I haven't seen him for a couple of days."

If there was ever anybody who needed firing for incompetence, it was Snake. None of his crew seemed to be a lot better. I wondered who had thought it a good idea to send them off unattended.

A wash of cold fear streaked down my spine with the answer. "Nobody."

"What's that?" Snake asked.

I shook my head and increased my stride. I dreaded what I'd find aft.

The chief looked up from her console when I stepped into the doorway of her office. "Everything going all right down here?"

"Nice to see you venturing so far from the coffee pot," the chief said. "Seems to be. I've had no complaints from the watchstanders. I'm keeping an eye on environmental. Penna's people seem to know what they're doing."

"We'll give him a raise when we get him back aboard," I said.

"A raise?"

"Sure. He's trained his people to do their jobs even when he's not here to supervise them. That's about as good as we can hope for."

"Well, he should have designated a successor," the chief said.

I laughed. "Yeah, probably but I'd wager the senior engineman might be lording it up a bit."

"Actually, the star is Schulteis," she said.

"The wiper?"

"Yeah. He's been working on his spec-three and pushing the other two to work on their next ratings."

"Spec-three?"

"Somebody told him he didn't need to take all the tests in between," the chief said.

"I wonder who told him that," I said.

She grinned. "You haven't lost your knack for motivating the crew."

"He on duty now?"

She nodded. "Should be."

"Thanks. I'll give him a pep talk."

She eyed Snake behind me and grinned.

I backed out of her office and continued down the passageway, sticking my head into engineering main on the way by. The crew looked relatively unstressed until one barked, "Captain on deck."

"As you were," I said. "Any problems?"

Three heads shook.

I glanced at the coffee mess, noting a stack of dirty mugs. I looked at Wallace. "You're lead on this section?"

"Yes, sar."

I cast a pointed look at the coffee mess before looking back at him with a raised eyebrow.

He gave a little double-take and winced, his face coloring. He looked back at me and nodded.

"Good man. Carry on."

Snake stuck his head in. "Isn't Tim supposed to be here?"

"He relieved the guy down in environmental," Wallace said.

I elbowed Snake out of the way and dropped down two ladders to get to the environmental section. "Mr. Schulteis, the chief tells me you're working on your spec-three."

"I am, Captain. About a quarter of the way through." He glanced at his tablet on the console. "It's tough sledding in places. I'm keeping notes for when Mr. Penna gets back."

"We'll be a while yet before that happens, Mr. Schulteis. If you get hung up, come see me. I was a spec-two in environmental in a prior life."

He grinned as if he thought I was kidding.

"Mr. Nunya, how are you enjoying life aboard?" I asked.

"It's Tim," Snake said. "Not Nunya."

I gave Snake a hairy-eyeball. "He asked to be called Nunya. I'm simply honoring his wishes."

Snake passed the sour look to his colleague.

"It's Tim, Captain."

"Well, Tim, how are you enjoying life aboard?"

"Boring with a capital bore," he said.

I chuckled. "Cheer up. I have a feeling things are going to get pretty exciting here shortly."

Snake stiffened beside me and Tim's eyes widened. "What do you mean, Captain?" Tim asked.

"In a few days we'll be at our destination. I'm not sure what that means for you, but Snake here says you're going to be heading back to Dark Knight with us. You must be looking forward to that."

Tim scowled at Snake. "Yeah. Thrilled, Captain. Delirious."

I walked down into the main processing areas of environmental, between the scrubbers and around the gray water processing tanks. Snake and Tim both followed me. "Mr. Schulteis?"

"Yes, Captain?"

"Do you have any scheduled maintenance?"

"Not this watch, Captain. We replaced some potable-water filters on the last watch. Scrubber two's on the calendar for tomorrow."

I nodded. "Thank you, Mr. Schulteis."

"My pleasure, Skipper."

I tapped a few pipes, peered into a few corners, and turned back toward the watch station, waving Tim and Snake ahead of me.

Tim wore one of the pouches. Snake didn't.

Something about the pouches bugged me. I'd seen them before but couldn't remember where to save my life. To save my life.

"Where's your ringleader?" I asked, sure that I hadn't seen the ringleader yet and a bit worried about the reason.

"Davie? He's asleep, I suspect," Tim said, earning another stare from Snake. He leaned back against the bulkhead and his pouch made a hollow, rubbery sound that reminded me of where I'd seen the pouches before.

I nodded and walked to the nearest emergency suit locker. I opened it and pulled out one of the suits, checking the tab.

"We check those every three months, Captain."

I grinned. "I know you do, Mr. Schulteis. I get the reports. You know how to get into it?"

"Oh, yes, sir. Under thirty seconds."

"Remind Mr. Larson to practice. He was the dead man on our last exercise, wasn't he?"

Schulteis grinned. "He's getting better. We've been working with him."

I nodded. "Good to hear." I racked the suit back in the locker and closed the door. "Carry on, Mr. Schulteis."

Snake followed me out of environmental and up the ladder to engineering. I stuck my head into the chief's office on the way by. "I figured it out."

She raised both eyebrows. "A puzzle?"

"Something like that. You remember the fire drills at the academy? The ones where you had to put on those breathing masks in the smoke?"

"Very well," she said. "I hate those drills."

"I did, too. I hated it worse when—as an upper classman—I had to lead those drills with the first years."

She chuckled. "Leadership begins at home."

"You know what I hated more than the drill itself?"

She shook her head.

"Having to carry the breathing masks around all the time," I said. "Not knowing when they'd spring a drill on us in the barracks or classroom."

She frowned for a moment before the credit registered. Her lips pressed into a line and she gave me the slightest of nods. "I can see that."

I started to leave and turned back. "Oh, I told Schulteis that if he got stuck on the spec-three course he could ask me. He seems pretty dedicated to improving his position."

"That was generous, Captain."

"He told me that Larson is working toward not being the dead man in our next hull breach drill."

The chief nodded again. "He was pretty embarrassed. Penna's been working him hard, too."

"Thanks, Chief. See you at dinner."

"Good to see you, Skipper. Call again."

We headed back up the spine. Snake glanced at me. "What's a dead man?"

"The last person to put his suit on during a hull breach exercise."

"Hull breach?"

I frowned at him. "Yeah. You know. When you get hit with a rock moving at some significant percentage of the speed of light and it punches right through the ship and anybody in its way?"

He stared at me for at least half a tick. "That happens?"

"Oh, yeah." I shrugged as if the prospect of having a ship with a rock-sized hole in it was an everyday, let's-not-worry-about-it kind of thing. Judging from the look on his face, he was thinking more like asteroid-sized and not the typical thumbnail-sized pebble. I smiled and didn't try to disabuse him of the notion. I was sure his own worst fears would work on him harder than anything I might describe.

CHAPTER THIRTY-FIVE
TELLURIDE SYSTEM: 2376, MARCH 20

I had to hand it to Mr. Reed, he led the ship a merry chase around the system before coming into range for the mega. When we got within hailing distance, I had Al try to raise them on voice. The chief joined us on the bridge, peering out at the ship.

"Traffic Local, *Chernyakova*. Over."

"*Chernyakova*, Traffic Local. Stand by."

"They don't seem too surprised," Al said.

"I would be surprised if they were," I said. "We've been swanning around here for a week."

The chief's tablet bipped. She pulled it out and read the message, then stuffed it back into the holster. She gave me one of her sideways grins and glanced at Snake standing in his usual spot at the back of the bridge.

"*Chernyakova*, Traffic Local. Sending you approach vectors now. Hold at outer markers. Over."

"Traffic Local, *Chernyakova*. Roger, hold at outer markers. Out." Al clipped the mic back onto her console. She opened a window, accepted the navigation instruction, and routed it to the helm. "Ms. Torkelson?"

"I have it, sar. New course locked in. We're on the beam."

"Thank you, Ms. Torkelson."

"How soon before we're there?" Snake asked.

"Ms. Torkelson?" I asked. "ETA?"

"Looks like about ten stans, Skipper. We'll be at whatever passes for outer markers here."

"Thank you, Ms. Torkelson." I looked at Snake.

He did not look like a man who was only hours from home after a long voyage. The sweat beaded on his bare scalp and he twitched almost nonstop.

"Something wrong, Snake?"

"No," he said, way too quickly. "Just glad to be back."

"I bet," I said. "Well, there's no use our standing around up here and watching Ms. Torkelson steer. Al, set navigation stations when we're half a stan out."

I joined the chief at the armorglass looking out over the bow. "Do I need to be worried?"

"Always, dear boy," she said. "But not about that." She tilted her head at the monster ship floating in the void ahead of us.

"We're coming down to the wire," I said. "It took me a long time to figure out what they wanted."

"Have to admit. It was clever to dangle the can that needed to be returned," she said. "How long have you known?"

"Couple of days. When I realized they weren't planning on letting us leave." I shook my head. "Just couldn't figure out how this gaggle of giggles was going to pull it off. We could have had them all bundled up before we cleared Dark Knight."

The chief nodded. "It took me a day to figure out why we didn't."

I nodded. "The guy in environmental is the only wild card."

"Davie? Yeah. He's the real deal. I've seen softer hull plates."

I sighed. "Won't be long now."

"Hull breach?" she asked.

"Keep an eye on environmental. It'll start there."

"What'll start?" Snake asked.

"We're due for some scrubber maintenance," I said. "You can tell because the ship starts getting a greasy sheen on the bulkheads."

The chief nodded. "It usually starts in environmental. It got ahead of us without Mr. Penna aboard, but we can deal with it once we're moored."

"Come on, Snake. I've got reports to sign and I need a cup of coffee." I led him off the bridge and down to the mess deck for a cup. I didn't really need to go to the mess deck but I wanted to keep him distracted until the mysterious Davie tossed the gas cylinder into the atmosphere recycling system in environmental.

I had Al set navigation stations half a stan before our projected ETA at the outer markers. As the ship eased into orbit with the mega, it became clear that the phrase "outer markers" did not actually mean what we were used to. There were no buoys. No physical representation at all. I pondered that as Ms. Torkelson brought the ship to zero delta-vee to the monster ship—our respective bows pointing at each other from a distance of a hundred meters. From the bow, the ship looked like a flower. Four cans locked around a central spine formed the petals. The bow nacelle formed the pistil, a ten-meter docking ring dead center.

"Pip is going to be so pissed," I said.

"Traffic Local, *Chernyakova*. Holding at outer markers. Over." Al released the talk button on the mic. "At least I think we're at the outer markers. Hard to tell."

"Roger, *Chernyakova*. Stand by."

"*Chernyakova*, Traffic Local. Sending docking approach vector. Sorry, we haven't got a tug. Over."

"Traffic Local, *Chernyakova*. Roger docking approach. Don't worry about the tug. We'll do our best not to scratch the paint. Out." Al clipped the mic down and tapped a few keys. "Routing docking approach to helm."

Ms. Torkelson nodded. "Docking approach vectors locked, sar."

"Take us in, Ms. Torkelson," I said.

She tapped the maneuvering jets to give us the barest amount of forward way. At this distance we had no visual reference to see we were actually moving, but I could see the numbers on the helm console ticking down.

At the seventy-five-meter mark I said, "Ms. Ross, pipe Mr. Bentley to the bridge, please."

Al looked at me, a question in her eyes but not her mouth.

I cast a backward glance at Snake.

"Mr. Bentley to the bridge. Mr. Bentley to the bridge."

The range to dock fell to fifty meters before Mr. Bentley trotted up the ladder and stopped. "Able Spacer Virgil Bentley reporting as ordered."

"Thank you, Mr. Bentley. Please take a seat at the engineering console," I said.

He frowned but complied. "Aye, aye, sar."

The approach lights on the mega's docking ring blinked amber when we crossed the twenty-five-meter range.

"Captain?" Mr. Bentley asked.

"I know, Mr. Bentley. Bear with me for just a little while longer."

Al gave me an odd look.

I glanced at an increasingly nervous Snake in his customary position behind my seat.

At ten meters the docking ring blinked red and Ms. Torkelson brought our velocity down to a bare crawl.

At five meters, the docking lights turned solid red, painting the bridge with a garish, bloody brush.

Ms. Torkelson swallowed hard. "Docking in three, two, one." She killed our velocity as the two rings mated with the familiar *ka-chunk* that could be felt the length of the ship.

"Helm reports docking, Captain. Docking clamps are locked. Welcome to wherever this is."

I heard a hollow, rubbery sound that I knew too well—the sound of a breathing mask going on over a panicky person's head.

"This is not a drill, Al. Hull breach now."

She slapped the alarm panel and the *wheep-wheep-wheep* sound seemed to split the ship.

I walked aft and pushed a hooded Snake out of the way, cracked open the suit locker, and grabbed the first suit. I continued past the locker to make way for the next person and let the old reflexes push me into the soft, flexible suit that was intended to save my life in the event of loss of pressure. Once sealed in, I turned back to the locker to hand out suits but everybody already had one.

I realized that Snake was crouched in the corner of the bridge with his hands over his ears, yelling "What are you doing?" His breathing hood muffled the sounds.

I crossed the bridge to him in three long strides and grabbed him by the scruff of the neck. I keyed the suit speaker on. "Fun time's over, Snake. Al, you have the bridge."

I dragged him down the ladder so fast he practically fell on the deck. I shifted my grip and frog-marched him double time down the spine. We met a suited Chief Stevens outside engineering main. She held one of the hijackers' weapons.

"Report, Chief?"

"All of ours are suited up. I've secured the blowers so whatever he's done down there is more or less contained for the moment. We can vent the ship on your order."

"Thank you, Chief."

She hefted the weapon. "Benny's. You want it?"

I shook my head and thrust Snake at her. "Hold this for me?"

She grabbed him by his arm and dragged him into a crowded engineering main, thrusting him in the corner with two of his compatriots. "Where's his weapon?"

"On the deck of the bridge, I suspect. He was a little rattled."

"This isn't over," Snake said. "You're docked now. We've got you."

The chief laughed.

"How many are left down there?" I asked.

The chief shrugged. "Coming and going. At least the Davie guy. Maybe one more. Larson hasn't come up yet."

I sighed. "So, maybe hostage." I looked around. "Who's got a weapons rating here? Besides the chief."

Murawsky raised her hand. "I do, sar."

I nodded at the chief who handed the weapon to her.

"You're my backup. If I go down, you get out and tell the chief. Got it?" I asked.

She nodded. "Run and tell, aye, aye, sar."

A flashing red warning on one of the terminals caught my eye. "Chief?" I nodded at the terminal.

She tapped a few keys. "That's cold," she said. "The gas is sarin."

"The old nerve agent?" I asked.

She nodded.

I looked at the three hijackers in breathing hoods that wouldn't protect them from the nerve agent. "Get them into emergency suits. Notify Al on the bridge. Find the other four. They never were the threat. Just the distraction."

"We could have just taken them all out and avoided this," the chief said.

"It's the only way we could be sure they didn't have a bomb aboard," I said. "We'll still need to run a sweep of the ship after they're gone."

The chief nodded. "I have some people who can do that for us. I'll get a decon unit on standby."

"Later. Come on, Murawsky. We got a bad guy to bag."

I dropped down the ladder with Murawsky behind me and got halfway across engineering before a frangible round *spanged* off the deck in front of me. The streak of glass pointed at the shooter and I tucked behind one of the Burlesons. Murawsky had cover behind one of the support stanchions.

"Hold your fire, Murawsky."

"Holding fire, aye, sar."

"You with the gun. How much do you want to die today?"

A woman's voice, muffled by a breathing mask, echoed around the engine room. "You can't get out of here. You're locked to a ship full of our friends and we're the only ones with weapons."

"Murawsky, one round only in the general direction of our misguided friend."

"One round only, aye, aye, Captain." She reached around cover and put a spike of glass into the bulkhead on the far side.

"So, clearly you aren't the only ones with weapons," I said. "You also won't survive very long in that hood."

"I don't have to survive very long. Only until our people come in."

"You don't understand. The people on that ship are our friends, not yours. Your friend Davie released a nerve agent. Sarin. You die from skin contact or inhalation. All of our people are in suits that protect us from it, and we're going to vent the ship shortly so there'll be no air. Your people put you here to die. They didn't tell you the gas would kill you even if you wore the hoods, did they?"

A long pause gave me hope that I'd reached her.

"If that's so, why am I still alive?"

"Because the chief killed the recycling blowers as soon as the hull breach alarm went off. All the gas is in the environmental section at the moment, but eventually it's going to seep out here. The longer you argue, the closer you get to dying. I'm in a suit. I can last a very long time, can even walk through the gas without being hurt. I need to get in there to assess the situation before we vent ship. I can wait until the gas kills you, if I need to. I'd rather not wait that long."

Another long pause.

"Listen. Do you hear the blowers?" I asked. "Throw your gun out and come out with your hands up. We'll get you into a suit."

The pause continued. I looked at Murawsky, who shrugged. I looked at the ladder down to environmental.

"Have it your way," I said.

I grinned at Murawsky and bolted for the ladder. The shooter had no angle on me so I made it without any additional shots.

Somebody had closed and dogged the airtight door at the foot of the ladder. I gave the handle a tug, just to prove to myself that the handle was blocked on the other side.

I sighed and sat on the step, keying my suit radio on and shutting off the external speaker. "Larson? This is the captain. Can you hear me?"

The channel remained quiet.

"Chief?"

"Go ahead, Skipper."

"We have one shooter here on the engineering deck."

"We heard."

"The airtight door into environmental is closed, dogged, and the handle won't budge."

"We can blow it out, burn it out, or wait it out. Your call." The chief sounded serious.

"I was hoping for another solution," I said.

"I figured as much but those are the only ones I've got. Did you try knocking?"

I tried pounding with my fist but the suit glove sounded like I was knocking with a pillow. I spotted a fire extinguisher in the rack at the top of the ladder. I crept up, snagged it, and pulled back before our shooty friend could get a shot off. One came, but I was already halfway back down the ladder.

The fire extinguisher made a much more satisfying noise when applied to the door.

"I knocked," I said.

"It sounded like you used a hammer," the chief said.

"I would have preferred a hammer. I used the fire extinguisher."

I waited for another few heartbeats and raised the extinguisher again but the dogging lever moved, the dogs withdrew, and the door swung inward to reveal a suited Engineman Larson holding a weapon aimed at my nose.

"Larson," I said.

I lowered the fire extinguisher so he could see my face better, then pointed at my sleeve where the suit communicator rested.

His lips formed an "O" and he lowered the weapon, pointing it at the deck.

"Mr. Larson, turn on the radio." I pointed at my wrist again.

He fumbled the weapon until I held out a hand. With a sheepish shrug, he handed me the gun and keyed his suit radio on. "It working now?" he asked.

"Yes, Mr. Larson. Where's Davie?"

He turned and pointed to a figure collapsed against the bulkhead, face down. He wore a breather like the rest.

"Where's the canister?" I asked.

"It rolled under the sedimentation tank, sar. I tried to reach it but I need longer arms. I think it's empty now."

"Chief? How do we clean up this mess?" I asked.

"Close the door and dog it again. That should help keep the gas from spreading."

"Al, you on?" I asked.

"Yes, Captain."

"Round up the rest of our guests. Get them into suits."

"We have somebody at the lock, Skipper," Al said.

"Trying to get out or get in?"

"In. They've been ringing the lock call for the last few minutes."

"Chief?" I asked.

"I've warned them about the gas," she said. "You can let them in."

"You heard her. My compliments to Mr. Bentley, if he'd open the lock and let them in, I'm sure we'd all appreciate it."

Larson pushed the door closed and dogged it again. "Sorry about that, Captain."

"You did well, Mr. Larson." I looked at the body on the floor and shook my head. "What a waste."

"What's that, Skipper?" the chief asked.

"They didn't give Davie any protective gear either."

"We'll save some of them," she said. "Enough to get some answers."

Eventually, I heard a knock at the airtight door and opened it to find a portable decontamination lock mated to the outside. Four people in full hazmat regalia stood outside. I stepped back to let them in.

One of them said, "We need to get you out of the hot zone, Captain."

I pointed to Larson and one of the agents escorted him up the ladder and through the outgoing lock.

"Can you give me the highlights?" he asked.

I pointed at the body. "According to Larson, he opened the canister and fell almost immediately. It's under that tank over there. The room's been sealed and the blowers are secured. It should be contained in this room. The chief has the sensor data."

He nodded and pointed out two of his compatriots. One of them pulled out a folding stretcher and laid it next to the body, while his buddy spread an open body bag on top of it. They rolled the body onto it. When they did, the smoke hood fell off.

I stared at the face. I felt a little light-headed and braced myself on the bulkhead.

"Skipper? You all right?" the agent asked.

"No. Yes. It's not the gas." I just stared at him. "Davie," I said. I took a deep breath and blew it out, letting the memories all play out in my mind.

"What is it?" he asked.

I swallowed the bile down and had to wet my lips before I could speak. "I know him. Percival Herring. Although I think he's also known as David Patterson."

The chief's voice came over the radio. "David Patterson, aka Percival Herring. There's a file on him. Murder. Green Fields, Diurnia. Greta Gerheart. Check for other aliases."

"He supposedly worked for William Simpson," I said. "Pip told me he was a TIC assassin and only moonlighted for Simpson."

"Anything else I should know about in here?" the agent asked. "We need to evacuate you from the area, Captain."

I shook my head and he ushered me up the ladder and into the decontamination corridor, where they washed the suit with soapy water and brushes before having me strip out of it and leave it on the deck. I stepped into the next room where I had to strip out of my ship suit while they showered me off. It was the first time I'd had to go through the process since the academy, but I knew what to expect and suffered the abuse as stoically as I could. The chief handed me a fresh shipsuit and unders, then turned her back to offer a bit of privacy while I changed.

"My tablet is still in the shipsuit," I said.

"You can get it back tomorrow. Along with your stars." She handed me an injector. "If your nose or eyes start running, your eyes hurt, tightness in the chest—use that. Just jam it against your thigh and push the button."

I slipped the injector into my sleeve pocket.

"How do you feel?" she asked.

"I need to take a leak," I said.

The chief looked at Larson. "Looks like the suit drills paid off. How'd that go?"

"He put his gun down and pulled that hood on. The hull breach alarm went off and I grabbed a suit and was in it while he was still fighting to get the canister out of its carrier. I had the suit on and checked with the bridge before he started to open the valve." He took a deep breath and glanced at the corpse. "All that practice saved my life. I'll have to thank Schulteis when I see him."

"You did good, Mr. Larson."

Four people in black and silver jumpsuits marched down the ladder to the engine room. The first guy in line stopped in front of the chief, standing not quite at attention. "Ship's secured, ma'am. We're running the rest of the crew through the showers and keeping them on the other ship for now."

"Good. I'll come over for a full debrief as soon as I can," the chief said. She looked back at me. "You sure you're all right?"

I nodded. "It just surprised me. I never expected to see him again."

She nodded at the guy. "That's all."

"Thank you, ma'am." He and his colleagues left the way they'd come.

"Interesting company you keep, Chief," I said.

She chuckled. "Handy helpers."

"What else do we need to do?" I asked.

"I want both of you to go to the med-bay and let the auto-doc check you out. I don't think it'll find anything, but I'd hate to be wrong." She looked at Larson. "You're off duty. I want this place isolated for a full day. Any residual sarin will have broken down by then and we can start putting the ship back together."

"Can we go that long without scrubbers and filters?" Larson asked.

"Yeah. We'll leave everybody on the mega while we void the ship. I don't want to restart the circulation until we've given any residue a chance to break down."

"That's why they used sarin," I said.

She nodded. "Probably."

"I don't get it, sar," Larson said.

"The gas is an old, old compound. It got overtaken by better ways to kill people. They developed some really vile stuff. Persistent as hell," the chief said. "Luckily, sarin breaks down into harmless compounds in a matter of stans."

Larson shook his head. "No. Why did they want to kill us if we're supposed to take the can back?"

The chief looked at me with a raised eyebrow.

"They didn't want the can," I said. "They wanted the ship."

Larson swallowed hard. "That was close," he said.

The chief clapped him on the shoulder. "It was, Mr. Larson, but right now you have a date with the auto-doc. Take the skipper with you and make sure he gets tested for me, would you?"

He grinned and nodded. "Skipper tested, aye, aye, sar."

The chief winked at him and turned to me. "Go. First principles."

"Feed the crew?" I asked, puzzled by the reference.

"Put your own suit on first."

I couldn't argue with that. "See you later, Chief."

Larson led the way up the ladder and I followed on rubbery legs.

It had been a near thing. Too near. I wondered if I had done the right thing by letting the hijackers have the run of the ship instead of scooping them up when I could. Would I have done the same thing had I known that Patterson was the ringleader? Had I missed a bet by not tracking him down sooner?

I'd never know.

But I also knew he'd never hurt anybody again.

Karma was a bitch, and I had just been reminded why I should stay on her good side.

CHAPTER THIRTY-SIX
TELLURIDE SYSTEM: 2376, MARCH 22

We stayed docked to the mega for two days. It wasn't much in terms of a liberty port, but we treated it as if we were on portside duty. I toured the mega's bridge with Al one afternoon. It didn't look that much different from our own. On the whole, the ship was a bit of an anticlimax.

The chief's handy helpers always seemed to be nearby whenever we went through the lock. They seldom spoke. I never heard them talking with each other. None of their jumpsuits bore insignia of any kind, except there always seemed to be one person with a circular gold badge on their collar tab. I could never figure out if it was significant. For all I knew, it singled out the person who did the best job making their bunk that morning.

The chief brought the atmospheric recycling system back online on the morning of our second day and spent the whole day making sure that the system hadn't been contaminated. She gave it her blessing at the end of the day, and we made plans to head back to Dark Knight the following morning. The crew seemed pleased by the news. After the voyage out, just going home seemed like a cause for celebration and, as a liberty port, the damaged freighter lacked the amenities that crews looked forward to. Or any amenities, for that matter.

Sometime during the second day, one of the black-clad helpers knocked on the cabin door.

I looked up from a fascinating report on the amount of damage the ship had sustained while venting the gas, as well as the estimated replacement cost of the suits we'd given over as evidence. "Yes?"

"Captain, we need to take the cargo as evidence. We have a replacement for you."

"And the equipment to swap the cans?" I asked.

"Yes, Captain. And the personnel to make it all work. The new can is yours to do with as you wish. We'll send you a bill of lading and sale so you won't have any trouble disposing of it."

"Thank you for informing me," I said.

He nodded, turned smartly on his heel, and left.

I wondered what—if anything—was in the replacement can. I supposed I'd find out on the other end.

Al called the crew to navigation stations at 0900, giving Ms. Sharps a chance to clean up from the morning mess. We settled in and Ms. Fortuner sent the request for departure clearance. The response came almost immediately. "We are cleared for departure, Ms. Ross."

"Captain, the ship is clear for departure," she said. "No shore ties. Lock is secured."

"Mr. Reed?" I asked. "Do we have a course?"

"We do, Captain. Sending to the helm, now."

"Helm shows course locked. Ready for departure, Captain."

"Thank you, Ms. Torkelson. Ms. Ross, if you'd do the honors?"

"Releasing docking clamps, aye, Captain." Al tapped some keys and the docking clamps released the ship. "Ship is free in space, Captain."

"Thank you, Ms. Ross. Helm, take us out."

"Take us out, aye, aye, sar." Ms. Torkelson tapped the bow thrusters once, just a tiny push to start the separation between our two docking rings. As we got farther away, she tapped them again and again.

"One hundred meters, Captain," Al said.

"Yaw one-twenty, follow the beam, if you please," I said.

"Aye, aye. Yaw one-twenty, follow the beam, Skipper," Ms. Torkelson said.

"How soon can we jump, Mr. Reed?" I asked.

"We'll need to bring the ship around to the proper vector, Captain. Estimating time to jump at just over a stan."

We puttered away from the mega on just our directional thrusters. We needed be going in the right direction more than we needed to be going fast. Ms. Torkelson played the helm like a concert pianist and I remained quiet, giving her a chance to focus.

The minutes ticked by, giving me plenty of time to ponder the vagaries of the cosmos.

I glanced at the chief, sitting at the engineering console on the bridge. I knew she'd spent at least some time in the engineering section of the mega. We hadn't had much time to talk with each other. Between coordinating the efforts of her handy helpers—who were still "processing" the crew of the mega, whatever that meant—and getting environmental up and running, I suspected she had a hard time finding time to hit the head.

I had time to consider the irony in Patterson's death. As much as Pip had seemed convinced that Patterson should be my target—even as he assured me there was nothing I could do to him if I found him—lying dead in my environmental section had never been how I'd expected to find him. Running across him in a bar? Bumping into him on the docking gallery of some station? Playing poker in any of the casinos? Sure. Doing the things that people did in stations.

Leading a hijacking operation against my ship? No. Never.

I couldn't fathom the odds that—of all the freighters in all the systems in the whole Western Annex—he showed up on mine. Not finding him until he'd been killed by his own boss, face down on the deck in environmental? Those were all just gravy.

"Coming up on it, Skipper," Al said.

"Mr. Reed? Do we have a plan?" I asked.

"I can't speak for you, Skipper, but I plan a long jump from here. We'll do a bit of recharge and then jump back-to-back with a long and a short that should drop us into Dark Knight day after tomorrow."

I laughed. "Too bad you haven't given this any thought at all, Mr. Reed."

He shot me a grin over his shoulder. "Exceeding expectation, Cap."

"Chief? Any problems with the course Mr. Reed has laid out for us?"

"None. Capacitor is full. We're going to carve it down a bit but we should be able to get most of it back before we need to jump again."

"We can jump any time now, Captain," Al said.

"Thank you, Ms. Ross. Mr. Reed, ready about. Hard a-lee."

He punched it and the stars shifted around us.

Pip, Mr. Keehn, and Mr. Penna met us at the dock. Pip looked fully recovered. Keehn and Penna looked contrite. "Gentlemen, it's great to see you," I said.

"Sorry to miss the movement," Mr. Penna said, his gaze fixed on the lock just above my right shoulder.

"Couldn't be helped. Your crew did a great job. You've trained them well. Kudos to Mr. Larson for his quick thinking and Mr. Schulteis for his attention to expanding his skills. I'm sure all three are waiting to tell you all about it." I looked at Mr. Keehn. "Glad to have you back."

"Thank you, sar," he said. "Would it be all right if I went aboard now?"

"Of course, Mr. Keehn." I stepped off the ramp and stood beside Pip. "We've got a lot to talk about. I'll fill you in as soon as we've checked in with Oscella."

He put a hand up to his mouth and stroked it down his chin. "Yeah," he said. "Lemme just say—in regard to Captain Oscella? Three words. Big brass ones."

"What?"

"You'll see. You're heading there now, I suspect?"

I nodded. "I had a message from her on the way in."

"You'll see," he said again.

"Oh, we have a new can. I have no idea what's in it. There's probably a manifest in your inbox."

"Where'd it come from?" he asked.

"I'm going with cargo faeries."

"Cargo faeries?" he asked. "You feeling all right, Captain?"

"Eh. So-so, really."

"Anything you want to talk about?" he asked.

"Yes, but not here. Ideally over a couple of Clipper Ship Lagers somewhere."

He frowned. "I'll drink to that," he said, but he didn't smile. "First round's on me."

The chief came out of the ship and walked down the ramp toward us. "Pip, you missed all the fun."

"Wasn't my fault," he said. "Blame that medic."

The chief just laughed. "I'm sure she was a tremendous help in getting you back on your feet."

Pip shrugged. "I'll catch you when you get back. You're gonna love the story *she* has to tell." With a jaunty wave, he climbed the ramp and disappeared through the lock.

"What was that about?" the chief asked.

"Got me. I don't know what's happened here but it was enough to impress Pip."

"That's a pretty low bar."

It's hard to put my finger on, but being back on Dark Knight Station felt like coming home in a way. It might have been the accumulated stress of having armed hijackers aboard the *Chernyakova*. It might have been that I felt much more at ease in the Toe-Holds. The danger wasn't over. The bomb in the HVAC still represented a serious threat. One I didn't know how we would deal with. That should have made me nervous. Instead, the chief and I strolled through the passages and throughways of the sprawling station as if nothing was wrong.

I did a little window shopping on the way, noting that I'd forgotten to change into civvies. I honestly hadn't noticed until I caught a look at myself in the glass. I glanced at the chief and noted she hadn't either.

"We didn't change," I said.

She gave me a side-eyed glance. "I wouldn't say that."

"Our clothes."

She snorted, but offered no additional commentary.

We turned the last corner and looked down Main Street toward the security barracks.

"That's new," the chief said, nodding at the fusactor building across the way.

The whole top of the building sported blue walls. As we got closer, I could see them flutter a little as the air currents wafted by. "Tarps?" I asked.

"That's what it looks like."

"Not exactly a lot of shielding," I said.

We walked past a newsie stand and the chief's entire face crinkled from the grin. "I don't think it was intended to keep anything in." She pointed at the stand.

"We're Growing Up!" blasted across the front display. A picture of the blue-clad building flashed up, followed by a teaser paragraph announcing new construction.

"It's to keep eyes out," the chief said.

I looked at the stand and then at the building. "Pip said Oscella had a story to tell."

"I'm looking forward to hearing it," the chief said.

We continued down Main Street and walked into the station security office. The officer behind the entry nodded to us. "Captain Oscella's expecting you." A door buzzed to the left. "Go straight through there. Up the ladder, she's the door at the end of the passageway."

Her office hadn't changed. She rose, a smile stretching across her face. "I saw that you'd docked. I'm sorry we didn't prevent that hijacking. They got in before we realized what was happening and you were gone before we could respond."

I shook her offered hand. "It worked out. Odd things happen when somebody's trying to force you to do what you were going to do anyway. What's with the building?"

"Cover story," she said. "Gave us the opportunity to block off the view so we could work up there without anybody seeing exactly what we were doing."

"You seem pretty relaxed for somebody sitting on a nuke," the chief said. "Should I assume it's no longer a threat?"

She nodded and waved us into her guest chairs. "Have a seat." She took her own chair behind the console and leaned back. "I know the general High Line perception of the Toe-Holds is that we're a backwater, but you don't survive out here, thrive out here, without learning how to deal with the people who just want to burn it all down."

The chief leaned forward in her seat. "So? Tarps to block the view. Faraday cage to block radio?"

Oscella nodded. "Yeah. It had to be running off a radio-based trigger, but we couldn't be sure of the frequency so we blocked them all. Once we had the bomb isolated, we brought in some imaging equipment and took a look inside. The radio was easy to find, but we couldn't be sure that cutting the radio out of the system wouldn't set it off."

"You weren't worried that the Faraday cage would?" she asked.

"No. If you're sitting on a bomb, you don't want it to go off just because your radio lost power. Having the receiver active but receiving no signals can't be a trigger unless you're planning on leaving immediately. A simple timer works better for those situations."

"You sound like you've faced bombs before," I said.

She laughed. "Several times every stanyer. The only people who have more experience with bombs is High Tortuga. You'd be surprised how often somebody thinks it would be a good idea to cripple the banking system for the entire annex."

The chief shook her head. "Doesn't surprise me in the least."

Oscella grinned. "In any event, not that many people have the knowledge or wherewithal to build a nuke. The design has been around for centuries but the technology to build them hasn't gotten any simpler or become any more readily available. You really have to know what you're doing to make one and you have to have—and be willing to spend—the credits to do it."

The chief leaned back and steepled her fingers in front of her face. I recognized the pose and waited for her train of thought to pull into the station, but Oscella continued.

"Anyway, once we knew what was inside the case, we were able to get into it and remove the reaction trigger so that even if the detonation signal got through, it wouldn't have a trigger to operate. After that it was pretty simple to take the unit apart, pull the bomb out, and rebuild the unit." She shook her head. "The bomb itself was inside the cooling coil. That HVAC unit was fully functional. It looked and acted just like the others."

"How are you going to find the trigger man?" I asked.

"We found one. When Dumaurier replaced that hacked sensor, he also put a trace-call into the network. When they tried to re-hack it, he traced the location, sent it to us. It was one of his network monitors on the far side of the station. We dragged the guy in. Turned up the trigger when we tossed his quarters."

The chief's eyes narrowed. "He still alive?"

"Yeah," Oscella said. "Why?"

The chief looked at me. "Ishmael, would you be a dear and disappear for about five ticks?"

Oscella's eyebrows rose so fast, I thought they might have attained escape velocity.

I nodded. "Of course, Chief."

I walked out of the office and left the building. Main Street seemed almost painfully prosaic. People walked, sometimes hand in hand, sometimes in groups, often just as individuals strolling or striding along the path. Each of them fully engaged in a life that teetered on the knife's edge. I wondered if they knew how thin that edge was or how near they walked to catastrophe.

I leaned against the building, as much to get out of the traffic lane as support, and let the memory envelop me, of that day, that evening, that single event that had nearly ended my life and taken Greta's. The knife's edge, indeed.

Oscella's almost cavalier attitude should have made me—at least— uneasy. "Oh, well. Another bomb. Best deal with it." I marveled that my inner self wasn't screaming "Are you mad?"

Something about the previous few days seemed to have desensitized me. Or perhaps reset my brain. Watching those idiots threaten my crew did it, perhaps. I had been less worried about one of them doing something on purpose than that they'd do something stupid out of ignorance. I still couldn't really believe Snake never understood that I'd effectively disarmed him—or didn't understand that taking the ammunition out of the weapon made it nothing more than a high-tech club.

A colder side of me could understand why that crew had been selected. When you're engaged in criminal behavior with unstable characters, getting rid of problem members of the crew had to be difficult. You couldn't just fire them. Killing them outright sends a bad message to the rest. Dropping them quietly out of air locks brings too many people into the mix. Whoever had done it must have seen it as a particularly clever ploy.

The critical side of my brain kept telling me I should have just rounded them up and stuffed them out the air lock myself. It would have been easy enough. I certainly couldn't have kept them. The ship had no brig and I couldn't think of a compartment I could have used as one.

I closed my eyes and rested my head back against the solid metal building. The image of David Patterson came unbidden. His eyes staring, tear-tracks across his face and snot crusted under his nose. Probably drowning in his own fluids as the sarin attacked his lungs. Betrayed by his own people. I took a couple of deep breaths and something inside started to uncoil.

Mal Gaines's question rose in my mind. "How did it make you feel?"

I thought back to the *Lois*, to working on my ratings, to the friendships and camaraderie I'd enjoyed there. A level of connection I'd not felt before. My cynical self tried to tell me I hadn't felt it since. Then I thought about the *Tinker* and remembered the *Agamemnon*. Even the family I'd left on the *Iris*.

I didn't have to go very far down that hole to bump into the *Chernyakova*.

"Ready?" The chief startled me.

"Yeah," I said. "I think I am. You all done with Oscella?"

She nodded.

"Do we need to wait around?" I asked.

"For what?"

"For your people to pick up the device and the trigger man?"

She gave me a glance and a small smile. "No."

"I'm planning on doing a normal four-day layover. I don't know if Pip has a cargo yet, but that should give him time."

"It'll give me a chance to go through environmental with hot water and disinfectant."

"Disinfectant? You expecting hijacker germs or something?"

"No, but sarin plays hell with some of the organics in there. I want to scrape it down, clean up any potential problems, and reset the area with fresh materials." She shrugged. "It's probably not necessary, but I'll feel better about it."

We walked a while without speaking.

"You seem different," she said. "You all right?"

"Yeah. No. I don't know. Seeing Patterson was a shock. Seeing him dead was ..." I shrugged. "I don't even know how to describe it."

"Anticlimactic?" she asked.

"Something like that. For so long he's been the boogeyman. The danger in the dark. Then Pip convinced me to come out here and find him."

"Confront your fears," the chief said. "See him as human."

"Think Pip was thinking that deep?" I asked.

She threw back her head and laughed. "Oh, hell, no." She stared me straight in the eye. "But you are."

"I don't think Pip's all that bad," I said.

Her jaw dropped and she stopped right in the passageway, spinning me to face her. "How can you say that?"

"He's never had friends. I might be the only one he's ever known. It's probably why we bonded on the *Lois*. Yeah, he's a prankster. He's been a lot darker lately, but I don't think that's even something he's aware of."

"Are you kidding? He's got family from Impromtu to Chiba. They run probably the single largest private shipping company in the Western Annex. The Carstairs brand is bigger than anything in shipping by a factor of two and I suspect the only company that's worth more is Usoko Mining. Manchester, Mellon-Merc, Pravda—none of them are close."

I shrugged. "Family is family. I didn't have much of one. Getting to know my father this late in life has been interesting and—in a certain sense—challenging."

I turned to continue walking toward the ship.

"His family is huge," the chief said.

"Yeah, but you don't really get to pick your family, do you? They're the people who accept you for who you are, for the most part. I know there are exceptions."

"Your point?" she asked.

"Friends are the people who pick you because they want to. They accept you for who you are, not what your relationship with them might be."

She frowned at me but kept walking.

Chapter Thirty-eight
Dark Knight Station: 2376, March 26

As soon as I got back to the ship, I had Al pass the word that we'd be docked for the full four days. I felt a collective sigh pass through the crew at the news. It hadn't been the longest trip we'd ever made by a long shot, but I couldn't remember a more stressful one. The reality didn't set in for me until the second day, when I realized nobody was threatening the crew, the ship, or me.

I sat in the cabin and looked at the shearwater on the bulkhead. My hands started shaking so bad, I had to put my coffee cup down so I wouldn't spill. The cabin door stood open and Pip took advantage of it by strolling in and taking up residence in a guest chair.

"Do you have any idea what was in that can?" he asked.

I shook my head and pressed my palms on the desk. "What?"

"Two hundred metric kilotons of refined tellurium."

"Did you sell it?" I asked.

"Sell it? No, I came to find out who it belongs to. There's a bill of lading showing the can came from Telluride but no delivery address."

"It's ours."

He blinked. "Where'd you get it?"

"Traded a bag of magic beans for it."

"What's in that coffee?"

"Nothing, but I wouldn't mind a shot of rum."

He glanced at the chrono. "At 1030?"

"It's five o'clock somewhere."

He got up, closed the cabin door, and returned to his seat. "Wanna talk about it?"

I shook my head.

"I'll stay and irritate you until you do," he said.

He surprised a laugh out of me and I felt the spasms releasing me. "He's dead. Patterson."

Pip sat up straight in his chair, staring at me across the desk. "David Patterson?"

"Yeah."

"Did you do it?"

"What? Kill him? No. What the hell?" The idea that he thought I might be capable of it left me shocked and appalled. "What kind of man do you think I am?"

He settled back, a smile playing around the edges of his mouth. "Well, I happen to know you were hijacked, flew out into the Deep Dark at gunpoint, and swapped that can of trash for a can of treasure." He shrugged. "I've heard that you visited the mega, turned over the hijackers to persons unknown, and thwarted a nerve-agent attack."

"Not in that order," I said.

Pip laughed. "Fine. Not in that order." He paused to look at me. "I didn't hear that Patterson was the deader. I thought it was just one of the hijackers that got caught in the crossfire."

"The people behind the hijacking gave the gang a canister of nerve agent. Sarin. Of the eight people aboard, the guy they had guarding environmental never crossed my path. I never knew he was aboard until they started dragging the body out and his smoke mask fell off."

"Smoke mask?" he asked. "Like at the academy?"

"Yeah. That's what tipped me off that they were planning on gassing us. The lot of them started carrying around their masks."

"But a smoke mask won't protect against nerve agents."

I nodded. "The only one who died was Patterson. He was the one with the canister."

"How badly did somebody want him dead?" Pip asked.

"They wanted the ship. I suspect that whoever hired him saw it as a good way to fire him."

"What happened to the rest?" Pip asked. "Everybody's being pretty tight-lipped."

"Somebody had taken over the station by the time we got there. They relieved us of the hijackers and the body, the contaminated goods, and the can we took out. They gave us a new can in return."

"Are these the good guys or the bad guys?" Pip asked.

I shrugged. "I'm calling them the good guys. They didn't try to kill us, commandeer the ship, or enslave any of the crew."

"That's a pretty low bar," he said with a grin.

"Given the number of people who've tried to do some variation on those over the last month, I'm all right with it."

He opened his mouth but closed it again without saying anything. He nodded after a few moments. "Good point. I hadn't looked at it that way."

"Do we have a can?" I asked.

"Not at the moment. What're you thinking?"

"Port Newmar. We need to have a stockholders meeting and most of them are there. I suspect the chief's about to leave us. Al might be willing to stay for a while." Mal Gaines was there but I didn't see the need to bring it up.

"May need to go roundabout," he said.

"Fine."

He paused and looked at me again. "You sure you're all right?"

"I'm relatively sure I'm not." I shrugged. "I'll get better."

"Dinner ashore tonight?" he asked.

"Yeah. Sounds good actually."

"Really?"

"Why did you ask if you thought I wouldn't go?" I asked.

"I just didn't expect you to give in so easily."

"Neither of us has that many friends."

He stared at me for almost a full tick. "We can stock up on Clipper Ship Lager," he said.

"As good a reason as any," I said.

He nodded a couple of times, almost as if to himself, before pushing himself out of the chair. "All right, then," he said, clapping his hands. "Meet at 1800. I found a great little bistro just off Main. Janine introduced me to it. You're going to love it." He headed for the door.

"Janine?" I asked.

He grinned over his shoulder on the way out the door. "My med-tech. You met her, didn't you?"

I laughed. "See you at 1800," I said.

The shaking had stopped. I couldn't be sure it wouldn't come back but I felt the need to move. I changed into my old comfortable jeans and an olive pullover, and slipped into my ship boots. I looked at the burgundy suit on its hanger and turned my back on it. That wasn't who I was. It might have been once. Not anymore.

I walked through the main portion of the cabin and stared at the blank wall again. Every time I looked at it, I thought about the *Agamemnon*. I grabbed my tablet, stuck it in a pocket, and left the cabin behind.

Ms. Cross passed me coming up as I was going down the ladder. "How's the painting project coming, Ms. Cross?"

"We haven't actually decided on what to paint there yet, but the committee is coming closer to consensus, Captain."

"The committee?" I asked.

She nodded. "Yes, Captain. I started canvassing the crew about what to paint on the spine. A couple of the engineers thought they should decide because they use the spine the most."

"What do you think about that argument?"

She took in a deep breath and blew it out slowly. "It has merit, sar. On any given day, way more engineers than deck division people use it."

"But?" I asked.

"Well, sar, it's our ship, too. I think having them have some input on what should be there is a good idea, so I recruited them to the committee. I got Ms. Torkelson to join, too. Ms. Ross agreed to be the tie breaker."

"Ms. Ross?"

"Yes, sar. She seemed quite intrigued by the project."

"How are you coming on your next rating, Ms. Cross?"

"I'm almost through the able-spacer work, sar. I should be ready when the next test period comes around."

"Well, done, Ms. Cross." As I started down the ladder something the chief said popped into my head. "Tell me, Ms. Cross, have you considered the academy?"

"The academy, sar?"

"Yes, the merchant academy at Port Newmar."

She laughed, almost a nervous giggle. "Not possible, Captain."

"Why not?"

"Well, for one, it's expensive. I don't have that many credits just floating around, sar."

I bit back on a laugh. "I used that line on my captain, too, Ms. Cross."

"What happened, sar?"

I did laugh that time. "I went to the academy." I gave that a moment to sink in. "You never know what's possible until you do it. Just think about it, Ms. Cross." I started down the ladder again.

"Thank you, Captain. I will."

"Good luck with your committee," I said.

As I passed the mess deck, I glanced in to see Al standing in the middle of the deck. She appeared to be staring at the bulkhead, deep in thought. Every so often she'd shift her weight or tilt her head. I grinned to myself and left her to her ruminations.

"I'm going ashore, Ms. Torkelson."

"Aye, aye, Captain. Do you know when you'll be back, sar?"

"I'm meeting Mr. Carstairs for dinner at 1800, but I should be back by 2200 at the latest."

"Thank you, sar. I'll leave a note."

"Thank you, Ms. Torkelson."

She keyed the lock from her station, but I turned back to her. "How are you doing on your next rating, Ms. Torkelson?"

"Spec-one helmsman," she said. "Very close to being ready for the exam."

"Get with Ms. Fortuner. She should have the dates. She'll need to know when you're ready so she can have the exam for you."

"I'm hoping to take it when we dock at Port Newmar, sar."

"Port Newmar?"

"Yes, Captain. Isn't that where we're going next?"

"It is, yes, but how did you know?"

She shrugged. "Corporate office for Phoenix Freight, isn't it?"

"Technically we're incorporated at Diurnia," I said. "But you're right. Most of the board of directors lives at Port Newmar."

She nodded. "You're overdue for a stockholders meeting if I've read the by-laws correctly. I just figured that after the last voyage, we'd be grabbing a can headed that way."

"You read the by-laws?"

"Of course, Captain. I mean, not everybody does, but I like to know the kind of company that's keeping me, sar." She grinned.

"Would you have left if you found something you didn't like?"

She looked down the passageway as if looking for help.

"It's not a problem. I'm just interested in your perspective as a member of the ship's company."

"Well, yes, sar, I probably would have." She looked down at her console. "I almost did."

"Are you comfortable telling me why?"

She steeled herself, stiffening her spine and raising her eyes to look at me. "Why I stayed or why I almost left, sar?"

"Whatever you're comfortable with, Ms. Torkelson. Nothing at all, if that's your choice."

She stared for a moment before making up her mind. "There are companies that say one thing and do another. The Phoenix by-laws are just boilerplate. They're the minimum required."

"And you almost left because of that?" I asked.

"No, sar. That's actually pretty common. It's probably smart. You can't get in trouble for not doing things you didn't say you were going to do." Her eyes glazed over a bit. "Did that come out right?"

"I got the drift, Ms. Torkelson. You have my attention."

"So, yeah. Captain. It's pretty common. So you have to look at what the company does. How they treat people. What they stand for."

"We don't measure up?" I asked.

She looked down.

"I would really like to know, but if you're not willing to say, I can respect that, Ms. Torkelson."

"So, you pulled me off the docks at Breakall, Captain. That counted. You rehabbed the ship. That was huge. It broke my heart every time I came aboard. You sank I have no idea how much into this ship to make it whole and you brought me along. For that, I thank you."

"But?"

"But you didn't seem to care. It was like after all the work, it was done. We're just going to go through the motions and make money and carry on like what we do doesn't matter." She looked ready take a fist to the jaw but stood her ground. "Sar."

"That's quite an accurate assessment, Ms. Torkelson."

"What?"

"Your assessment seems very accurate, Ms. Torkelson. You're right. What made you ship out with us again?"

"I wanted to give you, the company, one more shot. A new ship. A new crew. I knew there were lots of ghosts, lots of baggage. Not just you. Ms. Ross. Mr. Carstairs. Chief Stevens. Heck, even Ms. Sharps."

"And what have you decided," I asked. "Anything? Should I expect to replace you when we get back to Port Newmar?"

"I've decided that I was right to give it another shot, sar," she said.

"I'm pleased to hear it, Ms. Torkelson. Can I ask why?"

She shrugged. "Lots of stuff. The way you handled those hi-jackers. Ms. Sharps has a galley she's proud of. She sings in there sometimes when she thinks nobody's around. Kris Cross is going to be able spacer soon. You don't know what that really means. That was a girl who had nothing. Nothing. When we first shipped out, I wasn't sure she wouldn't hang herself in the head before we got back."

"Ms. Cross?" I asked.

"Yeah. Seriously, Captain. Have you seen her lately?"

"I just talked to her about the spine, actually."

"She seem like somebody ready to cash out her chips, sar?"

"No, Ms. Torkelson. She certainly didn't."

Ms. Torkelson shrugged, as if to say "I rest my case."

"Thank you, Ms. Torkelson. I appreciate your candor."

"You're welcome, Captain. Enjoy your time ashore."

I started off the ship but stopped at the top of the ramp. "Do we stand for something now, Ms. Torkelson?"

"Sar?"

"Before. You said you didn't think we stood for anything."

"Oh." She nodded. "Yes, I did."

"Do you still think that? Or do we stand for something now?"

"We stand for each other, Captain."

"Thank you again, Ms. Torkelson."

"Any time, Skipper." She paused for a heartbeat. "Can I ask you a question, Captain?"

"Of course, Ms. Torkelson."

"Weren't you scared? Taking that gun away from Snake. I almost threw up a little when you leaned right up against the gun like that. Then you just took it away from him like he wasn't even holding on." She swallowed. "Sar."

"Yes, I was scared, Ms. Torkelson. I was afraid of what he might do with that weapon. In my defense, I recognized it as an orbital defense weapon that I'd trained with at the academy. When I grabbed it from him, the safety was still on and the charging coil was off—it couldn't have fired even if he'd pulled the trigger. The biggest danger was of jamming my fingers trying to get the magazine out and clearing the chamber."

"Oh," she said. "It looked a lot more dangerous than it was then?"

"Afraid so, Ms. Torkelson."

She nodded and leaned forward a bit. "I won't tell anybody, sar."

"Thank you. Ms. Torkelson." I chuckled all the way down the ramp.

I strolled along the gallery and wondered if that's what Gaines had meant by asking "What will you stand for?" The truth was I really hadn't given it much thought. I really hadn't been thinking much at all. I'd been stupidly lucky taking Snake's gun away without getting my chest filled with glass. I'd been lucky that I spotted those pouches and that the lot of them had been incompetent in the extreme. I felt my hands start to jitter so I stuck them in my pockets and kept walking. I tried to distract myself by trying to reconcile the vibrant Ms. Cross with the picture Ms. Torkelson painted. I kicked myself figuratively several times, but at least my hands stopped shaking.

I'd been shopping at Dark Knight before with the chief, who seemed to know exactly where to take me. I thought about that a bit on the stroll. I took the short cut to Main Street, ducking through what would have been an alley in any city I'd ever been in.

Not like I was much of an expert on that. Odd that space had seemed so foreign in the beginning, but now I couldn't imagine living anywhere else. Of course, I'd been barely eighteen then. I'd lived more than half my life in the Deep Dark. I had no real explanation of why that made me feel like I'd accomplished something.

The Main Street looked the same, no matter what time of day. I wondered if there were times when there was more or less traffic. If the shops ever closed. I really had no plan in mind. No real goal. I just wanted to get off the ship. To not be the captain for a few ticks. Myself and my thoughts, loose on the world. I felt like such an idiot, but I smiled because I could.

I looked in the windows as I went. Much like those on the orbitals, shops displayed merchandise in various ways. Mannequins with clothing. Lots of clothing. Much of it a little bit garish.

One shop drew me in with a display of boots. I recognized the smell of real leather and oil as soon as I stepped through the door. An old man looked up from a work table when the bell over the door chimed. "Can I help you?"

"I might need a new pair," I said.

He snorted. "Ya do or ya don't. No matter. You look like a boot man. Spacer?"

I nodded.

He waved me over. "Show me."

I crossed the tiny shop and he peered down at my footwear. "You wear these all the time?"

"No. They're my comfy boots."

He glanced up at me with a grin that showed white teeth gleaming against dark and wrinkled skin that looked like it was only one step removed from leather. "Son, there's comfy boots and the wrong boots. These boots are nice and broken in. Show me the soles."

I felt a little strange lifting a foot so he could look at the bottom of my boots.

He nodded. "Yeah. Getting a little worn. Heels could use some work." He rubbed his chin and stared at my feet. "New pair's going to be stiff. Take you some time to break them in. They won't fit like those do for a while. What to do you wear on the ship?"

"Normal ankle boot."

"Rubber sole? Steel toe?"

I shook my head. "They've got a little tread on them."

"Basic spacer boot," he said. "So you're not an engineer." He eyed me up and down. "Not steward. Hands aren't red enough."

His eyes widened as he looked into my face. "Ah. Sorry, Skipper. I shoulda spotted that first thing."

"Not a problem. Honestly, I saw the boots in your window and the scent of good leather just drew me in."

He grinned. "So? Dress or casual? These look like they might have been dress at one time."

"I'm not much for dress," I said.

He nodded. "Fleet once," he said. "Probably still but you don't really fit in, do ya?"

I wondered what he saw when he looked at me.

"No matter. Come here. Sit down. Take those off and lemme look at 'em."

I slipped the boots off and handed them over.

"Put your feet on that plate," he said. "Lemme see what we're working with."

I spotted the glassy plate on the decking and rested both stockinged feet on it.

He looked up from his examination of my footwear and glanced down at my feet. "Yeah. Good. Stand up. Right on it. It'll hold ya."

I stood and looked down.

"Not like that. Atten-HUT," he said. "Eyes front. Knees slightly bent. You know the drill."

I snapped to attention and almost laughed.

"Been awhile since anybody called you to attention, eh?" He chuckled.

"Yes. Rather a long while," I said.

He pulled out a tablet and looked at the readouts. "That's got it. Nothing seriously wrong with the way you're standin'." He looked from the readouts to my feet a couple of times. "Yeah. That's good." He nodded and handed my boots back to me.

"So, what'd'ya think, Doc, will I live?"

"Oh, sure, but your days of playing piano are behind you," he said.

I laughed and slipped my boots back on.

"You want a new pair like those?" he asked. "But new? You'll have to break them in yourself, of course."

"Yes." The word popped out before I realized it. "How soon?"

He shook his head. "Next time you come back to Dark Knight."

"It'll be weeks. Maybe months."

He nodded. "You're not exactly the first spacer I've dealt with. I got a room full of boots back there." He jerked a thumb at the back of his shop. "Lemme set up your account. Take less than a tick. Next time you're here, swing by."

"Aren't you afraid you'll do the work and I'll never come back?"

He shook his head and started tapping on his tablet. "Half now to cover the cost of materials. Half when you pick them up. I might have made five or six pairs in the last couple of decades and didn't get paid. Still have the boots. New owner might come for them." He shrugged. "Don't matter. I'm doing what I like doing. I make enough from people who pay." He thrust the tablet at me. "Thumb that and we're done except for the color."

I looked at the sum on the tablet and thumbed it. "Black, please."

He nodded. "I figgered. Goes with anything. You can dress up or down and still wear black. Lemme flash you a receipt, Captain, and you can be about your business."

I held my tablet and accepted his beam. "Thank you," I said.

"Thank you for your custom, Captain." He tossed his tablet down on the table and returned to his work. "They'll be ready for you to pick up in three weeks."

I left the shop and noticed that he had a real bell above his door. I could still hear it jingling from the sidewalk outside. I stood there for a moment and wondered why I'd bought another pair of boots. Why it felt so good to have done it.

A shop window across the street caught my eye. I crossed to get a better look. The display showed two dolls in fancy dress sitting across from each other, having tea. An ornate teapot stood on a silver tray, the cups—too big for the dolls—on the table between them. Decorative tins of tea stood in stacks around them. Of course, I went in.

The scent of tea leaves filled the place. The mélange tickled across my nose with hints of jasmine and bergamot layered on a musky, black-tea base. I wasn't much of a tea drinker but the scent of exotic teas soothed something inside me. Several other shoppers wandered the store. The cashier did a steady business, his smile broad for each new buyer who stepped up to the counter. The long side wall held shelves of tea—some in tins, some in paper boxes wrapped in film, some in ornate wooden chests. I followed the wall all the way to the end, all the while wondering if I would buy some while arguing that I probably wouldn't drink it. Ms. Sharps already stocked tea for the crew. Brewing my own felt almost sacrilegious. The end wall held cubbyholes—every hole held exactly one cup, each different from the rest.

The wall reminded me of *Sifu* Newmar's studio with the wall of cups in the kitchen. I scanned the collection, wondering for a moment if she'd been here, if this shop had been the inspiration for her wall or—vice versa—some academy grad had settled here to establish the shop. A lot of the cups reminded me of styles she had. Simple round clay cups in dun and white, some ornately shaped and colored, some with intricate blue scenes of birds and branches, some with simple flowers. The sight was almost dizzying. I remembered an empty slot in Newmar's wall at the same moment I saw one of the fancier, delicate cups—red hibiscus trumpets practically glowed around the sides. I reached for it at the same moment another customer did, bumping hands before we both retreated.

"Sorry," I said, turning to her—a youngish woman, well, younger than I was by maybe three or four stanyers. She wore a leather jacket, much worn but clearly loved. I lost myself in the dark brown pools of her eyes. In short, she was stunning. Literally. She stunned me into silence for a moment that felt like forever but probably was only a few heartbeats. "Sorry," I said, again.

She withdrew her hand and cleared her throat. "We both want the same cup," she said.

I took half a step back and waved her forward. "I can find another."

"No, that's fine," she said. "It's not important."

A woman nudged her shoulder. "Nats? You all right?"

The first woman blinked a couple of times and looked over at her friend. "Yeah. Yeah, I'm fine. Why?"

The second woman—slightly taller with a hint of epicanthal fold—looked as striking as the first. Not as stunning as her friend, Nats, but with the command bearing of a senior deck officer. She placed her hand on her friend's shoulder as if to protect her from me. She wore an academy ring which gleamed in the spotlights aimed at the various cups. It didn't surprise me.

I took another half-step back. "Sorry," I said, a third time.

"They probably have a box of them in the stockroom, Nats."

A clerk hovering nearby stepped in. "Actually, we don't. Each cup is unique. Some are very old. My partner and I have been collecting them from all around the Western Annex. Estate sales, flea markets. You'd be surprised what you can find at a flea market." He winked at me.

I laughed. "I started out in a flea market. I've seen a lot of things there."

He gave me a nod. "Then you know." He scanned across the row and pointed out a different cup. "There, the blue hibiscus on the end. They're from the same source, the same maker. Both very old bone china. They may have come from the same set. At one point in time, it was fashionable to have a set with different colors of the same pattern on all the cups. The hibiscus was a common choice because the real flowers come in a variety of colors, making a tea service look like a garden of mallows." He smiled at each of us in turn.

"I can take the blue," I said.

She glanced at me and nodded. "I'd like the red."

Her friend narrowed her eyes at me. It wasn't quite a threat, and I wondered if she thought I might be one. Honestly, I didn't blame her being a little jealous of her partner.

The helpful clerk nodded. "Wonderful. Let me get some boxes for you."

He reached into a drawer under the display and pulled out two flats and some tissue paper. It took him almost no time to assemble the glossy white boxes, line them with tissue and nest the cups inside. He left the tops open and handed the blue one to me, the red one to her.

I thanked him and stepped away to pick up a canister of tea to go with the cup.

"You sure you're all right, Nats?" the second woman asked. She spoke softly but clearly didn't care if I overheard.

"Yeah. I'm good, Zee. Let's check out and head back to the ship."

I watched them complete their transaction with the cashier and leave the store. I couldn't help myself. It wasn't their looks, although neither of them lacked. It was the way they moved. Nats moved like a cat. She reminded me of Bev from the *Lois*. She had the same smooth, contained gait. I wondered if she was as deadly as Bev could be. Her friend was definitely fleet. The way she stood. The way she looked around the room. The ring gave away her academy background but she didn't strike me as engineering or cargo.

"Excuse me?" A man beside me pointed at the shelf I was blocking. "I just need to grab a can?"

"Oh, sorry." I stepped back, the spell broken. I found a kilo tin of green tea to go with the cup and checked out. The chrono on the wall behind the cashier told me I needed to head back to the ship and drop off my purchases. I'd spent more time than I'd realized.

I stepped along sharply on the way back. I told myself it was because I was late, but I got to the lock and felt a little let down that I hadn't been able to catch another look at Nats and her friend.

CHAPTER THIRTY-NINE
DARK KNIGHT STATION: 2376, MARCH 26

Pip, as always, found the places with good beer. The "little bistro" turned out to be the least likely looking restaurant I'd ever seen. To begin with, it had no chairs. The tables were on long poles bolted to the deck. They fell at about the right height for most people—a little tall for me and Pip, a little short for taller people. When he had said, "just off Main Street," he wasn't kidding. It was—literally—in the alley between two buildings, Tammy's Music on one side and a Fidelity Cargo office on the other. I never did figure out where the kitchen was.

He led me to a table and leaned his elbows on it, propping up his head in his fists. "Somebody will be along shortly." He nodded at a display on the wall of the music store. "Beers du jour. The pilsner is nice. The lager is terrific. The stout is so-so. Stay away from the wheat." He made a face. "Watery would be understating it and failing to convey the nature of the actual crime."

I laughed. "Judgmental at all, are we?"

He held up his hands, palm out. "I'm just saying. You might like it. I won't think any less of you as a person."

"Yes, you will."

"Yes, I will," he said with a shrug.

A guy on roller skates zoomed up to the table. I looked down at them. "Snazzy. How do you stand up?"

"Practice and a grav unit on my belt," he said. "Food? Beer? What?"

"I'll have the Squire Lager. What's the special?"

"Spicy barbecue pork loin sandwich. Side of fried potatoes."

"Real barbecue?" he asked.

"Got a pit and everything."

"How spicy?" Pip asked.

"Just regular but the pork has a bit of fire on it. It doesn't exactly bite you back but you know it's there."

"Yes. Skipper?"

"Got a porter?" I asked.

"Knight Time," he said. "Nice color, good heft. A solid brew with some coffee and chocolate notes in the malt. Light on the hop so you don't get bitter at the end."

"He's always bitter," Pip said.

The guy looked at Pip. "Really? That's the best you got?"

Pip shrugged. "I'm out of practice."

The guy looked at me with a raised eyebrow.

"I'll take it."

"You want the special or should I recite the menu?"

"Special," I said.

He snapped his fingers. "Darn, I was hoping to recite the menu. See if I remembered it from this afternoon." He shook his head and tapped on the table with a knuckle. "Be right back." He zoomed off.

"Roller skates? Is he really wearing roller skates?" I asked.

Pip nodded. "A little gimmicky and I can't imagine how much food and beer they spill a night."

A woman wearing skates circled the table. "Less than you think," she said with a wink and rolled away.

"Ya have to admit," he said. "It's different."

"I can't fault you there."

The guy slid to a stop and placed two pint mugs on the table. "Food's up in a sec." He was gone before I could speak.

"Can't fault the service, either," Pip said, taking a pull from his pint and sighing in satisfaction. "Not Clipper Ship but damn fine."

I tasted the porter and found it to my liking. I toasted Pip with the mug. "If the food's as good, we have a winner."

He clinked his mug to mine and we settled in.

The sandwiches lived up to the beer and, after the second round, I didn't mind the table height as much, but I was ready for a sit-down. We settled up and headed back to the ship.

"What do we do now?" I asked.

Pip looked at me. "I thought we were going back to the ship."

"Not now now. Now next."

"We only had two rounds," he said.

"We found the mega. Patterson is dead. Do you have some other secret mission to drag us around the Western Annex on?"

Pip looked down at the deck and stayed quiet for so long I thought he might be sleepwalking.

"Spit it out," I said.

"I quit. That was my last outside job."

"That's not going to sit well with your boss, is it?" I asked.

"Well, I haven't actually quit. I need to do a sit-down with them when we get to Port Newmar."

I looked at him, really looked. "You're serious."

He nodded.

"Is it because you got kidnapped and roughed up?"

"No. Not that. It's not the first time, actually. These people were amateurs."

"Yeah, our hijackers were, too. I screwed up on that one," I said.

He glanced at me. "Why do you say that?"

"Because I assumed that they were *all* amateurs. I only went out of my way to check out the Davie character once, but never made it a point to actually track him down. In the end, the only thing that prevented that plan from succeeding was his mistake in trusting his client."

"Not the way I heard it," he said.

"What did you hear?"

"Overlooking the star-struck renditions of the Captain and the Snake, you spotted the smoke hoods, alerted the chief who spread the word through the crew. The hull breach alarm killed any chance the plot had of succeeding in killing the crew. Even if Patterson had been wearing a full hazmat suit, the plot ended there. Dealing with him afterward would have been a lot dicier, but you beat him at his own game. Fair and square."

I shrugged. "Eh, I just keep thinking of things I could have done differently, better." I kicked an empty paper cup. It skittered across the deck and bounced off the bulkhead in front of us. I stopped to pick it up and crumple it into a recycle bin. "It took me forever to tumble that they didn't care about the can. They wanted the ship. They almost got it."

Pip slung an arm over my shoulder—which must have appeared comical because he was about three centimeters shorter—and leaned in. "This is what you do, Ishmael. You need to stop it. You're second-guessing yourself. In the heat of the moment, you're one of the best. I couldn't have dealt with that situation. I'd have probably lost the ship by smart-assing the wrong thug. It's not like you were out there alone." He craned his neck around to look at me. "The chief was there. Did she do anything?"

"No."

"How about Al?"

"No."

"So what would you have done to hold them if you'd rounded them all up? They were scattered all over the ship and you couldn't be sure to take them all down at once. You couldn't even take them down one at a time and keep the others from learning about it."

"Well. One of the coolers, maybe," I said. "If we'd moved on them while they were separated."

"You still would have had to deal with Patterson and he wasn't one of the stooges. He was dangerous enough that his boss needed to kill him. You've seen him work. Do you think you could have gotten the drop on him? His bosses didn't try."

I felt somewhat mollified. I still couldn't stop the debriefing in my head.

He pushed me to the side. "Stop it." He laughed and punched me in the arm. "Did you really wrestle that weapon out of Snake's hands, unload it, and give it back?"

"Yeah. Why?"

"You did it in front of the whole crew."

"So?"

"So, your crew watched you pour a coffee, stare down an armed intruder, get up into his face, take the gun away from him, unload the gun right in front of him, give the gun back, make him look like an idiot—"

"He did that on his own," I said.

"Shut up. I'm telling you what they saw. Then you basically ignored his ass for over a week, trotting him up and down the ship like a puppy dog while taking the short-handed crew to a pirate base and back after defeating the plot to kill them all and steal the ship."

I didn't know what to say. It made Mary Torkelson's revelations earlier in the day make a little more sense. "I only did what needed doing," I said.

He stopped in the middle of the docking gallery and just stared at me for almost a tick. "Say that again. Out loud."

"I only did what needed doing."

"Think about that. Meditate on the words. I'll wait." He propped his shoulders against a bulkhead, crossing his arms and ankles.

"I have no idea what I'm supposed to think about that."

"Start with 'only.' You only did what needed doing. That's exactly right. No wasted movements. No harebrained ideas. Only the things that needed doing. You didn't try to round them up, potentially setting the plot off early—or, heaven forfend, cause them to trigger a bomb you knew they were capable of detonating. You did what was needed. Necessary. You took care of the crew. You took care of the ship. You didn't even have a whole crew aboard—not that I'd have been much use to you, but Keehn and Penna might have served some purpose because that's—you know—why they're on the payroll to begin with. Get over yourself. Stop being an idiot. You won. Next time you'll do better. Next time you'll have practice. Next time you won't win by the skin of your teeth. Or with your head up your butt."

I stared at him. He seemed really angry—breathing hard, flushed face, fists actually clenched where his arms were crossed.

He took a deep breath. "Now. If we're through with the histrionics, I'll tell you what we're going to do next because we're docked and I'm the CEO of this operation. We're going to make a stupidly large profit on that can of tellurium and go call a meeting of our stockholders to tell them we're all getting stinking rich and we want to buy another ship. Then we're going find another cargo and keep going because that's what we do."

"Another ship? Why?"

"To get rich twice as fast."

"That's not how it works," I said.

He took a figurative step back and blinked at me. "You sure?"

I continued walking toward the *Chernyakova*'s lock. "Yeah. Pretty sure. We're getting crew shares and I'm getting captain's share. The company gets the owner's share, not us. That gets split up to the shareholders. We're going to get a piece of that but a new ship will only contribute the owner's share to the company, not to either of us."

"We're still going to get rich faster," he said.

"Well, yes." I nodded. "But not *twice* as fast."

He laughed and clapped me on the back. "Come on, we got cargo to move."

Chapter Forty
Port Newmar: 2376, May 15

The conference room at the Windbreaker took up half the top floor
and gave a gorgeous panoramic view of the bay and surrounding
coastline. I could see the academy's sloop beating to windward just
off shore.

Alys Giggone stepped up beside me, sharing the view.

"That went well," I said.

"It did. Was he serious about buying another ship?"

"I think it's just a negotiation position. He'd have to delegate
cargo-picking to somebody else and it would kill him."

She laughed. "You two scoundrels have done pretty well. Was
he right? You're going to just keep on hauling freight?"

I snorted. "That's all we were supposed to be doing in the first
place. Everything else just piled on to us."

"Keep telling yourself that," she said.

"What are you going to do now?"

"I need to go visit Margaret Newmar. I have a gift for her."

"How soon are you shipping back out?"

"We'll be here a couple of weeks all told. I want to give the
crew a chance to come planetside. They've earned a bit of sun and
sand." I shrugged. "I'll be spending a little quality time with Mal
Gaines. Try to get back into tai chi. The chief says she needs some
extra time in the engine room for some maintenance."

"You talked Al out of retiring, I hear."

"For now. I put her in for the captains' board. Even if she
doesn't pass it, she's earned a seat at the table."

"You think that'll keep her?"

"I don't know. Maybe. Maybe not. I don't know what happened that she got beached on Breakall. She hasn't talked about it and I haven't asked." I looked at her. "You know she's an artist?"

Alys nodded. "A good one, too. Have you seen any of her work?"

"Some sketches. She showed me a few pieces in her stateroom. She passed on the art show in Diurnia last time around. I'd like to make sure she has a chance at that again."

"You just need to get her there. Christine Maloney will do the rest."

"I suspect we can arrange that."

We stood there staring out at the sky and the sea for a few moments. "You seem better," she said. "Calmer."

"You remember when you met me the first time?"

"Neris, wasn't it?"

"Yeah. You gave me the speech about how signing the articles would mean my ass was yours."

She laughed. "I loved giving that speech. I can't tell you how many times I got it from my father. As far as I know, he got it from his."

"Why?" I asked. "Why did you love giving it?"

"Because every time I did, I found out something about the new member of my crew. It scared some. Completely broke a few. I used to feel bad about those, until I realized it was better they knew early rather than late. Some showed me the glimmer of greatness." She winked at me. "You weren't one of those, but I had to give you credit. You had grit. There were times I wondered if I'd made a mistake, but even when you had your head so far up your ass you were looking out your navel, you always looked out for the crew. Even when it wasn't in your best interest to do so."

"So why did you recommend me?"

"Because I knew you wouldn't do it. It's amazing how much of an obstacle a little paperwork is and how often people accept the filled out form to attend a program that dooms them to paperwork for the rest of their lives."

I laughed because it was so true.

"At the time I wondered if I would have to arm-wrestle officers to sign for you," she said. "For a nobody, you sure made some big impressions even before the academy. Cassandra still asks after you." She looked at me as if to gauge my reaction. "So when are you going to send some candidates my way?"

I shrugged. "Chief Stevens has a hot one. She's been after me to pass on some recommendations."

"Why haven't you?"

"I lost track of what I stand for," I said. "I held on to lessons I should have forgotten and forgot lessons I should have remembered."

"That's pretty navel-gazery. Gaines?"

"He's helped a lot."

"He's a good man," she said. "Did he give you homework?"

I chuckled. "He did. Miserable unanswerable questions that I couldn't ignore."

"I'd have expected no less. His business is pushing buttons."

One of Alys's aides stuck his head in the door. "Commandant? Your next appointment."

"Are they on the ground yet?" she asked.

"They're on final."

"Thank you, Remi." Alys looked off to the west where a tiny spot of light angled across the sky. "Duty calls. I need to go put my commandant pants on and go apologize to some alumni. Wish me luck."

"Good luck," I said.

She left the room from one door as Pip came in another. "That went well."

"The meeting? Yeah. You're not going to get the second ship."

"I don't want it," he said.

"What do you want?"

He paused and swallowed.

The action was so unlike him, it worried me. "What? What are you asking for?"

"A spacer academy in Toe-Hold space."

"A what?"

"A school for crew."

"You think they need it?"

He shrugged. "Yes. At least I think so." He motioned with his head. "Come on. We need to get back to campus."

"Why?"

"I've got three cases of Clipper Ship on ice and we're hosting a party in my cottage tonight. I want to make sure the catering is there."

"Why?"

"Why what? The party? Recruiting."

"What? Officers?"

"How many do you think we need?"

He shrugged, leading the way out of the conference room and into the elevator.

"I want to know what kind of upperclassmen we're putting into the field," he said when the doors had closed.

I frowned at him. "You want to recruit them into your data project on the cargo distribution model."

He shrugged. "Is that a crime?"

"No, I think it's a great idea. Will you need to be back for the conference? When is that?"

"Next spring. It's covered. I've got a company that handles it for me."

We left the hotel and stepped out into the early afternoon traffic in downtown Port Newmar.

"This place has certainly grown," I said. "I wonder if Erik James still has a studio here."

"We'll be here for a few days. You can look him up."

Pip struck off for the shuttle bus stop and I followed along in his wake.

"Why didn't we rent a car and driver?" I asked.

"You have any idea how much that would have cost?" he asked.

"Less than we'll spend on Clipper Ship Lager while we're here, I bet."

He shot me a dirty look. "Philistine. What have you got against the shuttle?"

"Nothing. It was just a question."

We got to the stop and jumped on the bus just as it was ready to pull out. We flashed our IDs and took seats near the front.

"Busy day?" Pip asked leaning forward to address the driver.

"Midday, midweek. Cadets are in classes. We don't run that many shuttles during the day."

"Still run on the halves after 1800?" he asked.

"Yep," he said. "Going in is almost always full. Thins out around 2000 and picks up again after 2200. Commandant runs a tight ship, she does. School-night curfew is 2400 and woe be unto the cadet who misses that."

Pip laughed. "I may have forgotten a lot about the academy but I remember that. Her father wasn't any different."

The driver laughed and pulled up to the next stop.

Chapter Forty-one
Port Newmar: 2376, May 15

They'd assigned me to the same cottage with the white roses as I'd had on my first return. Pip asked for and got one of the larger buildings closer to the admin tower. I was happy with my cozy cottage. When I'd arrived the previous evening, it had been too dark to see much. In the afternoon light, it seemed like home. Silly, I suppose, but I noted the roses had been recently pruned. Some of the stalks still showed the white scars of new cutting.

Inside was the same furniture. Why would it have changed? I looked around, remembering it festooned with my old clothing. Recalling how it felt to be embarking on a new adventure.

Gaines's question came back to me: *How did it make you feel?*

I wasn't supposed to answer it. Just let it linger. The feelings rose of their own accord as long as I didn't try to name them. It was the question that made me remember Alys Giggone's initial speech. Remember my early days on the *Lois*. If I closed my eyes and thought back, the sounds and smells flooded me. The melding of fear, excitement, triumph, and anxiety keeping me off balance. Except the words failed to express the feeling that I remembered. Poor boxes that lacked the scope or integrity to encompass what that feeling had been. Or at least the feeling I remembered.

This place I remembered. The sorting and shuffling, keeping and tossing. My absolute certainty that a correct answer must be here. The desperation that drove me into a partnership that I knew would be flawed from the beginning.

And yet.

And yet.

The afternoon had not yet gotten to the point of long shadows. I grabbed the cup and tea from my grav trunk in the corner and went in search of Margaret Newmar.

The path to the studio behind the gym still curved the way I remembered. The trees that had seemed barely taller than my head now arched high above. Here and there I spotted small plantings that looked natural, but consisted of species not native to the sector, let alone the planet. I snorted to myself. None of it was native to the planet, was it? The scent of green and growing plants gave the air a texture no scrubber could match.

The studio looked much the same. The beautiful weathering on the wood siding. The tall glass window wall reflecting the sky and trees. At night the lights inside turned the sanded floor into a stage where we danced to a silent rhythm.

The knob turned to my touch. The door opened. Inside I slipped off my shoes and bowed to the studio. The old forms coming back. A deep peace falling from the rafters.

Sifu Newmar stepped out of the kitchen at the back and smiled at me. "Ishmael Wang. How lovely to see you."

I bowed to her, student to master. "*Sifu*. I have a gift for you."

She returned the bow, equal to equal. "Your being here is the gift."

I crossed to her and offered the packages.

She took the tin in both hands, holding it to her face and inhaling. "A green. Lovely. Come. Sit. I'll make tea and we'll chat. Like old times, yes?"

She drew me into the kitchen and seated me in my old chair facing the wall of cups. My gaze went to the still-empty slot.

I placed the cubic box on the table and watched her moving through the familiar routine—cold water in the kettle, hot water to warm the pot, pinches of tea between two fingers and thumb. Rough measures. She seemed just as I remembered her. Memories are such traitors, happy to replace what was with what is. I'd been out of the academy for twenty-odd stanyers. She'd seemed so old then. Moving slowly. Deliberately. Wise. On the floor she moved with a fluid grace, her core strength beyond my own in the beginning. Even years later, I never matched her in grace or strength.

She poured water over the tea and clinked the top on the pot before turning to me.

"You want to tell me about it?" she asked.

The question surprised me. "About what?"

"Your last voyage, maybe?" Her sharp eyes glinted in the light. "You seem quite different."

"The man who killed Greta is dead."

She nodded. "Are you sorry?"

"Sorry that he's dead?" I asked. I shook my head. "No, why would I be sorry?"

"Sorry you didn't kill him." She crossed her arms and leaned against the counter in that way I remembered.

I took a deep breath and considered it. "No," I said after a few moments. "I never wanted to kill him. I only wanted justice for Greta."

"It's an old law," she said. "Eye for an eye."

"Doesn't make it a right one."

"But the notion of reciprocal harm? You think that's wrong?"

"I think I prefer restitution to retribution," I said.

She raised an eyebrow at that.

"I don't know," I said. "I didn't want to have to become a monster to beat a monster."

"What justice would you have preferred?"

I shook my head. "In the beginning, dragging him back to CPJCT for trial seemed the correct course."

"You changed your mind."

"Yeah. Pip tried to convince me that he was actually a TIC operative. That he'd never stand trial."

"What if he had?" she asked. "Would you have considered it justice if he were acquitted? Or if convicted and put out an air lock?"

"You mean if I'd pushed the onus onto somebody else?"

She smiled and waited.

"It's a slippery idea, justice," I said.

Her smile widened and the tea timer dinged. She selected two of the plain, round china cups with no handles, christening them from the pot over the sink before bringing them to the table. She poured the tea and set the pot aside.

We sipped for a few moments, the silence of the studio settling around us. The scents of old wood, new floor wax, and green tea wafted around my head. The tea rolled across my tongue and down my gullet, almost too hot to drink and warming on the way down.

"What else?" she asked.

"Not much. A nuke on Dark Knight Station. We docked with the mega for a while after the ship had been contaminated by sarin gas." I took a sip. "I ordered a new pair of boots."

"I heard Pip was snatched."

"Yes. He broke free but was still in the auto-doc while we were getting hijacked."

"Coincidence?" she asked.

"Probably."

She let that stand for a moment.

"I have no idea. It seemed all connected to the push to get the *Chernyakova* out to the mega."

"You think differently now?"

"They went to ridiculous lengths to get us to take that can. Pressuring Kondur. A nuke at Dark Knight. A team of truly incompetent hijackers. Kidnapping Pip."

"I heard they hit Kondur, too," she said.

"We asked him to dinner on the *Chernyakova*. He got jumped on the way back to his office."

"Sounds like a busy trip." She sipped her tea. "You saw Penelope and Quentin at Mel's."

"We did. Also Cousin Roger. Pip seemed to think it odd that they were having a private meeting with Malachai Vagrant."

"Not unexpected." She sipped her tea. "What will you do now?"

"Extended port call. The crew's getting some rest, the ship's getting some maintenance. I'm visiting my therapist. Then we go back out and haul some more freight."

"You have some time to spend here? We haven't danced together in too long."

"I'd like that. I'm out of practice."

"Most returning students are." She smiled and lifted the cover on the small white box. The blue flower practically glowed against the white china background. "Ishmael, this is lovely."

"It's probably not as old as the one that broke, but I thought it would make an interesting replacement and fill in the empty hole in your collection."

She held the cup in both hands, cradled like a bird or a kitten. "It's not the age or even the pattern. It's the heart that comes with it and the stories that surround it."

"The broken one must have had some stories," I said.

She gave a small smile, almost sad. "It's last story hasn't found an ending yet. Perhaps someday."

I finished my tea and stood. "Thank you, *Sifu*. I hate to drink and run but I need to get back to my cottage and get cleaned up. Pip's asked me to help with the party tonight."

"Party?"

"He's trying to recruit last-term cadets to join his research project."

She smiled. "Ah, yes."

She stood, gave me a hug. "Studio opens at 0600. I'll expect you."

I wandered down the path, still a little distracted by the conversation. I left feeling like we talked around the edges but never really dug into any part of it. It felt odd.

Two women came from the opposite direction so I stepped to the side of the narrow path to let them go by. I nodded without really seeing them, but as they passed I noticed one of them holding a familiar white, cubic box.

I looked after them just as the shorter one looked back in my direction. The same woman. They disappeared around a turn, the vegetation hiding them from view. I would have followed them but the fading light among the shade trees made me question. It happened so fast. It couldn't have been. "What are the odds?"

The walk back to the cottage took a few ticks. I enjoyed the fresh air and the sun's shadows lengthening across the parade ground. The two women occupied my brain while my senses enjoyed the view and air that hadn't been filtered.

CHAPTER FORTY-TWO
PORT NEWMAR: 2376, MAY 15

Pip's soiree went off without a hitch. The hired caterers kept the food moving. The crowd grew from a modest half dozen to around thirty or so upperclassmen. I expect that had as much to do with the word going out about the free beer as much as interest in the structural equation modeling of cargo distribution.

Pip, in an uncharacteristic spasm of common sense, limited the distribution of free beer to two per student. The party started to peter out relatively early and only a couple of students needed to be pried out of the house at 2200. It was a school night, after all. The caterers cleared away the mess, stashed the leftovers in the fridge, and left us to our own devices by 2300.

I grabbed a cold one from the beer cooler and rested my weary bones on a sofa across from Pip. "How d'ya think it went?" I asked.

He made the little teeter-totter with his thumb and pinky. "So-so. I only found one that knew what a standard deviation was." He shook his head and took a pull off his beer. "Not exactly a bust. I might have gotten a couple of people thinking about the project. They may be more interested once they graduate and get a job."

"You should have restricted it to those on the cargo track."

He shook his head. "I should have invited the instructors from the cargo track and had them bring a couple of their students."

"Targeted marketing," I said.

"I'll drink to that," he said.

"At this point, you'll drink to almost anything, won't you?"

He laughed. "No doubt. I'm completely beat. Between the shuttle, the stockholders meeting, and this party, I think a couple days of sleep would suit me fine. What's on your to-do?"

"Tai chi at 0600." I sipped my beer. "Do you have to check in with her?"

He shook his head. "I quit."

"No exit interview?" I asked.

"She hasn't asked for one."

"You realize you basically just told me more than I'm supposed to know."

One side of his mouth curled up and he winked at me. "I'm not telling you anything you haven't already worked out, and you might be surprised how much of it you're expected to know."

"What's that mean?" I asked.

"Never struck you as odd? How many times we've been tangentially involved in stuff that most people never hear of?"

"With you and the chief on board? Not even once."

"You think that happened by accident?" he asked, draining his bottle and placing it on the table between us.

"Not in the least. It was your plan all along that we poke the bear with a stick named *Chernyakova*."

He shrugged and stood. "So, I'm ready to call it a night. I've got a heavy day of loafing ahead of me tomorrow and I need to get my rest." He squinted at me. "Don't you have a date at some stupid predawn hour?"

I took another sip of the beer and left the half-full bottle on the table. "Yeah, I do." I stood and headed for the door.

"We make a good team," he said.

"It'll be interesting to see how we do without all the outside influences," I said, looking back at him.

He laughed and shook his head. "Hold that thought." He left the bottles on the table and wandered down the hall toward the master bedroom. "Night."

"Good night," I said, and let myself out. All the way back through campus, I wondered what he meant. He didn't seem to believe that his quitting would remove the outside influences. Considering all we'd been through, I felt pretty sure he could be right.

My tablet buzzed me awake at 0530, leaving me enough time to grab a coffee and a snack and slip into some gym clothes to make my way to the studio by 0600. The morning sun hadn't quite peeked up over the horizon, but a glorious silver and gray light show against a bluer-than-blue backdrop heralded its imminent arrival.

I arrived to find *Sifu* Newmar already working through some warm-ups.

"Am I late?" I asked, after bowing to the studio.

"Just getting started," she said. "At my age, I need to ease into the day a bit more gently than when I was only a hundred." She shot me a wicked grin.

I slipped off my shoes and joined her on the floor, echoing her warm-up movements, stretching my torso, tugging gently on the calf muscles and thighs. I felt stiff and awkward at first. My body found the memory and my balance shifted slightly. I felt the warmth through my core.

She stopped the warm-up and took the opening position, glancing over her shoulder at me. "Ready?"

"Yes."

She began the Jung Long form and we eased through it, languidly immersing in the movements as if rejoining a lover after a long absence. We finished and she stepped out of the ending position to turn and look at me. "You're rusty."

I laughed. "I told you that last night."

She nodded. "The rust is all at the edges. Your core is stronger. More balanced."

"I expect we'll knock that rust off before I leave again."

She grinned. "You need to practice while you're underway. In that great big ship there isn't enough room for even a Yang Short?"

"I'm planning on using the spine. Just haven't done it yet."

"That should be plenty of room." She nodded me toward the kitchen.

"Tea already?"

She shook her head. "I need to show you something."

She led me into the kitchen and pointed to the two tea cups on the table.

"It *was* her," I said. "I met her on the path on my way out last night but I wasn't sure."

"You met her already?"

"We both reached for the same cup. That's why I got the blue one." I glanced over at the empty slot. "I picked up the tin of tea to go with it."

She nodded. "Great minds."

"Was she a student of yours?"

"A long time ago. Last night was the first time I'd seen her since she graduated. She was the one that broke the original cup. Brilliant engineer."

"Dangerous woman," I said.

"Why dangerous?"

"She reminds me of a classmate here. Absolutely deadly in unarmed combat. Nobody on the ship could take her. Gwai Gwahr with a lot of other techniques."

"Beverly Arith," Newmar said.

I nodded. "That's her. This woman moves like Bev."

"Interesting observation. You noticed this from just a momentary observation in a shop at Dark Knight Station?"

"Hard to miss," I said. "Her friend is no slouch either."

"Zoya is the one people most often watch. Striking woman."

"Zee," I said. "The other one is Nats?"

"Natalya. Yes."

"So while everybody watches Zoya, Natalya is the real danger," I said. "Are they a couple?"

She shook her head. "Not any more than you and Pip are." She paused and gave me one of her looks. "Why do you ask?"

I knew I was busted but shrugged. "Just curious."

"Well, shall we dance?" she asked.

"That's it? You just wanted to know if we'd met?"

"I found out what I wanted to know." She smiled.

It was the smile that told me that she'd gotten a lot more out of our exchange than I had. We set up for another form and I made a bet with myself. I'd be seeing Natalya and Zoya again. Sooner rather than later.

"Zoya is a deck officer, isn't she," I said.

"Focus, Ishmael," she said. "Be in the moment."

I had a feeling that the other shoe, when it dropped, would hit me in the face. I was pretty sure it would be a woman's shoe. I felt the smile forming and schooled my expression.

CHAPTER FORTY-THREE
PORT NEWMAR: 2376, MAY 17

Mal Gaines leaned forward in his chair, elbows on knees, staring at me. "So, how are you?"

"I'm not sure."

"Give me the spectrum. What's on one end? What's on the other?"

I blew out a breath. "Well, the guy who killed Greta is dead."

"Which end is that on?"

"That's part of the problem. He's gone. That's over. Whatever that was."

He sat back and nodded. "Talk some more about that."

"Part of me thought I should be all 'Grrr. Bring me the head of David Patterson.' Part of me didn't want to be the person who thought like that, who felt that way. Mostly I just miss her and wish I'd been smarter about the whole crew relationship issue."

"Smarter how?"

"I know that the chain of command exists for good management reasons. That having people in relationships can get messy and ugly. In space, maybe deadly."

"Keep going," he said.

"But I've seen it work. At least from the outside it looks like it works. Family ships are common out there. Ships where the whole family works together. Pip's aunt and uncle make it seem like 'why wouldn't we be married to each other?' On the *Agamemnon*, the first mate and the cargomaster fell in love and started living together. I'm pretty sure they didn't break up when I moved on and she became the captain. You must see it in your practice."

"It's not uncommon," he said. "But it can get messy. Why do you think it's dangerous?"

"The relationship can cloud judgment."

"You believe that?"

I nodded.

"All right," he said. "Would you do anything differently as captain if, say, you loved the cook?"

"I wouldn't know until it happened, would I?"

He laughed. "All right. You faced down an armed hijacker. Got right up in his face. Pulled the gun out of his hands."

"Yeah."

"Why'd you do that?"

"He was threatening my crew," I said. "He obviously had no idea what to do with the weapon and could have easily killed one of them by accident."

"Tell me that first part again."

"What? He was threatening my crew?"

"Yeah. That part."

"He was threatening my crew," I said.

"Not threatening *the* crew. He was threatening *your* crew," Gaines said.

He stopped me short with that one.

"Which one of the crew would you have been willing to sacrifice?" he asked.

"None of them." The question lit a fuse in me. "What kind of question is that?"

He smiled. "Who's your favorite crewman?"

"Favorite? That's got to be like asking a parent which is their favorite child."

His smile broadened and he just stared.

"What?" I asked.

"What if—in order to save the crew—you had to jump out the air lock without a suit?"

"Why would I have to do that?"

"Why did you stand in front of an armed hijacker and dare him to kill you?" he asked.

"It's what any of us would do."

"Al?" he asked.

"Certainly."

"How about Tom Reed?"

"Of course."

"Your third mate. Ms. Fortuner?"

"Kim, and I'm certain of her. And Chief Stevens. Any of them. Right on down the line to the most junior spacer apprentice." The image of Kris Cross standing up to Snake gave me a combination laugh and cringe.

"What was that?" he asked. "That last bit."

"My junior SA is not exactly an imposing physical specimen."
I paused. "Intellectually, she's firing on all cylinders and she's got
the heart of a lion."

"So what? The image was funny?" he asked. "David and Go-
liath?"

"Something like that. Also frightening. Snake could have killed
her by accident."

"He could have killed you by accident," Gaines said in the most
matter-of-fact tone. "Why is it different with her?"

"The safety of the crew is my responsibility."

"And Ms. Cross? Is her responsibility to wait for somebody else
to take responsibility?"

"No," I said, but I stopped reacting and started thinking. I
remembered Ms. Torkelson.

Gaines's smile came back. "Tell me about it."

I settled back and took a deep breath. "One of the questions you
asked was 'What will you stand for?' I tried to think of things like
truth, honesty, and abstract things like that. In my head I always
heard the question differently. 'What do you stand for?' and that's
not what you asked, unless I've remembered wrong."

"You remember correctly. That alone is pretty impressive." He
paused. "Did you come to any conclusions?"

"It took one of my crew to tell me." I could hear her voice
echoing in the bare lock. "It was after all the dust had settled. The
danger behind us. Bombs disposed of. Hijackers locked up or dead.
She told me she almost left the ship the last time we were here
because she didn't think I really cared. About the ship. About the
crew. Anything."

"PTSD and depression are almost never invisible," he said. "They
just look like something else."

"She actually said that she didn't think we stood for anything
and she didn't want to be a member of a crew that didn't care. I
asked her if she'd changed her mind. What did she think we stood
for." I paused, thinking about her standing there in the lock and
facing me with her doubts and dreams on her sleeve. "She said we
stood for each other."

"Interesting young woman," Gaines said.

"Spec-two shiphandler. She's got the touch."

"Do you agree with her?" he asked.

"I do."

"Why?"

"Ms. Sharps asked about a piece of faulty galley equipment.
She was looking out for the ship and the crew even when nobody

else knew there was a problem. Ms. Cross found a safety issue in the spine of the ship. She came to the cabin and confronted me about it. She was right. Schulteis in environmental, a wiper, low man on the totem pole, got his senior watchstander working on advancing rank and probably saved his life by helping him drill with the emergency suit." I shrugged. "Those are only the ones I noticed lately. There have had to be others."

"Sounds like you had an interesting voyage, Skipper."

I laughed. "Parts of it certainly seemed like a curse."

"What are your plans now?" he asked.

"What do I plan or what do I expect?"

"Both."

"I plan to get the ship back out there earning credits. We've almost got it paid off and Pip's talking about expanding the fleet."

"Can he get that past the board?"

"Normally, I'd say 'no' but I'm not going to put anything past him. It might not be another Barbell, but he knows the fast packet trade cold. Compared to what we've currently got, that would be a cheap addition. His father would probably sell us Pip's old ship at cost."

"And what do you expect?" he asked.

"I expect to get smacked in the head by a falling shoe."

"As in 'the other shoe?'" he asked.

"That's the one. Seems like whenever I begin to feel that I have a handle on things, I find out that not only do I not have a handle—I don't actually have a clue."

He laughed. "Well, come see me when you get back to Port Newmar. You can fill me in."

I checked the chrono and saw that our time was up. "That went fast. You don't have any homework for me this time?"

He shook his head. "You've got a lot to chew on. Patterson's death. You found the mega."

"It didn't sink the *Pequod*," I said.

"You're not Ahab," he said. "Focus on processing all the changes that have happened since we first met here. That's a lot to think about."

I stood and shook his hand. "Thanks, Mal."

"See you next time, Captain."

Chapter Forty-four
Port Newmar: 2376, May 17

My tablet interrupted the walk back to my cottage: a message from Pip asking for my presence at his house "at my earliest convenience." Normally, I might have just shrugged it off as "Pip just being Pip." That phrase, used in a context where he—as CEO—outranked me, had me legging it from the administration tower to his house. Part of me hoped that it wasn't going to be what I knew it would be.

He met me at the door with a cold bottle of Clipper Ship and a bemused expression. "Captain, we have a problem." He led me into the dining where the chief, looking as unruffled as ever, and Al, looking excited with a hint of fidget, sat at the long table.

I looked at the chief first. "It's time?"

She nodded.

I looked at Al. "Retiring?"

"Not exactly," she said. She held up her tablet. "I'll forward you the message."

My tablet bipped and I flipped open the screen. "An artist-in-residence?"

She nodded. "Christine Maloney has run an artist-in-residence program for over a decade. She's invited me to be that artist."

"Did you apply?" I asked. "How did this happen?"

Al shook her head. "It's not that kind of program. She picks an artist who she believes represents an important voice. The term is a stanyer. It includes housing, an allowance for supplies, studio space, and a featured show in her gallery on Jett." She stopped and swallowed hard. "It's a big deal in the art world."

I looked at the chief, who gave me the biggest "who, me?" face in the Western Annex.

I looked back at Al and smiled. "How can I help?"

Pip looked at me like I'd lost my mind and fell into one of the chairs. "What?"

I looked at him. "You expected me to object?"

"Well, I thought you might put up a token bit of resistance just to let her know how much we value her contribution to the team." His pout wasn't really convincing, especially when he washed it down with a heavy pull from his beer bottle.

I pulled out a chair, plopped into it, and looked at the chief. "I didn't see it coming *here*," I said. "I should have. You've been invited to be a guest lecturer at the academy for the next little while?"

Pip's expression turned quizzical. "Why would you say that?"

"It's the most likely reason for her to leave the *Chernyakova* here."

"What's your second guess?" he asked.

"That her publisher is pressing for the next edition of the text she's been working on the whole time she's been aboard but it's not ready yet."

Al snorted and folded her arms across her chest. "He's no slouch."

"Both?" I asked, looking at the chief.

She nodded. "But I promised I wouldn't leave you without a chief."

"How did you get them to come in from Dark Knight?" I asked.

Her eyes widened for a moment before she grinned. "How did you know?"

"Serendipity. Never underestimate the power of chance to reveal that which you thought to be hidden."

"Fortune cookie?" she asked.

"Yeah. Plum Blossom over at Jett."

"I know it well. Jimmy Chin's an old friend."

"I ran into them in a tea shop on Dark Knight just before we left. Nats was buying a tea cup to replace the one she broke. I was buying one for Margaret Newmar because I knew somebody had broken one of hers. I saw a likely replacement in the shop. We both reached for the same one," I said. "I ran into them again late yesterday afternoon when I left the studio. I thought I was mistaken until I went back this morning and found the same cup on Margaret's table and got the rundown on a brilliant engineer and a frighteningly effective deck officer."

The chief gave a small shrug. "We have some paperwork that needs doing, and you're going to want to interview them before they sign in."

"Wait, you knew this morning?" Pip asked.

"No, I knew when I walked in to see both the first mate and chief engineer sitting at your kitchen table." I shrugged.

I looked at the chief. "When are we expecting them?"

"They'll be here shortly."

"You have any tea?" I asked, looking at Pip.

He shook his head. "Not on my provisioning order. Why?"

"At least one of them drinks tea."

"I thought this was a job interview," he said.

"Pro forma," I said. "I've seen these women. Margaret Newmar raved about them. The chief has hand-picked the engineer and, since they're a package deal and we need a first mate, too, I'm willing to bet Zee is almost as good as Al. They're both around our ages, they've been banging around the Toe-Holds for rather a long time, and they're both academy grads. Nats moves like Bev did and Zee has more command presence in her little toe than your Captain Roland had in his whole body."

The chief looked at me with a question in her eyes. "What makes you think they've been in the Toe-Holds for a long time?"

"The taller one, Zoya. She's fleet to the core but she wasn't dressed for it, didn't seem overly disoriented by being at Dark Knight. She fit in with the Toe-Holders almost seamlessly."

"What about Natalya?" the chief asked.

"If I had to guess, I'd say she'd either been born there or spent a lot of her life pre-academy there. Just the way she moved, her clothes. She didn't look like she was trying to fit in. She just fit in."

The chief looked at Al. "You're right. He's no slouch."

"Wait," Pip said, bracing his beer bottle on the table. "Wait. I know these names. Natalya, Zoya. Where do I know these names from?"

"They were neighbors for a while," the chief said.

Pip's eyes grew wide enough that I could almost see the whites all the way around his irises. "Oh, no. Statuesque. Drop-dead gorgeous. Took over when UMS17 got blown up?"

"Wouldn't surprise me," I said.

He closed his eyes and hung his head forward on his neck. "Aphrodite."

"The goddess of love and beauty," Al said.

The doorbell rang and Pip went so pale, I thought he might pass out as the blood rushed from his face. "Would somebody get that, please?" he asked.

Chapter Forty-five
Port Newmar: 2376, May 17

I went to the door and enjoyed the looks of surprise. I held out a hand to Natalya. "Hello. We haven't been introduced but I'm Ishmael Wang."

She seemed a little dazed but shook it off enough to shake my hand. "Natalya Regyri."

I offered my hand to the other. "Ishmael Wang."

"Zoya Usoko."

"Pleased to meet you both. Come on in. At least one of your friends is here."

Natalya looked at me. "At least one?"

"I believe you know Chief Stevens?"

She nodded. "Of course."

We walked into the dining room where the chief met them with effusive greetings including many huggings and exclamations.

Al caught my eye and shrugged.

Pip looked like he might pass out and was examining the floor for a likely landing spot.

The chief did the honors. "This is First Mate Alberta Ross. She's been selected for a prestigious position over in Jett."

Al stood and shook the offered hands but stayed clear of any incipient hugs.

"Natalya Regyri is my collaborator on the emergency Burleson collar, among other things." The chief looked at me like a magician pulling a rabbit from a hat before turning to Zoya. "Zoya Usoko, chairman of the board for Usoko Mining. Between them, they're two of the key players in ore and metal distribution in the Western Annex."

Natalya held up a hand. "Don't oversell us, Chief."

"Pull up some chairs," Al said. "Let's talk techy."

"Can I get you anything from the galley?" I asked. "There's no tea, I'm afraid, but I'm sure there's coffee."

Natalya nodded. "I'll take a coffee. Black, please."

I looked at Zoya.

"I know this is a job interview and all, but if there's another Clipper Ship ..." she said.

Natalya looked at Zoya. "Really? You're going there?"

"It's Clipper Ship. Of course I'm going there."

Pip looked up and the movement must have attracted their attention because both of them zeroed in on him like radar on a rock.

"Carstairs," Zoya said. She didn't look angry as much as confused. "What role does he play in this circus?"

"Chimpanzee," Al said, a bemused expression on her face as she looked from Pip to Zoya and back.

"CEO," I said. "Phoenix Freight. Also cargo master on the *Chernyakova*."

Pip looked up, struggling to his feet. "Long time, no see."

"You care to explain just what the hell happened back then?" Zoya asked. If her face were a storm, lightning would've been shooting out her nose and thunder out her ears.

"I was taken by surprise," he said, looking at where his finger traced circles in the moisture on the table. "I wasn't expecting you." He swallowed. Hard.

She shook her head. "I have no idea what you're talking about but my eyes are up here." She forked her fingers at her own eyes. "CEO or not, I'd appreciate it if you'd talk to me and not the table."

He held up both hands in surrender. "I'll do my best, Ms. Usoko. Let me get you a beer." He shrugged, being careful to look her in the eye. "We can talk."

I looked at the chief who shrugged. I noticed Al had narrowed her eyes at Pip and seemed to be struggling to hold in a grin.

"Have a seat," I said, waving the two women into chairs at the end of the table. "We'll be right back." I looked at Natalya. "You want a beer instead of coffee? We're all officers here."

"Coffee any good?"

"I don't drink bad coffee."

"Coffee, please."

"I thought you were a tea drinker."

"Because we were in a tea shop?" she asked.

"It's a logical assumption."

"Are you a tea drinker, Captain?"

I grinned. "Touché." I grabbed Pip by the arm and dragged him through the swinging door and into the small galley. I lowered my voice to a near whisper. "You wanna tell me what the very hell is going on between you and Usoko? Is it her money?"

He blinked a couple of times as if trying to process. "Money? No. She has money?"

"Usoko Mining? *The* Usoko Mining?" I rummaged in the cupboard for the grinder.

His eyes got big. "Her?" he asked, the word coming out like a quiet wheeze.

"What then?"

"Have you seen her?" he asked. "I can barely look at her without freezing up."

"We all noticed," I said. "What's the story?"

"She's gorgeous. Some kind of goddess sent to haunt my dreams."

"She's a talented and intelligent deck officer. Stop being a dumbass and go give her a beer."

"You don't understand. I've met her before. It's been stanyers and I cannot get her out of my mind."

"Must have been some meeting."

Abject horror washed across his face. "I was a complete ass. Rachel still rides me about it."

"Some things never change. Get a grip. We need to interview her for the first mate slot. We'll talk later."

He nodded, steeled himself, and pushed through the door.

I measured some beans into the grinder and pressed the button, getting some cold water into the reservoir by the time the beans were ready. I pressed the go button and went back into the dining room to see what fresh hell our CEO had rained down on us.

"It's brewing," I said, trying my best to be professional in a room full of cross currents and strange vibes. I looked to the chief. "I'm guessing that pulling jackets won't tell me much."

She nodded. "I can tell you that these two started the job that we finished in Telluride. Between them, they built the Zvezda Moya mining depot."

"That was really Higbee's doing," Zoya said. "We just put the blocks together after my grandmother placed the orders."

I heard the coffee pot finish brewing and held up a hand. "Hold those thoughts. Coffee's ready. I'll be right back."

A quick pass through the tidy kitchen gave me two china mugs full of coffee and I returned almost before the swinging door stopped flapping. I gave one of the mugs to Natalya and kept the other. I looked at the chief. "Now. Can we speak freely?"

She nodded. "They picked up the pieces after our friends detonated a bomb in a Usoko Mining station. They've known about it for a very long time." She looked at Zoya. "It's over, by the way. We found the base and fumigated it."

Zoya's eyes closed for a few heartbeats and then opened. "I knew there had to be more."

"We got the *Paisley* shortly after you went to Margary, but we've been trying to track the rest of them ever since."

"So it's really over now," Natalya said.

"The *Chernyakova* made it possible," the chief said.

"And now you're going to be here teaching?" Zoya asked, her eyes narrowing just a little.

"Yes, and finishing the next edition of the book, thanks to Natalya's insight," she said.

"And you've got a plum job elsewhere?" Zoya asked, looking at Al.

"Artist-in-residence at a gallery on the orbital at Jett over in Diurnia." Al's eyebrows rose only the slightest fraction.

Natalya glanced at the chief and then looked at Zoya, pursing her lips. "How fortuitous for us."

"Not exactly," Zoya said. "Correct me if I'm wrong, Captain, but a Barbell needs an engineering *chief* officer."

"You're correct," I said.

She looked at Natalya and shrugged.

For her part, Natalya's face seemed to fall a little.

"What's the hold up?" I asked.

"Engineering *first* officer," she said, raising her hand and giving her fingers a little twiddle.

The chief sat up in her seat and Zoya pulled out her tablet.

Natalya leaned over. "What are you looking up?"

"Qualifications for chief. Hush." Zoya said. She apparently found what she was looking for and shook her head. "You sly old fox."

"Thanks, I try," the chief said.

"What am I missing?" Natalya asked.

"You only need a senior chief engineering officer in good standing to certify your performance to make chief," Zoya said.

"That can't be right," Natalya said. "Don't I need to pass a board review?"

"The senior chief can waive it in favor of actual demonstration of performance," Zoya said. "It has to be something the chief has personally observed and is willing to testify to." She held the tablet so Natalya could read. "See. Right there. We saw this before in Margary. Remember?"

Natalya looked at the chief. "You?"

The chief nodded.

"You haven't seen my performance since we jumped that broken Barbell out of Zvezda Moya."

"Your point is what?" the chief asked.

"You don't know what I've done lately or what my performance is now."

"We worked together on that emitter yoke for a stanyer. I'm pretty sure you haven't gotten worse because I've got a copy of every performance review since you got the *Madoka* out of the yards. That capacitor design is brilliant, by the way. Who programmed the latching circuits? That doesn't look like Manchester code."

"She did," Zoya said. "I helped with some debug and testing."

"Chief Willoby was ready to sign your promotion last stanyer but you didn't have enough time in grade," the chief said. "If you like, you can take the exam and we can convene a board here at the academy, but I can tell you what they'll say."

I sat back and looked around the table. "So? Are we agreed that you two have the technical qualifications to be chief engineering officer and first mate in CPJCT space?"

Zoya nodded. "I think so, Captain."

Natalya nodded. "I'm a bit in shock but yes, Captain. I believe so."

I looked Al. "You wanna conference on this?"

She shook her head. "Your ship. Your call, Skipper."

"Chief?" I asked.

She grinned. "All the work I put in getting this together and you think I'm going to pull the plug now?" She shook her head.

"Well, there's only one thing left to do," I said. "Chief, Al, thanks. I think it's time for us to see if the four of us can work together. Let's get together for lunch tomorrow, shall we?"

Al gave me a lopsided grin and stood. "Come on, Chief. I've got a case of Clipper Ship in my cottage and I don't go on watch until tomorrow night."

The chief stood and headed for the door. "I could use another cold one, especially if you're buying. Have fun, kids."

The sound of the door closing sounded loud in the silence.

Natalya looked at Zoya and shrugged. "You have to admit. As ambushes go, it could have been worse."

"Grant you that," she said and looked across the table at me. "Captain?"

"Oh, she's been doing this to me for stanyers. I've learned to roll with the punches."

Natalya laughed. "So have you figured out who she works for?"

"I have some guesses," I said. "It's certainly not me. I'm just the handy cover story but I've learned a lot from her."

Natalya raised her mug in a toast. "I'll drink to that."

Zoya frowned, staring down the table at Pip. "What's your story, Carstairs?"

He looked up and took a couple of deep breaths. For a couple of heartbeats I thought he was going to hurl, but he shrugged. "I'm working on being a better person."

His answer surprised me and it must have shown on my face.

"What were you before?" Zoya asked, not exactly a challenge. Mostly curiosity with a little disbelief mixed in.

He stared at the empty bottle on the table near his hand. "Kind of an ass." He shrugged. "I've been a little bit obsessed for the last few stanyers. Off balance. I thought putting the company together and grabbing the *Chernyakova* would fill the void." He shook his head.

"You've always been an ass," I said. "Why change now?"

He shrugged. "We finished the job. All that stuff is behind us." He glanced at Zoya before looking at me. "I guess I just have a reason now."

"So how's this company organized?" Natalya asked. "You're the CEO and cargo officer?"

Pip nodded. "Yeah. It felt like too much conflict of interest for Ishmael to have CEO and captain. So, he's in charge of the ship. I'm in charge of the company. Underway, he's the law. Docked, it falls to me. Since I'm CEO, having me make cargo deals on behalf of the company makes sense. I don't have to get into the details of running the ship, and he just has to get the can from here to there without running into anything."

"How do you two manage?" I asked.

"Like the chief said, I'm chairman of the board for Usoko," Zoya said. "I hired a CEO who runs the day-to-day operations. Board has oversight and we meet about three times a stanyer to review the operation. That's in Margary. Will that be a problem?"

"We have a mandated board meeting here at Port Newmar—nominally—once a year. I think we can work around it. Pip's pretty good at finding a can going wherever we need to be," I said.

"What about the shipping company?" Pip asked, looking at Natalya.

"One ship. It's all we've needed. Usoko is our primary client. We run finished metals from Zvezda Moya in the Toe-Holds and deliver them all around the Western Annex. Manchester gets the lion's share but we also handle shipments to the other shipyards. Unwin gets a big slug. Higbee is another," Natalya said.

"Do you have to have a board meeting or anything?" I asked.

She shook her head. "Privately owned."

Zoya made a show of pointing at Natalya.

"You own it. Outright?" Pip asked.

"It's a long story," she said.

"It's one I want to hear," I said. "But I have to ask. You were first mate on the *Madoka*? Is that the right name?"

"Yeah," Zoya said. "She was engineering first. Her ship. She can be whoever she likes."

"How can you come work for us?" I asked.

Pip asked, "*Why* come work for us? Seems like you've got a sweet deal going."

"The second mate was ready to move up, but couldn't because I was in the way," Zoya said.

"I wouldn't be able to make chief without bumping Willoby, and we don't have a job to give him. He's a great guy and an amazing officer. I couldn't do that to him, the ship, or the company. When Chief Stevens suggested she could help me back at Dark Knight, I jumped on it. The only catch was we had to come to Port Newmar. We got a can coming this way and here we are." She shook her head. "I never suspected she'd actually be the one to give me the rank."

"She works in mysterious ways," I said. "If she ever shows up on my decks, the only thing I can count on is life is about to get interesting."

"You know that's a curse, right?" Zoya asked.

"First hand," I said, toasting her with my coffee up. "First hand."

She laughed and even Pip got in a little chuckle. It hardly sounded strained at all.

Chapter Forty-six
Newmar Orbital: 2376, May 19

We signed the necessary paperwork aboard the ship. Pip booked a suite at the Newmar Zenith for Natalya and Zoya so we could all have access to the ship during the transition. Al and the chief took a couple of days to pack up while Natalya and Zoya got familiar with the crew. Zoya stood portside watches with Al, eating on the mess deck and generally getting a feel for the ship. Natalya and the chief fell into what looked like an easy working relationship, reminding me they'd worked together before.

The crew seemed to take to the new faces readily enough. After a few double-takes, I noticed a lot of smiles in the passageways. I took that as a good sign.

As we came to the end of our two-week layover, I called a meeting in the wardroom. It felt a little funny to have Al and the chief at the foot of the table while the new people stood to the left and right of me. I took a pull off my coffee cup and glanced at Pip. His earlier spasms seemed to have subsided for the most part. I still caught him staring at Ms. Usoko once in a while. I couldn't blame him, but I hoped it would all work out.

Ms. Fortuner slid into the wardroom and I took my seat. Everyone followed suit.

"First order of business. You've all met in the passageways already but a formal welcome to our new people." I raised my mug to Zoya and Natalya in turn.

That got some smiles and murmurs of "welcome aboard."

"Second order, thanks to Ms. Ross and Chief Stevens. It's been an honor and a pleasure."

That got more smiles and a few knowing grins around the table.

"Are we all settled?" I asked, looking around the table.

"We're in the suite," the chief said. "I'm moving down to campus housing after you've gone."

"I've got a ticket to Jett on a DST packet in a few days," Al said.

"Nice when the owner sends a yacht for ya, huh?" the chief asked, with an elbow nudge.

Al chuckled. "It's certainly not something I'm used to."

"I'll forward the change of address to the captain's board," I said. "Maybe by the time your residence is up they'll have moved on it."

She nodded. "Appreciated, Skipper."

I looked to Natalya. "How's the engineering division looking, Chief?"

She grinned. "I'm not quite used to that title yet. The division is ready for space. Tanks are topped. Spares inventory is up to spec."

"Any problems with the crew?" I asked.

"No. They're a good lot. They seem to be taking the change in stride. Nobody's challenged me for the position." She nodded toward the chief. "I would have been surprised if she left me anything but a well-managed division. I'll try to keep it that way."

The chief grinned. "You'll be fine."

"Ms. Usoko?" I asked.

"I've met everybody in the division, I think. Al warned me about Bentley."

Everybody laughed.

"He's a good guy," she said. "All of them are top notch and a lot of them are working on their next ratings."

"I found that in engineering, too," Ms. Regyri said.

"It's a bit of a cause with me," I said. "I can be a little pushy about people moving up. Company policy to give them the title and pay even if their job duties don't change substantially. I'd be perfectly happy to have spec-one ship handlers on messenger watch."

Zoya frowned for a moment before she caught on. "Because everybody else is already spec-one something?"

I nodded. "I wouldn't expect to keep them once they get too far along, but I'd be happy for the *Chernyakova* to have the reputation that crew moves up and out."

Zoya nodded. "I haven't checked with Ms. Sharps yet, but I'll double-check on stores before we get underway. She doesn't strike me as the kind to short us on food."

I grinned. "I think you'll find your trust paying off. She and Pip have an arrangement going where the galley isn't an expense for the ship. The last two quarters it actually generated profit for us."

She looked at Pip. "Really? How do you do that?"

I thought he might revert to a stammering fan-boy but he took a deep breath and launched into his spiel about the amount of food we needed to satisfy CPJCT regs and how we never used it all so we traded in back-stock items, etc., etc.

I couldn't help notice that the more he talked, the more he loosened up. Or maybe it was that Ms. Usoko seemed to shed a bit of her reserve.

I let it go on for a tick or so and held up my hand. "Off line?"

They both nodded but Ms. Usoko leaned over to say, "Brilliant idea."

"Pip, I heard we have a can."

"We do, Skipper. Hydroponic supplies bound for The Ranch. Nothing exciting but we got a good rate."

"Anybody object if we pull out of here tomorrow? Any unfinished business before we go?"

Nobody spoke up.

"Good enough. Ms. Usoko, pass the word that liberty expires at 0600 tomorrow morning."

"Liberty expires at 0600 tomorrow, aye, Captain."

"Mr. Reed, do we have all the astrogation updates?"

"Everything that's come in so far. I'm expecting another batch tonight. I've got the mid so they'll be in by morning."

"We'll need to file for somewhere in order to get clearance for departure," I said.

"I know the drill, Skipper. What time?"

"Let's see if we can get at tug for 1330."

"1330, aye, Captain."

"Ms. Fortuner, can you get a full system backup off-site by then?"

"Of course, Skipper. Do we have a place to store it?"

"Get with Pip and rent a storage cube." I looked at Pip who nodded back. "We should have done it before."

"Captain?" Zoya asked.

"Yes?"

"*Madoka* kept backups at all the major stations in the Toe-Holds. Zvezda Moya was our home port, but we found it useful to be able to take an off-site more often than when we made it back home. We never needed them but it was cheap insurance."

"I like that. Pip?"

He pulled out his tablet and started tapping. "On it."

"Ms. Fortuner?"

"Aye, aye, Captain."

"Anybody else? Anything I'm missing?"

Nobody raised a hand so I stood. "All right. Meeting adjourned. Thank you, everybody. I'll be in the cabin if there's anything you want to talk to me about." I filled my mug from one of the carafes and exited the wardroom.

It only took a moment for me to climb the ladder but I had barely settled behind my console when Al showed up at the door.

I waved her in. "Close the door if you want."

She shook her head. "Usoko is ferocious. She doesn't need me dogging her anymore, so I'm off. I only wanted a minute to thank you, Skipper. Having you put me in for the captains' board ..." She shook her head. "I may or may not make it but just being put in? Yeah. Thanks."

"Don't start getting sappy on me," I said.

She snorted. "As if, but I wanted you to have this. The cabin could use a little decoration." She reached back into the passage and brought in a framed picture. It showed the *Chernyakova* coming out of the Unwin yards at Dree. I stood and walked around the console, drawn to the near photographic rendering and entranced by the play of light across the hull with the darkened yard gantries lurking in the background. She pressed it into my hands. "It's got magnets in the frame," she said. "They'll be strong enough to support it."

"It's amazing, Al." I could barely drag myself away from staring at it to look at her. "I'm—well, I'm speechless, I guess." I held it up to the bulkhead beside the door and moved it about a little until I felt the magnets pull against the steel supports behind the bulkhead panels. When I released it, it snapped to the wall and looked like it had always been there. I had a hard time swallowing for a moment when I saw her grinning at me. "I don't know what to say."

Her grin softened. "What we always say, Skipper. Safe voyage."

I opened my arms and she gave me a hug with back-slap flourishes. "Safe voyage, Al."

She stepped back, her eyes as damp as I suspected mine must have been. She came to attention and saluted.

I returned the salute.

With a final grin and a nod, she left the cabin and disappeared down the ladder.

I went back to my chair and admired the painting from afar. The pale gray ship slashed across the darkness of the yard and the stars beyond. It was never a view anybody had seen in person, but she'd captured the vision in a way that pulled to me.

The chief stepped into the open door frame like she'd been waiting outside for Al to leave. "Gotta tick?"

"Of course."

She entered and swung the door closed behind her. She stared at the painting for a moment before taking her customary seat. "It's something, isn't it?"

"I'm dumbfounded," I said.

"She's been working on that for weeks."

"You've seen it in process?" I asked.

The chief shook her head. "Nobody sees her work in process. I saw it the other day while we were packing up to move out. Zoya hid it in her stateroom until Al could present it to you."

"I know you picked them. Can I ask why them?"

"Gut feeling. They're both top notch," she said. "Natalya has mechanical skills that exceed my own. I'm a theorist at heart. She's a nuts-and-bolts, get-her-hands-dirty engineering officer. She's got the heart to help without helping too much. She's happy to see people try and fail, but has no patience for those who won't even try.

"Zoya has been on the bridge since she was a teen. Her grandfather groomed her to run a ship while her grandmother pulled her to the family business. She's a legend among the Usoko people in Margary—and probably in the Toe-Holds as well."

"That explains her command presence," I said. "What's the story with her and Pip?"

"Pip met them both stanyers ago. They were trying to recover from the UMS17 disaster and had a mutiny. The two of them managed to round up the mutineers and sent word to us to get them picked up. Rachel took Pip's ship—and Pip—over to do the transfer. Rachel said Pip had been reduced to stammering and staring at his shoes the second Zoya walked into the room."

"That must have been a great first impression."

"Yeah. The effect doesn't seem to have lessened much. I thought he was going to puke on his shoes when she walked in," the chief said.

"I have never seen him act this way around anybody. In all the stanyers I've known him, he's always at least attempted to be a player. He didn't always succeed, but he always wore that ladies'-man shell," I said. "Thank the heavens he seems to be coming around."

The chief grinned. "Zee is a force of nature. She might be just what Pip needs."

"You think she's going to rein him in?" I felt my eyebrows rise at the idea.

She shook her head. "No, I think she's going to make him look real hard at himself in ways neither of us have been able to."

I stared at her for a couple of heartbeats too long, apparently.

"Natalya isn't Greta," she said.

"But she might be just what I need?" I asked, a sour taste growing in my mouth.

"Don't put words in my mouth." The chief frowned at me. "She's the best engineering chief in the Western Annex. I wouldn't leave you with somebody who couldn't do the job on a daily basis and still rise to the challenges of Toe-Hold and High Line. She is just what you need because she's just what the ship needs."

I felt the anger beginning to recede a little. "Sorry," I said. "Just. Made my hackles rise a little."

She grinned. "Understandable." She rummaged in her pocket and pulled out a silver flask. "I need to get going myself. Natalya's got the job under control and I want to get down to campus and get settled. Here." She clicked the flask onto my desk. "I wanted to leave you something to remember me by."

I picked up the flask, smiling at the memories of having her spike my coffee. "I can't take your flask," I said.

"That's not mine," she said.

I flipped it over and found the inscription. "Presented to Capt. Ishmael H. Wang for meritorious service above and beyond the call of duty under hazardous and life threatening conditions. Core Worlds Navy Admiral Margaret Stevens." I had to read it twice. I looked up at her.

"It's empty. You'll need to fill it yourself." She stood. "Thank you, dear boy. Safe voyage."

She started for the door before I could move.

"Wait, is this a joke?" I asked.

She grinned. "No, that's a flask."

"But—" I pointed to the inscription.

"Oh, yes, well. Of course, it's a joke. A gift from an old chief who used to sail with you. Strangest sense of humor, but a good judge of fine rum. Right?"

I tried to think of something to say but couldn't get my mind around anything coherent beyond "Safe voyage."

She grinned at me again. "Never know. I might be back," she said, before ducking through the door, latching it behind her with a click.

I stared at the flask, pulled between the urge to lock it in the ship's safe and the desire to find a bottle of rum to fill it from. I settled for slipping it into a storage drawer in my console.

Ms. Usoko looked up from the watchstander's console. "We've reached the Burleson limit, Captain."

"I've the urge to go somewhere else, Ms. Usoko."

She grinned at me, her teeth white against her skin in the dimness of the bridge. "I believe Mr. Reed has a destination in mind, Cap."

"Is that true, Mr. Reed?" I asked.

"Well, Skipper, it's either jump or try to turn this boat around. I'd recommend the jump."

"Where are we going, Mr. Reed?"

"The Ranch, eventually, Captain, but for now?" He waved a hand toward the bow. "Somewhere out there. I hope."

"Close enough, Mr. Reed. Ms. Regyri, are the boys in the back ready?"

"Yes, Captain. Burlesons charged and ready. Capacitors at full. We can do two full jumps."

"Thank you, Ms. Regyri. Secure sails and sail generators for the jump."

"Aye, aye, Captain. Securing sails and sail generators." After a moment she said. "Sails and sail generators are secured, Captain."

"Thank you, Ms. Regyri. Mr. Reed? Ready about. Hard a-lee."

I heard his keyboard click and the stars moved to new locations in the sky around us.

"Jump complete," Ms. Usoko said. "Verifying location."

"Burlesons are recharging, Captain," Ms. Regyri said.

"Location set, Skipper," Mr. Reed said. "We're just a bit long and we'll need a short burn to get back on the path."

"Thank you, Mr. Reed. Tell me when you've defined short, if you would."

"Aye, aye, Skipper."

"Ms. Usoko, log the jump, if you would?"

"Jump logged, Captain."

"Thank you, Ms. Usoko. Where are we on the Burlesons, Ms. Regyri?"

"Sixty percent and charging, Captain."

"Short is defined at ten ticks and a few seconds, Captain. Programmed and ready."

"Execute, Mr. Reed."

"Execute burn, aye, aye, Captain."

The familiar rumble under my feet felt like coming home as the ship spun around its axis, twisting to point the bow to our next destination.

I had to give Chief Stevens credit. Natalya and Zoya had slipped into their positions like two hands into a pair of gloves. The crew meshed with them—perhaps even better than they had with Al and the chief. Sitting there looking around the bridge, I would have been hard-pressed to point to the new kids if I hadn't known who they were.

"What's the calendar look like, Mr. Reed?" I asked.

"Best course shows one more long, a short, then another long and another short one into the system, Skipper."

"That's an odd short," I said.

"It lines us up for the last long one to drop us for the approach, Captain. Alternate takes longer and we have to do a lot of short jumps with course corrections between."

"Thank you, Mr. Reed. I trust your judgment on these things."

"Thank you, Captain. I try to exceed expectations."

I chuckled a little and watched the countdown timer click over to zero. The rumbling under my feet stopped.

"Burn complete, Captain. We are on the beam."

"Thank you, Mr. Reed. Ms. Regyri?"

"Plenty of juice, Captain."

"Mr. Reed? Ready about. Hard a-lee."

The stars shifted again.

"Verifying position, Captain," Ms. Usoko said. "Logging the jump."

"Burlesons are charging. Capacitors at twenty-percent, Captain."

"We're where we need to be, Skipper, but we need a corrective burn here."

"Thank you, Ms. Regyri. Mr. Reed? How much burn? Hours? Days?"

"Still calculating, Captain."

"Thank you, Mr. Reed. Ms. Regyri, how soon before the capacitor reaches full charge?"

"Eight stans, Captain."

"Burn for seven stans, forty-five ticks and change," Mr. Reed said.

"Close enough. Mr. Reed, execute burn. Transfer updated course plot to helm."

"Aye, aye, Captain. Execute burn. Course plot to helm."

I felt the rumble and watched Usoko lean over to Torkelson on the helm.

"Helm reports course update, locked and on the beam, Cap." Ms. Usoko said.

"Thank you, Ms. Usoko. Secure from navigation stations. Set normal watch throughout the ship."

"Secure from navigation stations and set normal watch throughout the ship, aye, aye, Cap." Ms. Usoko made the announcement. "Logged, Captain."

I stood up and stretched. "Thank you, everyone. Well done." I turned to the ladder and slid down on the railings, ducking into the cabin. I left the door open in case anybody needed a word. I stood there for a moment, staring at that damned blank bulkhead.

I heard footsteps behind me and turned to see Ms. Regyri peeking in.

"Something wrong, Skipper?"

I shook my head but then shrugged. "Come in, Chief." I waved her into a chair.

She perched on the seat and I faced the bulkhead again. "When I made captain, my first ship was a tractor. The cabin ran across the bow and had a port." I spread my arms. "Almost all the way around. It looked straight out over the docking ring."

"That must have been quite a view," she said.

"It was. As long as we've been flying the *Chernyakova*, I've missed that view. It's silly, I know. That bulkhead is actually along the starboard side of the hull. Even if we could cut a port, the bow is that way." I put my left arm out. I looked at Ms. Regyri. "So, yeah. I was standing there cursing this bulkhead because it's not a window." I shrugged.

Her face lit up in a huge grin.

"What?" I asked.

"Something Margaret did just before she left the ship. She ordered a piece of gear and I couldn't imagine what it might be used for. She told me to tuck it away in the spares closet and that one day soon, I'd know what to do with it." Her smile never dimmed. "Now I know what she meant."

"What is it?" I asked, with a laugh. "Did she order a big sheet of armorglass?"

"Better," Regyri said, staring not at me now, but seeming to measure the bulkhead with her gaze. "This is going to be amazing."

"What is?"

"The window," she said. "Right there. Facing forward."

"How are you going to do that?" I asked.

"I visited Zoya's grandparents before Madoka died. They lived in a hollowed-out asteroid. Big sucker. Maybe a kilometer long. They had windows in the living quarters. Endlessly fascinating to sit on the sofa and look out into space. I loved it." She glanced at me, her eyes all but dancing in her excitement. "Konstantin, Zoya's grandfather, had installed these high-definition displays all around the inside of the living quarters. He fed them from cameras mounted on the outside of the rock."

I spun to look at the bulkhead, picturing in my mind what that might look like. "She ordered a big high-definition display?"

"Not just big. Huge. I didn't even know they came that big. I asked at the time if we had a bulkhead big enough to mount it on outside of the spine," she said. "You know that little 'I've got a secret' smile she has? That's all I got besides 'You'll know it when you see it.'"

"What are the logistics of this?" I asked.

"You're asking how soon I can get it installed?" she asked. Honestly she looked as delighted as I felt.

"Not to put too fine a point on it, but yes."

"I can hang it in less than a stan. Getting it connected? Do we have cameras on the hull?"

"Maybe," I said. I sat at the console and brought up the yard notes. I paged through the hull exterior work orders and found one for sixteen exterior hull-mounted cameras with a specification note reference. The link took me to a specification page showing the access information, reference to the camera controls, and a note. "For when you get your head out of your ass and begin to look forward instead of back. -MS."

I sat back in my chair staring at the screen. "They were installed in the yard," I said. "I'll forward the access information to you."

"This is going to be amazing," Ms. Regyri said. "I'll be right back."

I sat there staring at the note, lost in a tangle of thoughts and feelings, until Ms. Regyri dragged a stupendously large box into the cabin with the help of Mr. Dent and Mr. Harris. The sheer comical size of it made me laugh. It took all of us, with the help of Ms. Usoko who came to see what the commotion was about, just to get it out of the packaging and into position on the bulkhead.

Ms. Usoko and I stepped back to watch as Ms. Regyri worked with her crew to get the beast attached and powered.

"She's good," I said.

"You have no idea," Ms. Usoko said. "When we graduated and got chased out of Port Newmar, it was just the two of us in an exploration scout. She's come a long way since then."

I glanced over at her. "And you?"

She shrugged. "All I ever wanted to was to sail."

"Not run the richest company in the Western Annex?" I asked.

She made a rude noise. "You sign reports. You go to meetings. You have to deal with lawyers, accountants, and newsies. You make decisions that might eventually trickle down to the people who do the work. Here, I can see that the things I do matter in real ways. People's lives are made better, or at least not worse. The ship stays on course. The crew earns a share. I can help make that happen. Directly."

"You're a romantic," I said.

She laughed and nodded at the screen. "You're the one getting a window put in so you can look out any time you want."

I laughed with her.

Ms. Regyri dug around in the discarded packaging and returned with a remote.

The screen access menu popped up as soon as she powered it up and she scrolled through the options until she found "cam1-fwd." The view from the bow flooded the screen.

We all just stood there.

"Holy crap," Mr. Dent said.

"I couldn't agree more, Mr. Dent," I said.

He suddenly seemed to come to his senses and gave me a sheepish grin. "Sorry, Captain. No offense."

"None taken, Mr. Dent." I started to laugh. It was brilliant. I couldn't believe it. "This is perfect."

Ms. Regyri waved at the trash littering the cabin floor. "Mr. Dent? Mr. Harris? A hand with this if you please."

They folded the larger pieces of packaging around the smaller bits and soon had the area policed well enough that the only residue left was small enough for a broom and swab.

Ms. Usoko left without me noticing. Not surprising, since I had a hard time pulling my attention away from the view. The two crewmen piled the rubbish onto the grav pallet they'd used to bring the screen up from aft and towed it away for disposal.

"That should do it, Skipper," Ms. Regyri said.

I looked over at her, her face turned to the screen—an almost childlike delight evident in her smile and the glow in her eyes. "Thank you, Ms. Regyri."

She glanced at me and gave me a shy shrug. "Thank Margaret. She's the one who set this all up." She looked around the cabin before picking up her tool box. "Looks like they got it all." She gave me another glance and took a look at the screen. "I better get aft and make sure my people are playing nice together." She stopped at the cabin door to pull it closed behind her on the way out.

I looked at the door for a few moments, pondering Ms. Regyri's words. Margaret Stevens *had* set it all up. I wondered how far back her influence went and just what, exactly, Admiral Stevens might have set in motion.

I turned to peer into my new "window" and wondered what I might see looking forward.

The Golden Age of the Solar Clipper

Quarter Share
Half Share
Full Share
Double Share
Captains Share
Owners Share

In Ashes Born
To Fire Called
By Darkness Forged

Milk Run
Suicide Run
Home Run

South Coast
Cape Grace*

Tanyth Fairport Adventures

Ravenwood
Zypherias Call
The Hermit Of Lammas Wood

* Forthcoming

Awards

2011 Parsec Award Winner for Best Speculative Fiction
(Long Form) for *Owners Share*

2010 Parsec Award Winner for Best Speculative Fiction
(Long Form) for *Captains Share*

2009 Podiobooks Founders Choice Award for Captains Share

2009 Parsec Award Finalist for Best Speculative Fiction
(Long Form) for *Double Share*

2008 Podiobooks Founders Choice Award for *Double Share*

2008 Parsec Award Finalist for Best Speculative Fiction
(Long Form) for *Full Share*

2008 Parsec Award Finalist for Best Speculative Fiction
(Long Form) for *South Coast*

Contact

Website: nathanlowell.com
Twitter: twitter.com/nlowell
Email: nathan.lowell@gmail.com

About The Author

Nathan Lowell first entered the literary world by podcasting his novels. The Golden Age of the Solar Clipper grew from his life-long fascination with space opera and his own experiences shipboard in the United States Coast Guard. Unlike most works which focus on a larger-than-life hero, Nathan centers on the people behind the scenes—ordinary men and women trying to make a living in the depths of interstellar space. In his novels, there are no bug-eyed monsters, or galactic space battles, instead he paints a richly vivid and realistic world where the hero uses hard work and his own innate talents to improve his station and the lives of those of his community.

Dr. Nathan Lowell holds a Ph.D. in Educational Technology with specializations in Distance Education and Instructional Design. He also holds an M.A. in Educational Technology and a BS in Business Administration. He grew up on the south coast of Maine and is strongly rooted in the maritime heritage of the sea-farer. He served in the USCG from 1970 to 1975, seeing duty aboard a cutter on hurricane patrol in the North Atlantic and at a communications station in Kodiak, Alaska. He currently lives on the plains east of the Rocky Mountains with his wife and two daughters.

Made in the USA
Coppell, TX
16 January 2020

14542675R10186